Don Sanger lives with his wife and son in the South East England. He started his adult life with a degree in art and design. After a few unrewarding jobs, he settled in the building trade and later became a carpenter. He then went on to develop his own businesses. However, he is an artist, a writer and his greatest interests and passions are the study of philosophy, spiritualism and the mystical arts.

Don Sanger

AN APPRENTICESHIP TO A GHOST

AUSTIN MACAULEY PUBLISHERS™

LONDON • CAMBRIDGE • NEW YORK • SHARJAH

A CIP catalogue record for this title is available from the British Library.

ISBN 9781528908559 (Paperback)
ISBN 9781528908566 (Hardback)
ISBN 9781528958974 (ePub e-book)

www.austinmacauley.com

First Published (2019)
Austin Macauley Publishers Ltd
25 Canada Square
Canary Wharf
London
E14 5LQ

Author's Insight

All my life I have had what most people would call weird experiences. As a child, I saw ghosts and had strange dreams—well I thought at the time they were dreams—but many years later I realised that they were nothing of the sort. According to some experts on the subject, I was having OBEs or 'Out of Body Experiences'.

At the tender age of four or five, with my physical body in bed, I would often find myself floating around the bedroom ceiling. Being so young, no one had told me that this sort of thing was supposed to be impossible, so it didn't bother me in the slightest. Yet I would still wake up screaming; not because I was scared though; I was screaming in frustration because I wanted to venture outside. Try as I may, I could not open the curtains. Each time I tried, my translucent hands would keep going through the cotton material. And each time I would find my parents shaking me awake saying, "You are dreaming… You are only dreaming… Wake up."

On other occasions—more pleasurable I might add—I would find myself floating around in different parts of my parent's house. I played games on the stairs. It was a wonderful feeling to glide effortlessly up and down. But not once was I aware of my physical body.

However, in my early twenties, I had a conversation with some friends about 'Astral Projection', and thereafter, I began to practice it. This is the art and ability to leave the body at will. It was when I was practicing 'Astral Projection' that I realised that I used to do it quite naturally as a child. My experiences were not always favourable though, some were full of strange creatures with demon like qualities, but other experiences were nonetheless really quite remarkable, even beautiful.

Now… I'm not saying that this is a true story, but there are most certainly elements of truths with in it—I mean to say elements of my own experiences with extra stuff thrown—in to make it more interesting. This story and the messages retained within these pages are then—you might say—derived from the fruits and understanding of my own experiences. Although, the names and characters in this story are fictitious, and any resemblances to real characters are purely coincidental.

Introduction

For decades now, there has been a slow transformation of the human consciousness; a spiritual change that is felt deep inside every individual soul. It doesn't take a genius to realise that there is a shifting in our collective human psyche. We feel a personal opening in our spirit that exposes us to many unanswered questions: questions that science, philosophy or religions have yet to fully clarify.

More and more people are feeling drawn to the mystical, supernatural and the unexplained. Highly intelligent people searching for inner satisfaction and meaning that until now has remained elusive. As more turn their attention to psychics and mediums for a hopeful truth to be found with their lost loved one, we sense this change. This change can also be seen in our ever-increasing demands for such topical media generally expressed in magazines, books, films and television documentaries. Topical subjects like ghosts, do they really exist, and if so, do they have any answers for us.

This is such a story; a unique ghost story full of mystery and wonderment. A story never before told. A story with secrets untold since the beginning of time; powerful secrets, normally shared among a special few, ancient and wise individual souls, wishing to remain silent and anonymous. I have some incredibly exciting news to share with you. One of these anonymous souls have come forth to explain all.

We can all give our own interpretations of the mystery of life. We are born, grow old, and then we die. Why? Are we here purely for the experience or for some other reason or reasons? For thousands of years, man has pondered this very question. Many books have been written on the subject. All religions are founded on such thoughts.

And what of death? Why must we die? What's the point to it all? Is there life after death, or do we just switch off to a blank nothingness like a street lamp at the end of its allotted useful life?

Surely, if our soul continues on, then the only person to know of such things would be someone who had the fortune to experience it; someone who is already there.

If it were possible to clearly communicate with a ghost, what wonders could be told? If this soul had been observing humanity since the beginning of time, what would this entity know, and what powers could it summon? What could it teach us, and what marvels could be told?

Are you a deep thinker? Ever questioned the meaning of life?

Have you ever questioned the meaning of death?

Would you be excited to learn from someone in the know?

Someone possessing a special knowledge kept from humanity since the creation of the universe.

If you are ready for this knowledge and possess the rare traits that will enable you to understand these special secrets, there is an awakening in your soul. Everything happens for a reason. When the student is ready, the teacher will appear. You have the profile. You have what it takes to receive the unknown. What was it that made you pick up this book in the first place? What circumstances took place for you to receive it? I warrant you, this was no coincidence.

Chapter One

At last it was noon. The exit door banged against a steel post when I kicked it open. I was the first one out, jumped three steps and landed with a thud on the melting tar path. Behind me, as if they were alive, I could hear creaking old tables and chairs screaming as they were shoved across the studio floor. The other students were still in side saying goodbye.

"Yes…!" I hissed loudly, "end of the term."

I didn't dislike art college, on the contrary, I adored it, but I was not myself. My whole life had been turned upside-down.

As I walked along the soft tarred path, the birds were singing merrily. Sweeping across my face in warm currents of air was the sweetest scent of roses. As this soothing fragrance blew past, I took a deep breath. It was summer; what a beautiful time of year.

"Not for me…!" I shouted making my way down the main pathway to a huge gate at the bottom. I pulled it open with such force that it bounced back and hit me from behind. I turned and gave it a good kick and hurt my foot as I did so. I tried to convince myself that there was no pain and walked on feeling extremely bitter.

"Life is a strange place," I mumbled. "What's it all about, and why are we here? We are born. We eat and drink. We live. We reproduce get old and die…Why? What's it all for? What's the meaning of life, and is there a grand plan to life and the universe— for there must be a plan otherwise what would the point be to it all. Why must we die, and what happens when we do? Is there life after death? Is there a God…?"

I looked up to the sky. I was now pleading for help and bellowing at the top of my voice:

"Can anyone hear me?

Is it some kind of secret that we are not to know about? God help me understand."

Then, in my head other questions fought their way through: Do spirits exist? Do ghosts exist? What's the difference?

"I don't know…!" I shouted as if trying to communicate with something hidden in the sky.

"Questions…questions and more questions…leave me alone!"

Suddenly, appearing to come from somewhere deep inside myself—my spirit perhaps—I don't know yet, I heard a peaceful voice that said, "Stop torturing yourself and calm down…" But alas, outside the college gate was a two-way main road. I turned left. The cars on this busy road seemed unusually loud, and the noise drown-out any influence from this peaceful voice.

I took a short walk, and somewhere at the side of this noisy road, I found a public seat. I walked up to it, slumped down and buried my head into my hands. Oh no, the questions have started up again.

"Don… Don… Don, are you all right?" came a well-liked, familiar voice breaking through the monotony of questions.

Embarrassed, I sat up. I hoped that he hadn't heard me shouting. I smiled, and as usual, I pretended that everything was just fine. But not being able to cover up and continue with this falsehood, I slumped back into the seat, and then it happened. Something mimicking a ball had got stuck in my throat. I felt a tremendous force working its way up through the centre of my body, and upon reaching my head, I exploded. Tears poured down my face. I leant forward pushing my head into my lap; I tried to cover my entire body with my arms. I wanted the whole world to just go away.

Comforting me, I felt a hand on my shoulder, but nothing was said.

After a short while, I opened up, straightened my back, but I could not look at him. With faltering fingers I did my best to wipe the tears from my eyes. I took a deep breath and heard his sympathetic voice. "What's up…? Come on, tell me. Is there anything I can do to help?"

I shook my head.

"Has anyone been troubling you? Come on, tell me."

More questions, I thought.

"No…!" I snapped in a most distasteful manner.

Then through hazy eyes I saw many students giving me strange looks as they walked by. I had seen them before. They were from the same college, but none of them were my friends.

Gaining more strength, I raised my wiry body and uttered, "Oh, come on…! Let's go to the park."

It wasn't that far, but it felt like such a long journey. Apart from stopping to buy a few cans of beer, we walked in silence.

Billy was a good friend. I had known him for three years. We met on our first day of college. I was positioned next to him in a large studio. He was from an Irish family, a thin chap, blue eyes and short blonde hair. I had quite a number of friends at the college, but only a few I would call close friends, and Billy was one of them.

Just like me, Billy was a deep thinker so we could sit for hours talking about all kinds of deep philosophical things. But, he was a very deep person, and he seemed to be like it most of the time. He would sit for hours at his drawing board doing absolutely nothing but thinking. At the end of the day, he would pack away a clear white drawing pad only to return the following morning with this same pad full of ideas both written and drawn. I wondered whether he slept at night.

He was good at telling stories though. He liked the feeling of captivating people's emotions. He would be telling a story and then slowly, steadily, luring you to the final climax, and when he had you fully mesmerised, he would say, "That is it… Finished." He would just stand there laughing at you. Many times, I heard people begging him to finish the story, but he never did. Maybe for him they had no ending, I don't know.

I could now feel the sun burning my back. Wiping the sweat from my brow, I moved my arm across my face and blew upwards in a vain attempt to cool myself. I opened a can of cold beer and felt a cooling sensation as it trickled down my throat. I was feeling better now.

We walked through the park gates, and I started to feel guilty. Billy was a good, genuine, dependable friend, and I owed him an explanation for my behaviour. We had not spoken since we had left that public seat. I looked at him through the corner of my eye. He was holding his head down in melancholy.

"Sorry…" I said in a weak tone. He returned a smile.

"Don…there's something very wrong isn't there; please tell me. We've known each other for a long time. You can tell me. I might be able to help."

Still walking and unsure of what to say, I looked up to the trees.

I took a deep breath and said, "Billy, I am sorry, but you can't help me on this one; it's something that I must go through on my own. It's about my uncle Peter…" I paused trying to control my emotions.

"He is dying of cancer. I went to visit him yesterday, you know, just to see how he is, and well, you see Bill, he has been slowly dying for months now, and each time that I see him, he's worse. He lost his hair, and his body has ballooned. He grows larger and large by the day. It is the steroids that cause the enlargement, they told him .The cancer started on his lungs and worked its way up. He has two tumours in his brain."

Billy was about to speak. I stopped him with a motion of my hand, and I tried to continue but, the same hidden force was working its way up my body again. I tried to breathe. I swallowed and pushed it down.

"This on its own is enough…" I continued holding back the tears. "But last night across a table, close up, face to face; he placed one hand on mine, and with haunted weepy eyes he said, 'I don't want to die, Don.'"

As we walked, I looked at Billy's concerned face and cried out, "It's tearing me apart. It's not right to see a man as strong as my uncle used to be…pleading with me so weakly. What can I do? I can't help him. I feel so bitter. What am I going to do? I keep seeing his face in everything, and I hear his voice pleading with me, 'I don't want to die, Don…!' It echoes in my head. He is haunting me, and he is not even dead yet."

I stopped when I realised that I was hitting myself. "I love him…" I said in despair.

"We are so close. Some years ago, before he was married to Phyllis, he shared a room with me at my parent's house. He went through an unsettled marriage the first time around. He was desperate for a place to stay, and we provided it for as long as he wished to stay. He stayed for two years, and we became close friends. Now, the cancer is draining him dry. He no longer laughs…Billy. I've seen the pain in his face and felt the fear of death radiating from his body. He is already way past the final days of the doctors' expectations. They say that he is doing well, but he will not last much longer."

We stopped walking. Through glazed red eyes I looked at him expecting to see an anguished face. But instead, I was greeted by a warm smile. His face seemed somehow invigorating, and his blue eyes captivated my attention. Then, once again, he put his hand on my shoulder.

"I am truly sorry for you and your uncle," he said in a well-composed voice. "Just when you think that you have life all sewn up, and things are going your way—for you have to admit you are doing quite well at college."

I nodded.

"Then God presents one more great useful lesson. He prepares your uncle for the closing hour of his existence. He has conducted him through this strange—tortuous at times—beautiful labyrinth of a mortal life and will finally prepare him to die. Such is the peculiar system of our lives. Your uncle is not dying. He is merely passing on to a better place. All of his pain, torment, anxiety, fears and problems of this world will leave him. And yet, he will return. You will meet him again. Why…it is not the end, but it's a new beginning."

I couldn't believe what I was hearing. For a moment, I was speechless. *What a beautiful thing to say,* I thought. Yet, still not trusting my ears, I looked straight at him, and our eyes met. His face blushed red as no doubt the realisation of what he had just said instantly manifested in his mind.

"I am sorry," he said. "I must have just gone-into-one."

"No…! No…!" I replied, "What a lovely way to put it. Did you learn those words from a book or something?"

"No!" he responded with laugher, "They just flew off my tongue from God knows where."

Our eyes met again. "Yes…!" I returned, "I bet God knows them words very well."

We walked on, passing through a well-used tree lined grassy path.

The soil was dry and hard from the hot days we'd endured. The grass was brown and dusty.

"Let's go down to the lake," I said, changing direction.

As we walked, the woods became more dense, and the ground softer. I could smell the damp vapour of nature as a cool, refreshing breeze blew through the trees. My mood instantly changed. It was as if my bitterness had blown away on a current of air. And I thought of the comforting message Billy had given.

There seemed to be a hidden meaning to this message, I thought. I tried to remember the words. "He is not dying, he is moving on to a better place. And yet, he will return. It is not the end, but a new beginning."

The meaning to me was obvious 'the cycle of life'. I wonder, is this true? Could this really be true? My emotions took control of my senses as all logical reasoning was pushed aside. 'Reincarnation' the transmigration of souls moving from one body to the next, death and rebirth, like the changing of the seasons, one life after another in a never-ending cycle. Your consciousness drifting through time and space, learning more and more throughout each life duration, right through the history of mankind and...

"Look!" Billy shouted, crashing my train of thought, "look at the size of that bird." He was pointing a finger. I followed its direction, and there, high in the sky, I could see a large bird.

"I think it's a Red Kite... They are very rare," he said with excitement.

Its agile movements were alluring. We stood and watched as it slowly but gracefully glided over and above the cool waters. Using the warm air currents, it smoothly drifted on and on into a kind of dreamy endless 'timescape', seemingly lasting for ever, it gradually climbed higher and higher, then diminishing, it crossed the lake and faded out of sight. It had left me standing, transfixed on a now-vacant sky. I was captivated. Nature is so beautiful at times. It has a magical charm that strikes you unaware. Then came a faint, subtle voice from who knows where—intuition perhaps—it said, "There goes another soul on its path to..."

"Come on Don!" Billy shouted from some distance away.

I hadn't realised I was alone. Feeling somewhat foolish for being caught out but perturbed for losing a special moment, ran to catch him up.

'What time is it?' I asked curiously, not really knowing why.

"Two o'clock, why? Are you going?" he asked.

"No, of course not...!" I shot back trying to finish my first can of beer.

"Well, that's a relief," he commented laughing. "Come on, this looks like a good spot."

Close to the water's edge, we sat down under a sprawling oak tree. A cool breeze blew across the lake, it tantalised its surface before it fanned us on the bank. His choice was a delightfully cool place. I opened my bag and pulled out another beer.

"You're drinking a bit slow aren't you," came his mocking voice. "I didn't realise that we had started a race, Bill," I snarled.

"Okay, okay, no need to bite my head off. I was only joking," he said with resentment colouring his tone.

There was a silence.

While drinking my beer, I casually looked at Billy. I now regretted my words and actions. I should not have snapped at him that way, but, on the other hand, he probably deserved it.

He was looking out onto the lake. Bought from a charity shop, his clothes were similar to mine, a mix of ex-army and out of date designer wear. It wasn't our fault, we did the best we could on the money that we received from our student loan, but then again, I didn't mind because some people throw away some really descent clothing, and it gave me a good feeling to think that my money had gone to a worthwhile cause .

The money we spent on beer should have been spent on food, but this was the last day of the term, and the first day of our summer holiday.

"Life isn't all work and study," I said under my breath.

Poor Billy, he did look thin. I looked down at myself. I didn't have a great deal of flesh on me either—unlike my poor uncle, his body was not thin. Once again, I held a strong mental image of him that I would not forget. His torso blown up like a balloon, his face swollen to twice the normal size and below two very thin legs that had not properly been in use for many months.

"Poor Pete…" my Grandad used to call him.

My dear old Grandad, God bless him, what a wonderful fellow he was, I thought, *always laughing, joking and full of life.* Due to his sense of humour he called my uncle 'Poor Pete' because he had money, and he was always travelling. He would have three to four holidays per year. You didn't ask him where he had travelled but, where he had not, that was much easier. He was fortunate in that way because he had a high position in an American airline. He earned good money then. I hoped that one day I could do the same, and finally, get out of the second-hand clothes that I wore.

Some would have considered him very lucky though, for he was well-travelled, and apart from his first marriage, he led a very good happy live with my Aunt Phyllis.

Aunt Phyllis, what a wonderful woman she is, I thought. Like a guardian angel she had looked after him so well, catering for his every need, and I knew that she would go on doing so right till the bitter end.

Yet I could feel the bitter anger building inside once again. In a few weeks' time he would have been retiring. Why must he finish his life right at the point where he can finally relax and take things easy…? What a cruel world we live in. He will have to come back to finish off… That is, if it is possible. Is there such a thing as life after death? I did hope so for his sake.

I looked back at Billy. He was still gazing over the lake and like me in deep thought. He was sitting cross-legged and resembled a Buddhist monk engrossed on some unfathomable hypnotic state. He jumped startled when I called out his name.

"What do you want? You're not going to have another poke at me are you?"

"No," I paused, thinking about the implications of what I was about to say.

"Tell me Billy, and be honest. Do you believe in reincarnation?"

He looked at me with a puzzled smile. Turning his head to look at the lake again, he sighed and said, "I don't know, but somehow, I knew that you were going to ask me that question. It is one of those deep mystical questions. It's intriguing, I know."

He looked at me as if he had knowledge of something special.

"It is the unknown, the source of life and energy. Can it be passed on? How does it manoeuvre from one body to the next? It sends shivers up your spine, just thinking about it…"

Then, as if a dark distant memory had struck him cold, he quivered like there was something small crawling up his back.

"But I really don't know. I find it hard to believe that when the lights go out, there is nothing but darkness. There must be something more."

Feeling somewhat embarrassed to openly talk about this intriguing subject, I murmured laughing and mocking, "Maybe there is… How many lives have you had then…?"

"It might be possible!" he snapped. "What do you know about it anyway?"

He stopped and looked away, sulking.

"Oh… Come on, Bill, I'm only joking," I said softly, "it's just that this is an embarrassing thing to talk about. No… Really, I would like to know what your thoughts are on the subject." He glanced back at me unsure and smiled. He then lay back, leaning his head on a wooden stump that was protruding from the ground behind him.

"I have had some spooky things happen to me in the past, and they were no laughing matter," he persisted. "I will tell you about one, and you can give me your opinion."

"I promise that I won't laugh…unless it is funny of course."

"Well…there is something that started a while back. It concerns this old lady that I once knew." He delayed what he was about to say and sat up. Then, as if to be sensing our immediate surroundings, he cautiously leant forward and continued.

"Every time that I returned home from college, there was this old lady standing in her front garden by the gate, it didn't matter the time or what the weather conditions were, she was always waiting there. As I walked past, we would exchange greetings. Yet, not once did I stop to talk. Maybe she was lonely and had nothing else to do,

16

but she made me feel uneasy, every time. I'm not really sure why. She appeared to have a rather deceptive, sinister air about her too. I looked her in the eye once, and she seemed to look straight through me, chilling me to the bone."

To hear him better I also leant forward. I was now seduced by what he had just said, but then a thought struck me.

"Oh…no…!" I screeched loudly. "This isn't one of your anti-climax stories, is it?"

"No…!" he protested. "This is true."

"So what makes you think that she was waiting there just for you?

She may have been there all day, greeting everyone that walked past." He looked at me with a cunning smile, and moving closer he said.

"I know that she used to wait for me and only for me, because every time that I walked past, she would turn and go inside her house."

He lay back again waiting for my reaction. "That does sound spooky," I replied.

He pointed a finger at me, and raising it up, he looked down it out of the corner of his eye. "Ha…ha but, this is not what I wanted to tell you. This is not the unsettling thing that happened to me. It happened a few weeks ago, and you will be the only one that I have told."

He paused and looked around again and, as if to reveal something top secret he continued,

"I had this dream about her. In this dream, I was walking past her house on my way home from college. As usual she was standing at her gate. I was about to say good evening when she opened the gate and beckoned me to come in. Strangely enough…in this dream, her beckoning didn't concern me at all. I approached, and she led the way. She took me inside and showed me all over the house. I think we even sat in the kitchen and had a long conversation over a cup of tea. I woke up feeling a bit confused, but thought nothing of it."

He looked at me to see if I was still listening.

"The clincher is that on my way home from college that evening, I found out that the old lady had died in the night. I spoke to her family, and they let me look around the house and…do you know, the layout and interior of the building was exactly the same as in my dream. Don't you think that's eerie? I tell you…as I walked around that house my skin was alive, crawling all over."

He lay back again. Obviously feeling good about himself, and there was a silence.

I just sat there in contemplation. My thoughts drifted deeper and deeper, desperately searching for an answer to what he had just said.

Finally it came to me.

I tipped my head back and drank the last drop of beer from the can.

Putting the empty can back into the bag, I drew out another and opened it. I took one mouth full, leant forward and asked, "So what is your explanation to this experience?"

"I'm not sure. I can't give you a good answer. I have often thought about it but never really found a satisfied answer. Dreams are strange at the best of times, aren't they? What's your opinion?"

"Well…" I hesitated, "have you heard of 'out of body experience'?"

He shrugged his shoulders.

"It is when our spirit or soul is able to leave the body and travel entirely on its own. Maybe that is what happened to you. The old lady was dying and called for you to help her that night. She was unable to wake you up, but in her desperation she drew you out of your body."

"Yes…! Yes…! Maybe," he returned enthusiastically accepting my notion.

"Still this does not explain the other things."

"What other things?" I asked. "You mean that's not it."

"It's just that…" He stopped what he was about to say and turning the palms of his hands up, he shrugged his shoulders. I sat there waiting for his elucidation, but nothing could have prepared me for what he was about to say.

"It is just that…sometimes…please don't think that I am mad because I cannot express exactly what it is like, but sometimes I can feel her presence…her very being, bearing down on me. It starts with a heavy odour, and then its existence is felt with a light touch on your head and shoulders. In fact, I can feel it now, and she is sitting next to you."

The very thought of a ghost sitting right next to me, shook me rigid. Then I felt a cold, tingly sensation rushing up my spine, and on reaching the top of my head, it discharged, making every hair stand to an eerie awareness. I could not move. Paralyzed, I sat there waiting for something to happen. I looked out of the corner of my eye to see if this old woman was sitting there. A strong wind blew, and I listened to it in anticipation as it rushed through the trees. My heart raced as I waited for some unearthly apparition to appear. The wind dropped to a deathly silence. Then it happened. I felt a light touch on my shoulder. I leapt, shaking and brushing my shoulder as if something invisible was still there. "Tell her to go away…! Tell her to go away…!" I shouted.

Billy burst into laughter. He was laughing so much that he could not breathe. I watched his body jerking as he banged his hands on the ground. He rolled over and drew a breath and then another burst of laughter came out.

"It was a leaf," he said. "A leaf landed on your shoulder." He took another deep breath, and still laughing he muttered, "Oh…you should have seen your face. Oh…if only I had a camera, that would have been a great picture."

Suddenly finding humour in the whole situation, I sat down laughing with him. When we had finished, I was still puzzled by this presence that he sometimes felt. Was the presence of the old lady a part of the joke, or does he really sense this thing, I wondered, and if he does sense it, is it real? What is it? Is it his imagination, or is it a ghost?

I looked at him. He had a stick in his hand, drawing patterns in the soft peat and leaves, which he was using as a colouring medium. I sat there watching him make this masterpiece.

"Were you being truthful when you said that you sometimes sense this old lady," I commented.

"Yes…!" he said staunchly. "I do feel her around me sometimes, and I did feel her here earlier, but she has gone now, and I know what you are thinking. Did I see her sitting next to you? The answer is no. I am sorry, Don, but that part was a joke. I couldn't resist the temptation."

"But even so," I persisted, "you say that you feel this thing. Doesn't it give you the creeps?"

He looked at me and smiled.

"Yes it did at first, but I have got used to it now. I just try to forget it, mentally push it aside, and it goes."

He then looked down and carried on with his work of art. "Do you consider yourself to be a psychic," I asked.

"I do see unexplainable things sometimes, but whether that is being psychic, I don't know," he replied.

I finished off my can of beer and sat back against the oak tree now feeling somewhat intoxicated. I turned my head to look across the lake. I watched the surface of the water playing with the sunlight, flashing a million twinkles that resembled a blaze of jewels on green silk. I could hear birds on the trees singing. I leant over the edge of the bank. The water near me was calm and appeared dark in comparison to such a bright day. My reflection could clearly be seen. It showed a young 23-year-old from Surrey. Unlike Billy's hair, mine was curly, a darker blonde and a lot longer. The curls hung in ringlets down to my shoulders. They were the envy of many girls, I was told.

Gazing at my image there in water, I wondered how many others had done the same in the past. Back in history before the mirror was invented. Water was the only way you could see your image. I had a vague recollection of doing so many times in past lives. I tried to focus on one. My reflection started to move, and I watched like an old sage in anticipation half expecting my image to change into another person, or maybe an obscure scene might appear. There was a small ripple, then another slightly bigger destroying the image completely.

I looked up to find out the cause of the disturbance. There was a duck with six babies gently swimming by. I watched the little ones eagerly jostling to keep up. I wondered what their lives were like. I wondered what it would be like to be born as a duckling. It is sad, but even such a beautiful creature as a duck will eventually die.

Do we reincarnate, and if so, do all animals and plants follow in suit? Why not? If we have a spirit that can pass on, then surely they do too?

And what about ghosts…? We may be able to sense a human ghost, but can we sense the ghost of an animal or even a ghostly tree. It sounds stupid, but if every living thing has a spirit, why not…? Maybe spirits are interchangeable. If it is possible to reincarnate, then I could come back as a duck. Maybe the spirit in the oak tree behind me used to be a man.

"That's odd," I said to myself. "I have never had thoughts like this before." It was as though the information had somehow been given to me.

"You seem deep in thought," said Billy. "What're you thinking about?

I was about to attest my ill innermost thoughts, but fearing ridicule and everlasting banter, I thought better of it.

"Oh…nothing, just boring stuff you wouldn't want to hear anyway."

"Have you ever used the Ouija board?" Billy asked.

"You mean one of the board games for contacting spirits?"

"Yes…that's the one," he mused looking down at his creation. "What do you think of my creation?"

I stood up to get a better view. It was really quite good. It had plenty of colours, full of vitality—leaves, sticks, different coloured soils, wet and dry. It was remarkable. It reminded me of some work by the artist Andy Goldsworthy.

"Is it a Picasso?" I asked in jest.

"I wish it was," he answered with a crafty grin. "It would be worth a lot of money."

We laughed, and I sat down again.

"So what made you mention about Ouija board?" I asked, thinking that he was going to invite me to participate.

He glanced at me, hesitated a little and said, "It's just that the other day, Sarah and Michelle were telling me that they have had a go at it two or three times."

"Oh yeah," I said nonchalantly. "My girlfriend Sharan tried a few times too. It frightened the life out of her."

"No, listen," Billy snapped, "cause this is really strange."

I stared at him. He looked anxious.

"The first time they tried. They contacted a man called Tom. He told them that he had died in the house as a young man. A few days later, they made some inquires around the neighbourhood, and at one time, there was indeed a young man that lived there by the name of Tom, and to top it all, he died there in the house, but no one knew how or why it happened.

"They tried contacting him again, but the second time they were not successful. They tried again, and this time he came through. He told them he had died of an illness and went on to spelling out one of the girl's names, which turned out to be Sarah.

"Sarah asked how he knew her name and he replied, 'I know a lot about you. I follow you to college every morning.'"

"Can you imagine how Sarah must have felt after that?"

"Is that why they stopped doing it then?" I asked, waiting for a reaction.

"Are you kidding?" he said in exasperation. "Sarah is terrified. She wants to move to another house."

"But the others might have been pushing the triangular thing and influencing the outcome," I exclaimed. "They were probably playing a joke, and Sarah fell for it. You know what they're like anything for a laugh."

I thought about my girlfriend and the experience she had had. 'What about Sharan's experience then?' I said.

"Oh…yeah," he returned sarcastically, knowing precisely how much I think of her.

Nevertheless, I didn't react to his immature remark. I just sat there and did not say a word. It was probably only a couple of minutes, but it felt like hours. Finally, Billy could take no more and said, "All right you win, come on, are you going to tell me the story or what…?" I was just looking across the lake.

"Was it a séance or something that she went to?" he whispered, trying to initiate a spooky atmosphere.

"No," I said softly looking at him. "They were playing around with this Ouija board…"

I picked up my can of beer that was resting on a large root by the side of my leg. After finishing it, I squeezed the can flat and throw it into my bag. I pulled out another. "I am feeling quite pissed now, how about you?" I asked, opening my can.

"You bet…" was the reply. "So where and when did this thing take place?"

"It happened in Ireland a few years ago. Sharan, her cousin Melissa and some friends used to meet up regularly at 'Scrabo Tower'.

"This place is well known for all sorts of weird goings-on. It is said that witchcraft, devil worship and all kinds of rituals have taken place there throughout the ages. It is also considered to be haunted.

"One of them had made their own Ouija board from a large piece of white card. It had the words yes and no, all the letters of the alphabet and numbers from one to ten, but instead of a triangular object, they used a glass to put their fingers on. They tried using this Ouija board at home in one of their houses but were unsuccessful in contacting anyone. So, for a few nights, they took the board to meetings at Scrabo Tower. They would normally just mess around playing games, frightening each other. However, the last night they took this board is a night they will never forget."

I looked to see if Billy was listening. He was all ears and fully absorbed awaiting the climax of the story.

This is it, I thought, *I have got him. Now I can play him at his own game.* I looked at him with a smile and said smugly, "That is it…finished."

Being fully committed and intent on hearing me out, he started pleading. He was contriving every means to make me reveal the final outcome of the story.

"Oh…come on, Don, you can't stop it there. I know that's what I do sometimes, but that's me. That's my joke."

"And how does it feel?" I returned, butting in laughing.

"You can't leave it there…" he protested, "You know you want to finish it."

He was right. I did want to tell.

"Okay!" I uttered leaning forward trying to retrace my thoughts. "And so each time they took this Ouija board to this spooky place on the hill, they were hoping to contact an entity, spirit or something on the other side. They were very successful at this, but instead of contacting something unusual and mystifying, which you might expect from such a place, Sharan's late Uncle David came through. Session after session they contacted him yet, they grew increasingly uneasy about this spirit. Although he claimed to be Sharan's uncle, he was not answering their questions correctly.

And one evening Melissa was not happy. "That is not Uncle David," she shouted. "He would have known the answer to that question easily.

"The last time they got together at the tower was at midnight. She had told her mother that both she and Melissa were going to their friend's house. They went to the tower instead. Her mother would not have allowed it. To make matters worse, they stopped at a pub on the way. After a few drinks, the two girls went to meet four others at the tower on top of the hill.

"When they arrived, the others had already set things up. They gathered around a door on large metal drums they were using as a table.

"The room was lit with candles, and the air filled with incense.

"They all placed one finger on a wine glass which was placed in the centre of this homemade Ouija board. They then began as always by saying, 'Is there anybody there?' They repeated this a few times, and the glass started moving.

"Because Sharan and Melissa were drunk, they found the whole situation a scream. They were laughing, playing about and laughed even more when the glass started moving faster.

"There was a girl sitting to one side, writing and calling out the messages, 'Liars, bitches, lying bitches.' It spelt out Sharan and Melissa's names. The glass then slid across the table so fast that they all took their fingers off, but it didn't stop moving. The girls screamed as they all watched the glass moving, completely unaided, round and round the board. The room became very cold, and a high pitched ringing sound was heard from the glass in the centre. Then, without warning, it flew across the room and smashed against a wall. They all panicked and ran out leaving the Ouija board behind, and since that very night, not one of them has had the courage to return."

"I'm not surprised," Billy commented, moving about making his self-comfortable. "Who would go back after an experience like that?

Yes, that would have been quite an ordeal."

"Quite an ordeal…!" I yelped. "It put the fear of the devil into them. I doubt if they ever got over the shock. Can you imagine what it must feel like to see an object moving completely of its own free will, not knowing what might happen next? I don't think that is what you call 'quite an ordeal'. That is terror struck at your innermost being. It is what nightmares are made from. It goes against nature and science, human reasoning and everything that we perceive about the known world. If this could possibly be proved, it would turn science on its head. Man would have to go back to school for a rethink."

I stopped to apologise because I was not sure of what I was talking about. "I don't know where all this information is coming from," I said.

"I do…!" Billy said, "I wouldn't mock the spirits today."

"What do you mean," I asked.

"The information is coming from a spirit that has attached itself to you."

"Now that is not funny. You've already tried that joke on me once, and I am not falling for it again."

"But I'm not joking this time," he protested. "There is this ghost of an old man sitting right next to you."

Not wanting to be played around with once again, I didn't look. "It's time to go," I said.

It took all of my strength to raise myself from the ground. After managing to straighten up, I brushed the dirt off my jeans and bent down to pick up the bag of remaining cans of beer. The bag was unexpectedly light as every can was empty. I had no recollection of drinking them all.

"Come on, Bill, let's go."

"Don…!" he bellowed, "Did you hear what I just said."

"I know, Billy, there's a ghost at my side. Come on… Let's go," I replied dispassionately.

He got up, and from the way he had picked up his bag, I could tell he had no beers left either.

"That larger was strong," I said.

He nodded.

24

The temperature had dropped, and the shadows grew longer as we walked. As we drew closer to Billy's home, he asked me if I wanted to see the house where the old lady used to live. I declined saying, "That just the thought of it sent shivers up my spine."

He was laughing as we parted.

My journey home was always a long affair: two trains and a long walk at the end. Nevertheless, I was 'pissed', and so it did not seem as long as usual. At each train station, I watched people getting on and off. In my drunken state I was amused by the way people behaved when boarding. They always look around for a vacant seat, not the nearest seat or the easiest access, but the one with the most vacant space surrounding it.

I do the same. We all do. *What a strange, unfriendly lot us humans are,* I thought. No one looked at anyone, or so it appeared yet, all no doubt were secretly studying, as I was, every individual around them.

I quickly turned my head. My eyes met another, and I turned away. Why did I do that? I wondered. Why can we not look at each other?

"The moment that you do…you will have connected with that person…" a voice said.

Startled, I looked around to face the person, but there was no one near enough to have made such a comment.

The train jerked, and we started moving. We slowly gained momentum to a loud, unwilling whining sound. A whiff of strong pipe smoke hit my nose. I turned to see who was smoking because everyone knows that smoking on trains is forbidden, but to my surprise, no one had lit up. The strange thing was that although I could smell thick pipe smoke, it wasn't visible. I turned and gazed out of the window. The train was at full speed now, and I watched as the trees and buildings shot by.

The beers that we had drunk were defiantly taking effect now, because as I looked at the trees, I noticed something quite odd. I had not noticed this before, but some trees were travelling past the window faster than others. The trees in the background were small and travelled past slowly. The trees closest to me were passing so fast they were a green blur. *Why should this be?* I thought.

At that moment flying high in the light evening sky, passed a delightful luminous full moon was an aircraft. Again, it too appeared to be travelling slowly. Everyone knows that planes travel at vast speeds. So why did this plane not shoot past the window? The answer is obvious it appears that way because of the distance that I sat from it. It was the distance that caused the illusion of its slow speed.

Then a thought struck me. Maybe this is why the moon and the stars do not appear to move very fast across the sky. Although we are told that the earth, sun and moon plus all the other planets and stars are travelling around the universe at great speeds, they don't appear to do so when you look up to the night sky. The illusion is due to the vast distances between them and us.

"Wow…!" I mused, as if finding the riddle of the universe. Where did that information come from?

"Riddles indeed…" said the same mysterious voice.

Irritated, once again I quickly looked around, and once again, no one was next to me, but this time the people in the carriage were gawking at me.

The train stopped. With an effort I clambered out of the carriage and slammed the door. The smell of smoke had gone.

I walked merrily along, whistling and singing some favourite songs. On the way, I stopped to listen to a bird singing on a tree. "You're a bit late to be singing, aren't you? Why…you must be as drunk as I am." I stood there trying to mimic his song, and I must have been very good because he was singing back to me as if we were communicating. "It's a pity that I cannot understand you," I said, "We might have become friends."

I walked on laughing. A woman gave me a strange look as she was passing. *What's the matter with her,* I thought, *maybe she's a bit funny in the head. Yes, there're a lot of strange people about.* I laughed again and carried on walking.

I was still laughing when I opened the door to my parent's house. Closing the door, I could hear my mother calling from the living room. Entering the living room, I found my mother crying, and my father had a grave look on his face. My heart sank, my stomach twisted in knots, and I hated myself for being so happy, for I knew deep down inside what I was about to be told. With glazed eyes my mother told me that my uncle had died at 2 o'clock.

My heart sank even further, and the knots in my stomach turned into rocks. There was a silence as I tried to accept what I had just heard. My mother wept tears that ran down her cheeks. Her body was jerking as I put my arms around her. Over her shoulder, I saw my father vacantly staring into space.

The front door opened, and my two brothers were also told the tragic news. We all stood in silence not knowing what to do or say.

Silence can be a troublesome thing. Silence at a time like this can be so deafening, an atmosphere so static and yet somehow so alive. No one dared to speak.

"You know it is strange." We all looked at my younger brother Raymond who had dared to break the silence.

"We knew that he was dying, and we have known for well over a year now, and yet, when it finally happened, it was still a shock. I suppose death is so final that you can never prepare for it, no matter where or when it happens."

We all nodded and sat down in silence.

***

I lay in bed that night thinking about the unusual day that I had, the things that Billy and I had discussed at the park, Ouija boards, spirits, out of the body experiences and ghosts. But out of the entire discussion, something really intrigued me. I had never considered it before because I assumed that ghosts haunted buildings. Can ghosts haunt people? For the spirit of Tom seemed to have followed Sarah to college? What an eerie thought. Trying to pass off this negative line of enquiry, I turned over in bed and ordered my mind to search for something more positive.

Like a horror movie, I knew full well that these subjects would later play on my mind, but as I dropped off in my warm slumber, I drew great comfort in recalling the Red Kite that gracefully glided across the lake, as I did so, I could not help but wonder that maybe, just maybe, that bird was my uncle's spirit saying farewell as it passed over to the other side.

Chapter Two

Only a few days had elapsed since the tragic news of my uncle. Therefore, I was still feeling sad—no depressed. So, a few days, a few hours, nothing seemed to be real anymore, and I didn't much care either. I was sleeping a lot. I was going to bed early and waking up late. I even took to snoozing on top of my bed in the afternoons. My new odd sleeping habits had completely caused me to lose track of time.

Then…one night between the hours of nine and midnight, I had nodded off again. The timing wasn't unusual for sleeping of course, but the new sensations were. I had somehow found myself adrift—how or what caused this spectacle, I have no idea for I had not drank or taken anything out of the ordinary.

Quite unexpectedly, I found myself caught in a calm transfixed state. Some tranquil sensations slowly gave rise to an irresistible urge to continue. Gradually, I became conscious of an existence along with an awareness of perception. It was an awareness that was somehow familiar and yet immeasurable, a kind of realisation of thought and knowledge…not unlike a daydream. I was engrossed on some incomprehensible thought that I tried to gain control of…

I then became aware of an audible humming sensation that rhythmically pulsated up and down and engulfed my entire being. Finally, grasping control of my thoughts, I tried to move, only to find that I was absolutely powerless.

"Oh…my God, I'm totally paralyzed." Then, intuition told me that a life changing phenomenon was about to befall me.

My eyes instantly opened. I could now see—in fact, I could see much clearer than normal, but I did not understand what I was looking at. It was the shock perhaps—I don't know—but the information given to me from my eyes didn't seem to penetrate the clear empty void in my mind. The sight was somehow very familiar yet I could not remember why. Then the answer came to me in a flash.

"No…! No…!" I said panicking. "This cannot be…" Yet as the horror exploded, radiating fear throughout my entire being, this coupled with the cold sense of reasoning, I knew it had to be true. For there in my bedroom, through a small open window came a faint light. From the night sky, shone stars and a dim misty light of the moon; this faint light made it possible for me to see the most unimaginable thing. I appeared to be floating some two metres above my body.

There I was in bed. Well…at least the image looked like me.

I now became very confused because if that was me on the bed then who am I?

Wow…! I must be out of my body, I thought.

Then a dreadful feeling clouded over. "Am I dead?" I asked myself.

Yet much to my relief mainly due to some pulsating thrusts which appeared to be coming from my physical body, I knew different. My entire existence was gently vibrating to a pulsating hum that rhythmically tingled up and down what could only be my spirit. I purred like a cat suckling from its mother. What a beautiful feeling it was.

I was enjoying this sensation when the room started moving, no, it was not the room moving. It was me. I was moving.

Apart from this faint light coming in through my open window, the rest of the room was dark, although, with a little attempt to hold up what felt like my arms, I was surprised by an awesome sight for the thought had not accrued to me that being out of my body, I may not have any limbs. My arms and hands were translucent, made entirely of millions of colourful dust particles that glistened in faint starlight. I gazed at them in bewilderment, although, for some unknown reason, for a flashing moment, I remembered doing this many times before as a child or even as young as a baby. No…even before that.

Totally mystified, I turned to face the faint light penetrating the intense blackness; the open window caused a longing-full feeling of freedom. No sooner had the thought struck, I shot through the window, and before I realised what had taken place, I was flying above the clouds.

Glancing up at the night sky, I saw stars of jewels set in a dark blue ultramarine mist. Falling from space a small meteorite entering Earth's atmosphere dashed across the sky, then bursting into a life of its own, it flashed with a blaze of colour before creating a billion settling mini-stars. Although short lived, they extinguished floating to Earth as a pinch of smoking dust.

Reflecting from the moon, the clouds were a glow of white luminosity against the dark orange street lamps below. As I swooped down through the clouds, I watched as the streets became a body of orange seeming to spread endlessly before me. I felt like a God in the heavens peering down upon a creation that I could not remember making.

I had total control over everything. A moment's thought was a moment's creation. To wish to be somewhere is to instantly be there. I wondered what lay amid the street lamps below, and in a flash, I was soaring among the rooftops of various tall buildings.

I descended, and floating a metre or so above the surface of a vacant motorway, I willed myself to go faster and faster along this wide open road. I shot through a tunnel and realised what it was to be a bullet fired through the barrel of a rifle. Shooting out of the other side, I took off in the warm night air. I felt myself oscillate and then quiver with excitement as a rush of air seemed to blow straight through me. *What a fantastic feeling,* I thought. I just sizzled in the moon light.

Slowing down, I gently dropped like a large bird caught in a cooling current of air. Drifting over the roof of a large house, I saw a substantial number of people gathered in a vast, well-kept garden. Being inquisitive, I proceeded to find out what exactly they were doing there. My thoughts had struck, and in an instant, I found myself surrounded by them.

My head seemed to be at a similar height to theirs' so I assumed that I was standing on the ground. I took it for granted that I had a body, but not once did I look to find out. If I did possess a kind of body then it seemed strange not to be able to sense the tactility of material objects, since, it seemed that the entire material world was untouchable, I could not even feel the ground beneath my feet.

However, from my location, I could see most of the people very clearly, although some were out of view hidden behind trees. I stayed there for a while observing everyone.

Judging by the clothes that the people were wearing, it was a very important party indeed. Every man wore a black bow tie, a white shirt and a black suit. The women were adorned in ravishment. Their jewels sparkled as they gracefully moved across dark soft grass. They were all laughing, telling humorous stories and very much enjoying themselves.

I moved around the garden amusing myself by meandering in and out of each group, but something was very wrong. After some thought on the matter I realised that they could not see me.

As a kind of experiment, I found a large group of people beneath two spotlights. I imagined myself drifting towards them, and it happened just as I had wished. Amid this group of people were two couples talking. Beneath these bright lamps, I hovered right in front of them, but not one was able to see me. I lingered there trying to fathom out the situation. Then two of them walked away, and a third walked straight through me. It was then that I realised not only can these people walk through me, but I can go through them too. And what's astounded me even more was that I could go through people and/or penetrate anything and everything.

I had great fun piercing through whole groups of people and trees in one easy movement. Passing through a wall, I found myself inside a large dining room full of yet more people, eating, drinking and laughing merrily.

There was a very heavy smell of tobacco, the air was thick with smoke. I then had a strange feeling that someone was watching me. I scanned the room for a possible onlooker, and to my amazement, a bystander in the form of an old gentleman was studying my every movement. As I moved his eyes followed.

Feeling extremely curious as to why only he could see me. I willed myself in front of him.

Peering at him closely, I asked in puzzlement. "Can you see me?"

Returning a glance and like a wise old sage bestowing a fool, he simply said, "Yes… that's right."

He can hear me too, I thought. The realisation of this was just too much; this I could not understand. I had now lost all control and I did not know why. "Who is this man…?" I asked myself.

Then I realised that he was not dressed the same as the other men. He wore light grey trousers, a dark red button-down cardigan, a white shirt, and glasses, and now a big grin on his face.

Holding up a pipe with his left hand, he struck a match with his right and calmly puffed filling the air with more smoke. The smoke drifted around his bald head and played with the white wispy hair on the sides. He inhaled more, took another breath, and more thick smoke drifted out from beneath a white yellowing moustache.

When the smoke had cleared his wrinkled face, he smiled as if he knew—all too well, the situation that I was in.

"Why are you able to see me and the others can't?" I asked insistently.

He just smiled.

"You know why…" came the reply.

"Well…" I hesitated, trying to think of something to say. "I seriously believe that I am out of my body…"

I heard him laugh.

My mind instantly centred on my physical body. His laughter grew louder and echoed as his image appeared to be slowly diminishing. With this laughter, I could feel myself stretching, and the people's voices seemed to be rapidly reversing to a loud swishing sound and…

I breathed in and sat bolt upright in bed.

"Wow…! What a dream…" I sat there shaking with excitement. "Yes… Wow…! What an amazing experience. If only I could go back and do it all again. If only I could have more dreams like that, wow… I would never get out of bed."

I slumped back and could feel the adrenaline racing around my body. My heart was pumping as if I had run for ten miles. Like never before, I was totally infused with energy. It was as if my spirit and entire body had been recharged. "This is something that I will never forget," I said under my breath.

I lay there thinking it through, and it was quite some time before I finally calmed down.

As I lay there I began to wonder what had really happened to me.

Could I pass it all off and simply accept that it was all just a dream, or had I ventured out of my body? To dream is fine, but to come out of the body is a frightening thought, or at least the afterthought was frightening for the experience, well, that was bizarre but really quite beautiful.

I found it just so hard to believe. I was actually floating above my body. Although it was dark, the view of it was somehow extraordinarily clear. My body was totally at rest, and it didn't seem to mind at all that I had slinked out.

However, I could recall that whilst I was hovering there above my body, the question of death raised its ugly head. I obviously had not died but wondered could this experience possibly be related to the real event? Is this what it is like to die? You float out of your body, and you just don't return?

If this is true, then maybe I appeared as a ghost to the people in the garden. Well… It is a known fact that most people cannot see ghosts. This might explain why I was able to go through all material things since ghosts are renowned for similar tricks, are they not?

I turned over in bed, trying to sleep. My body was now relaxed, but my mind was still racing, searching for more answers.

Much later I had calm down. I was settling, just coasting into sleep when a thought came through thick and fast. Who was the old man? Who was the old man that was able to see me? This triggered my adrenaline again, and my heart jumped into action.

Judging by the clothes that he wore, he didn't seem to fit in with the rest of the crowd at all. So, what was he doing there? This puzzling thought had got the better of me. I was totally flummoxed and felt mentally defeated.

"Good," I said to myself. "Now maybe I can get some sleep."

Settling once again, I stretched out across the bed. Nicely spread out I could feel myself calmly drifting. I wondered if l might be moving out of my body again.

"That is it…!" I shouted. "Perhaps the old chap was out of his body too. What an awesome thought, two souls meeting outside of their bodies. On the other hand, what if he is dead? He would then have been a ghost and therefore did not possess a body in which case I had visited his world on the other side, in the land of the dead."

"No…!" This was a thought that I did not relish at all.

This was too creepy. I could feel every hair follicle set into motion as developing goose bumps spread throughout my whole body. My skin moved as if to retain a mind of its own. I turned over in bed once again, wriggling amongst the sheets trying to escape the eerie feeling.

"How can I possibly go to sleep now," I said, griping my teeth. It was a long night. I laid there tossing and turning for hours before finally feeling totally exhausted. I dropped off to sleep.

***

The morning greeted me with a bright yellow glow that struck a potent flash as my eyes opened. Holding them closed, I tried to move but a pain shot straight through my head.

"Okay…" I said to myself moving back the covers. I slowly dressed and made my way downstairs to the kitchen. It was ten o'clock on the morning of the day of the funeral. The house would normally be buzzing and full of life, but it was quiet, and I assumed the entire household was still in bed. Apart from me, my family had tried to draw their sorrows, but sadly this method rarely helps because you just wake up with a sore head, and your problems are still there. If you're a drinker then you would know this full well. And you would also know that you receive temporary relief which feels good at the time.

My two brothers were still in bed, but to my surprise, my parents were quietly making breakfast. My mother asked if I wanted to partake of a full English breakfast. My mother is a wonderful cook, and so I eagerly accepted.

After the breakfast some relatives came to visit. It was a bit early for it, but once again, my family sat talking and drinking to the memory of our dearly departed relative. And this was how the last few days seem to pass, day after day, for five days. No one in the family attended work that week. It was as if our lives had died with him. Hour after hour, day after day, they ate, drank and conversed their innermost thoughts and commemorations to 'Poor Pete'. In between my napping, I found out more about him in those five days than I ever did before.

He had a huge international stamp collection which he left to my parents, and the rest of the family was given small mementos. Placed into my hand was a green perspex keyring. I could hardly believe it. On the front was his initials PDFS.

I remembered making him this keyring when I was at school. Due to many years of wear, there were thousands of tiny scratch marks on its surface. In ten years, not once did he remind me of it so I naturally assumed that it was lost or thrown out. Tears trickled down my face. It's strange how such a simple thing can mean so much at times like that.

Today was another hot one made worse by the black clothes that everyone wore. However, when the time came, all were very punctual. The ceremony was well administered and so everything went as expected.

After the service, in great dignity taking our time with the vicar's steps, we walked slowly out of the chapel and into the courtyard. One and all gathered around a beautiful array of flowers which were meticulously placed on one side of a large circular section of the grounds. Each and every flower was dedicated to the memory of yet another 'heavenward' delightful soul.

As everyone stood looking and admiring this beautiful sight, there gradually grew silence. It was a deathly silence like I had not experienced before. Adorning his plight, we all stood in a calm motionless state. It seemed as if no one dared move or speak. I cannot remember hearing any sounds at all. Not even the birds were heard. The air was absolutely still, everything totally static, motionless as if the entire universe was mourning his loss.

I felt a kind of negative power taking over me. I had the same feeling in chapel but somehow managed to control it and pushed it aside. Then the unforgettable image of my uncle started to flood through my mind again.

"No… I mustn't cry…not in public," I said to myself. The colours in front of me started radiating from the flowers, they were getting brighter, creating an illumination so acute that I was forced to close my eyes. Only this seemed to make his sorrowful image more intense. Sick at heart, I tried to breathe but could not expand my chest. I tried to open my eyes yet there was no control. My body was shaking. Once again in desperation, I tried to breathe, but my chest still would not expand.

I was positive everyone had to be looking at me. Feeling shameful my eyes opened, and the flowers had turned into millions of grey particles that seemed to be drifting upwards. I felt a pain coming from my chest. Then I realised that the reason I could not inhale was because my chest was already full of air. I exhaled and just managed to stop myself from tumbling over. Breathing in the oxygen seemed to fill my body with life…positive life.

Feeling extremely embarrassed, I looked to see if anyone had noticed me being distraught. To my surprise, not one person was looking for they were all attempting to control their own anguish.

I heard a sweet gentle voice, it whispered, "There you are, I have been looking for you."

Trying to compose myself I turned around, and there, before me, was the light of my life. Sharan has a delectable face which was adorned with a gleeful smile. Her blue eyes sparkled in the sunlight, and her golden blonde hair blew as a cool breeze swooped gently by. Her beautiful face filled me with joy, and as if by magic, she had broken the depressive spell.

"Will you be okay?" she asked, "Only I have offered to help out with the food preparation. I will see you back at the house later."

Concurring, I smiled and just nodded.

"Don… You don't mind me going back now…do you?"

Pulling her close to me, I gently kissed her on the lips and whispered, "Of course I will be all right, and thank you for offering to help."

She smiled, turned and walked away with a joyful bounce. As she walked across the courtyard I couldn't help thinking what a lucky guy I am.

I turned to have a last look at the flowers, this was when I saw my loveable mum standing alone. I moved closer and asked of her wellbeing. Her red eyes seemed to light up as she clapped sight of me. For support I put my arms around her, and for a short while we stood in silence.

The love she had for me and my brothers knew no bounds, and here was a moment that I could show her mine. Then assuring me that she felt better she kissed me and went to look for my dad. I watched her anxiously as she walked off towards the crematorium.

My poor parents, I thought. They have suffered so much this past year for they were extremely close to Peter and Phyllis. They visited them most weekends and tried, I am sure, in desperation to squeeze a life time of visits into just one year. Together they would take Peter out on day trips whenever possible until he found it just too difficult to leave the house. My father is Peter's brother. He was a tower of strength and supported him mentally and physically right until the dreadful end.

Although he was putting on a brave face, I knew that he was badly hurt. "Life has dealt him the death card," I said to myself, "and he had seen the Grim Reaper." My mother was right to look for him because Peter was the last of his family to pass. His parents had long since passed over, and so he must have been feeling lonely. My parents have always loved and supported each other, and I knew that she would help to fill his empty battered spirit.

Not knowing what to do with myself, I slowly wandered off through a rose-covered archway and through a small garden of colourful flowers. I turned left and walked alongside the crematorium. Approximately halfway along the building I stopped to admire the architecture. It was a modern building, some thirty years old at a guess, and from an artistic point of view, it was quite appealing to me. The walls were natural red brick but laid in an unusual pattern, and the leaded windows were juxtaposed, revealing abstract interpretations of the Bible.

Although this building had an interest for me, I felt that the old Gothic churches were far superior in structure, design, and being old, they seemed to be more appropriate for our old customs and ceremonies. They offer a deep rooted connection with the past and gave us a sense of association with our long since passed relatives.

I stood there for a while amusing myself, trying to work out the meaning of each section of the glass panelling.

Through a small window that was a centre piece in its walls, I observed another service in progress. There were people inside mourning yet another person. We had not long walked out of there ourselves. "My God, it is like a factory," I mumbled. "One in and one out. I wonder how many they do in a day."

I could not bear the thought of my uncle being put on a production line so I turned in haste and was about to walk on when there was a familiar whiff of tobacco smoke. I turned around quickly expecting to see the old gentleman behind me but, to my surprise, there was no one there. Why would he be, he was only part of a dream. Feeling stupid for even thinking such a thing and somewhat puzzled, I carried on walking.

The grounds were enormous. Set in a rural area, the gardens looked as if they stretched for miles. The sun had appeared from behind some soft white clouds, and the heat was really getting to me so, I took off my jacket and tie. Better still, it was not long before I found a shaded seat. This took the form of an old oak bench. It may have been old, but placing myself upon it, I found it to be more than comfortable. I sighed in gratification that I had found such a cool beautiful spot.

Besides, trees and shrubs provided me with the delightful relief from the sun. In front of me was a large pond. "A sizeable expanse of water such as this cools the spirit and feeds the soul." I mused. Nature, a cool stream of air, the sun and the pond or earth, wind, fire and water the perfect balance of all things. I could still smell tobacco smoke but paid it no mind.

I sighed once again, trying to take in the tranquil atmosphere. The distinct beauty of the gardens alone was enough to sooth anyone's battered spirit. Feeling so warm and content after a while my thoughts started drifting.

Sitting very still I watched my scene as if to be orchestrated by an acute invisible composer. The wind gingerly played with the surface of the pond water and large floating green leaves bobbed up and down in unison. I saw a tiny water boatman skidding across the thin skin of the water's surface. Then breaking this thin skin were bubbles, and the water boatman disappeared, no doubt to a hungry koi cap for there were many. Although beautiful, I could see them, cool and lifeless like monsters from the deep awaiting their pray. I glanced up slightly, and there casting a black shadow over the water's edge stood awaiting a large long-legged heron.

There was a splash. I looked and saw a frog swimming for cover. And then I saw it, quite distinct and majestic; there among this sprightly pond life was one pure white lily. Being so pure and white, to me this lily somehow resembled a single lotus flower, and for a brief moment, I could recall a distant memory of such a site oh…so long…long ago passed.

I wondered if I had once lived before in India or the Far East. *Eastern Philosophies are very different to ours,* I thought. It is apparent to me that most people living in Asia and the Far East have a totally different attitude towards life and death. They don't appear to be so materialistic. Their lives somehow have more meaning, and they seem to favour and embrace ideas like reincarnation. Putting it lightly, this to us is very strange indeed, but it is a question of culture and belief… I suppose. Their ethos is a series of lessons to be learnt. When these lessons have been accomplished, you die and return for your next allocation, reincarnating time after time, life after life until you reach the final glorious height of refinement and that of enlightenment.

Many cultures have believed in such things throughout the duration of mankind. Ancient Egyptians and the Buddhist Lamas of Tibet are classic examples of this. To a Buddhist Lama, life is an utter chore. They work through life passionately accepting all of the burden, anxiety and pain of this life. Working and living in the grim hope of a better life next time around. They suffer the ache of each life until the eventual end and the termination of the physical for absolute freedom of the spirit. To us in the western world, such ideas are very difficult to accept. We tend to treasure life because we are not so sure of an afterlife. If it was possible to take a pill and extend our life, I am sure many of us would. Life to us is for the living, and our belief in an afterlife is not so strong.

"An afterlife that is for the birds," I remembered my dad saying when I was just a child.

Sadly our religious faith appears to be fading and giving way to a more vibrant calling the new answer for a new age, and we call it science. We have no scientific evidence of reincarnation so we choose to disregard it. Yet this does not help our grief with death, it makes it worse. Not believing in life after death, I feel panics us— it was panicking me—for when the time comes, death will then mean the end, and it will come to us all sooner or later.

Few people attend church these days. Save weddings and funerals I fear that the majority of people living in the west would not go to church at all. More than ever, we seem to be losing our churches to developers who are more than willing to turn them into luxury apartments. Money, big houses, fast cars, TV and the internet seems to be the new focus. As a nation, it's as if somehow, we have lost our 'Soul'.

To me, people in the west spend most of their lives hoodwinked, set on a narrow path of thought bound for the future. Given that our own health and family is good, most of us seem to soar through life working all of the hours possible, earning a living and pursuing a career. We contribute an entire lifetime stalking our own individual quests which will quite often have a connection with money. Most of us pay no attention to death…out of fear I guess, we just pass it off by saying:

"When it happens, it happens."

"You've got to die someday."

In our culture, death is something to be afraid of. We seem to find it too difficult to even mention it in any conversation. We live and want to be alive. The mere thought of death sends alarm bells ringing in our heads. After being informed that my uncle was dying, due the fear of death I remembered feeling scared to touch or even go near him. It was as if he had some kind of invisible contamination that was so contagious, one touch, and I would also die.

Quite often, we cannot even use the words death or dying either, preferring instead to phrases such as:

"We have had bereavement."

"The poor fellow has gone…"

"She has passed on…"

"He has passed over…"

Where have they gone to…? And past to where…? For a culture of people that are not supposed to be religious or believe in an afterlife, what strange phrases these are? Phrases left over from a bygone age, maybe, so deep rooted, we have forgotten the true meanings.

In the west, I think that we would all like to claim to be religious in case of what might happen when you die but sadly the idea of being rich is more appealing. Nevertheless, perhaps we use these phases with a grim hope that there is some kind of continuation after death strikes. Of course, there are some of us that believe in reincarnation, but I think that the majority just sincerely hope that it is so.

Individuals refer to their own death by saying,

"When I kick the bucket. When my time is up."

Yet rarely will we use the taboo words such as dead, death or dying. It seems as if by uttering these words, you will be attracting or inviting this terrible fate upon yourself. I personally do not like to use these wards because they somehow sound too final, as if that is the end of your existence, and there is nothing more but blackness.

I suppose if the truth be known no matter what faith or beliefs we have everyone fears death because no one can be absolutely sure about the final event.

And so, finally…why do we fear death so much? I think the answer to that is obvious. Death stands for the unknown, and what we do not understand, and what we are not able to prove, and what we cannot control, we will most certainly fear. If we knew for certain that to die would be a trip to paradise then we might all kill ourselves immediately.

I looked up to the sky, took a long breath and with a sigh, I hoped for my uncle's sake that he was in paradise or in his own utopia.

I lowered my head and glanced across the pond again. The only way to really find out exactly what happens when you pass on is to experience it first hand, and unless I was very unlucky that would be far in the future.

Having thought all of this through, I began to feel better about this whole situation. I was sad and held strong feelings for my uncle, but alas, there was nothing that I could do to help him. I knew him well, and he would not have wanted me to torment myself.

At that moment, I decided to wish him well and forever picture him laughing on a white sandy beach, just sunbathing with a pint of beer by his side. That to him, I am sure, would be utopia.

I took another deep breath and exhaled slowly. I could hear the air whistling through my nose as my chest deflated. Once more, it was as if all of my troubles were being blown from my body. I also realised that the smell of smoke had gone too.

I leant forward, stood up, but when I did so, I seemed to spring up and felt as light as air, as if a huge weight had been lifted from my shoulders. Turning to walk away, I found myself bouncing along the side of the pond. I must have been grief stricken for so long that I had forgotten what it was like to be back to normal.

I had finally accepted my loss, and the heavy spell was broken. Yet as I walked back to find my family, I could not pass off the idea that my uncle had somehow lifted it for me. Although, I could not be sure where some of these strange thoughts were coming from.

When I arrived back at the crematorium, it seemed that my family had already gone without me. I was just about to panic when I realised that they must be waiting in the car. I had obviously taken a lot longer than I anticipated because they were all waiting impatiently. I calmly apologised and joined them in a long black limousine. We pulled smoothly out of the car park and accompanied the traffic on the main road.

Although we were now the last car load from our party travelling at a normal speed, the atmosphere was extremely grim, and not one person spoke. This made it seem such a long journey back. My grief spell had broken, and so, I was feeling fine, but my family was still heavy hearted. I could not bear to look at them so I spent the entire journey gazing out of the window.

***

We arrived at the now solitary home of my Aunt Phyllis. It was a beautiful place set in the countryside of Hampshire, south of England. It was a three bedroom bungalow with large gardens, a driveway and completely secluded by trees. It was a home that Peter loved dearly. He was also a great lover of nature, a real country bumpkin you might say. He could be seen on the moors out walking his beloved black Labrador for hours at a time.

On one such an occasion, he invited me along. Somewhere along the trail he opened his hand to me revealing dozens of seeds, and with one swift movement, few were scattered among the undergrowth. "They will all be trees one day, and in a hundred years from now, here will be a forest of my making."

"Pete's wood," he said, laughing.

I was the last to leave the car and was greeted by his adorable black Labrador. "Dash!" I shouted, and the dog was all over me. I smiled, he wagged his tail and expressing a fondness, we petted man and dog.

He then greeted the rest of the family who received him with a loving embrace. We were then made welcome into my aunt's home. I was the last one in, but before I closed the door, I saw Dash sitting at the front gate waiting peacefully for his long lost soulmate.

I joined the assembly of people that had disbanded into the living room, kitchen and back garden. All waiting, it seemed for a bite to eat and drink. Sharan announced that the food was ready, and everyone slowly, politely, congregated around a large table of food in the living room.

Then, before I knew it, Sharan was standing in front of me with a plate full of all manner of delicacies. "I thought you might be hungry," she said with a smile.

Boy…was she right? Only, until I had been presented with such a delightful scene, I had not noticed my poor stomach was so empty.

"You are an angel," I replied eagerly accepting her offering.

I looked around for somewhere to sit but every place had been taken. Nonetheless, I ate the lot standing. Sharan remained next to me with a puzzling look on her face. Not knowing what was wrong, I asked if something was bothering her. Her expression broke, and she glanced at me with another smile.

"Oh…it's nothing, just that I did not know that your uncle had two daughters."

She then stood in silence, seemingly waiting for an explanation. I felt accused of withholding some vital information about my family.

"Oh…ha…are they here then?" I stuttered as I could not remember seeing them at the funeral.

"Yes," she responded, "they are in the garden and were asking about you earlier. Why don't you go and see them?"

She leant forward, took a piece of garlic bread from my plate and waited for my reply.

"I'm sorry, Sharan. There's not much to tell really. Some years ago, Pete and his daughters had a bad quarrel about politics I think it was. Well…that was the excuse, for I am sure that there was more to it than that. It was always something deep rooted with them possibly connected with his first marriage and their childhood, and so now he has gone, they are here to pay their last respects. They never kept in contact you see…"

I looked at Sharan and gently shrugged my shoulders and continued.

"But I have no quarrel with them, that was their affair, in fact, we used to be very friendly…"

"Are you coming into the garden?" she said, cutting me short. "It is such a lovely day."

Knowing how much Sharan loved to sunbath, I suggested that she should go, and I would join her shortly when I had finished eating. Enthusiastically, she turned and went out into the garden to greet the Sun.

I remained standing in the living room eating, drinking and casually observing the people around me. Much to my relief, the awful funeral atmosphere had gone, and everyone around me was talking.

"Then why don't you go and see a clairvoyant or a medium dear," said one woman to another as they walked past. A funeral can spark off this line of conversation, I mused.

Then a few relatives politely greeted me with a handshake and offered their condolences for the loss of such a fine man. I thanked them, and we spoke generally about the family and weather. It was as they casually walked off, I looked out of a window, and there, on the lawn, was Sharan talking to my two cousins. Like us, they were in their early twenties and full of life. They were always well-dressed and kept up with the height of fashion but...

"Wow!" How Pete's daughters had changed. They looked so different, so much older than I remembered. I could hardly recognise them. Despite the fact that they had obviously aged, somewhat their faces and physical appearance were so different and so much more mature. However, to me, they were now strangers. *How could this be,* I wondered?

After a little thought, I concluded that in biological terms the human body is constantly changing, and that every seven years, the entire physical body will have completely changed molecule by molecule.

I had not seen the girls for about ten years. "My God," I said to myself.

"I understood that, although these were the actual two sisters in front of me, they were also 'brand-new people' who had been renewing themselves over and over again. I cannot possibly go out to meet them, they are different people now," I said to myself. "They are now strangers to me, and I will have to get to know them all over again."

Then again, their physical bodies may have changed, but surely, their spirits would still be the same. And so all those years ago, it must have been their spirits that I had befriended and not their physical body. Therefore, if I go out to see them, it will not be our physical bodies that will recall a friendship but our inner spirits will because the inner person never changes.

"Oh, my God, where is all this information coming from?" I asked myself. There was a faint whiff of tobacco smoke once again. Oh...no not that again. This smoke and the strange thoughts that seemed to come with it were becoming quite disturbing so once more, I mentally pushed it aside and trying desperately to mentally focus on something normal. I looked down at the food on the table in front of me.

Shall I have some more chicken…no…how about a piece of apple-pie? But my stomach was full. I could not eat another thing. Then I remembered my mother telling me as a child; I could hear her voice clearly in my head saying, "Your eyes are bigger than your belly." What a strange thing to say. What did she mean by that? This used to bewilder me as a child. I would sit at the dining table with a mental image of my eyes being larger than my stomach.

I quietly chuckled at this amusing childish thought. Then for the first time in my life, I understood her riddle. The answer, of course, is that my stomach cannot accept as much as my eyes would like it too. I had obviously eaten quite enough.

What an amazing thing the mind is. It records every single sensation and experience throughout a whole lifetime, and in a split second, it can recall an event that took place some twenty years prior to the moment of thought. What an amazing feat of ingenuity. No human being could ever build such a device I pondered. And so I wondered what form of intelligent entity did? This question was very intriguing, and I hoped that one day I would be able to answer it.

In the hall, I was greeted by three men passing through to the room that I had just vacated. "What a lovely bungalow," one of them said. "And such an untimely death for Peter," said another. "Yes, just before retirement too," said the third man.

The first one, an old gentleman, leant forward, pointed to a drawing on the wall and said, "Is this one of yours, Don?"

I looked at it, and sure enough, it was one of my still life drawings of things that might be found in an old kitchen.

"Yes, that's right," I answered, blushing as he remarked on the good quality of drawing.

"A true professional," he said.

"Why…thank you! I do like your ring what an unusual symbol it has," I remarked, returning a compliment.

The symbol had a circle in the centre flagged by two arcs on a blue background.

He coughed with what seemed like embarrassment. He withdrew his hand from the drawing, and then as if to be concealing something mysterious, he quickly hid his hand behind his back. "Oh…yes…it was given to me by a brother," he replied with another cough.

The other men laughed mockingly at what I assumed to be a private joke because I did not see the joke at all. One by one, they shook my hand until the last one winked and whispered, "It symbolises moon fazes. We are members to a secret society." Still laughing, they walked into the living room.

I was intrigued. *What kind of secrets might they know,* I wondered? I felt the urge to go and ask, but somehow, I knew that they wouldn't tell. It would only lead to more ridicule.

Once again, I looked up at the drawing on the wall. It was a gift that I had given my aunt and uncle one Christmas. I was chuffed that they had kept the drawing because it was a great favourite of mine.

I felt a warm feeling inside as I pictured them freeing the drawing from the gift wrapping. They were so pleased to receive something so personal.

There was a tap on my shoulder, and then came the voice of my brother Steve.

"Hey…you look deep in thought, are you all right?"

Complying with his enquiry, I just nodded, smiled and generally commented that such a tragic event was taking place on such a lovely day.

He smirked and turned his head to look at the drawing that I had been pondering over. We both stood there for a few minutes merely gazing at it until an atmosphere became present.

From the corner of my eye, I could see him facing the exhibit on the wall. He might have been facing it, but he sure was not looking at it. His eyes were glazed. He was transfixed on some deep-rooted thought. I could feel tension building between us. *One of us will have to speak,* I thought.

"Where is he…?" Steve said breaking the intense silence. I looked at him with confusion.

"Where is he, Don…Where has he gone?"

He was being serious enough except that what he had said rhymed and caused us to laugh.

"My dear brother," I chuckled, "you couldn't be serious if you tried."

His smile dropped, and his face took on a stern appearance. Then he immediately adopted an ashen haunted look like he had just seen a ghost. I felt goose bumps all over my body.

This was totally out of character for Steve because he has always been the joker of the family. Out of three brothers, I am the elder, then Steve, some two years younger. I had known him all of his life, but never had I seen such a look on his face.

"I had a dream about Uncle Pete last night," he said looking around to see if anyone could hear. He then lowered his voice and moved a little closer.

"I dreamt that he was on a white sandy beach, beneath the rays of the sun, and I had had this feeling, that somehow, he had summoned me there, right to that spot. He held up a hand, in it was a lit, self-rolled cigarette, you know the type that he always smoked. He had a big smile on his face; he looked at me so wisely and said,

"Steve I am happy here. I can't tell you what a beautiful place this is, but I have a message for you. Please give up smoking. I died from lung cancer and smoking caused it. I would love to see you here in this gorgeous place, but there is plenty of time, so don't shorten your life by smoking."

As quick as a flash, Steve looked straight into my eyes, no doubt trying to capture my real innermost thoughts and reactions to his experience.

"So what do you think? Do you think that maybe he has somehow contacted me from the other side?"

I was sure of it, for as time passed, I was becoming more convinced of the reality of ghosts, and existence of the other side, and yet, I just stood there motionless, watching him trying to come to terms with his mystifying encounter. As there was no reaction from me, he carried on perilously trying to convince me that this had really been a terrifying experience for him. I could tell that this whole affair had taken a strong hold of him.

Then his approaching mesmerising stare loomed at me. His eyes magnified and appeared to emerge from their sockets.

"I feel the devil is chewing at my soul," he said. His eyes glazed over, tears ran down his cheeks.

I felt a sick gluttony in my stomach, and before I was sucked into this swamp of depression, I looked away, shook my head and focused back at him. He was now looking at the floor.

I put a hand on his shoulder.

"I'm sorry, Don…" he said mournfully, "this stupid dream has shaken me up badly; you know what dreams can be like?"

I did too. I had experienced and gone through my own fair share of hair-raising dreams. I took my hand away from his shoulder, and with a light nudge, I proposed that a stiff drink was in order. He looked up with a smile, and we walked to the kitchen.

We made ourselves comfortable at a pine breakfast table, and Aunt Phyllis kindly offered us a can of beer each. I drank some and proceeded to try and lighten the subject. I called our attention to

Phyllis's lovely bungalow. I reminded him, "It has three bedrooms, one en-suite, a large lounge, a dining room…"

"I know…!" snapped Steve, "I have been here before, remember…?"

I was obviously avoiding his sore subject and not asking the right questions. I knew that he wanted to decipher the meaning of his dream. I was going to say that his subconscious mind was telling him to give up smoking when he leant forward and came out with. "Do you believe in an afterlife or another world other than this material one?"

I could not say that I was not expecting this question, but the idea had been swirling around in my head for days.

My brain felt like a goldfish swimming around a bowl. This may seem a bizarre expression, but nevertheless, I was told that a goldfish has something like a three second memory. So, when swimming around its glass bowl for the first time—which takes it three seconds—by the second lap, it has forgotten the experience of the first lap. There, by each lap, seems to be a new experience. My brain had been going over the same questions which led to new answers which in turn led to more questions and new answers. My head was awash, *With goldfish in my brain*, I mused.

"Steve, I am sorry, but I really don't want to discuss this subject."

He leant back into the chair with a subdued expression. He had a problem, and I was not helping.

"Yes, I do believe in an afterlife," I reluctantly returned.

His face lit up. He leant forward again and was about to say something yet he stopped. His face dropped as he said, "so if that is true then uncle Pete might have seen my future, and if I carry on smoking, I will get cancer. Oh…God, the dream seemed so…"

He cut short and slumped back into the seat. He sat there deep in thought for a few minutes when suddenly he pulled out of his jacket pocket a full unopened box of cigarettes.

"That dream was so real," he continued, "that I will give up smoking right now."

He held them up with both hands, and in a kind of ritualistic manner, he twisted them, breaking every single one in the box, and before leaving the room, he hastily threw them in a bin. I stood up and went to join Sharan and my cousins in the garden.

I did wish that I could have helped him with his agony, but dreams are a personal matter. Yes, of course, I knew what dreams could be like, and how they can affect you, moreover, I am sure they have a connection with the other side—whatever that may means. Dreams can sometimes appear as normal as reality, other times totally mystifying, but they are always a personal affair.

I believe that it is possible to communicate with the dead—why not? Just because science cannot explain the phenomenon at the moment that does not mean that it cannot and does not happen. Who knows what happens to us when we are asleep.

Once upon a time, man thought that the earth was flat, and now we know that it is a sphere. In the future, we may find proof of the other side and be able to talk to lost relatives through special telephones. Until then we can only go on believing and hoping that what we feel is right.

I wanted to tell him about some of the dreams and experiences that I had been through: the out of body experience, the old man that I had seen, and the strange invisible smoke that seemed to connect with him. However, this would have led to a great deal more questions, and questions that I could not answer. I did not think that it would have helped my brother anyway so, I declined from the subject. I didn't exactly know what Steve believed, only he held that secret, but I never saw him smoke a single cigarette ever again.

I have asked many question, and most were never solved. I have had some strange experiences, and I have heard many told, only nothing could have prepared me for an experience that I had a few weeks after this talk with my brother.

Chapter Three

It was early morning, the sun had risen some two hours ago. I was in my room. Two weeks had passed since the awful death and funeral. I was preparing myself for a long college project. I had taken out my equipment and was at my desk with a blank piece of paper in front of me.

With pen in hand, I sat contemplating a long essay. This for me was never a good way to start any project. A plain white piece of paper always sent my mind astray. Without anything to hold onto, completely unanchored, my mind had gone back to my childhood.

I have always had an inquisitive mind. At a young age, my father nicknamed me Snooper because I was always snooping around, looking into cupboards and prying into everything. I was always asking questions. Ever since I was old enough to think, I have had the desire to seek the answers to many, possibly unanswerable questions. I felt as if to be driven by forces that I was only faintly aware of and did not understand.

I have always had weird things happening to me too. Even at that tender age, I used to have strange dreams, well… I thought they were dreams, but they were just so different than normal dreams. However, meeting the old man in that dream a couple of weeks ago had reminded me of similar dreams that I had as a child; dreams of floating out of my body. I would hover around the ceiling and try to wake up my brother Steve in the bed next to me. Other times, I would play on the stairs, but not once, could I remember feeling my feet on the steps. Oddly enough, once or twice, I even saw my physical body in bed. It didn't alarm me at the time because no one had told me that such things were not possible.

I suppose these early experiences were a kind of catalyst that led me on a philosophical path. For many years later, as a teenager I was always examining, exploring and enquiring for explanations about the meaning of life and the universe; questions that science and religion cannot answer or prove. I found life fascinating, but it was not long before my probing mind was unconvinced with the answers the experts give us.

For example, the science argue that everything that we see, hear, sense or imagine is a product of the mind, and that all thoughts are conducted in our brain. And that apart from the physical tangible objects in our material world and anything that cannot be detected with instruments of science or computers, cannot possibly exist. Therefore, things like floating out of your body is not possible, and ghosts cannot exist. They're a product of our imagination.

"No...!" I snapped suddenly, talking to myself. It was as if something had instantly taken passion of my thoughts.

"Well...science let me tell you this! You will never detect the presence of ghosts because they are not a product of the material world. Only things that are made from the material world can be detected in that world. The physical body does not sense ghosts, but the soul or spirit does because it is made from the same substance. The spirit senses the material world through the physical body. The physical body in itself is material made from earthy properties, fused in the mother's womb at 37 degrees when you were born. The two substances must then stay at that temperature. Failure to do so will result in a separation, and the obvious result is what you know as death.

Your physical body, your eyes and ears are made from the molecules derived from the earth. Therefore, you feel, see and hear physical objects because like your whole body, those parts are made from the same substance as the earth. This is how you live and experience the material world that you all share and live in. Your soul or spirit connects with the physical body, thereupon, it can experience and communicate through this earthy body. This is what you have come to accept as reality or the real world.

Alternatively, your soul or spirit is not from the material world. Its origin is very old, far more ancient than anyone's earthy body. It is made from other worldly matter. Therefore, you can sense or detect things outside of Earth's limitations. Your soul helps to connect the spirit world with the material world, bring them closer together."

"Wow...! Here we go..." I abruptly said as the feeling relinquished its hold.

Although fading, I could sense tobacco smoke again.

Trying to come to terms with these new thoughts that were somehow penetrating my mind, I shook my head.

Wow, that was weird but like a dream so easily forgotten, I instantly knew what I had to do.

I was about to write, to commit it all to paper, but when I looked down, I was shocked rigid. I had no need, for there before my very eyes was the unmistakable notation. The shock made my hands tremble in terror. I was horrified and astonished as the unexpected was so plain to see. It had already been written. It was not in my handwriting but, there it was in black and white.

I couldn't move. I was shocked and horrified to think that something had obviously taken me over but astonished at the information it had so clearly given. I sat there, gazing at it in bewilderment. Then, reading its content I couldn't help but admire the simplicity of such a complex subject.

Yet, after examining this passage for a bit, I realised that it made total sense only if we accept that we all have a soul. I was now convinced about it. Why else would I be having such experiences? And how would I be receiving this information if not through my spirit? I sat there just gawking at the sheet in front of me.

The only thing that was really puzzling for me though was the bit about our soul or spirit not being from our material world, and that it is very ancient. This being the case, what world was this passage referring to, and just how old was my spirit? This raised an interesting point, something I never considered before.

Trying to figure out this part of the statement, I looked away and just stared across my room.

Just how old is my spirit?

How many life times has it lived? When was the first life?

And what is its origin?

In wonderment I looked back at the sheet in front of me. I couldn't possibly answer any of these questions of course. And as for my spirit being made 'from other worldly matter', well, that just blew my mind completely.

Feeling somewhat defeated, I sighed. After all what was I to do with such information anyway? I was also quick to realise that to pursue this line of inquiry was going to take up a great deal of contemplation and time that I couldn't afford to give it. My college essay was still waiting my commitment. I had to make a start on it. So, reluctantly putting this strange script in my desk draw, I vowed to make a fresh start after a cup of tea.

Every year we are given a couple of weeks' work to be completed through the summer break. Most of the students would leave it until the last week or so, and then in a mad panic, they would tear through it like lightening. I knew this because some of my friends would phone asking how I was progressing. They were never pleased to hear that I had finished the project weeks beforehand. I liked to get it done straight away to stop the agonising thoughts of having to do it.

Moreover, and most importantly, I needed to keep myself occupied because if I didn't, something else would surely occupy it for me, that I had just experienced.

My grandfather once said, "When in a crisis, my boy, keep your mind occupied for an idle brain is a devil's workshop." He was full of sayings and proverbs to explain things, but the thought of my brain being a Devil's workshop was somehow not very appealing to say the least. But, nevertheless, his solution was correct. I needed to give my mind something to do.

The college project that had been set for me was very intense and so demanded a great deal of concentration. It called for an extensive amount of research on one artist leading to a final academic solution which took the form of a fifteen hundred word essay. I was enjoying the studying and challenges that the project had bestowed upon me. And to top it all, during this period, the house was quiet, and as everyone was at work throughout the day, I had no interferences from them which were a far cry from the disruptive atmosphere at Art College.

Yet, a few days later, all was not quite rational. The project was fine, but there were more strange goings-on. I could not pass off the feeling that something unaccountable was brewing up again; something disruptive was wilfully taking place and distracting me while I was working. The house may have been quiet, but every couple of days, I was interrupted by this same unusual smell of tobacco smoke. There never seemed to be any sign of smoke, just a thick whiff of its presence. The pungent odour would emanate, stay for a few minutes and then terminate as quickly as it came. It was extraordinary. This was not the first time that this had happened, of course, but previously, it came with information only, now it didn't. It was like it was taunting me.

One day, it presented itself three times, and on the third spell, it remained for a good ten minutes. Not accepting that it had anything to do with the old man, in total denial, I was furious and made a complete search of the room. Maybe, someone had left a dirty ashtray. It could not have been me that was one vice that I never took up. I searched the room but not a trace of tobacco ash was found. Why should there be? Steve had given up smoking, and no one else in the house smoked. I emptied the rubbish bin, yet still the odour persisted.

What could it be? Completely antagonised, I sat at my desk trying to decipher the origin of this intruding substance. Completely vexed, I could hear my heart pounding in the silent room. Then slowly as I listened to the hammering taking place in my chest, a stressful atmosphere developed. There was something in the room with me. I sat there waiting for something to happen, for something to move or something to appear. I looked around frantically feeling wildly horror-stricken at the possibility of a manifestation developing. My body was burning with apprehension as I awaited deliverance, but the odour ceased.

I slumped back into my office chair; sweat was trickling down the side of my face. This smell was a petty annoyance that was growing into something big.

By now, my mind had been totally drawn away from my work again, which no doubt was the fiendish ghost's intentions anyway for it was as though I was deliberately being tormented. I had to solve this problem, or I would not be able to concentrate. I tried to recall the first time that I had sensed it. Thinking back, I smelt it when I had been taken over and wrote that weird passage. And a few other times too, but most often it seemed quite faint, and it didn't really bother me too much. Yet it seemed to intensify more as the days went by.

Perhaps it was coming from outside? Standing up, I moved to the window and pushed it wide open. I took a deep breath half expecting to smell this strange smoke. A little warm summer's air blew in bringing with it the sweet fragrance of flowers that were growing in the garden below. I looked down at the flowers that had bloomed filling most of the area with a radiance of colourful beauty that had spread an affluent charm befitting to my now changing mood. Clearly, the awful smell had not come from outside, yet the flowers had reminded me of the grounds that surrounded the crematorium.

Of course, I smelt it at the crematorium and by the side of the pond. I was mixed up and down hearted at the time, but I could distinctly recall connecting it with the old man in my dream. How strange…

My thoughts were moving swiftly now, and things were becoming clearer. Even on the last day of the term, I smelt it. After saying goodbye to Billy, I was on my way home and boarding a train, the carriage reeked of this same brand of tobacco smoke.

Could this be included too as so many people travel on trains, anyone of them could have smoked a pipe.

I was trying to create a rational explanation, but deep down inside I knew that this was not the case. For a start, smoking is forbidden on trains, there was no sign of smoke, and it seemed to be the same brand. Plus, it accompanied a strange voice and seemed to propose odd thoughts.

I was now becoming more and more engrossed with the idea that maybe the odour was being caused by a ghost after all. That maybe the old man was not just part of a dream, but that he was actually a ghost.

As the realisation slowly developed in my mind, I felt a cold tingly sensation working its way up my back. My blood ran cold at the prospect of such an eerie thing pursuing and taking possession of me.

I pressed both hands against my face and in frustration. I made firm massaging movements on and around my temples. Then pushing my hands over the top of my head, I slumped back into the chair again. There I stayed for quiet sometime trying to fathom out these strange occurrences.

Then it finally came to me. How could I have been so slow? I now remembered what Billy had told me that day. He had seen a spirit at my side, and he said that it had connected itself to me. At the time I thought he was joking. Was I really being plagued by a ghost? The thought of a ghost being present each time I smelt the odour was a bit unnerving, but it seemed to be the only explanation.

"It has been following me everywhere…" I shrieked at the realisation of such a weird scenario. Is it possible? Can a ghost follow you around?

"Oh, my God… I am being stalked by a ghost."

"Why not…?" I had to say to myself. Sarah, one of the girls at uni, had a ghost following her to college every day.

Wow…the penny has finally dropped, I mused.

Yet, I still was not quite convinced. I needed to play with the idea for a while until I was truly satisfied that something was actually taking place. And so, later that evening, I asked my family if they had smelt any unusual odours around the house, but they just looked at me as if I had gone mad. Well, why not? I was questioning that myself. This had now become too much for me. Was I just getting paranoid over nothing, or just too dam slow to realise the obvious.

I even phoned Billy. And apart from laughing hysterically, he could not tell me anymore than I already knew.

Nevertheless, whatever I was thinking, up and until that point, I never solved the mystery. The phenomenon was indeed puzzling and somewhat strange, but as it turned out, there was a radical explanation for it after all. It divulged itself a few days after completing the college project. The ghost was finally about to make its presence known.

***

By the end of the period, I was so glad to have finally finished the project. I was exhausted. Mainly due to the stoppages, it had taken much longer than I had anticipated. However, it was worth all the effort because it was well received when I returned to college in the autumn.

Students like me are always short of money, and so through the summer, we would normally take advantage of the situation by taking up a temporary job. Most years, I was lucky enough to have one lined up in advance, but alas, the country was slowly drifting into a recession, and therefore, temporary work was scarce. My student loan was at its limit, so I was desperate for cash, and I was not going to allow the recession to deter me from work. Anyhow, I had worked so hard on my college project that I felt that I deserved a few days leisure before I went in pursuit of this new occupation.

It had been quite some time since I had seen my girlfriend. Every other day, we spoke on the phone, but I wanted to see her. The weather was still exceptional which is unusual for England. Everyone knows that it can be unpredictable. The sun was at its meridian, not a cloud in sight, and Sharan wanted to be out in its rays. Although I hadn't any money, Sharan talked me into going on a short two-day camping trip to the New Forest. She could be very persuasive and offered to lend me some money until I found work.

I was so glad that she had decided on the New Forest. It is quiet, the pace of life is slower and nature's essence would help to soothe and nourish my greedy philosophical psyche. Life in the countryside is natural, as the word suggests a connection with nature. On the other hand, life in our cities is not natural. It is full of man's desires, an endless domain of man-made objects with rushed disturbing procedures that we call work and all for an ever-changing commodity we call money. I knew that I would have to look for work, but for that weekend, I could feel free to enjoy some time with Sharan in the New Forest.

Little did I know Sharan had invited two friends along. Julie and Tim, a lovely couple had been friends of Sharan for a fair few years. I had only met them a few months previous to this occasion, and they welcomed me wholeheartedly as their friend too.

Early on the Saturday morning, we packed in Sharan's car and set off in convoy with Julie and Tim leading. We had been looking forward to this trip and had spent most of the night before talking about it. This was Sharan's first time in a tent, and so she was quite excited. She talked about nothing else all the way there.

On the way my thoughts dug up the mysterious tobacco smoke.

Sometimes, if you leave a problem in the abyss of your subconscious mind, it will work it out for you. My mind had resumed the problem without the answer. Not wanting to pursue as before, the agonising, torturous thoughts of what it might be I dismissed it, but I did wonder whether to tell Sharan.

Sharan and I held no secrets from each other, and so I could not help feeling somewhat guilty. She is also very level headed and would think me completely cuckoo so I thought better of it.

Some two hours later, we arrived at a beautiful camp site. To get onto the site required a drive off the main road, several miles along a narrow lane, we crossed a moor, went through a field of cows and finally, down a tree-lined dirt track where we were confronted by a site office; a small cabin in the centre of the woodlands. Nature was abundant. Without a care in the world sheep, chickens and ponies leisurely strolled across our path. When we approached darting out of sight, the rabbits were not so sure. We stopped at the office to purchase our tickets. The air was clear, fresh and full of nature's mating calls.

"What a beautiful place," said Sharan, getting out of the car.

After buying the tickets, we drove around looking for a suitable spot to pitch the tents. This did not take long, and in a matter of minutes, we had found an appealing patch of grass on a hill partly secluded by trees. The view was fantastic. Twenty minutes later, the cars were unloaded, the tents were up, and we were relaxing in the sun.

Sadly though, we were not sitting in the sun for too long. A huge cloud had drifted across dominating the entire sky, and the temperature dropped rapidly.

"That is typical," Sharan said, "our weather is just so unpredictable." Irritated, she stood up, put her hands on her hips and waited silently for a reaction from us.

I looked at her with a smile. *What a shame,* I thought, *her skin really was taking on a lovely colour.* It was obvious that Tim and Julie liked the sun too; their skin was so brown from the holiday they had had in Spain. They were both aged mid-twenties, had dark hair were slim built and were a bit taller than average. I felt that they had good taste in clothes too. They wore casual but designer wear.

"Would you like a beer, Don," Tim asked rummaging through the contents of a box.

I looked up and caught Julie looking at Sharan. From the expressions on their faces, I knew right there and then that I was not going to have that beer.

Julie then looked at Tim, and with a voice full of affection, she asked if we might explore the surrounding locality. I am sure that this was not quite what Tim had in mind nor I, for that matter, but under the circumstances, we thought it was a good idea. Sharan was also delighted. There was no sense in taking two cars so Tim volunteered to drive.

We spent hours driving and walking around the local towns and villages. There really are some beautifully quaint little villages in and around the New Forest. On our root, there were many old buildings including small thatch cottages, barns, shops and boutiques; all typically English, white with black oak beams. We pointed them out as we drove past and agreed that some were so ornate, they came straight out of a fairy tale book or the cover of a chocolate box.

If we thought that a certain town or village looked inviting, we would stop off and look around. In and out of the shops we were delighted to see so many wonderful things for sale. Sharan—like most girls—she loves shopping. I am sure that she's a 'shopaholic', she therefore could not resist the temptation to buy.

However, after a while, Tim and I thought that our time could be better spent elsewhere. So, like most guys, we found a quaint, little public bar. The ceiling consisted of very large oak beams that structurally held up the floor above. The walls were off-white in colour with dark beams strategically placed for decoration purposes. The whole place was decked out with rich antique furniture, pictures and all manner of bric-a-brac. It also appeared to have a very homely, welcoming atmosphere.

Inside, we casually but cautiously looked around. Moving closer to me and trying not to laugh, he whispered, "Who needs to buy from shops when you can have a better time in a house such as this?" Feeling frightfully devilish I returned an expression of evil delight.

After we received our drinks, overlooking the main street we sat at an old oak table near a window. Being hot and thirsty, I was longing for that first taste of icy-cold beer. Without muttering a word, I drew the glass to my lips and guzzled down a few mouthfuls of chilling, golden liquid. After satisfying my craving, I placed the glass on the table and looked across at Tim. He had drunk most of his and was sitting back in a soft chair with an expression of pleasure.

We sat there talking, laughing and drinking for at least an hour before the girls finally found our refuge. Tim generally asked how I was for I am positive he had sensed that something was amiss, but not wanting to turn our confab from a high to a low, I declined to mention my uncle Pete's passing. We talked by and large about our general interests and hobbies. We were deep in a conversation about fine arts when Sharan and Julie emerged from behind a wooden partition, carrying bags of shopping and, judging by their body language, very pleased with themselves too.

"We knew that we would find you in one of the pubs," they screeched in voices of chuckling laughter.

"Look at what we've bought," said Sharan as she proceeded to pull out the contents of her bags. I leant towards her and gently urged her not to pull everything out in the pub, but she snapped and accused me of being ungrateful because she only wanted to show me a shirt that she had bought for me.

She was good like that generous to a fault my girlfriend, always buying me things and still does. I then felt somewhat guilty, and after finding out what everyone wanted, I went to buy a round of drinks with the money I had borrowed. Walking to the bar, I hoped that I had enough to pay for the drinks.

Up until that point, everything was quite rational. We were all having great fun enjoying each other's company. But things for me were about to take on a sinister twist.

It was sometime later. We were on our way back to the camp site when we drove through a distinctively old village called 'Wickers End'. As we entered the main street, a whiff of the pipe smoke surrounded me.

"STOP!" I shouted, frightening the others half to dead. "Can you smell smoke," I asked.

They all shook their heads and looked at me in puzzlement. "Oh…ha…let's have a look around this village," I stammered.

The girls enthusiastically agreed. We stopped, reversed a little and were looking for somewhere to park when an old Rover pulled away, leaving us a perfect place to park, right in a cool-shaded spot too. It was quite strange the way it happened, almost as if the Rover had been waiting there just for us and drove away leaving the only vacant space in the area.

We casually got out of the car and proceeded to look around.

What a delightful little village it was. I am sure that it had not changed at all in three to four hundred years. Old buildings typical of the period lay either side of a narrow cobble-stone street. There were a number of small boutiques, gift shops and one antique shop that caught my eye. I left the others looking at clothes to browse around this single antique shop.

I had no intention to buy anything, but I love to look at antiques. There is something about old things that attracts me. Very old objects seem to have a presence about them which new items somehow lack. When you hold an antique, you hold something of the past. The person that made it, and the previous owner would quite often be dead. It is quite a haunting thought, but perhaps it is the dead owner that gives the object its strong presence. You see, a house is a material thing and so is an object. If a ghost can haunt a house then surely it can haunt an object.

After looking at the wondrous enchantments displayed in the window, I turned the arid handle which screeched as I calmly pushed the door ajar. An old musty antiquated smell, characteristic of the trade, hit out, and after abusing my delicate sense of smell, I coughed as if something had tried to invade me. Pushing the door further, a small bell rang alerting the dealer whom instantly came forth from among a bounty of jewels, ornaments, charms, regalia, etc.

"May I help you," came the voice of a charming, petite old lady.

She was quite short, thin, had long, white hair and wore a long black 1920's dress.

Feeling invited, I ventured further in, and while looking at an ornament, I gave a reply of what she must have heard many times before. "Thank you, I am just looking."

I then felt pity for the frail old lady. Well, the shop was, I suspect, her only source of income. I turned to her with a warm smile hopefully showing some concern for her welfare. Over the top of her gold rimmed reading glasses, our eyes met, and she returned a smile as a sort of thankful acknowledgement.

Then totally unexpected, it must have only been seconds, although, it felt like minutes, we held a fixed static state. Not being able to pull away, I watched her captivating gaze as she must have elicit some kind of futuristic prediction, because as she relinquished her control, looking away she politely said, "I am sorry dear, I am normally closed by now, but I knew that you were coming so I have stayed open for you. Pray, do look around, feel free to browse, and when you have found that which you seek, call me…but try not to take too long my dear. I must close shortly."

She quickly vanished into a room at the back of the shop.

I stood there, mouth open like a newly landed fish. Was I in water, or had I suddenly entered the Twilight zone? For it could not possibly have been reality.

What did she mean "I knew that you were coming"? How could she have possibly known?

"Perhaps the old girl is psychic," I said silently, chuckling over the amusing situation. "And what makes her think that I want to buy from her shop anyway?" *Perhaps the old dear has gone a trifle senile,* I thought.

Not thinking anymore on the subject, I drew my attention away and started to look around the establishment. Being a small shop with so many items, it was clearly impossible to display everything in a good orderly fashion, and so each object was placed wherever there was a vacant space. The outcome was a shambles but interesting. She had most of the usual types of things that can be found in all antique shops, such as Victorian furniture, china, cutlery and jewellery, plus some novelties to boot.

Walking around, I saw a lit display cabinet full of more jewels and china from different period and locations. I tried the cabinet door, but it proved locked, for therein rest assured, was exhibited the most awesome display of her most valuable stock. To one side of this cabinet, beneath an old foxfire were some war medals and to the right of them was a knife. It was a gruesome looking thing about twelve inches long with a baby deer's foot as a handle.

It was when I picked this knife up that I sensed someone watching me. Thinking that it was the old lady, I quickly turned to face her. To my surprise no one was there, yet my senses said different. I was so positive that someone was there in front of me. But how could they be if I could not see them.

This was all getting a bit too spooky, so while trying to keep my adrenalin reposed, I calmly put the knife down in its former position, and double checking I turned once again to make sure that no one was playing games with me; there was not a soul in sight. Yet, there, high on a shelf, covered in dust, displayed in its own box was a very old smoker's pipe. I didn't notice it the first time I looked, but then I was expecting to see a person standing there, and yet it seemed to me that this pipe had a presence of its own. Rather like the presence of a person.

Although I have never smoked and absolutely loathe the habit, this pipe was somehow appealing to me. I leant across and making sure that I didn't knock anything else around me, I tentatively picked it up. As I held it in front of me, it was vaguely familiar. I had seen it or one like it somewhere before, but I could not remember where. I had an odd feeling that I was not merely holding something of the past but actually held the very passed itself, right there in my hand.

The box was wooden and had seen better days, but judging by what I saw, at one time, it must have been of immense importance. The quality of workmanship was of an extremely high standard. The outside consisted of many pieces of different types of wood veneer arranged in a colourful pattern, commonly known as parquetry, including brass inlay and edging. It was a great pity, but some of the brass and wooden pieces were missing. I could imagine that at one time, the pipe and its box would have been very desirable objects indeed.

Pulling the pipe out, I put the box on a table and held the pipe towards the light of the window. It really was quite remarkable. The bowl end had been beautifully carved out of what looked to be ivory. The carved image was of a long, bearded man with his arms and legs wrapped around a chalice or bowl. The detail of the figure was amazing.

I could just make out minute fingers on his tiny hands and even curls in the long beard and hair. The expression on the man's face was of devotion, fidelity and faith in the divine object that he held. It was a work of art. Yet again a great pity as I assumed was due to excessive use over many years, but some of the carving had been worn away.

I peered into the top of its bowl. The inside seemed to be clean of ash, but a brown stain remained at the bottom. I then surprised myself by bring the pipe bowl close to my nose for a sniff, and the aroma shocked me rigid. The smell was of the same brand of pungent tobacco that had been haunting me for days.

61

I was so shocked that I just stood there gawking at it. Although I was physically looking at the pipe, my brain had now been 'shot'. My mind had taken leave of my body and taken up residence in a sort of no-man's land where I remained until an abrupt jolt brought me back to reality. Still looking at the pipe, I was awe-stricken, but I tried to reason with myself. Perhaps it was this pipe that caused me to turn around. It certainly had a strong presence about it.

Feeling rather stupid, I naturally convinced myself that I was only imagining things. Accepting the situation, I started looking around it and the box for a possible name or clue to its previous owner or something of its origin. With the exception of a small symbol on the side of its chalice, I found absolutely nothing on the pipe or the box. The symbol was of two curved arcs facing outward and centrally joined by a circle. It was exactly like the symbol I had seen on the ring of the man at Pete's funeral.

Feeling really quite puzzled to say the least, I commenced questioning the implications of the whole situation. Why would the smell of the residue in the bottom of the pipe be the same as that which had been haunting me? Conclusion, perhaps the brand of tobacco used in both situations was of a common type, and that the whole scenario was just a sequence of coincidences.

Although, at the time I would have welcomed such an easy explanation, I knew well-enough that there was much more to it than that. I had a hunch that the pipe was somehow connected.

Feeling totally frustrated, not knowing who to turn to, I asked myself, "What does it all mean, and what's the connection with me?"

"There must be an explanation," I said aloud. Then realising where I was, I whispered through my teeth in annoyance. "There must be a reason…there is always a reason or meaning behind any circumstance no matter how ambiguous it might seem."

I was not prepared to just write the whole thing off as a coincidence for there was much more to it; I was convinced of it. The smell of invisible smoke and the feeling of being watched as though to be stalked by some unseen, paranormal entity leading me to such artistry as seen in the elaborately carved pipe. These were not normal circumstances. These were not coincidences at all. Therefore, from that moment on, whether it is for the good or bad I was going to pursue this scenario and get to the bottom of this strange phenomenon.

Looking back at the pipe in my hand, I knew that my mind had totally run adrift, but I was now beyond caring. I had this overwhelming desire to pursue this bizarre adventure, *But where should I begin, and moreover, where would it all end?* I wondered.

Perhaps without realising, I had already started? All I knew was that apart from these strange sensations and unanswered questions, the only 'concrete exhibit' that I had to go on was the pipe, and where that fitted the equation, I had no idea.

And what of the old lady? She seemed to know somehow that I was coming. Had she been forewarned of my visit? If so, by whom or what, for that matter, because I didn't even know myself.

Picking up the box, I turned towards the cash desk which was located at the back of the shop. There watching and waiting for me with a delightful smile was the old lady. Delighted, I am sure, for her prediction had come true. I had indeed found, so it seemed, the very object that I was looking for.

Feeling foolish, I felt myself blushing bright red.

"She knows," I said under my breath. "She knew that I was coming, and she knew what I was coming for."

I moved slowly towards her thinking, *Oh…come on, Don, get a grip of yourself.*

Trying to cover up my embarrassment, I coughed slightly, and regaining some confidence, I calmly asked the price of the pipe but there came not a direct reply, just a silence as she was no doubt sizing me up for a plausible sale, hopefully befitting to my pocket.

"It really is quite a beauty isn't it?" She returned looking at it with interest. "Should it not have been in such a bad condition, it would have been worth a great deal of money or maybe even priceless."

She obviously wants quite a bit for it, I thought. With my head downward, and my heart full of gloom, I slowly put the pipe back in its box. I was about to put it back on the shelf when she said, "Fifteen pounds. I will take fifteen pounds."

With an anxious feeling that burst into a delightful zest, I put my hand into a pocket, drew out my last ten pound note, and before I could place it on the cash desk, she smiled once again and said, "Very well, ten pounds it is."

Right at that moment, ringing its bell, the door opened behind me. We both looked but no one had entered.

"He's a strange old fellow," she said.

Not knowing who she meant, I merely returned a glance back to the counter. She was kindly rapping the box and its content in brown paper after which she passed it back to me and politely bade me goodbye. As I walked towards the door, a thought stopped me dead in my tracks. Turning back once again, I asked curiously, "How did you know that I was coming here today?" The answer was yet another horrifying shock to be added to my seemingly never-ending list.

In a bewildered sort of way, she said, "Just before you arrived, some ten minutes before, an elderly gentleman came and told me that you were to stop by and would I stay open for you."

This was not the kind of answer that I was expecting at all.

"What elderly gentleman…!" I blurted out anxiously. "Did he give his name, and what did he look like?"

The answer made my blood run cold. I could feel my skin crawling as 'ice-cold fingers' lightly ran up my back. My hair stood erect, and my body was chilled to the bone.

She was now looking at me rather puzzled. "You saw him leave just now," she declared. "He is a strange one…friend of yours, is he?"

I took a breath and held the box tightly to my chest. I could feel beads of sweat developing on my forehead. "What the hell was happening to me?"

"Are you okay?" the old lady exclaimed.

I could not answer. Collecting myself, I reached for the door and quickly opened it. A breathe of cool fresh air swept my body reviving parts so, that I might move with ease. Closing the door behind me, the spell had broken.

I had never been so glad to get out of a shop in all my life, but the feeling that I had at that moment, I will never properly be able to describe. Although, I will say that I sensed an inkling of a divine revelation. Little did I know then, but I was on the verge of some Ancient Nobel secrets dating back to the beginning of mankind. And strangely enough, I was feeling very pleased with myself. I held the box close to my chest and jovially bounced back towards Tim's car.

When I arrived, the others were still shopping, and so I naturally stood at the car awaiting their return.

While I waited, my vigorous tone was suddenly curbed by the cold light of reason. What will I tell Sharan?

She will think me completely mad if I tell her that I had bought an antique pipe, and she would go loopy to find out that I had spent my last ten pounds on such a thing. Plus, I had no way of telling how she would react to the thought of some invisible smoke following me about, not to mention the old man and the unusual experiences that I had. What would anyone think, come to that? I was not sure of my own thoughts, let alone others.

My saviour took the form of Tim casually walking across the road towards me. I told Tim that the parcel was just an old box that I might repair for Sharan as a jewellery box. Accepting not to tell or thereby spoil a possible surprise, he agreed to keep it in the boot of his car.

On the way back to the camp site, my thoughts were constantly interrupted by the banter of the others.

"Come on, Don, cat-got-your-tongue," they said, laughing.

"If only they knew," I said to myself. "If only they had been through the same as me this past couple of weeks, they would not be laughing so much."

Sharan showed some sympathy for she knew of my uncle's passing. I had told her not to mention it to the others. It was too painful to talk about. Nevertheless, they were right, so pushing my thoughts to one side, I joined their vibrant repartee.

That Saturday night, surrounded by trees, we sat on a blanket outside the tents in the centre of a wooded camp site. With full stomachs, we were surrounding a fading barbecue. Drinking various varieties and strains of alcoholic substances, we were progressively penetrating the realms of drunkenness.

Sometime later, our stream of rippling mockery had ceased, and I noticed Julie and Tim acting somewhat strange. Sharan must have noticed it too because we both found ourselves staring at them. As we watched, they seemed to be acting as if they had just met. This was very strange because they had been together for approximately nine years. Although, to my knowledge, they had always been a loving couple, yet they still seemed to be overly affectionate. Sharan just could not restrain herself and so asked, "Is there something you want to tell us?"

They simultaneously looked at us both, smiled and playfully looked back at each other, but from a little sparkle in Julie's eyes, I knew their little secret which was confirmed by them immediately. Julie was going to have a baby. It was early days for them, and so the mother and father to be were obviously extremely pleased with the thought of a new arrival and a possible little 'treasure'. This was their first child, and so we were as delighted as they were to receive such news.

Yet due to cause and effect, this had caused the inevitable, and the effect was a long conversation about babies. We had been talking for quite some considerable time on the subject when my interest started waning. I tried to change the subject, but the flow was far too strong. I momentarily kept my mind occupied by listening to them conversing, but it was no good, my interest on the subject had completely dropped.

In my drunken state, their words became muffled, and slowly they had no meaning to me, just an indistinct utterance that gradually declined as I slowly and aimlessly looked about.

A faint glow from the dying barbecue caught my eye. It was so dull and yet so light in the surrounding black velvet night. In a tranquil trance like state, out of ashes and forever changing shimmering lights, I made faces. Each shimmer moved and flickered, sometimes quivering as if to be blessed with a life all of its own.

As I gazed at this spectacle display, a warm, gentle, whirl of air swept-by, stressing the ash members which in turn released millions of tiny fire balls. Drifting around, they sparkled like stars in the open sky on a clear summer's night. I was surrounded by them. They resembled groups of widely dispersed worlds floating in darkness—much like planets rotating around stars and all drifting through a galaxy somewhere in the outer limits of the universe. As I looked closer, each particle was an individual planet orbiting a blazing sun. If only I had a powerful enough telescope to see right into an individual world.

"Life is all around us no matter how small…" came the voice of the ghost. A slight, familiar sent of tobacco smoke surrounded me.

"Who is to say that there is no life there? Time has no boundaries. A minute in their world could be a million years. And just how big are you in comparison to the size of their planet? Your thoughts have created that world, and you are now its God.

Likewise…the earth is a speck of cool dust floating in a timeless universe. Compared to something much bigger, Earth is infinitely small. On Earth, you orbit a huge hot planet called Sun. The Earth is actually a cooled speck of ash floating around a hot burning cinder from a great fire. They are merely, collectively drifting apart and away from each planet's birth source—once ignited in the thoughts of the great one himself."

I carefully watched as the speck of dust turned into an Earth like planet, in orbit around a star much like our own Sun. There was a huge explosion a kind of 'Big-Bang', announcing a new beginning as billions of more planets were created, shooting and flying off in all directions. My heart jumped into action as I drew back, trying desperately to protect myself.

Reacting to my shock, Tim burst out laughing as he proceeded to throw another small log on the fire.

Hating him for it, and reluctantly recovering, I shook my head. "That's a good idea," I returned, throwing on yet another log. Being a bit catty, "Don't put too much on," the girls added. Backbiting, I replied, "Yes…dear!"

Feeling absolutely furious that my connection with the ghost had been severed, I peevishly returned to my spot on the blanket.

Throwing on some more sticks Tim whispered, "They'll be glad of it later." I nodded.

Just then, Sharan jumped up, rubbed her arms, trembled and shook as if particles of ice were being sprinkled down her back. Still quivering she ran into our tent, upset our newly made bed, pulled out a thick blanket, shaking it open, she threw it over Julie, leapt, and with one swift movement, she too was wrapped tightly within.

I casually looked at them, raised my eyebrows and sarcastically asked, "Cold girls?" I saw Tim grinning in the quivering reflection of the renewed flames.

"Look at that," he remarked, "we'll have a roaring fire in no time."

Although it was midsummer, and the temperatures during the day were high, it can get rather 'parky' at night. As the wood burnt, we huddled around its increasingly warm glow. I looked up briefly to see its reflections playing with the surrounding trees. With a warm smile I greeted the full moon as it appeared from behind some clouds…so smooth…so calm, they drifted gently by.

"Another beer…?" Tim asked, breaking yet another perfect moment. Looking at him across the flames, I reached out and clutched hold of another can. Sharan and Julie were pouring themselves more Prosecco, although Julie didn't seem so keen—she was pregnant after all.

Opening the can of beer, I heartily gestured cheers to Tim who replied, "Don't you just love camping?"

I nodded and reminded him that it was Sharan's first time.

"Oh yes…!" he reacted, looking at Sharan. "What do you think, Shaz?"

She was still talking to Julie but expressed that it was brilliant. I was glad of that because it meant that we would in future go camping for a whole week.

Looking back at the fire, the flames had now worked their way into the bigger logs. Leaning forward, Tim put even more bits on our rapidly growing 'heater'.

I was now feeling warm. Making myself comfortable, supported by a tree trunk, I leant my aching back on a thick sponge that I had found in the car. The relief was bliss.

"Comfortable boys…?" Julie sarcastically asked.

We all laughed at her quick wit.

Feeling warm and much more relaxed I began thinking about the ghost and the strange experiences at the antique shop. Who or what is this ghost? What was I to do with the pipe, and who was the ghost that the old lady had seen in the shop? I wondered if he was the same one from my dream, the same one surrounding me with invisible smoke, and the one feeding me with strange mystical ideas. It was impossible to tell because the old lady didn't give a description of him.

"Are you all right mate? You've been a bit quite all day?" Tim said across a now blazing fire. He moved around the fire to get a little closer. At a more sociable distance, looking into the flames as if to be contemplating a problem, he sighed.

"Look…" he finally said gesturing with both hands. "Sharan told me about your uncle passing away, and I must say that I am truly sorry."

"Thanks Tim. I'm just fine," I said calmly, acknowledging his concern. But little did he know that just this mere reminder of my uncle had set the questions going again. He had caused my 'philosophical door to open'. I had told Sharan not to tell anyone about Peter's death. I knew that it would set things off again.

As a desperate attempt, I tried to think of something else, anything to stop the questions. "The old man," I said to myself, "What about the ghost and the old man."

I looked back at Tim, who was now staring into the fire again. "Do you believe in ghosts?" I asked, and then watched as his face went pale.

"I'm not sure," he replied. "I've never seen one, have you?"

There was a loud snap from the fire making us all jump.

"Wow…! Did you see that?" the girls shouted, comforting each other.

It startled me too, but not in the same way. It was as if the ghost was trying to stop me from mentioning him.

"Does anyone know a ghost story?" Julie cried out, trying to increase the developing spooky atmosphere.

"Don does, he is quite good at them," Sharan called out.

I was not in a mood for stories, for unbeknown to them I had already met enough of my own creepy experiences for one day and

I did not want to encourage more of them by telling stories. I was sure to be too drunk anyway; I couldn't think straight. I shook my head as a negative response, and there drew a silence as no one could think of anything to say.

And so once again, I slowly found myself aimlessly looking about.

Peering into the fire, I observed the powerful glare that penetrated and dominated the entire atmosphere. I felt its warm glow radiating up my body, its energy so alive, so warm, so comforting and so commanding. As I watched, it grew brighter, seemingly captivating my thoughts and overwhelming me with calm.

And so yet again, my entire being was entranced. I watched the flames dance, creating glorious patterns which were a flickering display soothing my plight. As I lingered transfixed in this heavenly state, the inevitable happened. My mind was empty and free to wonder, and so my 'philosophical door' opened again. I could feel the burning onslaught of philosophical enquiry making its way to the entrance. I had already had so many questions that I wanted answered about the ghost without all of my old unanswered questions being raised. My mind was now filling up with:

"What is life all about?

"Is there a secret to life and the universe?

"Does God exist, and if so, why must we suffer so much pain in life?

"And, who is the old man? Is he a ghost?

"Do ghosts exist?

"Is there life after death?"

And the new ones. "How old is my spirit, and what's it origin?"

Questions and more questions, the fire was now roaring, its sticks cracking to my rhythmic charge of approaching questions. I tried to resist the temptation of asking another question, but the advancement was growing too strong. *What's the point? I can't answer them anyway,* I thought.

Oh…I wanted to cry out under the strain, but I knew to ask one would lead to another and then another. I sensed one coming to the surface. I was about to utter it when to my amazement the approaching assault of questions was seized.

My mind had somehow been mysteriously hushed, mentally suppressed and a deafening silence had descended.

There I sat completely spellbound over the silent, soft flickering of yellow fire light. I tried to move…but I had not the will, so I sat in sheer ecstasy for what seemed a whole lifetime in peace with a vacant mind.

I sensed a physical floating sensation, as light as air, I gently conjoined to some emerging aroma. Its maturation caused an awareness of its strength. It was getting stronger and stronger, thicker and thicker, until I was sort of cocooned within its enigmatic composure.

At that point I gradually regained some sense of reality, and my mind was somehow set free. My mind had been set free, and I was allowed to think once again, but I was absolutely horror-stricken, for I found myself completely engulfed in tobacco smoke. I felt alone, and a cold sickening feeling came over me. Fully conscious, I realised that I was still paralyzed.

What is this stuff, and what does it want? I thought.

I was now becoming more anxious as distress signals ran up and down my body. Not being in control, I was terrified. I felt smothered and so started to panic but all of my efforts were useless. I tried so hard but to no avail. Each time that I tried, I quickly became powerless and was exhausted.

I was not sure whether or not to be imagining things, but this smog seemed to possess intelligence. I was allowed to think, but I was not to ask questions or move.

I felt a smothering feeling taking me over again. Frustrated with a will to be free, I demanded to know what the hell this thing was, and even more to the point what it wanted of me. I insisted to know and be set free. Once again, my vibrant outburst of thought had completely stopped. I was now at the mercy of this strange substance.

And strange it certainly was for it seemed to possess an immeasurable intelligence that had soaked up all of my questioning, my energy and my whole being. All was silent, but I still could not move, and the strong pungent residue of tobacco smoke, like a cold, supernatural breathe, was yet still lingering around me.

"Oh…to be released from my bondage," I humbly asked. Feeling cold and tired, I waited. Then a message entered my mind, from where I could not tell, 'Perhaps telepathic'.

It said, "All your enquiries will be solved." For more information I waited a little longer, but nothing was forthcoming.

I mentally asked, "Who will give me these answers?"

I waited some more, and slowly an image developed in my mind's eye. My heart once again jumped into action. I was so excited at the prospect of something finally taking place.

As the image slowly evolved, I was simultaneously delivered some ten feet away from a dark figure. My bondage was disengaged, and shocks of terror ran down my body.

Did I really live such a bad life? I thought. I was sure to be dead, discharged to hell and was to be united with the dark lord himself. My body was shaking, and my soul was aching with fear.

I felt a dull pain in one arm, and Sharan's voice calling my name. I slowly turned to behold her beautiful smile.

She hit me again. "What is wrong with you," she exclaimed.

I breathed a sigh of relief and returned a smile.

"It's all been a dream," I said to myself. "She can hit me anytime—but wait, for," at the corner of my eye, the dark figure stood firm. I was terrified to look and pretended not to see him.

"DON…!" she shouted. "He wants you."

I didn't hear the rest, with vengeance ready to face up to my enemy, I turned to face the apparition, and there in the lustrous light of the full moon was the black silhouette of a large being. My body shook with fear and adrenalin, ready to take on the dark one himself. My life and my soul, I had everything to lose but not without a fight. I would not give in so easily. It moved forward into the light, my heart pounded with anticipation—only to my dismay, I had been duped once again. The light of the fire revealed a middle-aged man and his dog. It was the park-keeper.

"I am sorry to have startled you all…" he said politely, "only the rules are strictly no camp fires. So I must ask you to put your fire out." He then turned and casually walked away, calling his dog as he did so.

I sat there in disbelief. Reality had struck me home so hard that I felt a resentful feeling whirling around inside.

"What gives him the right to order us about like that," I snapped.

Sharan looked at me in dismay and straining a whisper, she said,

"Keep your voice down. He only wants the fire put out. You will get us thrown out."

She was right of course, so I sat quietly trying to accustom myself to the situation. We all sat for a few long full minutes looking at the fire. No one wanted to put it out.

Then out of the silence came the gentle voice of Julie. "Such a shame, I love to sit around the comfort of a warm fire, but you know he'll come back to check."

I was so tired. I considered fetching some water, but Tim had beaten me to it. As he poured the water, a cool black atmosphere took precedence, and with a hiss, some thick grey visible smoke accompanied the wind and blew away. Now it was the moon offering its silvery lustre, demanding precedence, being so white and so bright, just a white illuminating sphere of light; its tranquil influence had never so quite graced my soul alike.

Chapter Four

A month had passed since our little excursion to the New Forest. And once again, I found myself sitting in my room at the top of the house. My parent's place was an old Victorian, four-bedroom, detached house. It was and still is the oldest and highest house on the road. Being at the top, my bedroom was a loft conversion that stretched from the rear to the front of the building with one small window at each end and was, therefore, not the largest but most certainly the longest room in the house.

It was a bedroom/studio where I spent most of my time either studying or sleeping. It was a long triangular shaped room some 8 metres long with fitted cabinets down each side which narrowed the floor space too about 3 metres. White painted brick surrounded white painted gothic shaped windows at each end. The ceiling consisted of dark beams. From the central apex, they ran down both sides with uneven white plaster spread between each one. The floor was an expanse of clear varnished floor boards dressed with strategically placed rugs.

At one end, placed on a writing desk was a computer, next to this was a drawing table then an easel. At the other end of the room was my bed. The only thing missing was a wardrobe. Owing to the shape of the room, it was not practical to have a wardrobe, and so I was to share a very large one with my brother Raymond on the floor below. In some families this would have no doubt caused a social problem, but as I have mentioned before, we were and still are a very close family.

Every morning, I would go down a narrow staircase, and dress in my brother's room. I didn't often disturb him because he started work early and was, therefore, gone by the time I woke.

Anyway, one evening, I was alone in my room feeling rather fatigued and sorry for myself. I had been searching for temporary work for days. It was now ten o'clock on a Sunday evening, my bedroom window was open, and leaning out of it, I had a clear view of the entire road below.

I observed the occasional passer-by or the odd car being driven down our generally sedate road. The evening was warm, deliciously warm and typical for that time of the year. Gently raising on a windless air, a cool breeze gave tranquillity to my mood. Far away to the west, sun was setting in a blaze of orange adornment behind the distant roof tops of our small village, tinting the entire area with a warm reminder of the following day to come. Lengthening shadows slowly emerged with the surrounding night that suddenly fell, making the stars and street lamps glisten with a radiance of joyous quietude.

Down low, disturbing the mild, motionless, inaudible night air were two noisy drunks making their way up the road. They were singing at the top of their voices. I heard dogs complaining about their racket, then other dogs joined in—no doubt complaining of their fellow creatures barking—which in turn caused the dog owners to shout complaints at their dogs. I watched and listened to the drunks merrily singing as they staggered by, and then once again, a peaceful silence dawned.

What a strange effect alcohol has on the human mind, I thought. It somehow manages to alter not just our character but our whole perception of the world, about us and even the way we think.

Then, tenderly rising in a changing direction, in swirls of air, I smelt the food from a barbecue, accompanied by laughter from a nearby garden party. The association with this garden party, its smells and laughter, captured my thoughts, and my mind was instantly cast back to the night of the camping trip in the New Forest and to the bizarre seizure that had shaken me up so badly. I had no nightmares, but many sleepless nights trying desperately to push its association out of my mind. The horrific feeling lasted for days, and at the time, it seemed so unforgettable.

The night in question scared me so much that the following day I pledged never to drink again. But alcohol was not the problem, I knew that. I knew that merely giving up drinking was not the answer, besides, I was not a heavy drinker, just a little tipple at the weekends and that was all. I couldn't afford it anyway.

I stood there trying to reason with myself. Perhaps the sheer stress of my uncle's death had caused my imagination to run amok, and on that horrific night around the camp fire, it all reached a climax. I was in a kind of state between awake and asleep, coupled with alcohol, is it any wonder that my mind ran off its tracks.

"Yet, it all seemed so real at the time," I exclaimed voicing my opinion out loud.

Now quietly standing at the window I was becoming bored.

"Come on…what happened to the adventure," I stressed. What about the 'out of body experience', the intruding smoke and a possible connection with the ghost of an old man. At the time, I felt to be on a quest to seek the knowledge of life itself and all its meaning. It was the invisible smoke—in a bizarre kind of way—that seemed to be pointing me in the right direction of that quest.

Coming out of that antique shop, I was so excited and scared at the same time. I was dealing with the unknown, but the very thought of finally having all of the answers to all of my questions was so appealing that it exceeded, by far, any scary morbid feelings that I might of hand.

Gathering momentum, my bored mind was now getting excited about the prospect of a possible adventure.

'Who was the old man? Was hc a ghost?' In a strange sort of way, I wanted him to be. I wanted to talk to him. I wanted to have a long conversation, lasting days, for it would take that long to answer everything that I hungered to know.

Being dead himself, perhaps he could confirm whether or not life does go on after death. Or if he is real in the full sense of the word, then maybe the fact that he exists is prove in its' self. At the back of my mind I positively wanted to know, but negative thoughts kept on intruding.

"I am only young with a whole life time ahead of me," I muttered trying to come to terms with my morbid thoughts. "Why should I persistently concern myself with such things at my time of life?" I gave a little sigh.

But then again…what's the harm in it? Wouldn't it be comforting to find out that this was truly the case, and that death was not the end, just a new beginning. What if you could retain everything that you knew from a former life and attend school not with memory of that past life but with the knowledge of the adult that you used to be…?

A loud screech came from a car as it turned into our road. My body jolted to attention which caused my mind to focus on its powerful presence, the sound of its roaring engine and the tyres that swished across the tarred surface as it passed. I watched until it reached the bottom of the road wherc it flashed its break lights and rapidly stopped; it indicated, flashing left, the engine violently revved…and it was gone.

A pain shot up one arm, I had not realised that I had been leaning on it for so long. I moved to make myself comfortable.

The passing car had abruptly brought my mind back to reality. I was trying to recapture the significance of my scrutinising ideas, but I knew it was no good. I had to face reality. It was four weeks after the camping trip to the New Forest and nothing even remotely exciting had happened since then. Life it seemed was back to normal. I had started on my profound quest for knowledge, but it was short lived. It had all come to an abrupt halt directly after my nightmarish seizure.

My heart sank. I leant out of the window, still none the wiser. I sighed once again and lifting my left hand, I rested my weary head in its palm.

During each incident that took place, I had mixed feelings. I was scared, dreadfully scared, and at moments, excited too. I was dealing with the unknown, the supernatural, I was convinced of it. It was all new to me and, therefore, a shock. Back then, I wished everything to go back to normal. Now that everything was back to normal, I had gone through the experience and come out unscathed. Now that my mind had had a rest and finally eradicated the supernatural beast, I couldn't help but wonder whether or not the whole experience was just a product of my fanciful imagination, or was it all a dream. It all seemed so distant, so unreal, and I felt so empty. It must have taken place; were it not for Sharan generally talking about the trip over the last few weeks, I could quite easily have accepted that very notion. Strange as it may seem I now wanted it all to return. I was curious. I had hoped that something would have come to light by now.

Four whole weeks had passed and nothing. Not a single unusual thing had happened. In despair, I turned to face my room. As I did so, I was confronted by a wall of blackness which slowly, as my eyes became accustomed to the lack of light, turned into a dark funnel ending with a small gothic-shaped window at the far end. Faint orange shapes gradually appeared from the reflecting street lamps. Then a silvery shape appeared across the angled ceiling echoing the shape of my silhouette in the open window. Wondering what had caused the silvery light, I turned to look out into the night, and there high in the sky, just like the night in the New Forest, I was greeted by the full moon, as it appeared from behind some clouds. The clouds that surrounded the moon were a glow of soft white lustrous mist that swirled with the wind creating coils of vapour that twisted around, not unlike spirals of smoke from a pipe.

"That's it…!" I expressed loudly, "the pipe. I still have the pipe." I had completely forgotten all about the only tangible thing that connected me with the ghost.

My whole body was all of aghast, filled with tingling activity as I realised that maybe…just maybe the whole scenario was real after all.

"But why had nothing happened for a whole month? Why had nothing unusual taken place, and why had I not encountered a ghostly old man or at least something of the paranormal strata of things?" I said amusingly.

After racking my brain for a while, I remembered being told once, many years previous that all supernatural activity is governed, to a certain extent, by the phases of the moon or 'the lunar phases' he called them.

That's it, the answer to the puzzle, I thought.

Accepting this conclusion, my mind went blank as a soothing cool mood spread over my body. I just calmly hovered motionless as the implications of what I had just thought slowly developed in my mind. I did not feel empty anymore, my spirit had somehow been replenished, and I merely stood there in the darkness of the room bathed in silvery moonlight.

I waited for something to happen. I longed for something to take place, for this time I would not fight it off. I wanted to meet the old gentleman. There was so much that I wanted to know, and somehow I knew, deep down inside that he could help me.

Looking at the moon I pleaded for an appointment, that somehow in the abyss of the spirit world, I might be heard. Awaiting a reply, the moon's calming influence bathed my restless spirit, but alas, nothing happened.

Feeling somewhat disappointed. I sighed bringing my head down to view the road below. I am not sure how long I stayed in this melancholy state, possibly half an hour or so. I didn't know it at the time, but I was learning that sometimes to receive subtle messages from the other side you must be patient.

I heard two teenage girls walking. They slowly made their way down the road towards our house. Their steps made a rhythmic clonking sound as they drew nearer and nearer. Passing in front of the house, they stopped to light up cigarettes. Then continuing their rhythmic clonking, I watched as they walked to the end of the road.

Why would such young beautiful girls want to destroy their lungs, I mused. Such innocence tarred by ignorance.

This caused me, for a while at least, to think about the whole motive behind smoking and its greedy producers. It was while I was pondering over this subject that an idea seemed to pop into my head.

I immediately sprang into action, fumbling around in the darkness of the room. I frenziedly groped about for the light switch...*click*, the entire room was flooded with light that burnt, making my eyes squint. Using my hand as a shield, I scanned the room, trying to remember where I had hidden the pipe. Then feeling tremendously excited about my idea, I frantically searched among the clutter of my bedroom/studio. It was some time before I found it—would you know—safely tucked away under my bed.

With the box firmly held in both hands, I quickly returned to sit on a chair near the open window, and there I opened the box to reveal, once again, the mysterious ivory pipe. I sat there for a minute or two just admiring it. Once more, I gaped curiously at the sheer artistry on such a disgusting object.

As nothing unusual had taken place. No ghostly phenomenon or supernatural activity. My idea was to try and perhaps evoke something to happen. Akin to the way that we use a telephone or possibly a computer to contact another person, so spiritualists or mediums might use a crystal ball or even Ouija board as instruments for communicating with the dead. Conceivably the reason why spiritualists and mediums need to use these instruments for communication is because the spirits on the other side find it too difficult to reach us.

Due to fear of the seizure, I had fought so strongly against contact with the ghost that even my girlfriend found it an arduous task to get through to me. Around the camp fire she found it necessary to physically hit me in order to capture my attention. So what chance did an extrasensory message have to get through? Perhaps the spirit of the old man found me too difficult a candidate for contact. *Ironically, I may have scared him off,* I amusingly thought.

I had, therefore, began to view the pipe as a communicational instrument. What other reason would the hidden powers of the ghost have enticed me into the antique shop to buy with my last ten pounds an item connected with a habit that I absolutely loathe. It was an appliance for communication...what else?

There had to be away of contacting the ghost through it. The obvious answer for me was to smoke from it but the very thought of puffing thick smoke from its archaic spout made me sick to my stomach. Who knows what may come out of it.

Inside the box next to the pipe was a small sachet of tobacco. A couple of days after the weekend in the New Forest, I took the liberty to ask at a tobacconist what he thought the previous content or brand of tobacco had been in the bowl. After giving me a strange look, for this was no doubt an unusual request, he held it up admiringly and sniffed around a few times. "I have no idea. I have never smelt such a brand before."

I tried another, but he said the same. I was about to give up when I chanced on a third one in an older part of the town. He told me that the brand was rare, so old and strong that no one smoked it anymore. And yet, after a great deal of effort, he found some at the back of his shop. He even gave it to me saying, "No one would have bought it anyway, strictly for the real connoisseur."

Contemplating my motive and feeling rather silly for doing so, with a finger and thumb of my left hand I gingerly lifted the pipe from the velvet soft interior of the box. Slowly turning my hand, it lightly laid in my palm, weighing down quite heavy for such a small object, and what a beauty I beheld. To want the beauty as seen in the artistry of such a mundane item, someone obviously loved smoking the rare brand of tobacco very much. I had altogether let slip from my memory the sheer craftsmanship, so fine, so artistically executed, it was a pleasure to own. It didn't seem to matter that I was not a smoker. I just couldn't believe that I had bought it so cheaply.

As I feasted my eyes upon it, amusing myself with the concept of using the pipe as a sort of communication device, I steadily became absorbed in its overwhelming subtle presence. It seemed to emit some kind of hypnotic aura that was so appealing, I just had to smoke from it. No longer did its criterion disgust me, and no longer did the idea of smoking from it sicken me. Its charm so bewitching, the very thought of smoking from it, slowly became…oh, so irresistible, spurred on by the tantalising idea of talking to a real ghost.

I jumped out of the chair, nearly dropping the precious masterpiece to the floor. Trying desperately to regain control over my faltering fingers, I pulled them towards me crashing the box and pipe together, surely breaking both objects at the same time. My head flew-up, my eyes closed tight, and my body went stiff as I slowly looked down to examine the damage. Nothing was broken.

I gently placed both pieces on the writing desk in front of me and quickly leant over to the very drawer where I knew a box of matches would be. Opening the draw by the side of two candle sticks, I instantly found a full box seemingly waiting there for this special occasion. *Lit candles would be a good idea too,* I mused striving to plan a course of action.

They should help to enhance the unearthly, creepy atmosphere that I needed. By drawing my attention, they might help me to concentrate, and who knows they may even encourage the shady soul of the old chap to come forth.

Like a moth being drawn to a flame, not knowing the dangers or pleasures that lay ahead. Feeling scared and excited at the same time, my precarious task sent cold shivers writhing up my back. Violently shaking my shoulders, I managed to disperse the quivers and briskly set up the candles in positions, either side of my chair close to the open window.

After lighting the candles, I dashed to switch off the main light and lost no time returning to the place specially prepared for that part of my quest. Making myself comfortable and trying to free myself from all negative doubts that I had concerning this brave undertaking. I looked about me, making sure that the atmosphere was just right.

Two feet in front of me, resting on the edge of my writing desk, next to the pipe and its accessories was a white candle in a brass holder. Close to me on my right, in the centre of a small table was the other white candle in a similar brass holder. To my left, through the open window I saw a clear, dark night's sky full of glittering stars, and a bright full moon offering a subtle assurance that the time was just right.

I looked at my watch, it was almost midnight. It was indeed the right time, "the witching hour," I said, mocking struggling to lighten the heavy atmosphere that was now creeping around me. My eyes had finally adapted to suit the less subdued candlelight flickers that seemly caused the dark shadows to hide shivering deep into the corners and crevices of my attic room.

To pick up the pipe from the desk, I moved forward creating a shadow that grew longer and longer across the angled ceiling. I jumped as the nearing candle on the desk crackled at the side of my hand. Making best of my movements, panting, I grabbed the pipe, matches and sachet of tobacco. Tension had built inside me. Doing my best to restrain my breathing, and there, by slowing down my increasing pulse, I drew a long deep breath filling my body with the much needed oxygen, then blew out causing both candles flames to flicker wildly. Feeling slightly better, I leant back deep into the confines of the chair.

After a few minutes had elapsed, by degrees my sensitivities were much more at ease with the atmosphere, and my mind still seduced by its motive, I calmly brought the pipe and sachet close to a dim glimmer of light to my right, and there I might see better to fill its bowl with the rare 'arcane' granules of tobacco. I refer to them as 'arcane' because each granule had a strange red tint that changed hue in the flickering light, and its smoke, I hoped, would be penetrating the barriers to the other worlds.

On opening the sachet, the pungent odour was a dreadful reminder of the mysterious invisible smoke that had so often haunted me. Although, at the corner of my eye, appearing an attempt at my subscribing spirit, I could see the shadows creeping from their lair, my only sanctuary being the pious light of the candles, burning making the shadows quiver at bay. I pressed on regardless, determined to carry out my eerie calling.

After filling the pipe, heart throbbing, I eagerly fished out a match from its box, and I was about to strike it when an awful grave thought struck my mind instead. Conscience is a fearful thing. What if he is the devil? What if the ghost who was with so much difficulty restrained, should be deaths messenger, whom was yielding to an unbridled impatience or mistake the time and should think himself accredited to my soul tonight, instead of at old age; should I be tampering with such things that I knew nothing about?

Hot with tension, mouth dry, my warm clammy hand was stuck to the pipe, stressed fingers tightly twisting a virgin match, veins swelling under the pressure of a pounding heart, beads of sweat forming on the forehead... I struck, filling the air with a bright eruption of light.

Had I wronged anyone or anything enough to be cursed to Hell's damnation? I wondered. Encompassing and spinning in my head were justice, fairness and balance, with temperance, prudence and fortitude banging on an imaginary door. Nearing my fingers, I stared at the flame burning down the match stick. Heavy beads of sweat ran down the sides of my face.

It is only your mind playing tricks, I reasoned. I've come this far, too far to stop now. I must succumb to my fate, whatever the outcome.

I paused for a moment longer, and once again, trying to elude my shady conscience, I delivered the pipe to my reluctant lips, lit the tobacco and puffed, blowing the smoke straight out into the room. I did it again and again, filling the room with a thick grey smog.

Extinguishing the match, I watched…nervously as its coils moved gracefully, floating on the calm air before being drawn towards and out of the open window. Its smooth, placid movements caused a calm dreamy effect that clouded my anxiety.

I lingered there breathless in vigil watchfulness as the smoke on an eternal flight to the unknown was metamorphically dispensed by the strong outer currents of air. I wondered if it would truly infiltrate the boundaries of our material world and reach the nose of the hopefully wise and knowledgeable spirit that I had envisaged in the old man.

When the last remaining cloud of smoke had finally disappeared, my attention was drawn to the content still smouldering in the pipe.

There was yet more to be smoked. Feeling much more at ease with my situation, for much to my relief, the ghost had not suddenly appeared from the blackness, by degrees, my increasing confidence was returning.

I puffed some more, then getting totally carried away, I puffed drawing in more each time, but by sheer carelessness or just stupidity, I breathed it in, taking down a lung full of its thick smog that smothered my chest, blocked my air passages; I gasped for air, there was a slight pain in my lungs before I finally blew it out coughing and spluttering. Heaving with jerky movements, I struggled to catch my breath. Hanging my head out of the window, taking in deep gasps of air I eventually achieved control but felt very dizzy.

In about five minutes an hour had passed, the candles were a lot shorter than before, and the moon had moved a few degrees across the night sky—a sure sign that time had passed—but I had no recollection of it waning. I had no recollection of any paranormal activity taking place either. With a disappointed huff I blew out the candles. Drained of energy, in a weary manner I undressed and collapsed on my bed, but before drifting off into a dark slumber I planned for the following day to venture out and sell that no good pipe and its box to anyone who should have need of it for I at long last had 'given up the ghost'—if there ever was one in the first place?

Although, little did I know at the time, I had indeed started something irreversible.

Chapter Five

The night was a long slumberous affair that ended with a feeling of falling from a great height, a hasty jolt and something that sounded like a seat belt's...*click*, as I dare say, I must have clicked back into my body again. Ten past six in the morning and not an inkling as to why I had so abruptly been taken out of sleep, except that I had apparently just landed, for that was the sensation that I had received. Peevishly, I turned over and with absolute disregard for time, I was determined to return to whence I came, for perhaps an hour or more at least.

Sometime later, not so abruptly, I awoke again. This time it felt like more of a smooth transaction. It was warm, sunny, and the birds were still celebrating the new dawn. I slowly rose and as usual, laboriously put on my dressing gown. I glanced at the chaotic remains of candle wax, bits of tobacco and the pipe resting on my desk. Downcast and somewhat dazed, I made my way down the narrow stairs, to escape the sound of jovial contemptuous birds was a good enough reason. In the bathroom I somehow felt better, different and more, wide awake than usual. I had a feeling of jubilation and as light as air. I habitually leant forward to turn on the shower, but instead of turning on the tap, I abruptly woke up in bed. The feeling was most bizarre to say the least. "What the hell was that," I said to myself.

Thoroughly confused and full of disbelief, I once more rose from my bed. Everything was as before, warm and sunny, and the birds were singing. I put on my dressing gown and slowly made my way down the narrow stairs. This time, the hall clock chimed for 7.00am, and in the bathroom, I tentatively stretched out my right hand to turn on the shower. Yet once again to my astonishment, I woke up in bed again.

It seemed that my 'goldfish syndrome' had returned. I would get out of bed and go down to the bathroom where I would find myself in bed again. An endless cycle, it was extraordinary. I concluded that it must have been the after effects from all the smoke that I had inhaled.

On my third attempt, utterly bewildered, I rose from my bed. It was warm and sunny, and the birds were singing. I put on my dressing gown and slowly made my way down the narrow stairs. I tentatively entered the bathroom to turn on the shower, only this time, everything appeared to be normal. Somewhat dazed, I shook my head, trying my best to shake off the dreamy effect. Relieved, my bewilderment gradually eased, but the experience was just so disturbing that I had to shake my head again and pinched myself to make sure that I was not still dreaming. The pinch seemed real enough yet, my body felt unusually light, like I was floating. I shrugged off the feeling the best that I could and joined my brother Ray in the kitchen.

My brother seemed to be ignoring me. He could be like that sometimes. Normally, it was because he had a lot on his mind, so I didn't bother him. I decided against breakfast anyway. And before I knew it, I was on my way to those great historical places that have always housed many an antique shop preserved, Windsor and Eton. And my new mission, to sell the confounded pipe and its box to one of the dealers.

On the train as I idly watched the world shoot past the window, I got thinking about the pipe, and what I had tried to do with it the night before. "What was I thinking?" I scornfully said to myself,

"Trying to materialise an old man from a pipe, God…how stupid."

Feeling ashamed for being so easily taken in and seduced by my own wild imagination, I could sense agitation churning inside my stomach. "Just like Aladdin," I scoffed, "who rubbed his lamp and out popped a Genie. I suppose that I smoke the pipe and…"

I quickly rose, and putting my head through the train's window, the cool air instantly cooled the temperature of the 'furnace' burning inside me and to my relief, a sure deliverance from self-torture too.

I pushed my problem thoughts far into the unused cavities of my mind, utterly refusing to pursue its cursed issue any longer. Whatever the weird problem was, it was now at an end. I looked up to the sun shining its wondrous rays on the land. Trees were beautiful shades of green. It was one hell of a day to banish my ghost.

Fearing a train from the opposite direction, I pulled my head in. The train was full of people now, they had been jostling around for seats and clear opened spaces to stand, so when I returned to my seat, I found that it was no longer vacant. Disappointed, I casually looked around the carriage and directed my attention on the crowd of people immediately surrounding me.

The first person, standing to my far right was a middle-aged man, heavy-set, thick dark moustache, in a black suit, a coloured tie and tightly wedged between his legs was a black briefcase. *What clothing to be wearing on such a hot day,* I critically thought.

Next to him was a middle-aged woman with blonde hair, dressed in a dark grey short skirt suit. She too had a black briefcase, only hers was tightly wedged under one of her arms. She had beautifully shaped legs for her age. As I sat there admiring her legs, she must have sensed me looking, and I somehow knew that she was about to look in my direction. I turned my head quickly.

Sitting opposite me was a young man in dark blue overalls, wearing tired—as he looked—worn out old boots. Next to him, another young man in a brown uniform and wearing highly polished brown shoes.

The whole carriage was full of a mixture of people from all walks of life, from teenage to middle age. There were just two old people. We were bound for an industrialised town called Slough and so all were dressed not to suit the weather but dressed for work.

As I glanced around taking in the atmosphere, I noticed that out of some fifty odd people not one spoke, all that could be heard was the repetitive drudgery of the wheels polishing the tracks. I could feel everyone's gloomy presence spreading over me. Everyone looked so terribly sad. There was nothing unusual about this of course, I sighed.

"Well that's what work does for you," I said, caught in rumination.

It was Monday morning. Some looked to be still half asleep, but who goes to work with a smile anyway? The more that I looked at them, the more I seemed to be drawn into their dismal stupor. They looked so lost, almost as if to be dead. It was like a funeral procession.

Logically thinking, it was obvious, you work to live, and that is what they were doing. "But surely you work to earn money, and with that money, you can buy things you want, and you become happy, right?"

If this was so, then why did these employed people look so unhappy?

They seemed so empty and undirected as if not to possess a soul, just a mobile empty shell. "Had they sold their soul to the devil?" I asked myself.

The only answer was that they were caught up in the trappings of a habitual, dull, routine life. I was sure that way back in the history of the human race, deep in the channels of thought, there must have been a main direction, and yet that does not seem to be the case at present. Now the stream of our common united consciousness seems to have lost its central direction and to no particular purpose other than its wasteful performance of its own internal momentum. It seems to have lost the blue print of the grand plan, just a steady egocentric will to earn money and buy things. That is why all those people on the train looked so unhappy, they were disillusioned. Their united mind and spirit was lost. They had nowhere to go but 'dull old work'.

I had never noticed this in people before. "What an unusual cast of thought," I muttered to myself.

After slowly pulling into the station, the train eventually came to a grinding halt. The dense heaving of the masses seemed to force the doors open. They fought as if competing in a race. When we finally came to a complete stop, I sat quietly waiting for the surge to disperse.

The people on the Windsor train were so different. It carried many noisy passengers whom were dressed suitably for the hot weather: Light clothes that were full of wonderful colours. Their faces were not sad but cheerful—no, beaming with life—filling the carriage and my moving spirit with a delightful jubilation.

These people were not travelling to work, they were full of life, they had somewhere to go and curiously enough I felt that way too. What a wonderful feeling they had entrusted to me. The heavy emotional load that had weighed me down so, on the first train, was now gone.

What a peculiar thing it is, I thought, *that the emotions of complete strangers can be so contagious as if to transmit emotion across the space between us.* It was like we were all somehow connected. Perhaps our auras were touching. We were all moving simultaneously through space and time, and all were crediting glorious thought transference. They were not strangers. Each was a potential friend.

Standing directly opposite me, an elderly lady smiled and with an American accent asked the time. After informing her that I did not possess a watch, I wondered why she had asked in the first place, because I could clearly see that she had a watch.

As if reading my thoughts, "Yes I know," she answered, laughing. "You are no doubt wondering why I asked? My eyes are not what they used to be, and the hands on my watch are too small for me to see. Time has no meaning anyway." I couldn't see the point in her wearing it, but she no doubt had her own reasons.

She was a dear old lady. Wore designer glasses and had grey hair tied in a bun. She was somewhat frail in appearance, but exceedingly charming and judging by her clothes and jewellery, she was also very well-to-do.

"Oh, I do so love England," she went on. "You people are so debonair and at times so cool and reticent. Americans are sometimes far too open about things that we leave nothing to the imagination, nothing to explore, and your country is so green and beautiful, so full of history…"

She went on and on, talked nonstop throughout the rest of the journey. Within that span of time, she must have told me her entire life story.

No wonder the Americans see us as being so cool and reserved, I thought, *we can't get a word-in-edgeways.* Even so, there was something about her character that was really quite likeable.

Her whole life had been cantered on material gain. She was rich and wanted for nothing—material that is—yet until she had retired, she had not questioned the meaning of her life. She was far too busy making money, but in retrospect, if she had been given that time again, things would have been a lot different.

Towards the end of her 'story', I asked. "If you were born again with the knowledge that you have now, what would you have changed?"

Her answer was predictable, "To have my life again, all of my thoughts would not be directed at riches. We need money to live of course, you cannot live a day without it, but we need not be rich. Great wealth, I assumed, would make me happy, but it has only brought me sadness, lies and deceit. I am now dead, and I am no longer rich. I gave most of it away…"

"Pardon…! Did you say dead?" I asked in dismay.

She paused and looked out of the window, her eyes glazed as if drifting on a tide of reminiscence. "Yes…" she finally continued, still staring out of the window, "to have my life again I would direct it body and soul, a whole lifetime devoted to happiness."

She was obviously using the word as a figure of speech, but I had to ask, "Excuse me, lady, what do you mean you are dead," I chuckled.

She looked at me with dismay. "Yes, darling," she replied. "The meaning of life is not to be rich. Money is an illusion, a carrot dangling from a stick. The more you have, the more you want. The true meaning must be happiness, only…! I had not quite realised it before, not until now, when it is too late."

She could not have heard what I had said. Perhaps she was a bit deaf.

Her voice lowered and so did her head. "It was there all the time, staring me in the face. It has taken me a lifetime to work it out." Looking up, she returned to her gazing out of the window.

There is wisdom in those words, I thought.

Although there is a lot to be said about riches for it can at times create a great deal of happiness, yet to pursue riches for the sake of wealth and money itself, is pointless, and causes the opposite effect, great sadness. If wealth alone generated pleasure, happiness fulfilment of spirit, then all of the rich people of our world would be the happiest people alive. And yet, if this was true, why do so many wealthy people turn to drugs and alcoholism. They turn to psychiatrists, and the worst cases cannot take any more and commit suicide. Perhaps they felt empty, as if something in their lives was missing, and great wealth could not fill the hole. I am not suggesting that the poor are any different, but the point is great wealth cannot provide everything, it is not a panacea, so why do people see it as such?

I had drawn the same impression of the people on the first train. I feared that very few of them liked their job, if they did, then they would not have been so sad. They seemed to be unhappy, unfulfilled, lacking in spirit, failing to notice that their very greed for riches or ambition to do well has caused them the problem. Everyone wishes for a better life, to be happy, fulfilled and experience that feeling of achievement, and yet it is also possible to work too hard, for too many hours, for too many months, over too many years, that you lose sight of your original goal, which is surely happiness itself…is it not? That is happiness for yourself and your family.

Once again, as if reading my mind, the old lady stared at me and with a haunting look, all knowing and wise beyond her age, she said, "You are right, how perceptive of you my dear."

I felt a jolt and a tug as the train approached Windsor station.

Turning her head, the old lady was now quietly observing the castle on top of the hillside. I watched as each person in turn peered through the windows for that first glimpse of the famous battlements. One little girl asked, "Will they have swans and ducks." The atmosphere on board was so alive with enthusiasm.

The train pulled slowly into Windsor station. The reaction from the people on this train was totally different from the first. The old lady and I sat calmly with other passengers waiting for it to completely stop. No one even attempted to open the doors, let alone rush to get off, for they were in no hurry. Each person took their time to recover their belongings and then full of excitement—I could see it on their faces—complete strangers helped one another off. For they had arrived at their destination, but the train bound for riches, never arrives, never reaches its destination, and so its passengers must run to keep up with its momentum, only they run in vain.

In life you must board the right train, and while you are on it, take a good look out of its windows, for the meaning of life is not to arrive at happiness, but you must also enjoy the journey.

After helping the old lady off the train, I bade her goodbye, yet the strangest thing happened. I turned my head around, took a brief few paces forward, then turning back to offer her some guidance, to my amazement, she had completely disappeared. Had I been talking to a ghost?

Shaking off yet another spooky experience, I swiftly set off on the next stage of my mission, to Eton and the antique shops. Out of the station, I turned left to go down a hill which took me alongside the Windsor Castle. Looking up I admired the great walls that have protected many noble Kings and Queens throughout many centuries. How old they are, and what scenes they must have witnessed? If the stones could talk, what stories would be told?

Wasting no time, I moved on down a small hill and followed the road as it curved to the left away from the Castle and towards Eton. I was moving quite fast now, so fast, in fact, that on crossing a road, a car barely missed me and a second one would have hit me if I wasn't so quick to move out of the way. "Crazy maniac," I shouted. *He couldn't have seen me, he wasn't even looking,* I thought, *what's his problem?*

Composing myself, I pressed on eager to get rid of the pipe. So eager was I to sell the pipe, I almost went straight past the first of many antique shops. Without hesitation, I advanced through the door and up to the counter.

The dealer was helping a lady with an enquiry about a ring, so I waited. When the lady had finally left the shop, the antique dealer totally ignored me, turned and disappeared to a room at the back. I thought that his manner was somewhat ignorant, but I continued to wait. When he did not return, I realised that he must have seen the pipe in my hand. Perhaps he knew that I had come to sell and not to buy. My impatience got the better of me, so I immediately left.

Further along the road, I found another shop full of people. I moved swiftly to a third, and yet to my disappointment, it was equally busy. I could not possibly discuss business with the dealer being so occupied. I moved on to another only to find that the next one was closed. Feeling thoroughly frustrated, I sped off further down the road, not even considering the next shop which may have, by chance, a reckoning over my old piece of 'junk'. I felt ashamed to have been 'seduced' by such a distasteful object. I moved through the streets not looking or even caring were I was going.

I finally found myself at the side of a river. I assume it was the River Thames. I sat down on a seat and looked out over the water, wondering whether to throw the damn pipe and its box in the water. Were it not for the thought of contaminating the water I would have done so there and then.

I sat for a while watching the birds feeding on the bank. The tranquil atmosphere had a calming effect on my mind which in turn seemed to soothe my doleful spirit. I felt as if hovering over an endless transient path to nothingness. The feeling was quite beautiful until the dejected feeling returned. I then felt totally empty, and in a solemn mood, I moved on.

Further down the river, I watched boats bobbing up and down in the currents of the fast moving, green water. I could hear the faint sound of birds desperately singing in a vain attempt at changing my ever-increasing depressive mood. On and on I went, down the river, until finally the pathway opened out to a park.

Still feeling downhearted, I stared across a large field. Leaving the river behind, I don't know why it felt like the right thing to do at the time. I made my way towards a wooded area which seemed to be in the centre of the park. My mind wondering, I persisted aimlessly across this wet grassy field.

Yet, unbeknown to me for I did not know it at the time, I had had a calling. I was slowly but very surely being lured by some unknown subtle force. It had my full regard in its clutches, and it was reeling me in like a fish from the river. The closer I moved towards the trees, the more vibrant the greens in the grass became.

It was incredible. It seemed to almost come alive and move of its own accord. The colours of the trees were vibrant too, they took on a responsive shimmer which caused the leaves to oscillate in a heavenly display of colourful light.

With me in its clutches, I drew nearer and nearer, faster and faster until finally I plunged among the wondrous array of plant life. And there, to my disbelief, I felt to be floating in a spiritual pool of heaven-sent ecstasy.

I waited motionless in a timeless void of joyful embrace which slowly rose up my now vibrating body. Never before had I felt such power, never before had I felt such passion, and never before had I seen such beauty. All around me the woods teamed with life. As if to announce my arrival the birds were singing a melody. Squirrels darted in a playful dance across the branches, knocking leaves which forced the trees to relinquish them in an array of kinetic jubilance, full of colour, lingering and then playing with the warm air until finally each leaf had slowly and gracefully touched the softened ground.

There was a rustle of leaves, and out jumped a brown rabbit. It sat there curiously looking at me. Then in some unknown language that I somehow understood, it asked me to follow. Without hesitation, I followed this mysterious rabbit swiftly on root to somewhere in the middle of the woods. It was quite a journey across streams and past small natural ponds. Everywhere I looked, I had never seen such abundance of life. Then suddenly ceasing me in my tracks the rabbit stopped.

I casually looked to see what the problem might be. It was looking straight at me. Its eyes then seemed to light up in a kind of mystical knowing as if to hold a memory of an event which I had forgotten. And in a strange sort of way, this beautiful furry creature did look familiar. It reminded me of a rabbit that I had and loved as a child. I had named it Joey.

Gazing into its eyes, it held my attention while a telepathic message gradually, by degrees, filtered its way through. Seeming to laugh, it looked away to show me something in among the trees. "There are the water rushes," it said. You can hear soft voices singing in the wind. Weaving and dancing, the dragonflies play with the flickering sun light. Looking to one side the rabbit showed me a water boatman ski across the thin skin of a motionless dew pond. "And there beneath some sloth wood, a drowsy trout lay. Moving winds...are moving a breeze through the trees where wild brown berries and the reddest of cherries drop to the lake...and colourful, blooming flowers with a sweet smell of blossom that moves across the banks."

I was now hopelessly lost to an inherent stimulus that made me feel so wondrously alive, so 'deliciously' alive and dynamic. For the first time in my life I really felt part of the world, totally infused— no! I was the world. My emotions running wild I looked at the rabbit. "Go on, Joey," I whispered.

Turning in a joyful response, it continued running towards a destination that only it knew.

It seemed no time at all, while following this rabbit, I saw in the distance over the brow of a hill a bright light with rays that looked to be shooting straight up to the sky. Like sunlight only it couldn't be, yet on moving closer, I was not sure whether the light was coming from behind the hill shooting up or from the sky shooting down. If the light was coming from the sky, it was surely being reflected back by what could only be hundreds of mirrors. My adrenaline was racing, my body tingled with the thrill of excitement. The rabbit wasn't at all perturbed by the bright light, and we moved ever faster towards it.

Not even considering what this mysterious light was, without a care in the world, I chased on after the rabbit. The thought of it being a hostile energy of some kind did not enter my mind. I felt so warm and content, so ecstatically eager, so avidly devoted to embrace the light and force. I could not help myself. This force did not feel negative or malicious or even evil, it did not feel wrong, it felt Oh…so right. And following closely behind the rabbit, I shot over the brow of the hill. Closing my eyes, we plunged deep into the light.

There was a silence and a warm peaceful atmosphere surrounded me. I felt as light as air, so light, I could not feel my feet on the ground. I just lingered there floating in a timeless quietude. It brought comfort and tranquillity to my frenzied animated spirit.

Time appeared to lose all meaning, so how long I remained in this state, I have no idea, or indeed, did I care. I thought about moving, but the sensations were too good. My entire body had taken on more rhythmic vibrations that pulsated up and down my spirit, creating a cold tingle that shot up my spine and on reaching my head, I exploded with tears of pleasure which poured down my face. The rhythmic vibrations made me quiver in pure ecstasy. I did not want to move. I did not want to think. I wanted only to remain and rejoice for ever in this enigmatic state of pure bliss.

Then a horrific thought struck me cold. "Am I dead?"

"Is this what dying feels like?"

At the same time, I felt the beautiful rhythmic vibrations slowing down, drawing me back down towards a depressive mood which was about to sink to the pit of my stomach when I heard a soft friendly voice:

"You are not dying."

My mood and thoughts instantly changed, and the vibrations once again leapt into action, and once again my entire being 'sizzled' with excitement.

Wondering where the voice had come from, I courageously opened my eyes only to see an intense bright light. I quickly closed them and slowly tried again. It was sometime before my eyes became accustomed to the light. Yet, still all that I could see was a pure white illuminated light.

I heard the voice once again, this time more audible and distinct.

"You have been summoned here at my request." It paused, then moments later I heard.

"Your future is in review," it added.

I instantly felt the level of vibrations increase to a high-pitch hum, as it did so, the light dimmed and there to my surprise, sitting some twenty feet in front of me was the old man that I had seen in my dream.

I guess it was a dream. I was never really sure. He appeared slightly out of focus so I blinked hard and concentrated, and his image cleared. It was defiantly the same person.

He was surrounded by a mystical blaze of colour. I looked into his eyes, they lit up as he must have seen the surprise look on my face. He then burst into tears of laughter.

I am not entirely sure why, but I too laughed. Perhaps I felt foolish at the situation that I had found myself in. It may have also been the result of shock, or that his laughter was contagious, I don't know, but we laughed. I felt so happy to be alive.

Calming down, I asked, "Where are we?"

"Where are we?" He mimicked, still laughing.

"Where are we? He says. Where are we? Wouldn't you like to know?" He said, not able to contain himself. "Oh…the look on your face," he chuckled on.

Now feeling somewhat ridiculed, I demanded an answer. "Where are we?" I asked sternly. "And who are you? What do you want from me?"

He stopped and looked at me with a warm smile. His face took on a mystical glow which seemed to light up my spirit. He looked so knowing, so aware as if to retain the grand total of the mysteries of the universe right there inside him.

"What would you like to know?" he said in a calm, friendly voice.

Feeling like a mere mortal talking to a god, I timidly asked.

"Where are we, and what is this place?"

Then came the most obvious yet unexpected answer. "Why...we are in the park of course," he exclaimed with a mischievous smile.

Feeling surprised and somewhat stupid, I looked around me, and sure enough we were indeed surrounded by trees in the centre of the park. I looked back at his mocking face for an answer, but why would there be. I had not left the park so why would I be anywhere else but in the park.

He was sitting there on a log still smiling, waiting for a reaction. He was exactly as I remembered him in my dream. He had not even changed his clothes: A dark red cardigan buttoned down the front, a white shirt, black trousers and shiny black shoes. He wore glasses. His head was balding with white wispy hair to the sides and back and a narrow white moustache. He did remind me of someone, but I could not recall who.

"You have something for me, don't you?" he said suddenly.

"I...I...don't think so," I replied hesitantly.

"Is that so," he murmured, scratching the side of his face, "then what is that in your hand?"

I looked to see where he was pointing. "Of course, the pipe must be his. I remembered him smoking one in my dream."

"You mean the pipe. Is it yours?" I retorted.

"Yes...Yes boy, I lost it, long...long ago. You have no idea how long I have waited for this moment."

He seized it from me and eagerly opened the lid and took it out of its old secured container.

"Argh...yes...many a night I have spent in the light of the moon smoking from this pipe. Many a night I have spent looking at the stars contemplating the universe and its creation. Do you know I could sit drifting in and out of thoughts on an endless 'timescape' for ever smoking from this pipe? Thank you...thank you, my boy."

Then putting the pipe and its box on the log next to him, he looked at me and said, "Now I must do something for you. How can I help you?"

"I...I...don't know," I replied, hesitating once again.

"You wanted to know where we are," he continued, "and as I have already mentioned we are in the park, but what I think you meant or what you was referring to, was the wonderful experience you have just had."

"You know about that?" I exasperated.

"Yes of course…" he said, "I should do. It was I who made it happen. You have just experienced 'pure positive life force'. You didn't leave the park, you became part of it. You were the park, and the park was you."

This was all far too much for me to grasp. My brain was 'hurting'.

What is this old fellow talking about? I thought. *Yes, it was a wonderful experience, the best I had in my entire life or might ever expect to have in the future. It was a pleasurable enough experience, life changing even, but what did it have to do with this old man, and who or what was he?*

I looked at him in wonderment. Not sure what to do, or what to say, I finally asked, "Who are you?"

Then with a warm delightful glance he divulged his identity.

"Firstly, I am the best friend you will ever have or likely to want. Unlike you, I am pure spirit, what you would probably call a ghost."

"But…ghosts don't exist… Do they?" I said in disbelief.

"Then how do you explain my existence?" he replied.

"I don't know. I'm confused. I can't explain it," I declared. "Sit down next to me, and let me explain."

Then to my amazement, I did not just move to sit next to him, I floated and hovered by his side. I sort of tingled in animated space.

"You asked for me," he went on, "When you heard of your uncle's death, you were in torment and called to the winds. Your plea was heard. You were dreadfully distressed. You asked many questions but none were answered. Now is the time. Only now may you be shown and taught some of the mysteries of life, magic and the universe. When a pupil is ready, and only when he is ready will a teacher or guide appear. You are ready, my boy, you are indeed ready."

He winked and laughed again. I somehow felt lucky as if I had been given a test and passed with flying colours.

If that is so, I thought, *then why me, and what had I done that could be so great as to be bestowed such a prize.*

"You are wondering why you out of everyone?"

His query alarmed me. *My God,* I thought, he can actually read my mind.

"Well…firstly, you are not the only one. There are many such as you, and you all have one thing in common. You are all inquisitive. Most people find life in the physical world difficult. In fact, if everyone were truthful, all would admit this to be so for the physical plain is at times hash, cruel and at best most would say agonising with little if any rewards.

"They just carry on in their work day after day, week after week, month after month and year in and year out with the occasional alcoholic drink as a vain attempt to get out of their monotonous existence. They didn't start out that way, but this is what they quickly resulted too.

You, on the other hand, and those like you are different. You are inquisitive. You are questioning things. You are showing the first signs of further development and the first signs of awareness. This will finally allow your soul to move on to the next level for there are many."

He continued laughing again as if to be taunting me over something I and humanity had not quite grasped. It seemed that we had been put to some test and had failed. *What could it possibly be,* I pondered, *what had we failed to see or learn?*

Feeling humiliated yet honoured to have been picked out of so many, trying to be clever I finally asked, "So what is the riddle of life then?"

He immediately stopped laughing and looked me straight in the eye; his face provoked a fiendish grin of contempt that shocked me to the core. His face then softened to a smile as he answered.

"All in good time, my boy…all in good time." He moved a little as though making himself comfortable and went on.

"You, like every living thing, are in various stages of development. Some have started, others like you are on a more advanced level. There is an awakening taking place in the world today. It has taken a long time, millions of years, in fact, but now, finally, humanity is becoming aware of itself and its maturity. Through the development of knowledge, communication and various learning capabilities taking place internationally, man is on the brink of discovering something new, something until now believed to be impossible.

"Man is the most acute of all living things. The human being is so intelligent yet so incredibly stupid. Alas, evolution has been a learning curve, and some like yourself are now becoming aware of your capabilities. You have realised that there is more to your life than just a physical existence. You are not sure of your thoughts yet, things other than the physical cannot be proved to exist, therefore you doubt whether your feelings about this subject are true. Nevertheless, the point is you are questioning things, and there are many of you."

He paused for a moment to see if I was following him. Receiving an affirmative he pressed on.

"We call you the 'learned ones', and you are to guide others to the next level of evolutionary thought."

Feeling humbled and unsure of myself, I asked, "But…How am I supposed to do this? I'm not the sort to lead people. No one would listen to me, and as sure as hell, I cannot lead the world."

"My dear boy," he exclaimed, cutting my flow of despair, "you are defeated before you have even started," he chuckled. "Always negative, the human race is full of negativity, always first to assume the worst and always on the defensive."

"Not necessarily," I responded defending my own attributes. "I sometimes think positive. I don't always think negative."

"This is true," he answered. "This is why you are one of the chosen few. You are showing signs of divine qualities. You are to be taught the real secrets of life and the universe, the 'Grand Plan' as intended from the beginning of time—you and your friend."

My heart skipped a beat and seemed to lodge itself in my throat as an eerie feeling crept over me once again. 'We are not alone?'

"Yes…" he said, "you and your friend."

"What friend…?" I returned timidly looking around for an expected mysterious figure but nothing was there. No human, no animal, not a being to be seen. I looked at him totally puzzled.

He laughed once again in amusement. "You cannot see this person, but this friend is defiantly with you," he repeated. "Not here and now as you might expect but in another time. Across space and time this person's thoughts are with you. You know who I am referring to, don't you? You can feel your spirit move and tingle as the spooky realisation develops right there in your physical body. You now seem tense and not quite sure what to believe. Your heart is now beating. Believe it or not, we have what is called a spiritual connection. There are many forms of haunting…my friend."

Not knowing what he was talking about, I tried to press for further information about the secrets of life and the universe. Hoping that just possibly this old man may have some answers to the riddle of life. He had said some strange things so far, some I could not understand and some just completely incomprehensible.

Perhaps he is off his head, I thought. A complete lunatic, yet somehow, I found him intriguing. So, like a moth drawn to light, I asked, "What am I to do?"

He looked at me with glee. I had obviously asked the right question.

"First," he said, "you must attend a school of learning, and I will be your teacher. You will learn mysteries and the secrets behind life, and then you will make others aware. You will not need to be a leader, and you will not be asked to control people merely to guide them, if and only if, they should ask. That is all. All will be revealed bit by bit, that you may understand fully.

But first, I'd like you to tell me your feelings and experiences of life thus far."

Being put on the spot, my mind was completely blank. "Well, I don't know," I said, trying to think of something interesting to say. Try as I may, not one appealing thought came through. Then trying to shine some light on my dull life I half-heartedly said, "I am at art college, and one day I hope to be an artist or a designer."

He nodded and motioned me to continue.

"When I finish college, I hope to find a good job, settle down with my girlfriend and raise a family and…" I paused for a moment.

He prompted me further. "That is what you have planned for the future? What about your past?"

"There's not much to tell really, only that I have attended school."

"Yes! Yes!" he said enthusiastically, "go on."

"That is it," I replied. "What else is there?" I looked at him wondering what else he wanted me to say.

With a warm smile he asked, "What about your inner feelings? How do you perceive your life?"

"It has its ups and downs," I answered, generally reflecting over my experiences. "Sometimes, I feel good and other times I feel bad, just like anyone else, I guess. More down than up, I might add. Sometimes I feel as if my life has no meaning, a complete failure."

"And why do you think that is?" he asked.

"I don't know," I responded. "Everything can be going my way. Life can be going according to plan but for some reason I'll feel depressed. I don't know why. That's just the way life is I guess."

"And would you like to be happy all the time?"

"Of course I would," I exclaimed. *What a stupid question,* I thought. *Everyone would like to be happy all the time.*

"And what would it take for you to be happy all of the time?"

I thought for a moment.

"I see," he ruminated, picking up on my thoughts. "So, to be rich would make you happy? To win the lottery perhaps."

"Yes," I said excitedly, thinking that he could somehow grant me a wish.

"To always be healthy, never ill and be very rich, that would definitely make me happy. I could come and go, do as I pleased. I wouldn't have to work. I could travel the world and really see life," I said.

He smiled.

"And, when you have travelled the world what then? Would you not get bored and feel depressed once again?" he enquired.

"I don't know," I said. "I would like to give it a try though."

"And how would other people see you? Would you have friends?" He asked.

"Are you kidding," I exclaimed. "Everyone would want to know me. I could buy them things and make them happy too."

"Supposing that you are correct," he said, "then all healthy rich people must be very happy with their lives. Do you think that is true?" "I guess so," I weakly returned, for I knew it could not possibly be true.

"Then why do you suppose so many healthy, wealthy people turn to alcohol, drugs and commit suicide. Some even become trapped in their large secure houses, cut off from the outside world, bored, lonely and very unhappy. They are full of fear, cannot go beyond the boundaries of their own premises. There is security all around them stopping the world from getting in and them from getting out. Some end up like the old lady you met on the train."

Whoosh, there it went, a cold tingle up my back. This old fellow was full of surprises.

"How do you know of her?" I asked in astonishment. "Were you there? If you were, I didn't see you," I exclaimed.

"Oh yes, my boy, I was there, but you would not have seen me." He returned laughing. "I have been with you for quite some time, much longer than you might like or understand, but that is not important right now, you are an inquisitive person. You are questioning life, and all I have done is ask you questions. So from now on, I will give you some answers."

Leaning over, taking his pipe out of its box, he pulled some tobacco out of a pouch, filled the pipe bowl and struck a match. I was amused to actually see his smoke for the first time. I watched, feeling as if in a halfway-world, unsure of what I was seeing, and what I was imagining. Floating between us were clouds of blue smoke rising in layers. Gently rising clouds of smoke swirled thickly up and down. As they turned, a million points of light reflected from each particle, sending forth dazzling beams of colourful light. From my vantage point, I could see a rainbow of colours fanned by a breeze. Turning red, it, at times, almost flared into flames and fast dying sparks. Then given fresh life, the vibrant smoke rose in ever thicker columns of blue to form trailing paths above and behind our heads. Rising higher, the smoke formed yet another cloud. Wreathing and twisting on faint air currents, it seemed like a thing alive, like a creature, though dimly seen, breathing and turning in sleep. For some time, I gazed, hypnotised with a fantasy that I was within a living being, watching its life and the sway of its organs, I heard the sounds of the body, of life itself.

The smoke cleared, and there he sat motionless, looking at me with an expression of amusement, as if to be playing a game, and this was his favourite. He looked different somehow. His clothes seemed lighter, and some hair had taken root on top of his head. The park seemed to be clearer too.

"You say that sometimes you feel a failure, and life has its ups and downs," he said, breaking the silence. "You have also mentioned that lots of money would path the way to happiness. To win the lottery would solve your problems."

"Yes," said I, agreeing with his reflections.

"Then let me tell you that you are already a lottery winner. You are a winner, you just cannot remember it."

"Yes…that's right," I replied sarcastically. "I'll draw a few thousand out of the bank tomorrow."

"There are many types of lotteries, and there are many types of banks," he retorted. "You have no idea how lucky you are. You are indeed a one in a million. You have won the jackpot."

"How could that possibly be so?"

"Unlike me," he continued, "you are three parts. You are made up from three types of matter or bodies, a mind, a physical body and a spirit or soul, known simply as the mind, body and spirit. You are extremely lucky to have all three, and you are indeed fortunate to be alive and possess a beautiful physical body. No matter what you consider it to look like, it is yours and only yours to do with as you please. You have no idea because you cannot remember what it takes to possess such a body of matter.

"Firstly, there is the actual physical making of the body. This was not by chance. Using a process that took evolution millions of years to accomplish; your parents would have made love possibly many, many times, dispensing, sometimes misusing many millions of sperms at each session, totalling billions over many such encounters. Then out of so many of those encounters, one time was just right. You and millions of others were dispatched, and you, the lottery winner, succeeded above all the odds and came through a billion to one chance. Additionally, as if that was not enough, millions of pregnancies fail around the world every year due to illness, accidences, abortions etc., and to top it all, as if this was not enough, millions of babies die at birth or during the first three months of life."

He looked me straight in the eye. "And you and your body are living proof of success, the final result of a perfect successful winner. Do you still consider yourself a failure?" he asked in conclusion.

He was right of course, the odds of success on that kind of scale were very slim, very slim indeed. *I'm clearly not a complete failure,* I thought, feeling much better about myself, but this had not taught me much of the so-called mysteries of life. He had mentioned a mind, body and spirit. I desperately wanted to know more. I desperately wanted to learn his secrets.

"That all concerns my physical body," I said questioningly. "You say that we have a mind and a spirit too. The mind or brain, I can understand but what of the spirit or soul? Would you please explain?"

"Some would say that your mind and spirit are one and the same. This is not true. They are two, complete and separate entities. One is the brain which is a physical component and part of the body, the other is subtle and not of the physical world. Both work together, hand in hand. Thoughts are created by your spirit or soul if you will, and your brain is the earthly organ that puts the plan into action. They interact with each other producing the thing that you call 'Yourself, the you.' What you think you are as a human being?"

"But surely, my thoughts are made in my brain," I enquired, disbelieving his notion.

He sighed, pulled a pitiful face and shrugged his shoulders. "Yes, sadly, this is man's denial of his spirit. After millions of years in the development, the human being still finds it hard to accept that he has a soul, and that there is a spirit world. Even in your time, science cannot proof it, and so the greatest minds alive cannot accept it as a fact."

He paused for a moment.

"Let me tell you, my boy, they will never proof it. They will never proof it because it is not physical matter. Only things of physical can be proved physically, and only things of spirit can be proved spiritually. Spiritual things such as plants, animals and humans alike all have a spirit which can and does detect the spirit world because their main component, their spirit is very much part of that world.

"Man has been very clever, with the machine. Among other things, man has built the car, the air craft, the space craft and the computer, but all are dead. Everything that man produces has no soul. Yes, the objects function alright, and they work, and yes, you can communicate with a computer, but it is only as good as the information that is fed into it. It will never, ever, think for itself. That is done by spirit, for only a spirit or soul can think and feel as well as communicate. Man cannot make spirit, he is not a creator, although he would like to think so. Everything that man makes is spiritually dead."

I thought for a moment and tried to imagine what it would be like to experience a computer thinking for itself. Then an eerie feeling can over me. The very thought of a computer thinking for itself was spooky, for it would be like communicating with something alive, another person perhaps or a ghost, either way, it would surely possess the one ingredient every living thing has in common. This could only be a spirit.

"Supposing for now, I accept that a computer will never think for itself, and that there is a spirit world. Are you saying that we cannot prove that there is a spirit world, and that no machine or computer can ever detect or communicate with the spirit world?" I asked, trying to come to terms with his idea.

"Man will never fully detect the existence of a spirit or spirit world through the aid of any machine, computer or anything made from physical matter. However, it is possible for a computer to communicate with the spirit world, yes."

"How's that," I asked, jumping enthusiastically.

"It happens all the time," he said, smiling. "All living things or beings have a spirit. Humans have a spirit, therefore, when a computer communicates with a human, it is contacting a spirit. That spirit is of the spirit world, so at that point in time, the computer is in connection with the spirit world."

I turned away for a moment's contemplation, then returning my focus on him, I asked, "If we cannot prove the existence of spirits and the spirit world, how can we possibly accept the idea of possessing a soul?"

"You cannot, unless you work with your inner feelings and thoughts. Ask yourself truthfully, 'have I a spirit, or am I just a soft bulk of fleshy matter.' Go deep, search out that innocent, subtle voice, the inner being, the inner you and know this: nothing can live without a soul. No plant, insect or animal, let alone humans."

"But, how do I know that I am not just thinking with my brain," I exclaimed.

He started to laugh again. "Always in denial...always in denial." He repeated, tittering at my expense. "There are many forms of life, and all have a soul. What is the difference between a log and a tree? A tree has a spirit, and a log is a dead piece of wood. It has no soul. A tree, on the other hand, has a soul but has no brain, yet, although very slow, it can think."

This was just too much, I creased up. The idea of a tree thinking for itself was just too much to bear. I could finally laugh at him. The old man was a laughing stock. I could hear the whole world chuckle. *What a hilarious joke,* I thought, laughing on. *He really is a crackpot.*

I continued laughing for a while until suddenly he said,

"How else would the trees know when to blossom and grow their leaves?"

I stopped my laughter immediately and looked straight at him. He leant back with a discerning glance. Then striking a match, he puffed bringing his dead pipe back to life.

"Every living thing has a soul," came his voice through a blue cloud of smog that slowly withdrew and gently blew away in the wind.

"Every living thing has a conscience and is able to think. Contrary to man's popular belief that you think with your brain, you do not. You think with your spirit or soul—it matters not what you call it, it is what it is.

All trees and all plants possess spirit. These are known to some as nature spirits, and those spirits are able to think, just like all

103

spirits, only very slowly. They know when to blossom and when to grow their leaves. They understand that insects can help them to germinate, so they produce beautiful coloured flowers to attract them. This, of course, takes intelligence to accomplish. Like all humans and animals, they produce their offspring and live and work with the seasons. They do all this without a brain but think with their spirit like you and I. They then die and move on to a further development, possibly an insect or whatever the individual spirit needs for further advancement.

No matter how small something is, if it lives, it has a spirit, and if it has a spirit, it can think. Look down there at the life in the grass."

I looked to find a small mound of earth with thousands of insects running on and around it.

"Ants, for example, are very intelligent creatures," he went on. "They communicate and are very social. They dig their own tunnels build their own houses and raise large families. They even grow their own food, so, there is clearly intelligence there. This must take brain power you would think, and just how big would their brain be, or do they, in physical terms, actually have a brain? It matters not, for they think with their spirit and all their collected spirits, their thoughts put together are connected with the spirit world at large."

This was so difficult for me to take in. Everyone that I have ever known, have been taught from childhood that we think with our brain, and our brains were the key to intelligence. Yet, the old man had to be right. There did seem to be a hidden intelligence behind nature, and we know for sure that not every living thing has a brain. So where was the thinking done if not by brain?

I thought about my own life, and how I perceived the world around me. I tried to imagine myself with a spirit. "Where is it, and just how big is it?" I asked myself. "Am I now thinking with my spirit or with my brain?"

I pondered on the idea for a moment trying to get used to the concept. I was not sure whether I ever believed in having a soul before, and yet here was this old chap trying to convince me that not only do I possess one, but I actually think with it to. The whole notion was just so bizarre.

Then, completely out of the blue, I started to think about my grandmother, and how she, after a long life, had died due to the cause of a stroke. I went to visit her a few times, and when I did, I was constantly amazed at the fact that she could not communicate. She would mutter sounds, the same sounds over and over again as if she was trying to say something. On one occasion, I gave her paper and a pen, hoping that she could write or draw something, but she failed even to do that. The doctor told me that a stroke causes the brain to malfunction, and that the part of the brain which is normally used for communication breaks down. He said, "In most cases, the patient is totally unaware of this and he or she still tries to communicate. It is like being trapped in your own body. You are unable to talk or make anyone understand you."

From what the doctor had said, I took it to mean that although her brain was not working properly, she could still think and was totally aware of herself, and that she, in the doctor's words, was 'trapped inside her own body'. What did he mean by trapped, and just what was it that was trapped? Could this have been her spirit, and maybe, a thinking spirit at that?

What if the old fellow is right, I thought. *What if we do think with our spirit?* Then, suddenly, it was as if I had been struck by a bolt of lightning.

"Oh...my...God," I said. It was so obvious. "Why had I not realised before. How could I have been so blind?" The realisation had finally struck home. The penny had finally dropped. There, sitting in front of me with a smile on his face, was the ultimate confirmation of a pure thinking spirit.

The old man was as he had told me a ghost or a pure spirit. The existing proof that spirits do exist and can think. He could somehow, completely without a brain, be an animated presence that could absorb, detain, ruminate and valuate its experiences. Then after judging the incoming information, be able to connect with another such as I and impart the conclusions of its findings, not only without a brain but also without any kind of physical body. *How could this be so,* I wondered?

The only explanation from my point of view could be that possibly, just possibly, we all sense, feel, think and experience with our soul/spirit and not with our brains at all.

I looked back at the old man in wonderment. He raised his eye brows, and with a gleeful look in his eyes, he smiled.

"You have just realised haven't you," he remarked. "Don't be ashamed, my lad, most of humanity still doesn't believe. The functions of the brain and how thought is created have and still are considered to be the product of brain and only brain. The brain has always eluded and will continue to elude all of the great minds alive. They still don't know how thoughts are created, and they never will, for as long as they study the physical matter of the brain."

He stopped talking, and there was silence.

"Who are you?" I asked. "Do you have a name?"

"I have been called many names," he said. "You may call me 'Jak'."

I sighed with a kind of relief and an assured thought that I had finally accepted his existence if existence is the right word to use. *If I can see and hear him, then surely he must exist,* I mused.

"Yes, I do exist," came a reply. I had completely forgotten that he could read my mind.

"How is it that you can read my thoughts," I asked.

"That is a question among many others that will remain unanswered for now. Your first lesson is over, and it is time for me to depart. You must allow yourself time for this new knowledge to develop. Your spirit is on overload at the moment. Newly acquired knowledge is like a seed, it needs time to grow and become part of you."

"When will I see you again," I beseeched hopefully. I didn't want to give the 'seed' time to develop. I wanted to know more. I wanted so much to learn from his mind. I felt sure that he had the answers to all my questions. I wanted to know the answers there and then.

"All in good time, my boy, all in good time," came his answer.

He rose from the log seat. "You will learn of these things when you are ready. Don't be disappointed, I said that you will be taught bit by bit. This is the way of things. To learn slowly is to develop quicker.

This might be puzzling to you at the present, but you among others are very aware. You are open minded, and only an open mind can accept new knowledge, new ideas and take advantage of them, but this must be done slowly. Like a great Oak tree, it slowly develops and grows from its small acorn. You will know of these things. You will slowly learn, and most important of all, you will then understand them. Time is one of the secret keys to the 'Great Knowledge'. If you are not ready for the knowledge, you will not understand it. Let it grow and develop, my boy. Let it grow and develop, that you may learn the new. And one day you will truly understand the way of things."

He then disappeared, leaving me alone in somewhat dimmer surroundings. I remained motionless, wondering what to make of it all and just what had really taken place. I was not quite sure of myself. "Have I gone completely crazy," I said, "or did I really experience that. Was he truly here or did I imagine it all. It sure seemed real enough."

Totally bemused, I started for home.

Across the park, I stopped to look at the trees, shrubs, flowers and any animals that appeared long my path. Wondering whether they had indeed a spirit and could their spirit think, and if so, were they aware of me standing there looking at them. What did they make of me? Were they contemplating me as I did them? Could they communicate? Were they passing comments about me? I shook myself in disbelief that I was even thinking such thoughts. Walking through Windsor to the train station, I tried to shake of the thought. I tried to bring some sort of reality back to my existence.

By the time I had reached home, all the silly thoughts of spirits and souls and ghosts and the old man had gone. My life was back to normal. The questioning of life and the spirit world had gone too. No longer did it matter whether I had a spirit, or furthermore, whether I think with it or not. And as to whether I believed in possessing a spirit or soul. I did not care.

On entering my parent's house, I saw my brother as he opened the front door dressed for work. I bade him goodbye, but as if I did not even exist, he passed me, not acknowledging me in the slightness. Alas, yet again, this was nothing unusual, he could often be moody.

Well…he is certainly late for work this morning. I thought. *What on earth could have taken him so long, for I must have been gone for a few hours…that's strange?*

I swiftly moved up the stairs, entered my bedroom, and there I found the reason why my brother had not seen me at the front door. There in front of me was the reason why my trip to Windsor had been so bizarre. For there, lying in my bed was my own physical body. There was a rush. I breathed in and sat bolt upright. It had all been a dream. I gave a sigh of relief. But how come I just saw myself in bed? I looked at my clock. I had been out of my body for 10 minutes.

Chapter Six

It was pleasant indeed lying in the long grass on a summer's day. I watched clouds drift playfully across a beautiful blue sky. Birds flirted joyously, circulating in the warm upward currents. The warm, calm air brought tranquillity to my idle spirit. It was lunch time, and I had half an hour to rest my poor, weary body. I had finally managed to secure myself a job for the summer break. I was helping to erect large marquees during week days. In the evening and weekends, I would meet up with Sharan. Not once though, did I mention to anyone about my strange experiences, thoughts and unusual meeting with the ghost called 'Jak'. It had been a couple of weeks since my bizarre contact with him. I laid there bathing in the warm sun ruminating, as I did from time to time, over the implications of this whole intrigue.

For the entire day and many days after my rare encounter with the ghost, I could not stop thinking about him or the strange way that it all took place. Not to mention the most enlightening things he had told me. Unlike most dreams which are easily forgotten, this experience was somehow all so real. I could remember the entire affair and could not for the life of me, put it out of my mind. And then to return home and find my body still in bed asleep was amazing—no astonishing. It could not have been a dream. Therefore, it must have been an 'out-of-body experience'.

He had planted a thought seed right there in my psyche, and it was growing. The worrying thing was that I felt good about it too. So good did I feel, I wanted to tell the whole world about it and would have done so if I had not thought them to consider me completely mad. So, for the time being I would keep it to myself, at least, until I found out more. Then and only then I would have the courage to reveal all. Yes, I had high hopes of yet another encounter with the wise old fellow. Finally, I had come to accept his existence, and I was no longer scared.

I leant over snatched a thick blade of grass and began chewing the end. As the sweet sensation materialised on my palate, a puzzling thought sprang to mind. If I had had an out-of-body experience, why did I still have the pipe and box in my bedroom?

When I met Jak in the OBE, I gave this piece to him. He called it his 'long-lost pipe'. What confused me now was, if I was out of my body, how could my spirit have taken the pipe to Windsor when it was a material object? Moreover, if I travelled without the pipe, how could I possibly have given the pipe to Jak when I did not possess it at the time? "Mmm," I mumbled, "that's what you might call a paradox." I chuckled, gratifying my own notion. Then the most obvious, though for me, unwanted answer filtered its way through. "Perhaps I was only dreaming after all?"

"But it was so real," I said to myself, trying to find another explanation. Alas, nothing came forth. I sighed.

I laid there for a little longer observing the wild life around me and playing with the idea that everything possessed an intelligent soul. I watched a bird fly to its nest and feed its young. I watched how a field mouse cleaned itself after eating, and I watched ants gathering food from a young bird that must have fallen from its nest.

"Nothing is wasted," I said to myself, "...the cycles of life."

I imagined the young chick's soul, much like a human child's soul, I would suspect, leaving its body after death. Where next...? What would it become? Would it be born again as another chick, or could it be born as something else?

I could feel this line of questioning opening up another door to another realm of thought, when I suddenly smelt pipe smoke. I frantically looked about. I saw no one. I stood up and looked around, only to see our team of workers starting back on the marquees, but sadly Jak was not to be seen.

"Are you going to do a bit today?" One of them shouted, hurling abuse my way. It was a new friend called Gareth. He was another student, quite a big fellow of about twenty years old, he had dark hair, a goatee beard and could normally be seen working in nothing but shorts, a real sun worshipper. I would often talk to him on our lunch breaks, except on this particular day, he had taken the morning off and was now starting back.

"Yeah...you can talk," I returned with a friendly reply.

After a short greeting we both joined the others and set to work.

We were working on a large field, just outside Windsor Great Park, erecting marquees for a dog show. There were many people about, and everyone was in good spirits. All bar my friend Gareth that was. Unfortunately, completely unbeknown to the rest of the team, including myself, Gareth was withholding some tragic news.

He had put on a brave face. In retrospect, I really don't know how he could have possibly coped.

We had all been hard at work for some two hours or more. Gareth and I were hammering large metal pegs into the ground. As I worked, my arms grew more and more tired, and after the last swing of the hammer which sunk the peg into its correct depth, I stopped for a breath. But it was not until I looked in Gareth's direction did I realise that there was something wrong. He had hammered three pegs to my one.

I stood there watching, absolutely astounded at the rate that he was pounding at the metal. He was like a man possessed by something evil. The energy that he had tapped into or called upon must have been tremendous. Whatever he had evoked looked to be reeling through his body. I could see the hard metal head of the peg flattening and burring with each forceful blow, until finally, he threw the hammer to the ground. He straightened up, placed his hands on his hips, puffing and panting profusely. Then he feasted his eyes upon me. I felt the hair on the back of my neck raise up as my body went cold. I did not know what to expect. For a brief moment, I stood on my guard, ready to defend myself, but instead of continuing his fearsome act, I watched as a stream of tears ran down his cheeks. Putting his hands over his face, he drew back in dignity. Then his entire body jerked with the pain he must have been feeling. He started to walk away as our boss approached.

Our boss was a tall, slim man in his forties, and like the rest of the team, he wore jeans, t-shirt and trainers. He was a fair, thoughtful boss unlike his brother. They were both part owners of this small family business.

"You had better go after him," he said, "I believe his mother is dying. I will see you tomorrow."

After a short walk in the direction of Windsor town centre, Gareth had calmed down, enough to be able to talk anyway. He apologised for his sudden outburst saying that he could not hold it in much longer.

That is a curious expression, I thought, *to hold what in?* We all use this saying from time to time, but just what exactly do we mean?

We seem to be referring to a kind of energy that gives us great strength. What is it, and where does it come from?

Gareth decided that he needed a stiff drink. Saying that it would calm his nerves. So we stopped off for a glass of beer or two at an old pub called the Royal Oak.

I had often talked to Gareth on our lunch breaks. Over the course of a few weeks, we had built quite a friendship. At university, he was studying law. This among many other subjects we had discussed over many a sandwich and a cup of tea. He was quite open-minded, so occasionally the subjects had got deep and philosophical, but not once had he mentioned his mother. I suppose everyone harbours a secret, for I had not told him about my strange experiences.

We were sitting in the pub for about an hour, making what you might call small talk. I did not want to upset him anymore than he already was, so I did not mention his mother at all. I thought that given time he would open up, and I hoped that when he did so, I would be able to help.

After a while I turned our small talk into something more interesting for me, which was the power that Gareth had tapped into.

"I know you were distressed," I said to him, "but how did you feel, and how would you explain it?"

"I don't know," he replied. "I felt this incredible energy stirring inside me. It seemed to be growing more and more. I had no control over it. It was steadily growing, building to such a magnitude that I could not stand it any longer. I had to lash out. Wherever it was coming from, it seemed endless. At one point, I felt like I could lift a truck…no trouble."

"Would you say that it felt like it came from the outside of your body or inside," I asked eagerly.

He thought for a moment then I heard him say, "I suppose both. It felt like a never-ending power coming from within and yet from the outside, it was weird. I seemed to have conjured up this force when I was in deep thought about my dear mum."

He then proceeded to tell me about his mother and the grave tragic car accident that had befallen her. Despite the fact that her body had suffered a few cuts and bruises, she had been for many weeks and was at the time still in a coma.

I looked at him in despair. Words failed me.

"I don't know what to say," I uttered.

He looked at me glassy eyed, and yet with a calm unemotional voice he said with great understanding, "You need not say anything. No words from any language could heal my suffering. What I need is a miracle." He lowered his head.

We both fell silent, and for a moment, we gazed into our beer mugs.

My mind started to drift, I casually looked around an empty bar. It must have been too early for any more customers. It was a very old pub with dark over hanging beams and oak-panelled walls. I was trying to guess its age when I heard.

"Do you believe that your body has a spirit," Gareth asked shattering the silence.

This question was totally unexpected, and of course, after the experiences that I had had, I was sure of it to be true, but I was curious as to why he had asked such a question. And I knew that this field of enquiry would only lead to the inevitable, that being the subject of Jak.

In retrospect, I didn't really mind people finding out about my ghostly encounter. I was just afraid of their reaction. Souls, spirits, ghosts etc., have never been proved to exist. I felt that there had always been a question mark over people who claim to have seen such phenomena. I did not want Gareth to think that I was one of them. So I thought that I would probe him for more information first.

"Whatever made you ask me that?" I enquired.

With that, he pushed his half-filled pint of larger to one side and leant closer. Our eyes met, and his face took on a disturbing distortion of torment. He was worried about something. The look on his face was telling most of the story, but the details were retained, that was about to come.

In a soft, haunting voice he whispered, "She visits me in my sleep. My mum comes to me at night."

A familiar shiver ran up my spine. I did not quite understand what he meant though. "Do you mean that you have dreams about her," I asked in earnest.

"No!" came his answer. "Sometimes I wake up, and there she is at the bottom of my bed, watching me?"

My entire body went cold. I could feel goose bumps all over, and my spirit tingled with joy. I knew this feeling well. I watched his eyes light up. He was well aware that he had moved my spirit. He smiled complacently.

"How often has this happened," I asked in dismay.

"Oh…three or four times I suppose. At first, I thought I was just having bad dreams, but the last time, I shook my head, and she just vanished, leaving me sitting up in bed."

"So, it wasn't like a dream at all," I enquired with a sarcastic side glance.

"No…not at all like a dream," he said adamantly. "You don't believe me? I knew it, I should have kept my mouth shut." He turned his head away with embarrassment.

"No! No! I do believe you," I exclaimed. "I just was not expecting you to come out with such a thing. It's been a bit of a shock. If it will make you feel better, I can tell you about some weird experiences that I have had."

He turned his head to face me and smiled reassuringly.

I then went on to tell him all about my spooky experiences and the strange manner in which it had all manifested itself. To my surprise, he did not find my tale at all strange, moreover, he was fascinated by the idea and when I reached the part of my story where Jak had said that we all think with our soul, he clapped his hands saying:

"Yes…! Yes…! It has to be. It makes so much sense. It all fits. Why did I not see it before? I now know what has been happening."

He drank what was left of his beer and bringing a hand up, he wiped his mouth clean. He then grinned and sighed totally contented.

"You are right," he went on, "we do think with our soul. My poor mum has been coming to me for help, and I have been pushing her away in fear. She has been travelling out of her body, desperately seeking my help."

His eyes became glossy once again, and tears appeared, dropping to the table. "I know what to do now," he persisted. "I must try and help her to return to her body…thank you for that."

This is not quite the reaction that I had expected. I only told him because I wanted him to know that I did believe in his plight. I merely wanted to console him. Yet, here he was acting as if he had found the miracle that he had longed for.

"What makes you think that you can help her," I asked anxiously.

Picking up our two empty beer glasses, he stood up, leant closer and whispered, "When she visits me next time, I must convince her to return to her body."

As he walked away, I remained motionless in total dismay. This was like something out of a horror movie, although, in a strange sort of way, he did have a point. I sat there mulling over the implications.

"Why not," I said to myself. "I had been out of my body so why couldn't she have been? Perhaps that is what being in coma is. You travel outside your physical body, and you cannot find a way back.

I thought about the ingenuity behind the instruments keeping her body alive and the complicated systems it must have been using. His mother, of course, would normally do this intricate operation for herself. So why couldn't she? Her brain must have still been alive, or she would have been clinically dead. Why couldn't her brain tell her body to stay alive? To me, it was obvious. It's not your brain that keeps you alive but your spirit. I thought about his mother's body, like an empty shell lying in the hospital bed waiting for the vital part to return, the intelligent part, the part that could do what the sophisticated instruments themselves were doing, keeping her body alive; the part that Gareth called mum.

At that moment, Gareth returned from the bar with two pints of lager, placing them on the table, silently sitting opposite and slumping back in the chair. He then stretched out his left arm, and griping the glass gently with the tips of his fingers, he turned his beer, deep in a thought.

"I have been thinking," he suddenly said, "if my mum's spirit can travel out of her body with possibly her full faculties, as you say, then surely the spirit must carry on independently after death."

"I don't know," I replied, "unless it is your mother's animated physical body that is feeding her spirit and keeping her soul alive."

He went silent again and continued turning his beer glass.

"No!" he shouted, breaking the silence. "It's the other way around. It is the spirit that gives life to the physical body. Without the spirit the body cannot live."

I picked up my beer and sat back assessing his conclusion. I considered him to be right but something puzzled me.

"If what you say is true," I converged drawing his attention, "Where does the spirit get its energy from?"

"What do you mean?"

I supped another mouthful of beer, making him wait for my answer.

"In a healthy situation, the body needs energy…right. It gets that energy from the food and drink that we take in. If what you say is true that the spirit gives life to our body, where does the spirit get its energy from, if not from our physical body? Let's face it, everything needs energy to exist."

"I see what you mean," said he, cutting in with enthusiasm. "Like a ghost… For a ghost to exist completely independent from the physical body, it will still need energy to live."

"Yes," I returned, "and where do ghosts or any form of spirit or soul get its energy from?"

"I don't know," said Gareth, "but I bet that there is a connection with the powerful energy I experienced this afternoon. That was truly something else. You cannot get that kind of energy or power from a dish full of food. I can tell you that for nothing."

He paused to drink some beer and on his second attempt a new thought had hit him. His body jerked as he tried to swallow. He could not get it out quick enough. He was now coughing, trying to control the liquid going in and the words coming out.

"I am sure the Chinese have a name for it," he finally muttered. "If it is the same thing, they call it Chi, and it is supposed to flow through meridian lines around the body. These are kind of imaginary lines that channel a vital energy believed to circulate around your body."

"Supposing this is true," I replied, "and it is the same energy, this still does not tell us where the energy comes from."

Right at that very moment we both inhaled a powerful aroma of pipe smoke. This was of course very familiar to me, but Gareth was totally shocked.

"It's just like you described, completely invisible. Where the hell is that coming from," he abruptly cried out.

Then a look of terror came over his face. We both looked around the bar, there were now some people surrounding us, but no one was smoking. I was hoping to see Jak but was disappointed again. I looked back at Gareth. From the look on his ashen face he was totally spooked.

"Do you think that is Jak's pipe?" he whispered cautiously. "I guess so," I responded shrugging my shoulders. Unfortunately, Gareth was so spooked-out, we had to leave.

Outside the pub, the odour had completely gone. We had also realised that the time had raced ahead of us anyway. So, I wished him good luck and offered his mother a blessing. We shook hands and said goodbye. He left walking in the direction of the train station. I watched as he did so. Head stooping in melancholy, he walked across the road. I did feel sorry for him.

I, on the other hand, was not to take the train home this time. I had decided to take a long walk instead.

My walk home was about five miles or more. I am not quite sure why I decided on this walk for I had never done it before. Perhaps it was to help me ponder over the implications of our conversation, or just to help me clear my head. I have no idea, but walk I did.

My journey would consist of a long road to and through an old village called Datchet. This meant walking alongside the grounds of Windsor Castle, over a small hump back bridge, along the River Thames, through the old village to another long road beside the M4 motor way, into my village and home, perhaps an hour's stroll.

The walk past the castle, through to the bridge was just fine, but as I approached the river, the familiar smell of tobacco smoke surrounded me once again. Only this time, I could somehow feel Jak's presence getting stronger by degrees, strong and intent. At this point, noticing a wooden public seat, I thought that I would take a rest on the river's bank.

It was a beautiful evening. We must have been drinking all afternoon, and it was now quite late. I sat gazing as the cool evening breeze that created ripples on the water's surface. I listened to the light wind playing with the leaves in the trees. In the dying light of the sun, I saw bats 'zigzag' in and out, sending me the sound of their sonar as they shot past, but in the midst of all this beauty, nothing could I smell more than Jak's tobacco smoke.

This odour did not bother me anymore because I knew very well of its subtle origin. On the contrary, I desperately wanted to meet its master once again. There were still so many things that I wanted to know, so many unanswered questions, and I knew deep down inside that Jak had all the answers. And so, there I sat, heart and soul fully immersed in the ghost's aroma. I waited for a while half expecting him to appear. Nevertheless, to my utter disappointment, nothing happened. Feeling completely let down, I looked out over the sparkling water of the river. The display of light and the sheer beauty of surrounding nature helped me once again to conserve my tormented soul.

I knew that somehow I needed to take control of the situation. *Perhaps I could encourage him to appear,* I thought. *Perhaps, I could even summon him to me.* I laughed at the prospect of summoning what I could only describe as a supreme being.

However, this thought plus the outburst of laughter made me wonder whether it was at all possible. Not to summon him to me, that would be disrespectful. Only the idea of encouraging him to appear was, I dare say, intriguing. I played with the idea for a while until I reached a conclusion. Spiritual mediums and clairvoyants do it all the time.

I had read it in a book and seen it in films many times. A group of people gathered around a table, all hands joined to form a circle.

They would never speak inwardly, always aloud, saying, "Is there anybody there?"

Feeling very foolish, I looked carefully about. *This could be extremely embarrassing should someone catch me,* I thought. I then tried calling out like a medium at a séance.

"Jak, if you can hear me please show yourself."

"I know you are here. I can smell your pipe smoke."

"Are you there? Jak, please give me a sign."

I patiently waited for a couple of minutes or so and tried again.

"Please, Jak. I know you are here. If you can please show yourself."

My nerves were on edge, my senses alert. I sat quietly poised on the edge of the seat, waiting for something to happen.

I waited and waited but nothing was heard and nothing developed.

Feeling rather despondent, I cast my eye back to the river. The sun was disappearing beneath the horizon, leaving a bright orange blaze that spread across the sky. The surface of the river turned into a million sparkling jewels that seemed to have life all of their own.

What beauty? What energy? What power? I mused unconcerned.

"That is it," I shouted. My heart jumped into action.

"That is it," I hissed excitedly through my teeth. "Maybe Jak needs more energy to come through…more energy to materialise. Perhaps that is why I cannot see him. He needs energy. This is what Gareth and I were talking about earlier. Maybe ghosts do need a kind of energy after all."

I thought back to the time that I met Jak. We were both saturated in an intensive, all powerful energy that made me feel so vigorous, so alive, so spirited, it was as if to be life itself; he called it 'pure positive life force'.

I continued thinking on these lines when a possible answer suddenly hit me.

At the end of a séance, mediums claim to feel exhausted.

Moreover, the people gathered around the table, must it seems join hands. Conclusion…the ghost is using their energy.

Maybe I could give Jak some of my energy, I surmised.

I gave the matter some serious consideration until finally, I had convinced myself and decided to at least try.

And so there I was on a warm summer's evening on the river's bank, seated upon a wooden park bench, immersed in a ghost's aroma and about to encourage an appearance. I closed my eyes and tried to concentrate on Jak's image. It was probably only for a few minutes, but it felt a lot longer. I just sat there with my mind centred on his identity, trying to encourage him to materialise in front of me.

Other thoughts would try to distract me from my goal, but I just passed them aside to focus solely on his warm character and distinctive image. I tried to concentrate an energy existing inside me. I imagined it getting stronger and stronger, growing more and more vibrant. It felt like a kind of warm quiver that seemed to be expanding as it grew in strength. To my delight, it actually felt as if I had aroused something real.

The energy seemed to be coming over in rhythmic palpitations up and down my entire body. It was the same sensation that I had when I was out of my body. I then tried to concentrate on sending some of this energy from myself towards the image that I was creating. I imagined this giving power to the very core of his being. As this energy grew, I would will it to become an entity all of its own—hopefully being Jak. I would cut it off from myself, and it would exist completely self-supportive. The more I concentrated, the clearer his image was becoming. I could feel the very essence of him coming through.

It is working, I thought. My heart started to pump into action as I tried sending out even more energy towards my point of focus there some ten feet in front of me. As I did so, Jak's aroma seemed to grow even stronger. I was completely consumed by it. Over my panting breathe and throbbing heart, I could actually feel something in front of me.

But then some bats' sonar struck me, breaking my concentration, but all was not lost. I fought back, doing my damnedest to retain my intention. The energy in front of me was still there so I pressed on regaining my concentration. I continued pouring energy and intensifying my thoughts into my creation, but something was wrong. I had somehow lost all positive thought. It seemed that the bat had caused my mind to switch from good to bad thinking—bats, Dracula, horror movies… It now felt like the whole thing in front of me had turned to a negative energy. I quickly tried to absorb this energy back into my body, but it was too late.

Intuitively, I knew that something dire had taken place. I had lost control of the situation and could no longer smell Jak's pipe smoke.

Full of fear to open my eyes, I remained seated, absolutely motionless.

My heart still pumping hard, I could feel the vile energy racing around my body. The trees rustled, and once again, the sinister sound of a bat swept past. There was a deathly silence, yet I could still sense something in front of me. Terrified at what I may have created, I squeezed my eyes even tighter, praying to God that the outcome would be a favourable one.

A twig snapped directly in front of me, making me jump. My heart seemed to stop, as I heard and smelt a hot, foul breathe. This thing was almost touching me on my face.

Quivering at the prospect of being able to spawn such a vile creature, I knew that I had to deal with it somehow. With this thought in mind, I reluctantly opened my eyes to behold the head of a huge evil looking beast. It snarled, baring its teeth it drooled, no doubt at the sense of my fear. I felt the hair on the back of my neck raise as my entire body went frozen.

The beast has just sapped my energy, I thought.

Then, totally unexpected, and much to my relief, I heard a voice calling, "Lucifer. Come here, boy."

It was a beast alright, a very large black beast, but nothing that I had made, just a large Rottweiler dog. It had taken me by surprise. I just sat there dumbstruck, watching it bounce triumphantly towards its awaiting master who took the form of a big villainous looking man in a rough leather jacket and rough torn jeans. Pointing in the direction of the pathway, he goaded the dog along with a stick.

It was the bounce in the dog's step that alarmed me now: so buoyant, so dynamic, so vibrant, far more life than was usual for that type of dog. More like a Whippet than a Rottweiler.

It had left me feeling so cold, empty and lifeless. It seemed to me that it had taken all of the energy that I had created and more. I could not deduce it any other way. *The dog had somehow taken a large part of me; how odd,* I thought. Quite how or why it had done this, I could not tell, but I could not explain my loss any other way.

I watched the dog at play, darting in and out of the trees, running in front and then behind his master. "What's got into you, boy?" the man shouted raising his stick. "I knew very well what had got into him."

I watched them both walk out of sight. Then I set off to finish the remainder of my journey home, vowing never to delve into such matters that I could not control or understand. From then on, if Jak wanted to communicate with me, he would have to do the running, not I. I had had enough.

I walked home that night feeling so disappointed. I had been let down once too often.

"Why do we never get what we want in life at the moment we want it," I said to myself, thrusting out a fist in anger. "Nothing in this life is ever just given to you. You always have to work so damn hard for everything."

Chapter Seven

The day on the bank of the river had left me feeling angry and frustrated. This whole scenario had left my mind in limbo, and once again, I had embarrassed myself. Had I finally gone over the edge? Was I about to realise that I was going mad? I worryingly pondered over the subject. I even had my girlfriend and her family worried. They knew that something was wrong. In fear that my suspicions were right, I still had not the courage to tell them. Yes, I had told Gareth that day, and he was quite taken by the idea, but he wasn't in a good frame of mind at the time either.

However, moving swiftly on, another couple of weeks later, I was safely tucked up in bed and dreaming about being among thousands of what seemed to be city people. I had no idea who they were or where they were all going. The scene was of a large body of people, generally meandering about in different directions as you would normally find in such a large busy city. I was just standing there, gazing at them—much like when you might be daydreaming in the day time. No one seemed to mind so I remained motionless, just taking in the scene, when suddenly it occurred to me that I might be dreaming. I was not sure at first, but being true to myself, I questioned it anyway.

"If I am dreaming," I said to myself, "I should surely fly." With that, and not a care in world, I lifted up my arms and in sheer delight, I rose up and took off, saying, "Yes… I've managed to leave my body again."

I looked to see the city of London peering through the gaps in the white fluffy clouds. I felt so wondrously light and alive. Once again, it was as if I had the entire world at my command. Feeling like a bird, I glided among clouds and swooped down through warm air currents not knowing at all where I was going. Suddenly, I was aware of a powerful attraction. Whatever the attraction was, I could not pull away, it was far too strong. It was luring me. On a kind of invisible rope, I was being reeled in. I had no choice but to surrender and be delivered as unwilling easy prey. There was an unexpected flash, and before I knew what had happened, I found myself back on the riverside bench in Windsor.

Everything was just as I remembered it on the evening I walked home from the pub. The cool evening breeze that played with the surface of the water, the light wind rustling through the leaves of the trees, and there were even bats darting about; their wings were seemingly waving to the orange setting sun. Only this time, there was something delightfully different, and that was the captivating black silhouette of Jak standing at the water's edge.

"I am impressed," he said, after a short period of silence.

I was speechless, mouth open in awe, I gawked at him. Offering total admiration, like a creature to its creator I stared with unmitigated bewilderment. I had not understood a word that he had said. Struck dumb, somewhat cut off, I was unable to communicate, until his approaching form struck a faint glare of moonlight that had filtered through the trees.

"Pardon…" I muttered, trying to recall what he had just said.

"I am very impressed," he repeated. Then slowly turning, he drew himself closer until some ten feet in front of me he stopped. His face took on a kind of aluminous glow that directed my full attention. He smiled. His friendly presence fed me a calm spiritual assurance that released any sense of foreboding that might have been lurking about the inner chambers of my being. My spirit relinquished all anchors for it was quite some time I had yearned for this moment. I longed once again to be with this friendly ghost, and now that the moment was here, I was again speechless. My mind was adrift and completely blank.

All was silent.

"I'm…imper…I'm…impressed," I babbled trying to react to his complimentary remark, "impressed, with what exactly?"

"You have actually summoned me here," he declared. "Bless my soul, you have actually brought me to this place. I am very impressed. I underestimated you, boy."

"I…didn't really mean to Jak," I exclaimed trying to defend myself.

"Nonsense, boy," he went on, "you knew exactly what you were doing. You are so very aware. I had no idea that you could comprehend so much. This puts a different perspective on things entirely."

He turned, walked a few feet towards the river again and quietly stood in contemplation.

I felt warm and excited at the prospect of finally being entrusted with his secrets. *Could this really be true,* I thought. I patiently waited for what was probably half a minute but seemed like a lifetime. Then without warning, he quickly turned and looked straight at me, his big blue piercing eyes lit up, and then as if something was reaching straight through to my spirit. I felt my soul expectantly being examined.

"Mmm…mmm…you are a bright little cookie, aren't you," he pondered, "naturally psychic too. Mmm…let's see, you must have picked it up in a past life somewhere. Ah, yes…mmm…"

He mumbled on talking to himself while supposedly scanning my soul or examining my attributes, I am not sure what exactly, but he was having a good probe anyway.

"What do you mean I am naturally psychic?" I asked zealously, breaking his train of enquiry.

He huffed and puffed then shook his head. "What…What's that you say, boy?"

"I said, what do you mean I am naturally psychic?"

"Ah…" he pulled away to a comfortable position.

"Yes, my lad, you are indeed naturally psychic. No one has taught you this…have they? Not in this life time anyway."

This was too good to be true, at long last, my suspicions were to be realised. *So we do actually reincarnate after all,* I thought.

"You mean that I have lived before then?" I asked.

"Oh yes, many times," he said, "and in one of those lives, you were taught and were very aware of your psychic ability. Since then you have been increasing your perceptions, like millions of others, who have and are making such enquiries. Nevertheless, I am especially impressed with you, because not only are you aware that you possess a soul, but you are also aware of spiritual energies or 'life forces' that surround and interact with your soul."

I was quite taken back by this remark. I did not mind taking the credit for being aware and able to acknowledge my spirit, but I was not sure that I could possibly be rewarded credit for the acknowledgment of the powers that he had in mind.

"I'm not quite with you," I asked, somewhat flummoxed.

"Then what about the dog," he remarked with a side glance. "The big black dog, did he not run off with some of your spiritual energy?"

"Oh…that, yes he did, well…it appeared that way at the time," I returned fervently.

I paused and sighed. Then a change of thought caused a rush of energy that filled me with excitement. Hardly able to control myself, for I was not sure how long this session with the ghost was to last, I had to cut to the chase.

"Please Jak, tell me how it all works. What is the riddle to life and the universe?"

With that, he turned to one side and roared with laughter. His image started to fade, and I thought for one awful moment that I was losing him.

After a while his laughter stopped, and amid a cloud of tobacco smoke that had suddenly appeared, his image returned, saying, "You don't ask for much do you, my boy."

He then moved to take up a seat next to me on the bench.

Taking another puff from his pipe, he blew a stream of smoke that moved off circling in coils that gently turned, growing larger and slowly, like I had seen before, they faded in warm currents of air. "Life is like those coils of smoke..." he said at long last, "never-ending expanding coils that takes one whole lifetime to make one turn, for ever expanding. You then take another and then another. There really is no need for me to tell you this because you and everyone else already know this. You just refuse to believe. You and like most people are a prisoner of your own illusions. Fear is the biggest illusion of all. You all cling to your physical body for dear life. You are terrified of death."

"But how do I know for sure that there is life after death?" I asked, trying to come to terms with his doctrine.

He looked at me laughing again. "Why? Did you not agree that you have a soul? Have you forgotten that you are out of your physical body as we speak?"

Oh my God! I thought, *of course, I am out again.*

I felt a rush of energy racing through me, rhythmically tingling my spirit, and then the wind blew a cool breeze that went literally straight through me.

"Your whole life is a dream," he said, "and when you die, you will wake up. You will then remember everything. All of your past lives, what you learnt from each one, and what you need to learn from the next life. There are untold millions of souls trying to come through at any one time to experience, once again the physical plain. You have done this, many times before, you just cannot remember. That was part of the deal that you had before you past over."

I paused for a moment's thought then asked: "You say that it was part of a deal that is as maybe, I can only take your word for that, but why? Why are we not allowed to remember our past lives while we inhabit the physical world?"

He looked at me with an all-knowing mystical smile. "If you could recall you're passed life or lives, you would live as the same character over and over again. Your soul would not develop. You would not start afresh and learn something new. Through evolution, your soul would not develop. Each person would continue to live out the same life, time after time. Thereby, creating a self-imposed hell. A murderer would continue to murder, alcoholics would continue to drink, and drug addicts would continue to take drugs, etc."

I could not move. I remained motionless in dismay as he delivered more of his sermon.

"What I am saying is that everyone is born with positive objectives, attempting to bring forth the knowledge contained in the spirit world. For all of you, history has been a long process of awakening. When you were born into the physical realm, you, of course, ran into problems of going unconscious and having to be socialised and shown the cultural reality of the period. Apart from that, all you can remember are those gut feelings, those intuitions that you hold toward certain things or ideas.

Unfortunately, you constantly have to fight uncertainties and fears. Often the fear can be so intense that you fail to come through with what you originally intended, or you may have distorted it somehow. Everyone and I mean everyone, goes into the world with best intentions. Are not all babies born innocent until sometime later corrupted?"

I stalled trying to think of a good response. "So, you think that murders and thieves, for instance, would have really come through to do something good?"

"Yes of course, originally. All murder is rage, and all theft is jealousy. It is a way of overcoming an inner sense of fear and helplessness."

"What about the bad souls that are easily corrupted. Is there no hell for them to go to?" I exclaimed.

"On the inner plains, there is no time, not what you would call time anyway. Depending on your personal development, you can be reincarnated into the distant past or alternatively into the better developed future. Or you might live the same life again. It is all a process of learning. You should learn by your mistakes, that way your soul will develop. A murderer, for example, may return to become a victim, but there is no hell, as you say, no hot fiery realms," he said, laughing.

I hovered motionless for a while, trying to take this all in, hoping that I would remember all this when I awoke. *If there is no hell in the spirit world,* I thought, *then perhaps the physical world is hell?*

"No, the physical world is not hell," he said, picking up on my thoughts. "There is no place call hell. As individuals and as nations, you make your own hell. The same is with the afterlife. If you carry lots of bad negative energy when you die, alike attracts alike, you will go to a hell of your own making. You carry this heavy negative feeling in the form of guilt when you are alive, and you take that heavy burden with you when you die. You have no doubt heard of the term, 'the guilt will eat you up'. Well, it does well and truly, for without your body, all you become is an entity full of thought, and if guilt is all there is, you will burn in a hell of your own making."

"If you have this burden, is it possible to rid yourself of it?" I asked.

"Of course, boy, but there is no panacea and no miracle cure; each individual knows what they have to do to rid themselves of the burden. They must look inward and ask their soul, and that little voice inside will tell them what to do. They will know when they have succeeded, the heaviness held in their heart and the knots in their stomach will disappear.

On the other hand, if you carry lots of good positive energy such as love, you will go to a heaven of your own making." He paused for another puff of his pipe.

Focusing my attention and thoughts, I found myself questioning Jak's convictions. If the physical world is not hell, I contemplated, then why is there so much suffering in the world, for I was sure that not everyone deserved to suffer.

Throughout my short life, I had seen, heard and spoken to many people who had suffered. If the truth was known, I would assume that everyone suffers at one time or another. Our history books are full of such accounts like war, famine, disease and disabilities of all descriptions. It seems that we must all accept a great loss too as part of our lifetime of grief.

I had grieved such a loss with the death of my uncle and would, of course, experience more in the future, yet some of us seem to have a whole lifetime of nothing but torturous pain and suffering.

There is a belief that you only suffer due to something that you did in the past, a karmic payback of assorts, for a wrong doing of some kind which may have taken place in a past life. I have always found this answer a difficult one to accept for the reason that I am sure that not every single individual is naturally evil. Jak had already said that our souls come into the world with natural good intentions. So why must we all suffer so? Why must there be suffering at all?

I looked at Jak. He was smiling back at me, his pipe poised at the side of his mouth. He was really starting to annoy me now. I was sure that he had all the answers, but would I have time to hear them. I was also fully aware that he had read my thoughts too.

"Why…oh, why must everyone suffer so much?" I screeched.

His face changed. He appeared agitated at my outburst. His image started to fade once again. Just a haze of grey mist remained, where he must have taken yet another puff from his pipe.

That's it, I thought. I have offended him.

The wind blew and the grey mist disappeared. I was alone. My own presence now seemed to be waning, and my concentration dying. I was losing hold of my present existence.

"Everyone must endure suffering," came his voice like thunder; it shrieked through the ether. "Every living entity must know and learn from suffering. No one could ever know the true meaning and wisdom of suffering unless they experience it first-hand. Everyone learns something when they suffer…" His voice was now echoing through a colourful mystical cloud. I tried to focus my entire thoughts on his image and character, desperately willing him and myself to return.

The colourful blur descended to unveil our return to the side of the river.

"Please don't be discouraged," he said in a warm comforting tone. "Sorry, but you will have suffered far more than you would want to remember, my lad."

"Why though, what's it all about? Why can we not live in a heavenly realm instead of a torturous one?" I implored.

He laughed at me saying, "Are you telling me that you have had no joy in your life, and the entire world is a disaster? Are you so disappointed that you had ever lived?"

"No, of course not," I returned, "but why must there be suffering at all?"

"I love the way you question things," he replied, "that shows courage and foresight. However, to answer your question, you first need to know and understand the principals of life and its indispensability."

He moved back slightly in order to refill and light his pipe. "An old habit that I picked up from when I was alive," he murmured, puffing like a chimney.

"You see, it's like this, life in the physical realm is a school of mystery. It is the quickest, most effective means to acquire knowledge. There is no other channel, sphere, spectrum or mass quite like it. It is unique. There is, I must say, no substitute…a wondrous creation," he paused and smiled.

"What you, your friend and everyone alive don't realise is just how lucky you all are…"

There it was again. *What friend,* I thought, looking around in anticipation. And once again there was no one there.

"There are countless millions of wanting souls…" he went on, "waiting to embrace what you experience every day. Life is a beautiful thing to experience. Yes, you will experience suffering, but once participated, you long for a return. For those awaiting spirits, it is part of their personal, spiritual journey of development or evolution of their soul. They have all, like you, experienced the physical world many, many times throughout the history of the planet, as microorganisms, plants, insect, animals and some as humans too, many times like you have."

My mind was in a spin. "I don't quite follow you," I said, "what do you mean by evolution of the soul, and what has this got to do with suffering?"

"You understand the concept of physical evolution do you not?"

"I…think so," I weakly replied.

"By analysing old bones dug up from the earth, man is now aware that over the course of millions of years, certain physical changes to animals have taken place."

"From caveman to modern man, you mean?"

"Yes, my boy! That is it… Exactly what I mean."

"Ah…yes, Neolithic to Homo sapiens," he affirmed looking up, amusing himself. "Yes…precisely, but let's not forget the pre-historical animals that changed to form into all of the animals in your present period."

He looked at me to see if l was following him. I just nodded.

"As physical evolution, so spiritual evolution," he purred, "they run side by side." He stopped, for he knew that I still had not grasped the meaning of what he was trying to say.

"Let me try and put it into simpler terms," he went on, "each and every living entity, no matter how large or small, has a soul on a steady path of development, whether they are as small as microbes and insects or as large as trees or elephants. They all have a spirit or, if you prefer, a soul. Every soul is developing long side with the evolution of plants, animals and humans; as the physical world evolves so does each and every soul with part of the spirit world."

He looked straight into my eyes, and my spirit shrank, for intuition told me that what he was about to say was something that my soul had always known. I suddenly felt alive, my spirit tingled with elation as he delivered each and every word.

"You already know, don't you?" he asked, "you know deep down inside that you have lived before.

You have been plants, insects, animals as well as humans, many, many times in each category in that order too. How else would you explain the superiority that all humans hold over plants and animals? As a human, you are more advanced and spiritually further down the evolutionary track.

Human babies are quick to learn because they have lived before, half the time they are not learning but merely remembering knowledge from previous lives. This is sometimes called a gift. If you show extraordinary skill in something, people say that he or she is gifted. Mozart, Beethoven and Michelangelo are classic examples of this. Mozart was writing his own music at the age of seven. A young child cannot learn in a few years what it takes a musician a lifetime to learn. Mozart would have been continuing what he had learnt from a previous life. Remembering old skills, of course, gives children a head start in life.

Every soul starts out as something simple and small, increasing its awareness after each incarnation. Plants are not aware of animals or humans, some animals are a bit more aware and can relate to humans, like dogs or horses. You, on the other hand, can relate and understand plants and animals extremely well because you used to be one."

"Wow! What a revelation," I said to myself.

He paused for a moment, presumably allowing me time to take on board his esoteric mystery.

This might explain why there is a limit to how much animals are able to learn, I thought. Like chimpanzees, they cannot talk due to the undeveloped voice box that they have, and yet some have been taught sign language. Moreover, some types of birds, like parrots, are physically able to talk; these among other animals have the means to communicate, but all lack the intelligence of human beings.

"That is correct," said Jak, picking up on my thoughts. "Animals are inferior to humans because their souls have not developed enough to take the information. There is a limit to how much you can learn in any one lifetime.

Man is where he is today because of the evolutionary developed souls that are coming through, each generation becoming more intelligent than the next. I am sure that you will have noticed what man has achieved over the past one hundred years. Most people could barely read a book last century. Now scholarly records are being broken all of the time. Science and technology are prolific...Why man can even fly? Do you not think this to be strange? Thousands of years of underdevelopment, then in just a few decades, humans have walked on the moon, and the whole world watched in awe from their very own television set, not to mention the changes computers have made to the world."

I was awe struck, for he was right. Man has suddenly developed so quickly and in such a short period of time.

"So, my children will be more intelligent than I am then?" I suggested.

"No, not necessarily," was his answer. "That will depend on the child's own personal development. That is, it depends on what stage its soul is at, along its own, individual, evolutionary spiritual path. The more lives he or she have lived, the more intelligent he or she will be.

To a certain extent, you can tell by the speed at which children can learn. Although, this is not always true because some start off slow and flourish later. What matters is the total capacity of knowledge at the end of each lifetime. The more that you learn in this lifetime, the more you will know and understand at the start of another lifetime, and the more you will comprehend of life the next time around."

This was truly amazing to me. I just stared at him. I was not sure what to say or how to think. He had just blown my mind and the concept of everything that I had ever known about myself with it. My life would never be the same again. What this ghost had said could, of course, never be proved, but in a strange kind of way, the idea did seem plausible.

Plants do seem to possess some kind of knowing. They follow the sun across the sky and work with the seasons. "Some plants can even catch flies so there must be intelligence there," I said to myself. Yet plants are clearly not as knowing as animals. Animals are clearly much more astute. I had heard many dog owners try to give claim to the intelligence of their animal. Some even say, "Their dog is more intelligent than some humans; it's just unable to talk."

Furthermore, it seemed to me that some humans are barely able to show the intellect of an animal. Some even mimic animals. They prefer to live in the open air and scavenge for food from waste bins. Perhaps these scavenging humans are new to the human form and are remembering their lives as animals, otherwise what would be the logic behind the way that they live.

I looked up, Jak had moved to the water's edge. Sensing my attention, he turned to face me. Our minds met and in a soft voice he whispered.

"The realisation has finally sunk in, hasn't it?"

"But what's it all for?" I asked in dismay.

Laughing, he then proclaimed that I would have in time worked it all out for myself, but to save time, he would give me a clue.

"Just see it all as an adventure. It has been a process of events that has nurtured your soul into what it is at present. And I might say a fine specimen indeed. Without the many incarnations, it would not have been possible for you to have taken the human form that you currently possess.

Mentally take yourself back to your birth. Completely as a knowing, reincarnating spirit at a kind of subconscious level, of course. As soon as you were set free as a sperm in your mother's womb, you knew precisely how to swim from the memory of being a marine organism like a fish. You knew exactly where you were going. You knew that it wasn't just a race. Having previous knowledge which, of course, gave you a massive advantage over the rest, for you had done this so many times before; you left millions of others behind. You knew not to linger and headed straight for the awaiting 'life capsule'. You knew how to enter and divide the cells in the egg from the memory of when you were once bacteria. You knew how to set growth in motion from the memory of being a plant. You knew what to expect at birth because you had been through the process time after time as animals, and for you, many times in the human form.

And your parents showed you how to look after yourself. What I mean is they taught you how to take care of your new body, for when you reincarnate this can differ from life to life, but you already knew. You were not quick to learn, you were merely remembering knowledge from previous lives."

"But…how is it possible that I can, as you say, remember things that I had learnt from previous lives and yet cannot remember actually living the life or lives themselves?" I implored.

"You can if you try," he continued, sniggering.

"You have gained much knowledge from your present lifetime, but can you remember where and when you obtained each piece of that knowledge. You may recall some, but normally the information gets stored as general knowledge. You don't always remember the experience that brought you the information in the first place."

He stopped, "Mmm…no, that does not explain it very well," he then thought for a moment and had a puff of his pipe.

"Ah…yes put it this way. Due to an injury to the head, some people claim that they cannot remember who they are. This you may know as amnesia. They suffer with a complete loss of memory. They are able to live a normal human life using the knowledge they learnt, yet they cannot remember who they are, or who they used to be. Some sufferers go on to live a completely different live. This would be similar to a reincarnation."

He puffed firmly on his pipe once again.

"The thing is," he went on, blowing smoke towards the river. "Will you remember where you got this information from when you wake up in the morning?"

"Yes…I'm sure, I will," I muttered. Although the very thought seemed to echo a realisation of what I was doing and had once again caused an unwanted reaction.

"I am out of my body." I tried to resist, but all of my concentration had suddenly directed itself and centred on my physical body. It was too late to change anything now.

There was a swishing sound and a jolt as I woke up in bed.

Without a moment to lose, I grabbed a pen, paper and frantically wrote, determined not to forget a single detail.

Chapter Eight

This last encounter with the ghost had made me feel somehow different about the whole affair. Since, I had summoned him to the meeting, I now felt more in control and not so foolish. Perhaps now was the time to let someone else in on the mystery, someone close who might understand. *Gareth, it seemed, had taken an astonishing interest in these mysteries so why not others,* I thought. A week had passed though, before I had gained enough courage to reveal the esoteric knowledge that Jak had imparted to me.

It was by no means an easy decision to make. The reason being, I dearly wanted to disclose it all to Sharan, but she was quite sceptical about such things, and if she thought me mad then I was running a risk of losing her. However, I figured and hoped that her ghostly experience at Scrabo Castle would have been enough to open her mind and accept the weird mystery for what it was. I considered her to be highly intelligent, level-headed, down to earth and more to the point. I knew that she would give me a straight answer. If she thought me foolish, as sharp as a razor, she would cut me to the quick and tell me straight. On the other hand, if I could win over her sceptical mind, then perhaps my own sanity would no longer be in question. Then again, Jak had warned me that not everyone would be ready for such a revelation. *Maybe her spirit is not developed enough to accept such a truth,* I thought. Yet something deep inside me, call it intuition or just fate, it matters not, I knew that I had to tell her.

And so, one warm Sunday afternoon during picnic in a park, at great length I might add, I told her the whole story of what I had experienced, from my uncle's death, the mysterious smoke, the pipe, the out-of-body experiences and 'the unorthodox school of mystery'.

To my utter surprise and joy, not only did she grasp and understand the meaning of it all, she took an instant liking to the mystical concept and said, "The ghost Jak was captivating." On the contrary, and much to my delight, she was so enthralled that she wanted to know more and more, and added, "I know that it can't be proved, who cares, but it's a comforting thought to know that there is a meaning to our lives and that it does not end when we die."

She leant forward, and on offering a glass of wine, she tittered, "Of course this gives credence to the existence of ghosts too, such as the one that we contacted at Scrabo Castle." She shivered, trying to shake of the spooky feeling.

I was so pleased that I sighed with relief and laying back on the blanket-covered grass, a silence descended. She must have been deep in assessment though for she subsequently said,

"Mmm…kids seem to be more advanced and learn quicker these days. Take my niece Megan, for example, she can read adult books, and she's only five years old, and with total surprise to her mum, she is showing flair for the Spanish language too. As you know, our family is Irish, so god knows where that comes from…" She laughed at her own joke and then suddenly paused. "She is truly gifted, like yourself. You have a gift for art…" She continued talking and smiling; her face was an array of delight. I watched her pleasing movements as she played with her long blonde hair.

She was right, I did have a rare talent for art. I could draw before I went to school. It was a skill that I seemed to have always had. Could this have been knowledge from a past life perhaps?

"It's a known fact," she continued, "that children are physically maturing early. More and more babies are born with hair now than ever before. Older children are also developing early too. They go through puberty at an earlier age now."

"What are you getting at?" I exclaimed.

"Don't you see, it's not just their souls that are fast developing, their bodies are too. Kids are definitely maturing earlier…"

"Oh…I see what you mean," I replied, cutting her in mid flow, "and did you know that each generation is growing taller as well," I added. "What's that got to do with it?" She asked, delaying her next sentence.

I just looked at her for a moment, and with a playful smile I said: "I am taller than my Dad, and he is taller than his Dad was. Each generation is getting taller."

"Meaning…?" she sharply remarked.

"Have you ever been to the Tower of London," I asked. "You should see the size of the armoury there. It's all so small, especially 'King Henry IIX's', and he was considered a large man in his time."

"And your point is," she enquired with an air of nonchalance.

"Well…it's all part and parcel of the same thing," I asserted, "bodies developing not just faster but taller too."

"I see what you mean," she murmured, partaking of some wine.

Her eyes were now glazed as she looked fixedly on the park. She had obviously shut off, deep in contemplation.

After taking some wine and with great care, placing the glass in a safe place, I slothfully returned to my comfortable position on the thick tartan blanket. Bathing my half-clothed body in hot sunlight some clouds moved in warm currents, playfully across a light turquoise sky. I closed my eyes, and for a brief moment, I felt as if to be drifting. I light-heartedly gazed at the redness of my eye lids, and moving my head, I idly trifled with the colours that appeared.

"Jak is right!" she suddenly squealed, shattering my quietude. "Jak is right," she reiterated, "evolution of the soul, evolution of the physical. Both work side by side. Spirits becoming more and more intelligent, physical body's becoming more and more defined. From ape to man, less and less hairy, Oh my God!"

"What's wrong," I asked, anxiously sitting up.

She looked at me laughing as if she had seen something scary but funny. "Take it to its extreme," she sniggered. "Taller, thinner, more intelligent, large brain, no hair; you only need to add mixed races to create grey skin and add large black eyes and what have you got, an alien. What they call a Grey," she shrieked.

"Are you saying that these Grey Aliens are highly developed humans…meaning us in the future?"

"Could be," she returned giggling.

I lay back on the blanket. She was joking. I was not so sure.

Sometime later, after most of the food and wine had gone, a dark cloud appeared on the horizon. Fortunately, it seemed to be drifting close but away from our general direction. A cool wind picked up, blowing the bottom of the blanket over the dirty cutlery and plates. It was time to pack up.

We worked quickly, for we knew that the weather can change so fast in England, one minute warm and sunny, the next cold and wet. Realising the dark cloud was still moving away from us, our fast pace across the park slowed to a stroll and the joyful atmosphere, like our mood had turned to melancholy.

I sensed that Sharan needed comforting. So, putting my arm around he shoulders, I gave her an affectionate squeeze. "What about the suffering?" she said softly. "What suffering?"

"You asked Jak why we have to suffer. So why is there so much suffering in the world?"

She had me stumped of course. Owing to the fact that Jak had failed to tell me, I was unable to answer this important question. "Why is there so much suffering in the world?" I just looked at her blankly.

"He didn't tell you, did he?" she said.

"No... No, he didn't," I reluctantly answered, "but I shall ask him next time," I added, trying to reconcile my inadequacy.

"How do you know you'll meet him again?"

I looked at her with a smile. "I'm not all together sure how I know, but meet him again, I shall."

She looked away for a moment, and then on turning to face me again, she dubiously asked, "This out-of-the-body experience, can anyone do it?"

"I don't know," I replied. "I don't see why not. Why should it only be restricted to me? Perhaps, everyone does experience it, they just don't realise when it happens."

I paused for a quick thought, and then said, "Maybe lots of people do experience it, they just put it all down to dreaming. What's more, maybe that is why we need sleep. Our spirit needs a rest from our physical body. Perhaps we all travel out of our bodies, but on awaking, we are unable to recall the experience. How many times have you woke up knowing full well that you were dreaming but could not remember one detail of that dream?"

"Oh, many times," she said. "In fact, I know that I dream every night, but rarely do I remember what they're all about. Sleep has always been a mystery," she added, "even to the experts. A while ago on TV, there was a documentary about sleep. They couldn't understand why sleep was so necessary. Most people could get by with eight hours sleep, and some needed twelve hours, but they had found that some others could live on far less sleep. One woman only needed fifteen minutes sleep per night. The point they were making was that everyone can rest their body by sitting or lying down. This woman would get physically tired and needed to rest her body but would burn her night lamps till early morning at which time she needed to sleep for fifteen minutes. Why? What happened to her in those fifteen minutes that she was unable to get by just relaxing?"

She looked up to the sky, waiting for my reaction, except I was still contemplating a reply. A bird swept by catching our attention. We watched its unrestricted movements, floating freely into the distance until it disappeared.

"For all we know, sleep could be a release for us, a release from our temporary bonds," I muttered. "Perhaps sleep allows us to function in the way we truly are, as free entities." Jak even said, "Our lives are dreams, and when we die, we wake up."

"Wake up to what?" she asked. I watched as a haunted look appeared on Sharan's face. "What's it like?" she murmured, supposedly trying to control her inner fears. "What's it like when you have these out-of-body experiences, and when did it all start?"

With a view to focus on the question at hand, I instantly stopped walking. "Do you know, I am not entirely sure when it all started. After the first meeting with Jak, I could suddenly remember leaving my body many times before, and yet, before this phenomenon, I had no recollection of the previous experiences at all. So my first experience of being out was not my first but one of many. It has opened a door to a world that it seems I have long forgotten."

"What were those previous experiences like?" she enquired, moving on along the path.

Quickly scrutinising my mind for a possible first occurrence, curiously enough, I could not think of an actual first time. My memory could only summon up many.

"I don't entirely know when it all started," I replied, walking faster trying to catch up. "As a child, I can remember floating around my bedroom ceiling, trying to open the curtains but my hands would just go straight through the material. In frustration, I would wake up screaming in the night, and my parents would try to console me by saying that I was only dreaming. They would then invite me to their room until I settled down again."

"Go on," she asked excitedly.

"I can also remember playing on the stairs without my feet touching the steps. I would sometimes float, drifting slowly up and down, and then at other times, I would whizz up and down. It was all just a game to me."

"How weird, but can you actually remember what it was like, the sensation I mean, of coming out of your body." She stopped and waited for my answer in anticipation.

"There are a number of sensations," I said. "Sometimes I would feel like I was just floating and at other times, I could feel and hear sort of strong vibrations that seem to ripple through my body in rhythmic pulsations."

"Scary," she responded.

"Other times I might be, well… I can only describe as dreaming, when I am, somehow, able to control the dream and make things happen. Like the will to fly sends me soaring to the sky."

"How do you known that you are not just dreaming?"

137

With a smile of assurance, I acknowledged her remark, for it was a fair question indeed.

"It is different, Sharan. It is so, so different. You have such a wonderful feeling of freedom. Free from the bonds of your torturous body pains. Not until you experience this do you realise the constant pain that your body inflicts on you. You can move freely, expand or contract and even penetrate material objects, even doors and walls are not a problem. Everything seems so wonderfully colourful too. Everything seems to radiate a kind of colourful energy. It is as if you can actually see energy in colour. And you become so aware of your spirit, you are spirit…" I laughed. "We all are. Our physical body is just a puppet to be disregarded when it's finished with."

"Why did I not realise all of this before, wow…!" I laughed in private amusement.

"You feel at one with the universe and not a care in the world," I added. "Everything is so clear. Everything makes so much sense."

I couldn't believe what I was saying. I had somehow suddenly realised how wonderful my experiences had been. The enthusiasm had surged through me like a bolt of lightning.

"Yes, but dreams can be like that too, can't they?" she asked.

"No, it is hard to explain, you need to experience it to know the difference. Besides, I have looked down at my body lying in bed just before an experience and sometimes on my return."

"Does it not scare you though?"

"Yes, if I am honest…it has been scary at times, but the rewards are so worth it," I added.

"Mmm…the very thought of being out of my body scares me. I would feel so insecure, so vulnerable." She paused and a look of despair came over her face. Looking around, so as not to give the news to possible prying ears, she moved closer and asked in a timid voice, "What if you can't get back to your body? Oh…Don, say you won't do it again," she anxiously asked, pulling away. "It's dangerous. You might not come back. Promise me, you won't do it again."

"It's not as simple as that," I returned. "I don't have any control over it. Jak seems to summon me to him—although he claimed it different last time. He has pursued me not I to him. I might have encouraged it a bit, but he came to me first. Besides, it's not a scary experience anyway."

She shrugged her shoulders. "I still think it is dangerous." Her head hung low as she continued to walk the path.

"Have you ever had a strange dream or experience that you could not explain," I quizzed, catching her up.

"No!" she snapped.

"So you've never felt like you are floating and then jerk yourself awake?"

She stopped and looked at me curiously.

"Have you ever felt and heard a kind of click, like you have just clicked back in. Surely you have had the feeling of falling and dropped into bed?"

With that, her face blushed red.

"That is you returning back to your body," I said.

"Oh, don't…" she cried out, shivering trying to shake of the feeling.

"You have though, haven't you?" I insisted.

"Come on…!" she snapped, ignoring my questioning. "We'll be late for the train."

We spent the next fifteen to twenty minutes briskly walking to the station. After a while my arms and shoulders were growing tired from carrying the picnic equipment. Sharan offered to lighten the load by taking some off me. We had not spoken too much along the way so breaking the ice, I asked:

"Does this equipment feel lighter to you now, than it did on the way to the park?"

"Of course, it does," she replied, "there is no food and drink in the bags."

"Ah, yes, but we have eaten the food and drank the wine," I said.

"The question is, are we carrying the same load on the way back?"

"Oh…you are such a fool sometimes," she uttered smiling.

We continued along the road for about a mile, reaching the outskirts of the park, we turned left into the town. My little joke had done the trick though, for at no time were we quiet. We laughed and messed around all the way.

We then stopped at a few shops for Sharan to add to her collection of shoes—as if we didn't have enough to carry. I didn't mind too much really, for each stop gave me an opportunity to rest. One shop even had a sofa for me to sit on.

At long last, we reached the train station some two hours later and well after our original train. On entering the train station, little did we know it at the time, but we were in for a bit of a shock. Following closely behind us was a short old lady. She had apparently been pursuing us for quite a while. We were about to walk on to the station platform when Sharan discovered that her purse was missing, and in her usual stressful manner she panicked. It was while Sharan was displaying this act of anguish that this old lady appeared.

She was short, petite, had long grey hair tied in a red bow at the back. She wore a brightly coloured dress. The startling thing that was immediately apparent was her club-foot and one leg longer than the other. With the aid of a walking stick, she had managed, at great effort I am sure, to follow close behind us. With a warm, friendly smile, her eyes lit up as she caught our attention, and in a soft voice she said,

"I am sorry to disturb you my dears, but I saw this purse drop from your bag."

In total dismay, Sharan accepted the purse saying, "Thank you, thank you, how can I repay you. It must have been so difficult trying to keep up with us. Thank you. You are so kind."

"Oh…please my love, thanks is not necessary," the old lady replied.

Then came the most unexpected remark of all.

She turned to walk away and quickly turning to face us again she asked. "Are you a learnt spirit?"

"Pa…Pardon," I stammered trying to gather my wits and compose myself.

"I see that you are," she replied with a smile and an old wise sparkle in her eye. "Then you will know that there is no need to reward or repay me. You need only to help others when the time and circumstances pose themselves. I thank you for this opportunity, and I wish you good luck." She then turned and walked off.

Sharan and I just looked at each another in total dismay and instantly burst out laughing. Although, a cold shiver had run up my back, for this was yet another uncanny moment that for now would remain elusive.

We boarded the train and later made our way to my parents' house where Sharan had been invited for diner. We had an excellent meal cooked by my mum, and then we all relaxed drinking tea in the lounge afterwards. It was while we were relaxing that we had yet another revelation that seemed to confirm that Jak's assumptions were correct.

Watching the national news, we were informed, among many other items of news that back in Aug 2004, school leavers had record passes at 'A level' standard . 95% of all students that sat such exams had passed with 'flying colours'.

Sharan and I looked at one another in awe. We whispered that it must be true and that Jak must be right, this cannot be a coincidence. We were both so excited, especially I, because now I no longer felt stupid about the subject.

Then out of the blue, for I thought he was hard of hearing. My Dad said, "That's nothing. It was on the news yesterday that kids in America are passing degree standards as early as 12 years old, and one boy had been presented with a Nobel Peace Prize. How are these kids able to do such a thing?" he went on. "How can such a young brain cram so much information in and in such a short period of time? It takes most geniuses a lifetime to achieve such a feat. How on earth is it possible?" He then stood up and went to make some tea, laughing and shaking his head in disbelief as he did so.

Sharan and I looked at each other and smiled. We knew the answer. For us, there could only be one explanation that our souls move from one life to another gaining more and more knowledge through each life or reincarnation.

That young lad who had won the noble prize must be very advanced, I thought, *experiencing far more life times and grasping far more knowledge than lots of people put together. In effect, he is the product of many people put together and the sum total of all the lives he has been as many people. He is then many people in one body, and many people put together are very knowledgeable.*

At that precise moment, as a kind of recognition I guess, I could smell Jak's smoke. Acknowledging his presents, I offered a kind of telepathic thank you.

"Are you thinking what I am thinking?" she asked shattering my thoughts. Then moving closer so that I might hear her whispering, our eyes met, and she said, "Well, it is obvious isn't it, each generation is becoming more and more intelligent. This is clearly shown with the A level results. There has been a record level of passes. The human race has never been as intelligent as it is at present, and what of that young boy," she continued, "if the theory is right, which I think it is, he must have lived many human lives to have achieved such knowledge."

"Yes, then we were thinking the same," I replied.

"But where is it all leading too, and what's all this knowledge for?"

"What do you mean what's it all for? I'm not following you, knowledge is knowledge and that's it, isn't it?"

"I don't know, maybe I am reading too much into it again, but who is in the lead?"

I looked at her in puzzlement.

"If we have all lived many lives and have become more aware and wiser after each life and some of us are more advanced than others, then who is in the lead, who is the leader? Who among us has lived the most lives?"

I felt a surge of excitement rush into me. "I see what you mean," I retorted, "the first humans I suppose, those that have lived the most lives, they would surely possess the most intelligence of all and would be the top people in their field of knowledge."

***

The day after these conversations, the subjects would constantly be raised in my mind. I could not help but wonder if there were any grounds to our ramblings. I was intrigued, do these advanced souls really exist? I decided to do some research on the matter and was astounded to discover some super intelligent children that just might fit the description. Like most people these days, my research was mainly carried out on the internet. And to my surprise, there seemed to be lots of information about children possessing advanced knowledge.

There is a term in psychology literature called a child prodigy. A child prodigy is defined as a person under the age of ten who produces output in some domain to the levels of an adult. In the Collins English Dictionary, a child prodigy is a child with a very great talent.

Some of these children are physically advanced. They have entered Olympic standard competitions and won medals, gold, silver and bronze. Others are more mentally advanced, they seem to possess the same mental abilities as adults. But unlike most adults, they seem to have very high IQ levels normally from 100 to 147 and some even claim to reach the level of 200. Studies show that most child prodigies are often found in music, mathematics, art and chess, but they can be found in all areas of study.

I looked up the famous composer Wolfgang Amadeus Mozart born 1756. He appears to be the first recorded child prodigy. He could read music, play piano and started composing at the age of three. He wrote his first song at the age of 5. He went on to play the violin and performed before European royalty at the age of 17.

This to me was insane. How could a child of 3 years old possibly read music and play piano to such a high standard as to compose in front of an audience. Surely the records were wrong.

I then found a list of child prodigies. Now, this list was amazing. There are practically 200 names of very talented people. There are no doubts about it that every one of them had outstanding abilities and had achieved amazing levels of knowledge at such young ages. But among this list a few people were of great interest for me:

Carl Friedrich Gauss (1777–1855) made his first mathematical discoveries as a teenager. But when he was only 3 years old, he watched his father add up his accounts and corrected him.

Promethea Olymia Kyrene Pythaitha, born in 1991, is an American child prodigy with an IQ of 173. She started reading at the age of 1. Started learning college level mathematics at age 7 and at the age of 13 became the youngest student to receive a bachelor's degree.

Colin Carlson, born in 1996, earned a bachelor's degree in Biology aged 12 and a master's degree at the age of 17.

Balamurali Ambati, born in 1977, finished high-aged 11, was a college junior by the age of 12, and he was a doctor at the age of 17 years.

Sunny Sanwar, born in 1989, could fluently read, write and speak six languages by the age of eight.

H.P. Lovecraft could recite poetry at the age of 2 and wrote long poems at the age of 5.

Lope de Vega could read Latin proficiently at the age of 5 and wrote his first play at the age of 12.

Mohammad Hossein Tababai, born in 1991, memorised the entire Quran at the age of 5.

John Stuart Mill could read and understand several dead languages by the age of 8 and studied scholastic philosophy at the age of 12.

Hildegart Rodriguez Carballeira knew six languages by the age of 8 years.

John Barratier could speak German, Latin, French and Dutch at the age of 4.

Nathan Leopold (1904–1971) could speak at the age of 4 months; it is said that he had an IQ of 210.

Now, how is all this possible if we think with our brain. Research told me that a child's brain is not properly developed until the age of 3. So how can a child of 4 months speak, and a little girl of 12 months start reading.

But, of all these talented kids, the two that intrigued me the most were the boy who could read dead languages at the age of 8, and the little boy of 5 who had memorised the Quran. Now, I am speculating of course, but these two boys must have gained their knowledge from past lives otherwise, this just doesn't make sense.

I then looked at videos on YouTube, and my mind was blown away. It is one thing to read about child prodigies from a list, but it is quite another thing to see them in action. I saw kids of 3 and 4 years old, reading music, playing piano, violin and drums at the level of master musicians.

This was all speculation, of course, and neither I nor science could ever prove such wild claims, but were these advanced souls the ones Sharan and I spoke of that day? I hoped that maybe Jak could give me some answers.

Chapter Nine

For many weeks I tried to contact Jak in my sleep. I would lay quietly in bed trying to catch the moment between being awake and sleep. With ardent concentration on Jak's image, I endeavoured to project my spirit from my body, but alas, some weeks had passed, and I was unsuccessful. The nights were drawing in, and the days were getting shorter. Winter was on its way. Then finally, one evening, dosed in melancholy, I was sitting in my bedroom, elbows on my desk and with hands supporting my weary head, I peered out of the window. The view was like my mood, gloomy, over cast and raining. I had given up trying to contact Jak. The task had proven once again to be far too difficult, and not even a slight whiff of his agreeable smoke had I been able to appreciate since our last meeting.

Hour after hour, I must have sat gazing hypnotically out of that window, my blues sinking ever deeper into a timeless state of hopelessness and finally, to a state where I felt to be doomed forever.

Then suddenly, quite undetectable at first and growing continually stronger was for me the most welcome odour of all, Jak's invisible pipe smoke. Except this time, I could visually see it appearing all around me.

Then I heard it. The sound of Jak's laughter close behind me. I quickly turned, and there he was standing in the middle of my room, engulfed in a moving cloud of colourful smoke. He was, as usual, in a state of hysterical laughter.

"Hello, my boy," said he, chuckling amusingly, "I thought I would pay you a visit."

"Where have you been," I cursed like a spoilt, unruly child. "I have been trying to contact you for ages. Why have you not come?"

My melancholy had now turned into anger. I could feel adrenalin surging through me, boy was I angry. Like a bubble about to burst, I seethed with uncontrollable fury.

He instantly stopped laughing. "There is more to life than sadness, my lad. Sure, it might be raining, but there is good and bad in everything. You need only to look for it."

The wondrous look on his face, his soft voice and eyes blessed with an enchanting command, he had instantaneously depleted my anger. I felt as a puppet might under the control of a master.

Without doubt, it was definitely Jak, but he looked a little different. His hair, though still white, was much longer, and his face now supported not just a white moustache but a long white beard. His clothes were different too. The white shirt, dark red jumper and black trousers had been replaced. Complete with hood, he now donned a full-length dark brown monk's habit.

My return smile elevated his confidence in me, and I was compensated with a slight nod and a wink.

"Please tell me, Jak, where have you been? Why am I not able to contact you when I wish?

There are so many things that I wish to know. So many questions I wished to ask. I feel so empty and unfulfilled. I cannot explain why. I know that the weather does not help, but it cannot be totally to blame for I can feel just as bad sometimes on a fine day in the middle of summer, and there seems to be no reason for it, what so ever."

With a smile, he gazed at me in silence, seemingly deep in thought. It was at this point that although he was surrounded in colourful smoke of his favourite brand, for I could clearly see and smell it, he did not appear to be smoking. Furthermore, he did not have the pipe that I had previously given to him either. Being all together puzzled at not just the missing pipe but also his change in clothes. I asked him about these changes.

"Ah yes," he muttered, blowing away some remainder of smoke that had drifted between us. "I knew at some point that you would notice this fact, and indeed, I owe you an explanation."

He then moved in one swift movement from the centre of the room to one side. He turned to face me, and for the first time ever, his face took on an odd sinister appearance, and his voice became very harsh as he divulged his next point.

"You see, my lad, matters in the spirit world are very different from the physical world. You already know by experience what some of those differences are, yet others, I dare say, must be explained.

The reason my appearance changes from time to time is because of your expectations of me. When I first appeared to you, I took on an image of an old man very similar to your grandfather, whom you loved so dearly. This was not entirely my doing. I merely cleared my spirit image and allowed your emotions to dictate the outcome. The love that you hold for your grandfather had a direct effect on the image you saw. Now I am the image of a monk. Doubtless to say, you think me wise, and your image of an old wise man is what you see before you, a long, white-bearded monk."

This answer I was not comfortable with, and it sent alarm signals racing through me. I gasped in horror at the very idea that he could change his self, for what then was his true image, and who or what had I contacted and been communicating with all this time. I couldn't believe it. Had I truly been cheated? A worrying thought then came to me. Surely, there is only one entity that could be so deceitful.

I instantly shut off my senses, tightly closed in on myself and trembled as fear laboured its way through my being. His mocking sounds echoed around me. Feeling like a little mouse mischievously preyed by a cat, I shivered, paralyzed to a small space in the room. I could not move, neither did I want to.

My anxious thoughts then brought back his words that played on my mind, *I cleared my spirit image and allowed your emotions to dictate the outcome*. Over and over again, I heard it echoing in my mind.

"No, have I truly been deluded all this time?" I said to myself. My soul quivered at the very thought of what the final outcome might be. My emotions and deluded mind were now conjuring up a new image for him, or was this his true identification, I had no way of telling. All I could see in my mind's eye was a hideous creature with horns and pointed tail. I tried so hard to banish the developing image, but my anxiety kept on feeding it. Then once again, I heard his laughter. I was surely doomed then. I waited in silence. Compact to the size of a small furry creature anchored to the spot, I awaited my inevitable lot. As a jittering spirit, I couldn't do anything else but wait in the darkened room.

I could hear the rain against the window, there was a flash and a creak of thunder—as if I needed its extra sinister assault. Then it stopped. I waited until the silence was becoming too stressful and still nothing happened.

Perhaps he has gone, I thought, *or perhaps he really is playing cat and mouse*. I decided to sit it out.

After waiting for what felt like an eternity, curiosity got the better of me. So, I cautiously opened up expecting to be shocked by his ugly true self.

To my surprise, I neither saw nor heard a thing. With taunted spirit, I looked tentatively around the shadowy room. My fiendish friend had gone, yet was I still shocked to the core. Not of an ugly creature, but my very own physical body slumped over my desk. I had looked down upon my body before, only this time everything felt different, and to me there was only one conclusion.

"No…!" I cried.

"Sharan was right. She warned me not to pursue things. I've done it now," I wailed.

In desperation and hope that just maybe my feelings were wrong, I focused intensely on returning to my body, but it would not accept me. I tried over and over again to no avail. I could not get back. Fear ran through me like electric in water.

"Oh…God help me, please…! I promise to be good," I whimpered.

Right then, at a point when I thought a blazing fire was about to consume me. I heard his gentle affectionate voice.

"Fear is a dreadful thing, boy. It is the cause of much suffering."

His tone then became all together softer. "I am not the evil one, my lad, it is the negative force inside you that is evil. Fear is the devil. It is the nonentity, the negative energy, the antimatter. It is completely opposing and destructive.

Fear is the negative energy which closes down, draws in, contracts, runs and hides.

Fear makes you cling, grasp, hoard and worry. It is counteractive, causing financial depression and world money markets to slump. It is cold, greedy and rejects, causing prejudice and famine.

Fear makes you panic, attack, fight and makes war possible.

Fear is draining, non-living, shrinks the spirit causes confusion, suspicion and mistrust.

I am not evil, boy, fear is. Fear is the negative force, and the devil is not a creature with horns. The devil is the sum total of all the negative energy in the world, and what feeds the devil is fear and negative thoughts.

Evil is what you feel inside you right at this moment. You feel the devil's presence indeed, but it is not I. He is not next to you. He is inside you. You are full of him, and it is putrid. It stinks, makes you feel ill, and if you continue with this thought process, you will be doomed forever in its filthy pit. Is there any wonder you feel scared, worried and panicky, you need to flush him out…!"

Feeling relatively encouraged by his definition of the devil, I fearfully asked, "If you are not the devil, then why have you tricked me, and why am I dead?"

Once again, I heard his laughter, only this time it seemed warm and loving as if to be laughing for me and not at me. I watched apprehensively as he silently appeared once again in the centre of the room, still dressed as a monk and then with vibrant blue eyes and a warm kindly smile, that which could only be imagined of angelic eminence. He held out his palm, and in a soft gesture I heard him say:

"You are not dead, Don, and I have not tricked you. You tricked and scared yourself. As in all cases, your ignorance let the devil in. Your mind could not explain my existence. It could not explain how or why I change my appearance and so jumped to the wrong conclusions. Your lack of knowledge caused confusion, suspicion and mistrust, inviting fear which plunged you to the depths of hell and a hell of your own making."

"Then why can I not return to my body," I timidly asked.

He drew nearer. I pulled back, reducing myself as compactly as possible. Guardedly, I looked up, his huge spirit towered above me. I never realised that he was so big.

"Would you accept a small shivering wreck into you?" He said, sniggering. "Look at yourself, boy. You are too small for your physical body. This is what happens when people die of fright. Their spirit shrinks so much, they cannot get back."

I looked around, and sure enough, I was about the size of a peanut. Not only was his spirit huge, but my own physical body towered above me too.

Slowly looking back at Jak, I was completely at sea, totally bewildered. He gleamed in anticipation.

What beauty I saw in that man's eyes. "Could the devil radiate such love," I said to myself. "I think not. Wonder of wonders, then who or what is he?"

His entire spirit glowed, bleaching his monk's habit white.

Immersed in a bright colourful aura, he smiled.

It is an image I will never forget.

Gracefully raising both hands, his palms were turned towards me. I felt a tingle as my spirit seemed to absorb some of the colourful atmosphere that surrounded me. This immediately invoked a wonderful feeling of pleasure. At the same time, Jak appeared to shrink to my size.

"Look!" he said, pointing in the direction of my physical body.

I was now the same size as my counterpart and the look of bliss that I saw on its face, tears ran down my physical cheeks. I remembered such a feeling the first time Jak and I had met.

"Now your body will accept you," he said. "Be careful, though, if you go too close, it will snap you back."

I felt so good, so fulfilled, the empty fearful feeling had totally disappeared. I felt a flutter, like energy building inside as if something sensational was about to happen.

"What is this stuff?" I asked in a shriek of merriment.

"I have told you before boy, it is 'pure positive life force', complete opposite to the negative force you encountered just now. That is all you were lacking."

Is there any wonder that he is always laughing, I thought. *Being full of this stuff all the time, so would I.*

"But what is it, and how does it work?" I giggled uncontrollably. "First and foremost, I must apologise for putting you through that dreadful experience," he said, "but it is the way of things. The best and most effective way of learning anything is to experience it first-hand. I am sorry to say that this is one of the reasons why every spirit must experience great suffering and loses. To experience is to learn. I can now explain some of what has taken place.

As I briefly explained earlier, your only crime was ignorance. Ignorance is dangerous. It is dangerous to the physical body and dangerous to the soul."

His serious expression and tone instantly brought my bubbly spirit into touch. Fascinated, he had my full attention.

"As in all cases, your ignorance was at fault. Your mind could not explain my existence. It could not explain how or why I change my appearance, and so jumping to the wrong conclusions, your lack of knowledge caused confusion, suspicion and mistrust, inviting fear which plunged you to the depths of hell.

"Lack of knowledge can only do this. Ignorance is the root of all evil. It can cause fear, and when it does, it is most destructive. It accepts no mercy.

You asked me in our last meeting why there is so much suffering in the world. I tell you this, boy, it is of man's own making. Out of selfishness, fuelled by fear, ignorance and greed, a deadly concoction. Man worships the devil."

"No this cannot be," I exclaimed in the name of humanity.

"Then why is your entertainment so full of destructive action? Night after night, in the so-called civilised world, you read or watch the moving pictures, filling your mind with war, horror, thrillers, murder mysteries, and science fiction.

Modern man loves the thrill of being scared, and as if that was not enough, the entertainment companies produce ongoing soup operates that teach you how to have an unhappy destructive life where murder, adultery and greed are a normal way of living."

He was now laughing once again. "I tell you, your minds are so full of fear and greed that you cause your own suffering. You get a thrill out of seeing others suffering. Night after night, you 'worship' the dark side. The newspapers are full of bad news. The publisher will tell you that this is so because 'only bad news sells'."

He looked straight at me. "Do you still maintain that it isn't true? Do you still deny that you worship the devil?"

"We have comedy programs, they cannot be considered negative or bad, surely?" I asked.

"Ah yes," he continued. "You mean the ones that poke fun out of other races of people, the poor downtrodden unintelligent people in society, breeding dislike and hatred or intolerance towards other people because they are different."

Although I loathed to admit it, he did have a point. I thought of the endless hours I had spent watching such horror or actionpacked movies, and how the destructive action, the killing, so graphically detailed thrilled me with dread and excitement. I was appalled at myself for ever thinking in such a way.

"What does this mean?" I asked sorrowfully. "Why do I find such entertainment thrilling? I am a good person at heart. Deep down I am not a devil worshipper, but I hate to say it, I do find such action or scary films exciting. What is wrong with me?"

Full of mirth, Jak burst into laughter.

"Oh…how much I love these conversations with you, boy." His sounds of merriment were loud and echoed around the room.

Have I missed something, I thought. I patiently waited for him to calm down.

"No, there is nothing wrong with you, lad. You can't help the way you are. You have been taught to think this way. This was part of the plan of things. Throughout your various incarnations, from very young to old age, you have been taught to fear. You must watch for your enemy and beware of the dangers. You have experienced many wars and been directed in the skills of survival, be the fittest, the most victorious and successful of your kind. To love and have compassion is a weakness. So, you strive to be the fittest, most triumphant, successful being alive. Your life is very competitive, and so if you find yourself losing in any situation, you become scared. Your biggest fear is losing, for you have been taught that to lose is to be an outcast or not to survive at all, and so, of course, you choose the action fear sponsors, for that is what you have been taught by all of your 'parents' through many life times.

There is nothing wrong with you, Don. In fact, you are one of the more advanced souls, and there are many like you. You are all part of the plan."

"What plan?" I gasped.

"The plan," he returned, "the meaning to it all."

I could not believe what I had heard.

"Are you saying that our lives are not just played out at random, and that there is a plan behind it all?"

His face was full of exhilaration. "Why...you don't think that all your efforts have been for nothing, do you?"

"Well I was rather hoping that there was a meaning to our lives otherwise what would be the point."

Then in a sudden fit of excitement, I could not help myself—anyone in my position would have wanted the same thing, I am sure.

I had to know the secrets, the mysteries behind our lives. From the beginning of human existence, man has quest the meaning of life and the elusive plan. I had to know. I had to know the Grand Plan of things.

Perhaps it could answer the mystery behind our bizarre, diverse lives, and why we feel the need to compete and fight each other and, why some seek greed to become rich and famous. Why do we enjoy the dark side so much? What makes it so intriguing? I had to know.

"Jak!" I finally burst out. "What is the Grand Plan?"

Holding up one palm, he turned his head away in a negative response. My emotions dropped, for this could only mean one thing. I was not to be told.

Then turning his head to face me, he lowered his hand. "I once told you that you are ready for such knowledge, but there is much for you to learn first. Knowledge, you must always remember, is paramount.

Knowledge is the key to the plan, and the only way to gain true knowledge is to experience things first-hand. To experience, is to remember forever. Someone can tell you a story of their life. You could read someone's autobiography or watch a film about a person's life, but you will never know the real truth of that life unless you live it.

To live a life is to experience, to experience is to acquire knowledge, the more knowledge that you acquire, the less you fear. If you were able to know everything that there is to know about life and the universe, you would fear nothing, for you only fear that which you do not understand."

He paused, and I watched as his big eyes drew nearer.

"And my clue for you boy, the clue to the Grand Plan of things is knowledge. You must try to learn everything."

"But there is only one entity that could possibly know everything." I exclaimed.

"And it's not the devil," he said. "The devil lacks great knowledge and wishes you to know even less. 'He' sends his gremlins to tease and hold you back. Great wars have been fought due to lack of knowledge and understanding. To understand your enemy is to make a friend, and to have a friend you must first be one.

A moment ago, I was your enemy. Shortly after, when you knew and understood me better, you didn't fear me, and so we are now friends, and the devil was defeated."

He looks away as if to be contemplating something. Then looking back he continued.

"The reason I change my image from time to time is simply because I can and so can you. I can read your mind, and I know what you like and can change to suit your wants. Only a true friend would do such a thing.

Whilst you are outside your physical body, you too can change your appearance. Although, whilst you remain alive, it is comforting to maintain the same shape as your physical body, and it is easier to return. When you die, you disregard your physical body to become, as me, pure spirit."

He stopped for a moment to look and sense if I was still following him.

I smiled in response.

"As I mentioned to you before, your life is a dream, and when you die, you finally wake up. You will wake up to a realisation of what you are, pure spirit. It is when you have become pure spirit once again, you will remember everything. You will remember not just the life that you are living now but all of the lives previous to it. You will then once again, be in a position to assess the progress of your soul.

It is at that point you will realise there is no need to continue to be the image of your old self 'Don'. You will then retain the total knowledge and memory of all those lives or incarnations you had before. You can then, as I, adopt anyone of your passed identifications, if you so wish.

The point that I am making is, when you return to pure spirit, you don't really have an ID. You will just be energy or I prefer to call it pure spirit. You will have become, once again, like all spirits 'that what you are' or 'I am what I am'."

He waited for a moment, allowing me to take on board this special esoteric knowledge.

"I am a bit confused," I declared. "You say that you are a ghost and that you are pure spirit. You say that you can change your image too. My question is: you seem totally different from ghosts that are said to haunt old castles and manner houses. Why? They don't seem to be able to change as you do.

And another thing, Jak! Where is the pipe that I gave you?"

His eyes lit up with delight. "Excellent questions, excellent questions indeed.

The pipe that you gave me on our first meeting was a very old pipe. It belonged to me some lifetimes ago when I lived as a young man in the south of England. Your grandfather smoked a pipe, and so I used my old pipe to help create his image, that I might encourage you to follow its subtle influence."

"Well it certainly worked," I replied, "but where is it now?"

"Why? It is right there in its box, in the corner of the room where you left it," he said.

I glanced over and sure enough, there it was, although, I was not sure whether I had left it there or whether he had just placed it there prior to my glance.

He laughed at my reaction.

"Ghosts, you are quite right, there are many types. A ghost is a soul without a physical body. Most people would relate this to an eerie thing that swishes about in the dead of night making creaks and groans, causing the hair on your head to stand up. This type of ghost is just a poor lost wandering soul which refuses to believe that its physical body does not exist anymore. Again, out of fear the spirit of the dead person will not accept death so wonders about according to the habits of his or her previous life.

Other ghosts have an agenda or score to settle. A strong healthy person who may have been violently killed in some way may seek vengeance and cannot rest. The hatred traps them in a time warp where there is no escape, sometimes reliving the episode over and over again, until during centuries the will becomes dissipated and the soul moves on.

Both types of ghosts become poor mindless wandering waifs that can occasionally be seen by the living. Yet quite often, like you experienced earlier, their fear or hatred shrinks the soul so much that the living may only see of them a small ball of colourful light."

"You mean an orb?" I said, bursting in with excitement. "Call it what you will, boy, it is what it is."

"And what's the answer for those ghosts?" I asked. "Must they go on aimlessly captured in the past?"

"Of course not, like you, all souls must learn to open up. They must learn to accept what they are. And knowledge is the key, boy. You must learn all you can about anything and everything.

Did you know that there are still people in the world that have never stepped foot outside of their village?" He went on, "Like trapped ghostly souls they fear beyond their own little world. They are not living. Their life is a habit, and they feel safe doing the same things day after day, week after week, month after month, year after year, and they will feel safe doing the same things after death too.

You and every spirit must learn to open up, accept the world for what it is. Learn all you can in this life and the next; only then can your soul develop, only then can the world advance, and only then will you find peace in your heart, free from fear and the devil."

He stopped, and I felt his large blue angelic eyes as if taking stock over the future of my soul.

"Are you willing," he said, "Are you willing to open up and escape from your habitual existence?"

"Yes," I answered, but a cold chill had swept over me. I felt the negative feeling, once again, fear was shrinking my spirit.

"Please…Jak, you are not going to tell me that I am really dead," I stammered. "And that you are my messenger gently filling me in?"

"No, my boy, you have much living to do yet, far more to experience as does every existing soul, dead or alive. The world has much to learn."

He then raised his arms in a kind of ritualistic manner, filling my soul once again with his 'pure positive life force' and on holding the pose he recited something similar to this:

"Let me now implore you to observe that the path to enlightenment is darkness visible, serving only to express that gloom which is the result that cold selfish thoughts have made. It is

155

this mysterious veil which the eye of human greed cannot penetrate unless touched by that glimmering light within you rests. Yet even by this wondrous glow that you feel therein, you may perceive yourself to be at the door of death, and when this incarnated, life shall have passed away, the world again will receive you into its cold heart.

Let life's experiences mould you. Let the emblems of fatality which be set before you, lead you to reflect upon your inevitable destiny and guide you to ponder over the most interesting of all human studies, the knowledge of yourself.

You must be alert at all times and act on your allotted task wiliest you so live. You must always listen to the voice of nature, for as long as you dwell in that perishable frame. You will guide it as it will guide you. By inflicting pain, it will remind you of its mortality and with compassion, you will heal it so."

His voice tapered off as he slowly lowered his hands. "Please don't worry, my dear boy, you are not dying, you have just taken the third step on the path to wisdom. You are becoming aware of what you really are and learning the truth of yourself. You are opening up as I once did. You are expanding, becoming greater than you were, you and your friend."

Alarm bells were now once again ringing. There he has said it again. I thought, *Is he just playing with me?*

Once again, I looked around expecting to find someone next to me, and once again, I found no one, and yes, once again Jak was in stitches without ever an explanation.

This was really annoying me, but I did not want to give him the satisfaction of me asking him once again who this so called invisible friend was. Feeling completely vexed though, I sensed a surge of negative energy race into me, seemingly filling my spirit with instant pulsating anger.

"If you are so clever," I retorted, "Why is there so much suffering in the world? I don't just mean us fighting wars. What about the long-term sick, deaf, or people with cancer. Like my uncle Peter who finally died after many months of pain; old lonely people too, good people who have died of the cold in their own homes, and young people dying in accidents."

I looked away, my anger was such that I couldn't bear to look at him.

"Babies dying at birth," I added, "what did the parents do to deserve such a loss and innocent children being abused or sometimes murdered."

A feeling of nausea came over me, a heavy sickening sensation suppressed my spirit. In a vain attempt to stop this downward spiral, I looked out of the window to find something to focus on but the world outside was raining tears of sorrow. To look inward, I closed off my senses. All I could see, hear, smell, feel and taste was the vile stench of the sufferance of the physical world. I was lost once again to a pit of disappear and hell.

Then, just as what I thought to be the point of no return, for depression held my soul captive, a warm sensation took place on what felt like someone stroking my head. I immediately opened up, to find grief stricken Jak lightly touching the top of my spiritual body. A stream of tears ran down his cheeks.

"Out of the ashes of pain comes love," he said.

His glassy blue eyes, the anguish, the torment that he must have been feeling had distorted every contour of his face. My vicious attack must have evoked some dreamful memories from previous lives that had instantaneously held his spirit bedevilled. His haunted expression chilled me to the core. I could not believe that I had done this to such a happy soul. But yet, this is what we humans are like, I suppose. Always ready to save face, scared of losing. I looked away in shame.

As I did so, I was surprised to find that our environment had changed. My bedroom and its contents had been replaced by what looked to be the remains of a forest. It was a forest, only the tops of the trees had been mowed, leaving their trunks at exactly the same height. *What could possess the power to do such a thing,* I thought.

"Yes," said Jak, "our pitiful souls have shrunk. Our sorrowful thoughts have caused the positive life force to disperse, leaving us as just tiny masses of hopeless nothingness. We are no bigger than a spec of dirt. What you see before you is your bedroom carpet."

In sheer wonderment I glanced back at the sorrowful mess that I had created. Tears were still flowing freely, like an erupted ice cap his soul was melting.

"It is a dreadful thing, boy, but everyone must know and experience suffering. Throughout your many lives, as I, you have suffered greatly. Every single individual, man, beast or plant, by the time they reach old age, will have suffered many times. The world must know pain before it can understand love. There can only be peace on Earth when every soul has experienced war first hand, the loss of a loved one, agony, anguish, discomfort, distress, hardship, misery, pain, torture, sickness and prolonged illness. Every single soul must know of, understand and experience suffering."

"But…why?" I asked scornfully. "Surely our souls can develop without such deliberate afflictions. Must we really be put through such torment to become good souls?"

"Don't ask me," he returned, leaning forward wiping tears with the back of his hand. "For it is self-infliction. Every soul since the beginning of time has had a free run. Free to develop as it wished. And everyone has sought all kinds of suffering first. Many times old wise souls have been sent to help and save the Earth, guide the hopelessly lost, greedy, pessimistic souls of the physical world, and many times all in one way or another, the wise old souls have been subject to torture brutally and murdered. All of the religious books of the world are full of such barbarism.

The old 'learnt' wise souls that have been featured as the main characters in all books of wisdom. They became wise through their own suffering and tried to teach this to others, but alas, one of the worldly wise said, 'You cannot put an old head on new shoulders'.

And so, every soul must suffer and learn. It is sad, I know, but it is the only way."

I delayed a reaction to think for a moment.

"Do you mean like Gandhi," I said, "was he sent to create peace on Earth?"

"Yes, of course he was, but he was not the only wise old soul.

Everyone has their own favourite hero or saviour, as every religion worships its own God, Gods or Goddess. It matters not which path you are on as long as you feel good about it. There have been thousands of such wise old souls over thousands of years, working faithfully towards a better world, a peaceful world where every living soul works for the whole and not as a greedy individual. Where love and compassion is openly practiced and not behind closed doors, by that, I don't mean sex in public…" He laughed, "I mean showing love, offering affection and compassion to every living thing.

Sadly, my friend, this can only happen once every individual soul has lived through much suffering. The more you have suffered, the more sympathetic you will be to others."

He paused for a moment, seemingly scanning my spirit once again. He then smiled as if the answer to a puzzling question had come to him. "Why didn't you join the army when you finished school?" he suddenly asked.

Shocked and baffled at such a question, I was not sure how to answer.

"Why have you not joined the forces?" He went on, "It'll make a man of you, teach you discipline and skills."

"No…No, I could not possibly," I cried out, sensing more fear slithering through my tormented spirit.

"I know," he replied, "you have experienced that one too many times before. You cannot remember, for you are not supposed to, but trust me, my boy, you have killed and been killed may times, and the experience was so bad that you cannot bring yourself to do it ever again. You are now a peaceful loving person, searching for the truth, like millions of others in the world, souls that have already experienced the terrors of war. They, like you, need no more.

"Yet, even in peace time, millions of individuals every year actually volunteer for such an experience. Yes, they volunteer to be trained in the art of killing and risk their lives to do so. They may tell you it's for the excitement, the adrenalin rush, the 'buzz', but every new soul needs the experience, just like we did the first time around."

Mmm… I sighed trying to come to reason with all of this new knowledge. Then a conclusion came to mind.

"What about Hitler?" I said, breaking the silence. He glared at me with a curious pitiful smile.

"If the soul of Hitler had suffered war and torture first hand in a former life, he would never have led his people to war, and millions of people would never have suffered torture and death."

He nodded in agreement, then drawing closer I watched as another tear slowly dropped from his cheek.

"The world must know the dark side before it can understand the light," he said.

"Yes, you have suffered my lad. Just like many millions like you. You are indeed an old wise soul. You cannot remember but let your spirit guide you. Listen to the subtle inner feeling, that intuition, that little voice is your soul showing you the way."

Once again, he raised his hands towards me, and once again, our spirits grew larger. On reaching our normal size, I heard him say, "I will send you someone to help you towards your next step on the path to wisdom…good luck."

There was a rush as I found myself back in my physical body. My neck was aching where I must have been leaning awkwardly. However, this did not stop me from frantically writing until early morning, at which time the rain had stopped, and the birds were merrily singing. I tried to remember every detail.

Chapter Ten

I knew full well that my journey to the station would take me longer than usual, but I found difficulty in raising a heavy body from such a warm comfortable bed only to defy the cold relentless winds heard from my warm slumber.

I was now late.

Our unpredictable weather had become predicable. The cold northern winds blew across the icy surfaces that crackled a crispy crush beneath the soles of my stiff laden ex-army boots, where in, my numb feet, moved loosely about the old leather. I shivered in a long old inadequate ex-army trench coat. The streets were so oppressive that I hesitated, half inclined to go back. The walk to the train station would normally take me about ten minutes or so but laden down with portfolio and art equipment, I moved slowly repenting with every step. Then pounding the footpath, I ran with all my might. I could hear the train approaching the station and knew that I was about to miss it, nevertheless, I would give it my best shot. So, after extreme effort up an embankment, hurdling two flights of stairs, I ran along the platform like a madman. And yes, I was right. I missed it.

In sheer dismay at my own stupidity for not leaving the house earlier, I dropped my equipment, and in a cold sweat, I inhaled and puffed out cold fresh air. With every puff my breath turned to mist and every puff, like the workings of a steam engine and almost as if I were giving it the power, I watched the train move out of the station.

"Damn it!" I shouted, for at the Langley station there was no warm waiting room. I would have to wait in the freezing cold for the next one.

The wind howled through the lonely station cutting through my clothes as if I were stood naked. In a vain attempt to infiltrate some circulation, I shivered and stamped my feet on the hard surface of the platform, but what little effect it had. Cursing myself, I vowed never to make this same mistake again. "I must leave the house much earlier," I ordered myself.

The following train arrived about forty-five minutes later, making me wait much longer than I would have ever anticipated. I was frozen to the bone and could hardly move my stiff joints to load my art equipment aboard the carriage.

It was while I was loading that I heard someone shouting, "Stop…stop…wait…"

I had finished loading, the train was about to move when I surprised myself. I stepped back onto the platform again, and knowing well enough that the train could not leave with the door open, I waited, much to the dismay of the driver, for this young fellow to hurdle two flights of stairs, as I had done, then he ran like a madman towards me and to the only open door available.

"Thank you…thank you so very much," he said.

What had surprised me was not so much that I had obviously done this young man a favour, but before my dreadful experience of the freezing cold platform had taken place, I knew for sure that I would not have stopped the train, and the young man would have had to endure the same experience as I had just had. In fact, I might even have sat and laughed at his misfortune, not knowing what he was about to experience.

"And yet, had I truly saved him from the experience?" I said to myself, or would he be late tomorrow and have to wait for the next train, as I did, in the freezing cold. I may not have saved him from a wicked experience of the future but one thing was for sure. My bad experience had made me, if only a small amount, a better person.

Sitting in that train, this little episode had sent my thoughts back a few weeks to my last meeting with Jak and the idea that we all must suffer and that to experience suffering makes you a better person. I was only in my early twenties, and although Jak had intimated otherwise, I had not experienced a great deal of suffering, but what suffering I had endured in my short life had most certainly made the bad experiences memorable, and I had always learnt something from them, no matter how large or small.

To experience then was and is the best way of learning, and to experience things extremely bad, or good for that matter, makes these episodes memorable, and we learn from them.

My mind was cast back to a time when I was a child and to a time after being told so often to watch and beware of the roads. I had not listened or perhaps not understood the dangers until experiencing an accident with a motorcycle. I was playing football on the road when this motorbike came racing around a corner, and before I knew it, I was tossed into the air like a rag doll. Luckily, I only suffered minor injuries, but the shock I will never forget.

The strange thing is that this accident may have saved my life because ever since then, not only have I been cautious when crossing a road, I also have a fear of riding motorbikes. Thousands, possibly millions of people around the world every year are killed on such machines. I thanked the lord for giving me that bad experience, for I will never be found on a motorbike, and therefore, I will never come off one.

As a child, I could remember a time whilst playing, I ripped up one of my mum's magazines. Being a wise lady, she did not shout at me or slap my legs; she lovingly asked me to fetch my favourite book. After doing so, she held it in front of me saying, "You really love this book, don't you?"

"Yes," I innocently answered.

"Good!" she said and ripped up my wonderful book before my very eyes. The pain that I felt in my little heart was excruciating but the suffering was worth it because it taught me to value other people's property. And I have never forgotten it.

As a boy, you would never see me run a key up the side of someone's car, smash windows or wreck telephone boxes because as a boy, I had already suffered and understood the bad feelings that such acts can cause. No gain without pain, I suppose.

As I grew older, I was made aware of bullying. I was abused both verbally and physically by my friends at school. I complained to my parents, but there was nothing that they could do. Except one day, my dad told me to hit them back. Full of fear with the thought of retaliation, I told him it was impossible. He told me that when the time was right, and he assured me that I would know exactly when that I should hit the bully straight on the nose. "But make sure that you hit him hard. Hit him hard enough that he will not come back at you. Hit him too soft, he will."

One day, the pain of the bullying had become just too much. I had obviously suffered enough because a sudden change had taken place inside of me. I have no idea why it had happened at this particular moment but my heart jumped into action. The boy with all the mouth was standing right in front of me and all his so called mates surrounded us. My attention was immediately centred on his nose. Then turning my back to him, I gathered a tight fist. There was a sudden surge of power, and I hit this bully smack on the nose. The poor fellow went flying backwards, blood all over his face.

I was never to be bullied again by any of the boys, but after that occasion, a strange thing happened. All of the boys continued to bully others, except for the one that I had hit. He had completely stopped. In fact, he even seemed to be grateful for the lesson that I had taught him. Moreover, we became good friends.

Many years later, we were still very good friends, and he told me, "That was the day you had knocked some sense into me."

Some bullies go into adulthood still bullying and never learn the wisdom of being a victim, I thought. But I bet that they grow old, bitter and lonely, because no one likes them. Who can truly love a bully?

No doubt many leaders have bullied their way to the top. Managers, businessmen, not to mention politicians and world leaders, causing bad feeling, stress, poverty, famine and of course war.

The train pulled into Slough station. I watched as people got off and got on. Coughing and sneezing could be heard throughout the carriage. The doors were closed, and once again we were rolling along the track.

Opposite, now sat an old man, somewhat shrivelled in his old age. Blue from the cold, he shivered, complaining bitterly about the weather and what life he had had and that no one cared and how after his wife had died of stomach cancer, his family would not visit him.

I couldn't help but wonder whether I was sitting opposite an old bully that had not experienced the wisdom of being bullied. Then turning his head to look out of the window, I noticed a bad growth on the side of his neck, red and scabby; it looked really painful.

"There are many types of suffering," I said to myself. "We cannot be blamed for all of life's sufferings. Suffering at the hand of someone else is one thing, but we as humans or animals, for that matter, cannot be blamed for long-term sickness caused by viruses, for example."

I thought of my uncle Peter and how much he had suffered with cancer. What is there to be learnt by experiencing that kind of suffering? This was a subject that Jak had seemed to be avoiding, and this would have to be the subject of my next meeting with him.

The train pulled into Maidenhead station. It was my stop. I had now returned to college, and for the next few months, this would be my daily routine. I was dreading it.

After arriving very late for a lecture on modern design, I slipped in unnoticed at the back of a large group of students. The morning flashed by, and before I knew it, I was standing in a queue waiting to buy lunch.

It was when I was standing in this queue, however, that I overheard a girl talking about a reoccurring dream that she had been having, featuring a man called Jak. Craning my neck, I listened.

"Could this be the same Jak that I have been communicating with?" I asked myself. My heart jumped into action, the adrenalin shot around my body. I was shaking with excitement and could hardly contain myself. I was about to ask there and then, outwardly asking in front of all her friends...what does he look like? But I thought better of it.

Turning my head away, the queue started to move, and I had to move with it or cause trouble for myself, but I would not forget her face.

Later that afternoon, I described this girl to Billy and to my delight, he knew of this girl. "She is a friend of a friend," he said and promised to introduce me sometime.

"Her name is Julia, cracking looking girl, isn't she? I can understand your interest."

"No, Billy, you misunderstand."

"Yes...like hell I don't..." he quipped.

I had told Billy all about the ghost that he had seen beside me that day at the park and the experiences that had taken place thereafter, and like Gareth and Sharan he was fascinated, so I mentioned what I had overheard her say about a similar character she had dreamed about. He was most interested and set up a meeting with her in the canteen the following lunchtime.

It turns out that she had had quite a number of these dreams concerning a character called Jak. They seem to have started not long after the death of her father. She was tall, slim, attractive looking girl, long dark hair, well-dressed and very articulate. She didn't dress or act weird. Not the kind of person that you would normally associate with this sort of subject at all.

I asked how he appeared to her. She described him as, "Quite an old Chinese gentleman, shaven head with a very long, thin white moustache, quite portly, in an orange robe, like a Buddhist monk— although, I have known him to be different." She murmured.

"Different... How?" I asked.

"When the dreams first started, he appeared to me as an old friend that I once knew," she paused for a moment, trying with great difficulty to make herself understood. "Well, yes he was definitely an old friend, only...ah...I cannot remember meeting him before. Does that sound stupid?"

She looked embarrassed and was looking around the canteen to focus and hopefully change the subject no doubt.

"Does he laugh a lot?" I asked, attempting to bring her mind back on track. She looked straight back at me, our eyes met, and the expression on my face must have given me away.

"You have met him too, haven't you?" she asked.

I saw such pleasure in her face as if she had finally found someone to open her heart to and someone who could relate to her experiences. She even said as much at a later date.

Billy told me that you had similar experiences, but I was not sure because some people are a bit funny about such things.

"Yes, he does laugh a lot," she continued, "he can't help himself, as you would well know. He is full of himself, but he always makes me feel good at the time and for days after."

This had to be the same ghost, I thought. *It was obvious but how strange. Who had heard of two people dreaming of meeting the same person, let alone a strange ghost? How bizarre is that?* I pondered.

Nevertheless, it was good to be able to talk and relate to someone else about these bizarre experiences, or I was sure that in the end, I would have been thrown in a nuthouse.

"You say that he changes his appearance," I asked. "Please explain."

"As I was saying earlier, when the dreams first started, he appeared to me as an old friend, but I could not remember meeting him before, and as time when on he seemed to change, bit by bit until he became a Buddhist monk."

"Why a Buddhist monk?" I asked curiously, for I had consequently told her that my ghost changed form too, which was directly influenced by my beliefs.

"Curiously, it is the same as your Jak," she returned, "in that he picked up on my own belief system and changed accordingly. I am a strong follower of Buddhism and somehow he knew it."

I told her some of the things that he had taught me. She was fascinated then added that among other things, he had helped her to lose weight. I was astonished.

"Yes," she said, "I was not always this thin. I have lost five stone."

"In what way did he help you? I mean how is that possible," I quipped with a glance of suspicion.

165

"Yes, it sounds incredible, doesn't it? But it is true. It works like this. It is quite simple really. Most fat people are so large because of the large amounts of food they eat. This is evident, but the crux of the matter is why do they desire to eat so much? Everyone likes food, it is an essential part of life, without it you will die, but fat people are infatuated by it, why?

The fact that fast food is so readily available and so strongly advertised does not help. I know from experience but no one forces you to eat so much. In fact, a true friend would encourage you not too. So where does the problem lie? It is in the reason for that desire in the first place. Most fat people would agree that they comfort eat when they are unhappy. Healthy foods like vegetables, fruit and salad have no substance so they mainly go for foods with a high fatty content to fill them up. They also lack energy, so crave for anything sweet to fill the energy gap. The fatty food satisfies their hunger, and the sweet content gives them the energy they need.

In time, some come to realise their weight problem and turn to all manner of diets and health companies to help. After a struggle, many succeed and loose the desired weight and are proud and quite rightly so too. Even so, they have not got to the root of the real problem, and much to their disappointment, they put it all back on again.

Some big people are very happy with their size. Some even try to promote the idea that big is beautiful. I cannot condemn that at all, but the fact remains, there are many overweight unhappy people in the world. Diets help, but they don't solve the problem.

My buddha friend told me that the reason I ate so much was because I felt empty. "You feel depressed, lonely and empty inside, don't you?" he asked. "You will eat and eat as a desperate attempt to fill that void, that hole, that emptiness inside, which at times is so emotionally painful, it needs filling that you may feel better."

He told me that fatty foods are an ideal filler, only it makes you put on weight. This in turn makes you dislike yourself and causes more depression. People make things worse by calling you names, making you lonely, down-hearted and empty. You lack drive, self-esteem, vitality, you need more sweet, sugary foods for energy and plenty of stodgy food to fill the gap. Add boredom to the equation, and you have a binge on your hands. It goes on and on, an endless cycle. You feel good and a whole person when your stomach is full. He said, "…and so food becomes the most pleasurable thing in your life. You draw comfort from it. Yet, all in all your body is constantly being drained, and you are trying to fill it up with the wrong thing.

You feel good and a whole person when your stomach is full, but alas, you are not a whole being. You are spiritually dead."

He told me that I was lacking in spirit energy, That I have lost all belief in myself, and that I have a soul as well as a physical body. I was over feeding my physical body and starving my soul. "It is your soul that is empty, not your physical body," he said.

He stressed that I needed to feed my soul. That empty void that you sometimes feel in your stomach is your soul craving for positive life force. Positive life force does not only fill the emptiness inside, it gives you the will and energy that you need causing you not to desire so much food, making you lose weight, and you will feel whole and good about yourself again.

"Wow! It obviously works, from what I see in front of me," I returned, "but what of this positive life force he talks of? Do you know what it is and how it works? For I have experienced its power and the wonderful feeling it gives you myself, only Julia, where does it come from and how do you get it to fill your stomach?" I asked eagerly.

Perhaps now I would find out what this mysterious force is and how it works, I pondered. I leant forward waiting in anticipation for the answer I had for so long awaited. Jak had withheld it from me. Being so evasive, he had covered it in a veil of mystery, seemingly only to be known by the worthy. Perhaps now, at last, the mystery would be revealed.

"I'm sorry," she sighed, "I could tell you, but there is someone else who can explain it better than I. See Lucinda, she is the one in the know."

"Who is Lucinda," I enquired in disbelief, trying not to show my discontentment.

"She is a medium and knows about this spirit you call Jak and his powers. She's the one to ask."

"But you just said that Jak helped you. You, therefore, must know how it all works—surely?"

"Oh…yes but," she faltered. "Don't get me wrong, I know how to raise the energy. I was given certain mental exercises to follow, but how it all works, I am not so sure. Lucinda is the one to ask."

I couldn't help the feeling of being duped once again. Disappointed, my heart sank. There was no point in getting angry with Julia, she wasn't to blame, on the contrary, here was someone else who had met Jak, and it seemed from what she was saying that there was also a third party too.

"So who is this Lucinda again," I asked candidly.

She suspiciously looked around the canteen. Then with the utmost of caution she learnt towards me, and in a low voice, I heard her say, "I am sorry for not being much help, but I promised not to tell anyone about this secret energy source because not everyone is privy to its blessings and not everyone would accept and understand its potential. Anyway, Lucinda will help you. She has helped many like us searching for the truth. Like us…!"

I heard alarm bells ringing in my head. My jaw dropped, and unnervingly, I slumped back in my chair. I shook my head trying to come to terms with her assertion.

Could this really be true, I thought. It was now apparent that Jak didn't only visit me, and that he also visited others, like Julia and a possible third, but now she was claiming that there are many of us. The very idea was astounding.

"It is hard to believe at first, I know," she whispered. "He has a kind of following, a group of believers. They have formed a sort of secret society, and Lucinda is one of the leaders. She can help and train you. She is a mystic or psychic and a medium—I'm not sure what the difference is. She can contact the dead, read tarot cards and the crystal ball. She can help and train you in a way that you will understand.

I have got to go now. I am late for the studio. I will give you her phone number."

I watched her walk out of the college canteen. I was absolutely dumbstruck. What had I got myself into? I was also late, only in the context of things, college seemed unimportant. I slowly got up to make my way to the studio.

I felt as if to be in a trance like state. How, by just having a few dreams, could it all come to this?

I reflected back to my uncle's death. Back to when it had all started and back to the first time I had met Jak in a crowded room of people. I sifted through the course of events concerning the pipe, the mysterious smoke and the out-of-body experiences. I seemed to be searching for something. Something was missing from Julia's claims. Then it struck me. She referred to the experiences as dreams, whereas for me, they were defiantly out-of-body.

Yet, that was by the by. I was now getting myself deeper into something else. "Who are these groups and followers of Jak?" I asked myself, "and what do they want?"

This had put a completely different light on Jak altogether. Are they a strange cult of devil worshippers, waiting to lure me into their den? My last meeting with the ghost wasn't exactly comforting to say the least. Although, I had to give Jak his due, he did explain why he had put the fear of the devil into me.

***

At lunch time the following day, just before my return to the studio, Julia quietly asked me to meet her outside. She gave no particular reason just asked me to be alone.

Later outside the college library acting all suspicious, Julia gave me the telephone number to this medium called Lucinda. I was most apprehensive and could not shake off the idea that I was, somehow, being set up. Then my suspicions were confirmed.

"I told her all about you over the phone last night," she said. "She is such a lovely lady, and she would be delighted to meet you." Being so apprehensive, I was not inclined to comment.

"Oh, please say you'll go," she whimpered.

"First tell me who she is and what's this secret group. I don't want to get caught up with some obscure religious cult and have to attend rituals. That is not me at all."

"No," she replied chuckling, dismissing my comments at a whim. "It's just a group of ordinary people like us who have been contacted by this same ghost. As Lucinda is a medium, she has regular contact with him and can, therefore, help us with any problems that we have concerning him. As a medium, she normally charges a fee but to contact Jak or give advice concerning him, her services are free."

With the agreement that Julia came and formally introduced me, she had persuaded me to go and see this medium. In addition to this, I knew that it had been quite some time since my last meeting with Jak, and for all I knew, it may be the last unless I made some effort. Even more to the point, he did say that he would send someone to help me, so maybe this chance meeting and conversations with Julia were meant to be?

Chapter Eleven

An appointment had been set for me to meet Lucinda. On that day, my Dad dropped me off at 7pm outside a large house in Upton Court Park, coincidentally, just outside Windsor. To avoid a bombardment of questions I had told my Dad that I was visiting a friend.

Unfortunately though, Julia had let me down, the excuse was 'too much home work to do'.

I thanked my Dad for the lift and closed the car door. As I turned to face the house, I heard the car pulling away.

I was alone.

It was a dreadfully dingy night, the sort anyone would have expected for the time of the year and the sort of night anyone but myself would have stayed at home. I therefore, could not blame Julia for doing so.

The house was situated off a narrow unlit country lane, making it difficult to see at the best of times, only this particular night things were far worse. There were no street lamps and no moonlight. It was very dark, overcast and wet from a down pour we had endured that afternoon.

The entrance to the house was very grand with two large iron gates that were wide open, exposing a long driveway covered in coarse gravel. In the far distance, the house was a black shadow among leafless trees and a dark grey sky.

I took in a deep breath for courage, but my nose was insulted by a damp earthy odour of decaying leaves. With arrant repulsion, I started towards the house, kicking shingle with every step, which in the dead of night simulated a thousand soldiers marching until much closer to the building I stopped. Apart from a faint glow coming from a window on the top floor, no lights were on, the house was in complete darkness. It was a huge house, the remains of an old manor house, I had been told, converted into apartments, yet there were no parked cars, and there was no sign of any residents.

"Strange," I said to myself.

I stood in silence for a short while, debating whether or not I had been dropped off at the correct place.

It was a spooky sight, for sure. From what I could see in the dark shadows, I guessed the old house to be Georgian, built in the 18th century. Although, it had unusual turrets and some overhanging gargoyles with the most grotesque faces.

The wind picked up causing the tall bare trees to move. The branches creaked under the strain of their own weight. There was now a hostile presence in the air, a presence so profound as if my soul was shrinking inside my body, my spirit drew in. My blood ran cold, fear shot up my spine, and my heart at once thumped into action.

I hastened towards some stone steps that I was told led down to a basement apartment to the right of the building. Panting, running down the old steps, I suddenly plunged myself into pitch black darkness. I immediately stopped dead in my tracks, and for an agonising moment, I stood still trying to catch my breath. Nothing could I see, and nothing could I hear apart from my own pounding heart that seemed to be trying to get out of my chest. Looking back and up, I saw the dim light from clouds as they passed the arch entrance at the top of the stone stairway. It seemed that I had entered an old servants' passage way. The air was quiet, so…so quiet. I then became aware of pain coming from the area of my chest. I had not realised, but in the tense moment of it all, so as not to disturb the atmosphere, I guess, I was holding my breath. I tentatively let the air out in short nervous bursts. Doubts, once again came into my mind. "Am I in the right place, or am I trespassing?" There was only one way to find out. So with baited breath, I continued forward. Using the wall for guidance, I curst Julia with every hesitant step.

Further along the dark passageway, I saw, to my surprise, a soft flickering light and a door which was left open.

"Come in, Don," came a cheery voice from within.

Pushing the door further open, I apprehensively peered in.

It was immediately apparent that the light was coming from a blazing log fire that illuminated a small room with wavering, yellow shimmers reflecting on the walls. Timber snapped and creaked as blistering embers emitted a warm sensuous invitation.

Then quite unexpectedly a short, petite old lady with long grey hair emerged from a small kitchen. She was wearing a brightly coloured dress and black boots. Supporting her balance, she leant on an old well used walking stick. It was then that I realised, she had a clubfoot.

"Have I not met you before?" she asked politely.

"Yes," I returned excitedly, "at Windsor train station. You recovered my girlfriend's lost purse."

"Ah…that'll be right. Wheels within wheels," she said mysteriously. "I hope you didn't have to much trouble finding us on such a dark night. I'm sorry about the lack of light in the passage way."

"That's okay," I answered as if the spooky experience was nothing.

"Please take a seat by the fire. It is a dreadful night, I shall make you a nice hot cup of tea."

After closing the door behind me, I found myself a comfortable armchair, as Lucinda had suggested, right near the log fire. The warm atmosphere and the friendly natured old lady had calmed down my hysteria.

As my eyes became accustomed to the flickering light of the fire and the warm cosy atmosphere. I looked around the room. In comparison to the rest of the building, it was insignificant, like a bed sit you might say, because apart from the kitchen door, there was only one other, and I assumed that led to the toilet. Opposite me at the far end, presumably the rear of the premises was a long window clad in dark red velvet curtains. The room itself was full of antiques on a flagstone floor. This room was truly remarkable for there were no modern appliances at all. No television, music equipment or computer, not even a small radio. The old lady was obviously living in a complete time warp.

There was a sudden snap, and pieces of red ash shot out of the fire and making me jump, they landed directly in front. Then I saw them, two aluminous green eyes staring intensely at me. The hair on the back of my neck stood to an eerie attention. It was a black cat lying on a chair in a dark corner. The creaking sound must have startled it. "Would you like biscuits with your tea?" I heard the old lady ask from the kitchen. This promptly broke the cat's hypnotic gaze, and like a creature returning home, the aluminous eyes disappeared into the darkness.

"Yes, please…thank you," I replied, trying to control my jittery senses.

She entered the room carrying, all in one hand, a small tray of cups and saucers, a tea pot and biscuits. I offered to help, but she wouldn't hear it.

Placing it all on a coffee table close to my side she uttered, "Please help yourself to the green tea and lemon, it's probably not your usual brand but it is nonetheless very good for you." She then continued around the room lighting candles and incense. "I do so love the atmosphere that candles make, don't you?" She said blowing out a match. "Far more natural than electric lamps," she declared before I could answer.

She was right about the tea, it was not my usual brand, but the lemon did smell quite refreshing. I poured out the tea and handed her a cup as she sat on a sofa opposite me. Holding the cup between her palms, she looked at me searchingly.

There was a long silence until a presence was felt amidst the air that surrounded us. Our eyes met for a brief moment before I turned to look into the flames of the fire. From the corner of my eye, I watched her sample some tea and then she sat back into the soft confines of the sofa. And that is when I noticed it. On a long chain around her neck, the size of a large coin was a medallion. On this medallion was a familiar symbol, just like the one I had seen on the old man's ring at my uncle's funeral, and the symbol I had seen on Jak's pipe. Like so)O(. A circle flanked by two arcs. I dearly wanted to know the connection and the meaning behind it, but somehow, the thought of asking didn't feel appropriate. And yet, the atmosphere was now too intense. I had to say something.

"This is a magnificent old house, how old is it?" I finally asked.

Yet, to my apprehension, she did not answer. This baited a question. Perhaps her hearing is not so good, and she, therefore, didn't hear me? I was about to repeat my question when she finally replied,

"Yes, it is very old. It is nearly three hundred years old and was a beautiful house at one time, owned by a lord...don't you know...until the great fire that is. It was then turned into apartments. The entire house was gutted apart from this very room."

"Where are all the residents to the apartments?" I asked.

"Oh, they have all long since moved out to make way for a hotel." "Who is the person living on the top floor?" I enquired.

"There is no one on the top floor," she said with a look of puzzlement.

"Ah...but there is," I exclaimed, confidently placing my cup on the side table. "I saw a dim light."

"You could not have done," she insisted, "the power in the entire building has been cut off...ah...unless," she paused, "unless our resident ghosts are back."

A familiar chill ran up my back and a 'crazed' vibration took my inner being. Only this time, it was not a feeling of dread, more a feeling of pleasure. My skin tingled up and down my body. It was wonderful.

"Yes," said she, "the 'Great One' is right, you are ready. I see it in your eyes."

"Who are these ghosts," I returned, ignoring her last comment.

"That's of no concern to us right now, they rarely come out anyway. Let's get down to what concerns you. Julia tells me that you have had the pleasure of meeting Jak. Please, tell me about it."

She did not have to ask twice. I spent the following hour or more telling her all that I knew, and throughout the entire story, she sat in silence. When I had finished, I took a breath and sighed, waiting for her reaction.

"Yes, you have indeed experienced the 'Great One'," she said wholeheartedly. "Except no one really meets him, he is an experience, something that happens to you. I too have had the honour of his experience, for it is an honour, a great honour, believe me.

Many times, since I was a young girl and long before, I have had experiences of him."

"Do you mean in a past life?" I asked in earnest.

"Yes, only he is not known to me as Jak. Jak is a modern name that he has given himself. I know him as the "Great One," but for many people, like you, he is known as Jak. He has many names and can take many forms."

"Please…" I enquired, "in all honesty, if he has many names and takes many forms, how do you know that we are talking about the same person or being?"

"A good question, a very good question, only the answer is very simple. It does not matter what he is called or what he looks like. He remains the same and nothing can change that. If, for example, you had your face changed by plastic surgery, disguised your voice and wore different clothes, it would not matter what you called yourself, you would still be the same being inside. The same spirit or soul that is what makes you what you are and nothing can change that. That is what makes you an individual. That is your character the inner you, the one you refer to as I.

I call him the "Great One", simply because he is great, and there is only one of him. Call him what you like. He is what he is."

I thought for a moment, for she did have a point. How does anyone define who they are and what makes anyone different from the next person. It can only be the inner you, the spirit within.

"I agree," she said, picking up on my thoughts. "It is a known fact that identical twins can look the same, speak the same and even dress the same. And more, they have the same genes and will have been brought up the same. Yet, only those close to them will tell them apart, for unlike their physical bodies, they have completely different spirits inside."

I sighed in conformation as another question came into my mind. I looked straight at her and asked, "These other people you talk of, the ones that have also experienced Jak, who are they, and what is their opinion?"

"Oh…just very ordinary people. People from various walks of life like postmen, bank managers, builders, office personnel, teachers, shopkeepers, housewives, etc. It doesn't matter who or what they are in the flesh, it is the development of the soul that is important, not how much he or she has in their bank account or how much they spend on their designer clothes. That is all an illusion. I am a medium," she went on. "That means that I am able to communicate with the dead and the worlds beyond our physical existence. I sometimes use the tarot cards and crystal ball as aids to work with. People come to me for help and guidance. With my aids and help from the other side, we, hopefully, direct their lost souls, and the 'Great One', through me, has been a blessing many times."

"And yet…!" she shouted unexpectedly, leaning forward. "There comes a time when someone like yourself visits me, not for help or guidance but to ask as to who the 'Great One' is?"

She slumped back into the sofa laughing.

"Well done…well done, there are not many of you but your numbers are increasing all the time. Some see him as just a friend, for others he appears as someone noble, and yet more often than not, he can take the presence of a deity. Julia sees him as a Buddhist monk, for others, he is just a bright light. I know many who say that he takes the form of an angel."

"What would you say that he is?" I asked. She paused and looked into the fire.

My heart sank. Had I said something wrong?

"Okay," she muttered with a continued hypnotic gaze on hot orange cinders. "You were right to ask. It's just not an easy thing to put into words. He once told me that he is a Diva. By that I don't mean a famous female singer. A Diva to him is a Divine Being, one who is well beyond the human state, an entity that has attained to the necessary level of enlightenment and purity and can no longer return to a physical form. He is a body of energy, an entity of pure

175

positive power pertaining unconditional love for all developing beings, souls, spirits and the like."

She looked back at me with a contented smile. "Are there others like him?" I asked.

"Oh yes," she returned. "Only most have attained such high status, they are beyond our comprehension. I have tried to contact them, but their bright 'etheric light' was too intense for my psychic eye."

I looked around the room deep in wonderment. My eyes jumped from candle to candle as I searched for something to say. Crossing the centre of the room, at our eye level, there was a vapour of incense floating like a wave. It moved soft and graceful as if to know where it was going. I couldn't help but wonder whether Jak was present, but I had not the nerve to mention it.

"What does he want with us?" I finally asked.

"I should have thought that was obvious," she came back. "He wants us to be like him. He is training us. You have an apprenticeship with a ghost."

As if it were not connected to my body, I felt my entire being tingle. I was not quite sure whether it tingled in dread or excitement. "Oh...don't look so worried," she said with a warm, friendly smile.

"You can pull out at any time, besides, it's not that easy to accomplish. You will have to work for it."

She rose from her seat, placed another log on the fire and walked to the kitchen saying, "time for another cuppa, I think."

I sat there totally bewildered. "What exactly were we being trained up for?" I had to ask myself. "Not in my wildest dreams did I ever think that I was being coached on some course. Although, Jak had mentioned a kind of training school, that I did recall, but I had not realised that things had already commenced."

I waited anxiously for the old lady to return.

"What do you mean that I have an apprenticeship with a ghost?" I asked instantly.

She roared with laughter. "Don't worry, it was just a term of phrase...then again, what else would you call it? He is giving you the benefit of his knowledge, and that is what a teacher does, right? Also, in our profession, to people in the know that is, it is called "The Craft". Therefore, if Jak is a craftsman, you must be his apprentice." She continued laughing and mocking just like Jak sometimes did. I waited for her to calm down and return to her place of comfort. The flames were now gathering around the new log, and the room lit up with vibrant incandescence, filling the atmosphere with a warm gratifying embrace.

I watched her sip tea. Then placing the cup to one side, she asked,

"Of course, you do want to see him again, don't you?"

"Oh yes…do I," I spurted out with uncontrollable zeal. "Only, I find it too difficult. He is so elusive and hard to contact. He normally contacts me…you see. I am afraid that he may stop before all my questions have been answered."

"Yes, we all have great many unanswered questions, and the 'Great One' has helped many spirits, but it has always been difficult for the variant worlds to connect. Souls that have passed over are persistently trying to contact the living but, because so many people deny the very existence of the other worlds beyond the physical, spirits find it too difficult to contact us.

The "Great One", on the other hand, is different. He has found a way. He has found a unique method, all of his own making and can break through the barriers that separate us from them."

"Can you remember the dates he had contact with you?"

I gave her a rough idea. It was the best I could do without consulting my notes.

"Mmm…just as I suspected," she said, peering into her diary. "On or close to a full moon, that is when the energies are at their strongest."

She was still looking through her diary when I asked, "You say That the spirits are continually trying to contact us. How are the living supposed to know this if we cannot see or hear them? How do we know for sure that there is a spirit world or worlds beyond our senses? For all I know, Jak could just be a figment of my imagination."

She laughed, "I know you don't mean what you say, but to answer your question, nothing can exist without it. Everything would be separated including you and I. We would not be able to communicate. We would be distinct entities detached in worlds of our own. We are not. There is something between us. Something connects us.

Every word that I use is a sound that travels at great speed, from my mouth outwards, spreading throughout the room, penetrating the walls and ceiling. With special equipment, it is possible for someone to pick up my voice outside the building. This is proof that this stuff between us can go through walls. In fact, science will tell you that a great many things travel through this stuff.

I am not talking about air, for air is made of gases and is only part of this stuff. It has many properties, and many energies flow through it. It is a medium of space by which a great deal of vibrations or waves travel through, penetrating all physical matter. Science can detect some things within it, like radio waves, sonar, gamma rays, geomagnetism, and so on.

We also know that light is made up of photons, a quantum of electromagnetic radiation energy, which has both particles and wave behaviour. All this and more, science has discovered about this stuff between us. We can see light, smell gases and hear sounds, but radio waves, radiation and gamma rays, for example, are beyond our senses. We cannot see or hear them, but science tell us that they do exist.

In fact, there are great many wave energies or things travelling through this stuff, far beyond anyone's imagination, and ghosts are no exception. The spirit world is just another small component of the whole thing. Our senses cannot detect or prove that gamma rays and radio waves exist, but they do. Science cannot prove that ghosts exist or that there are worlds beyond detection, but I, as a medium, assure you that they do definitely exist.

I hear and see spirits all the time, and I tell you many are desperate to contact the living. Countless times I have had disturbed clients claiming they had seen a recently passed friend or relative. I tell them they have nothing to fear and that they are only afraid because they believe that ghosts don't exist. Quite often, the spirit of their loved one is only trying to say that they are alright, and death is nothing to be afraid of.

Not everyone is able to sense a ghost's subtle existence, and so the spirit of desperate recently departed try other means. They may stop clocks and watches, jump cups out of cupboards, objects personally related to the deceased move on their own or disappear and then reappear. They do not mean to cause fear to the living. They merely want to say that they are okay."

"Yes!" I said, eagerly jumping in. "Someone very dear to me lost her baby boy at birth. On the day of the funeral, six relatives including myself, went back to her house. Within fifteen minutes of our arrival, six doves landed on her garden fence. One relative commented saying how unusual it was to see doves in the middle of winter. Another pointed out that there were six doves and six of us. Then a third said, 'It's a sign. It is a message from your little one.' The strange thing is the birds remained until everyone left, some two hours later. What caused the doves to land, no one could tell, but all have since reported that it was a spooky experience."

With an all knowing smile, she said, "Yes these things are spooky to sceptical people. For instance, if you have been indoctrinated from a child, and everyone around you has doubts about the existence of a beautiful bird called a stork, and that storks were only a myth, possessing magical powers then to see one would send waves of fear or joy through your body. It's all an illusion.

You and everyone are taught to fear, and most people fear the unknown. Things that science cannot prove, cannot possibly exist, so say the scientists. But ask them this: Did gamma rays and geomagnetic energy exist before they proved their existence, or have they only existed since they discovered them? The answer is, of course, that gamma rays and geomagnetic energies have always existed…and I tell you this, so has the spirit world." She pursed for a moment's reflection.

"Besides, it is obvious. Let's look at it another way. The "Great One" himself once said, 'That it is common sense, by reason of there is an opposite of everything: male and female, black and white, light and dark, hot and cold. In all energies like electric there is a positive and a negative. There is an opposite of everything. Nothing can exist without its opposite equivalent. And so, we have this physical world, full of matter and a spiritual world full of its opposite, non-matter'."

She paused and looked at me with a smile. "I am sorry to be bending your ear, but I am so passionate about the other side. I see, smell and feel it all the time. It is a part of me. It is a part of us, all you need is an open mind. If you believe in it, it will reveal itself to you, but you must be prepared to meet it halfway."

We briefly stopped. Both of us were in deep contemplation.

I reasoned from Lucinda's interpretation—for she had indeed laid a full conviction—that I had succumbed to the same conclusions from my own experiences anyway. That the spirit world or worlds, the other side, the beyond, or whatever one wishes to call it, does doubtlessly exist. After summarising the situation, I asked curiously, "How can I meet Jak halfway?"

"I was rather hopping you would say that," she said, "since that is what you are here for."

I felt my spirit tingle with joy as if I had been lightly touched and praised for a good deed. The back of my neck tingled the most, like a brief contact had taken place with invisible fingers from beyond.

179

"You feel them, don't you?" she remarked. "You are surrounded by three spirits right at this moment. Don't be afraid, they are welcoming you."

Normally, like anyone else, this exposure to unseen life would have freaked me out, yet somehow it really did feel like a welcome and blessing. I then felt a very cold sensation down one side and someone blowing in my ear. Then the feeling ceased.

"There…you have been approved. This is most unusual at this early stage. You may consider yourself initiated into our hallowed order, congratulations and welcome."

"I don't understand," I uttered bemused.

"It takes some people months, even years, to be accepted like you have…" she went on, "some never attain it at all, and yet you have been invited instantly. This can only mean one thing. You are already a member to our ancient institution. You must have joined in a past life. That would explain your natural, psychic ability. You have been trained in these arts before, you just cannot recall the occurrence."

"No, but I do remember Jak telling me as much. He too said that I must have been taught how to use my abilities in a past life."

"Mmm…he did say you were ready," she muttered under her breathe. "Okay, so you want to meet Jak halfway?"

"Well yes, as long as I don't have to die first," I answered wittily.

She laughed and held a curious grin. "Of course, it will be a while before your next meeting with him. The energies at this time of the year are not very strong. Spring will be a good time to try, so we will make plans for then."

"Is there no possible way that we can do it sooner," I asked disappointedly.

"Sorry…but no," she replied hastily. "I sense that your spirit energy is low, so first of all your spirit will need charging. Do you feel depressed and low spirited sometimes?"

"Yes, I do…a feeling of emptiness, and quite often, there doesn't seem to be any explanation for it at all," I expressed with an agitated memory of such a period.

"Oh, there is a reason," she said. "There is always a reason for the way one feels. And what do you do when your feel that way? Don't tell me, you go down the pub like most other men and drown your sorrows."

I nodded.

"Some people drink to fulfil their spirit, and others, like Julia, eat too much. Both are extremely bad for the body when taken excessively. I will now teach you another way."

She moved around in her chair, making herself comfortable before continuing.

"Your body is made from physical matter. For it to function as well as it does, it needs physical energy, such as food and drink. This everyone knows. But for your body to function well, you must eat and drink natural foods. Not from cans or frozen but, fresh unhampered foods from nature herself. Try to stay away from processed foods as much as possible. And eating raw, fruit and vegetables are much better for you.

Nevertheless, we all have a soul or a spirit body too, and it also needs feeding. This is not so well known and is a big problem in the world today. Violent crime caused by binge drinking is on the increase and will continue. Obesity too is on the increase, people are eating far too much junk food. All in all, it is because they are unhappy. They feel empty inside, unfulfilled and resentful. The extreme cases, of course, turn to drugs.

What they don't realise is that it is their soul that needs feeding not their physical body. It is their soul or spirit that has been starved and has shrunk to the pit of their stomach. That is why they feel a kind of knot or emptiness in that area of the body. Excessive amounts of alcohol and food can help temporarily. It sort of fills the emptiness for a while.

Your soul has a body too, and it needs feeding. Once fed, your spiritual body will expand to the size of your physical body, making you feel whole again. When this is realised, your empty, depressed feelings will go, and you will feel elevated. But let me warn you." She leant forward to emphasise the point.

"These things are not to be taken lightly. What I am going to teach you are secrets known and passed down to mystics, sorcerers, magicians, witches, shamans and healers throughout the ages. They are quite simple in context, and anyone can learn them, but alas, they are so powerful, seers and sages—like you once were, no doubt— spent lifetimes to master them. It is said that in ancient china alone, knowledge of these secrets required payment of a king's treasury or even his life.

The energy or food that you will be giving your soul is none other than life itself. Its correct name is 'Vi Dei' or 'God's Force' but we refer to it as 'life force' because that is what the 'Great One' calls it. He also calls it 'pure positive energy', but I am sure that he will explain that part himself.

This energy, I'm talking about, is well known to adepts or followers throughout the world. It has many names in many languages, such as vital energy. In China, it is called Chi, Indian Yogis call it prana or kundalini. To Tibetan Lamas it is Tummo, and in Japanese Ki. The ancient Greeks referred to this energy as pneuma.

When your 'life force' is strong, your body will be vibrant and active yet when weak, the opposite occurs. In order to be strong, healthy and happy, your 'life force' must be abundant and flowing smoothly. This is your first step.

Just so you may get a feeling for this energy, I will set you a little exercise which you must practice. You may do this sitting as you are or lying down, the choice is yours. It does not matter so long as you are completely relaxed."

I was quite comfortable where I was, so I remained seated, totally intrigued for what was about to come next.

"Hold up your hands as if praying."

I did so.

"There is a reason why you must hold your hands this way when praying. Now you will learn the secret of holding your hands thus kept from public knowledge by the clergy for over two thousand years. Close your eyes and separate your palms slightly as if holding a small football. Now clear your mind of everything and concentrate on the area between them. In a while, you will feel a kind of magnetic force. I then want you to move your hands and play with it. While you are doing that I will make us another cup of tea."

With my palms slightly apart, I did as she asked and concentrated on the empty space between them. At first, I felt nothing…nothing at all.

So, I tried to relax. Then I had another go. I focused all my attention and centred what could only be my entire spirit into this vacant space.

Then, at that point, I moved my hands a trifle closer, and that is when I felt it, a slight magnetic resistance. I opened them up again and very slowly, I brought them closer once more. I felt another tiny resistance.

"Did you feel anything?" Lucinda asked, returning from the kitchen.

"Yes, I think so," I replied, "a sort of small magnetic pull and push."

"My word, just as I surmised, your energy level is indeed very low. I want you to practice this exercise for two or three minutes at least once a day. You must be somewhere very quiet and relaxed as possible. In time, with plenty of concentration you will notice that the magnetic feeling will get stronger, a kind of spongy feeling. You may also feel that parts of your body will seem heavier. I have even known people to experience squeaks or whistling sounds coming from their body. This is perfectly normal and nothing to worry about.

I would like to see you again in a couple of weeks to see how you are progressing. And don't forget to eat plenty of fresh fruit and veg. You must look after your physical component too, you know."

We fixed a time and date. I drank my tea, thanked her for all the help and advice, and then bade her goodnight.

"By the way," she said as I was leaving, "it's not worth even trying to contact Jak at the moment. Like I said, his energy levels at this time of the year will be too low. For the same reason, he will not be able to contact you either." With that, flickering from the soft light of the fire, almost begging me to ask, was her medallion. I only had to point at it.

"A symbol of our order," she said. "You deserve one too, don't you know? Well…you are more of a member than most have credit for. This symbol is many thousands of years old. It symbolises the moon fazes, a source of mystical power. See you in a couple of weeks…goodbye!"

It was way past 11 o' clock, and I needed plenty of sleep for college the next day, but in the light of all this information, I knew that sleep would be out of the question.

Chapter Twelve

I spent the next two weeks practicing the exercise Lucinda had set me. I even got Sharan and my family to try it—although, I dared not tell them of my informant. They all reported feeling something. Some felt it stronger than others, yet not one could describe the sensation, let alone explain any reason for it. It was not until I mentioned electric and magnetic force that they agreed, it was something along those lines.

I practiced the exercise twice a day, once in the morning and once in the evening. Each time I tried it, the force grew stronger. It is quite difficult to describe the sensation, but the magnetic force seemed to mature at each session. I began feeling a kind of soft spongy like texture. This progressed into a feeling of playing with treacle or putty. Then one day, it was so strong I could scarcely push my palms together. It felt like I had created something really powerful and seemed as solid as a building block. It was remarkable.

Meanwhile, unbeknown to me, Sharan had been practicing this exercise too, but stopped when she heard squeaking noises coming from her elbows. I had not heard any unusual sounds and still continued the exercise, except parts of my body did feel somewhat heavier. I also felt strange sensations at times when breathing.

What surprised us both were the wonderful sensations when making love and an incredible feeling of well-being generally. We both felt it. It was a tremendous emotional uplift. This was quite amazing considering the time of year. Usually during the winter months, like everyone else I guess, under clouded skies and through long dark nights, I would normally be feeling pretty glum.

Alas, one morning at college, I was full of the joys of spring in the middle of winter. I was clearly out of sync with the rest of the students. One even asked, "What are you so happy about?" On which I replied, "I don't know. I just get high on life."

Something had definitely happened to me, "but…hey, who cares. Don't knock it," I said to myself. I did feel good. This to a lot of people would be a feat in itself. It was to me if the truth was told, but I did not, nonetheless, feel any closer to my goal. I could not wait for the next meeting with Lucinda since she had promised to help me with my principal aim. That was, of course, to meet Jak halfway. It had been quite a number of weeks now since my last chat with the laughing ghost, and I was eager to return.

The days had past quite swiftly, and before I knew it, much to my glee, I was back in Lucinda's armchair. The weather outside was marginally better but still very cold. However, the discerning old medium had not disappointed me. She had a hot blazing fire going, candles and incense were lit, and making my entrance easier, she had replaced a candle in the passageway. The warm secluded atmosphere was a far cry from the cold elemental exterior.

"How have you done with your excise?" she asked placing a hot cup of tea at my side.

"Very well I think," I prudently answered.

Placing her stick at my side, she held up her arms and in one soft movement, the palms of her hands were positioned close towards me.

Then, as if sensing something invisible, using soft graceful movements, to and fro, our spirits seemed to embrace and our souls connected.

"Excellent," she said softly, retrieving her stick. She moved slowly to her usual comfy place on the sofa, and then putting her stick to the side of the fireplace, in her own good time she sipped tea.

"Do you feel any different?" She asked, peering over the top of her cup.

"Oh yes, I feel marvellous," I responded, trying to control my elation.

"You should be. You are very charged. Have you noticed anything unusual?"

"Oh yes!" I returned, "Like you said, parts of my body feel slightly heavier. My hands, the lower part of my torso plus, I do feel, how can I put it a lot more together."

"Good! That was the part of your spirit body that needed feeding. Your soul was hungry," she said.

"Good! This is not only pleasing to the spirit, it is also a tonic for your physical body. There are many schools that work with a deep penetration to the spirit. Tai Chi and Yoga are two such schools, and should you wish to pursue this path then either one would benefit you tremendously. In fact, you should try one, the experience will do you good. In general, these schools are excellent for raising the spirit, boosting your moral and guarding you from depression…"

"May I stop you there?" I asked politely.

My interruption was unexpected, but she, nonetheless, stopped and smiled.

"When you were explaining the exercise to me the other day, you said that it was the secret behind prayer. Did you mean that prayer does not work and that it is only a means or an exercise to summon life force?"

She laughed and shook her head. "I can understand why you have asked such a thing, but you have misunderstood. The act of placing your hands together in prayer is to help you focus. It is also an exercise to help, as you say, summon life force. To pray in the real sense of the word, you need not use your hands at all. You merely focus your mind.

"Now then, getting back to our subject matter, you do want to receive Jak…?"

"Oh yes, of course, without question," I pleaded.

"The reason for you to learn this shrouded exercise is firstly to bring your spirit to a good healthy condition. It can—among other things like the schools that I mentioned earlier—boost your fitness level and can be a great addition to any training exercises. Increasing strength, giving you energy, greater awareness, and it really boosts your immune system. You need to be very healthy because…"

She stopped and looked straight into the fire. "I don't want to alarm you, but there are risks involved."

"What kind of risks?" I asked in dismay. I had not considered any risks and was now very apprehensive.

"Do you not think that leaving your body is risky?" she said raising her eyebrows expectantly.

"Why? Of course," I replied, sighing with relief. "I have done it before, so I will do it again."

"Very well," was her response. She rose up from the sofa. "I will make us another cup of tea, and while I am away, you will have a good opportunity to practice summoning some life force."

This old girl can't half drink some tea, I thought.

"This exercise, by the way, goes by a very old name and was much sort after at one time. I will explain later." She turned and entered the kitchen.

With that, I feverishly threw up my palms. Fearless and completely aroused for the task in mind, I became profoundly focused. I was deeply centred on the area between my palms when

186

she returned. I was so deep in concentration that I had not acknowledged her placing the teas and returning to her seat.

"What does it feel like?" I heard her say.

This broke my concentration, and the energy force ceased.

"When I first tried it, the force seemed quite faint. Since then, I have sensed it getting stronger, spongy like, then a sticky putty feeling, and of late, it has become almost solid, like hard rubber or even a builder's block."

"Very good," she remarked. "Do you recall that at our last meeting, I told you that some of the things I will be disclosing to you are secret, and that some are very old...very...very old indeed, passed down through the ages?"

I nodded excitedly.

"The thing you call hard rubber or builder's block, which is possibly more appropriate word, has a very old name called 'Noster Lapis'."

She looked back into the fire again, staring as if gathering some thought. I waited in suspense with no preconceptions of what she was about to say. All was quiet apart from the sound of hot shifting ash in the fire. I watched as the shimmering light from the flames made her shadow dance up and down the back of the sofa. I saw incandescent lights play with the contours of her face.

She looked back at me with an enlightened glance and a smile. There were stars in her eyes as if she had just submitted to or candidly summoned an answer to a perplexing question.

"It is the 'Great One' himself. He wishes you to take the next step on the path to wisdom," she whispered joyously.

A rush of excitement seized my body and launched my heart into action. I did not know what the next step was or what it entailed, but she sure had evoked my spirit, it seethed with wonderment.

"The invisible block which you held in your hands has a very old mystical name called Noster Lapis meaning "our stone". Its inexplicable powers have been the subject of many popular myths and legends. Although very few found out its true meaning, many Knights have been commissioned among others to find and discover its secret powers, for it was thought to be something physical, like a powder or even a cup. It was and is also said to be mystical and to possess magical powers capable of healing the sick, curing wounds and diseases. This part was and is correct, because faith healers still use it today. It also goes by another name Lapis Philosophorum. But what may interest you is that it has yet a third name. A more modern name, you might say. I am sure that you will have heard of this name." "Yes!" she said, laughing. She came nearer. Her eyes were full of glee.

"What you felt between your palms is known by very few as 'The Philosophers' Stone'. The Philosophers' Stone is reputed to be a special substance created by the alchemists of old to be capable of changing base metals, like lead, into gold. This has been taken literally. It has been a clever smoke screen. The real meaning to this secret has been passed down to selected groups or fraternities, generation after generation for thousands of years."

With an all knowing smile, she slumped back into her seat.

"If you don't take it literally by manipulating 'The Philosophers' Stone' you can turn the heavy metal in your stomach to pure desirous gold. The alchemists called it the 'elixir of life'. The energy or life force that you have been summoning can and does cure many ailments and restores health. This is the same power faith healers have used throughout centuries and thus, still do today. More to the point though, the alchemists found that it could actually prolong life, for it is the very essence of life itself."

She paused, no doubt to see if I was still following her. I sure was but could not decide whether she was pulling my leg or not. Her face looked very sincere so there was no cause for laughter. I just stared at her waiting for a reaction, that I might make a decision and respond.

"That is right," she said, picking up on my thoughts. "You have understood correctly. For centuries, historians, theosophists, theologians, people into divine doctrines and the like, have been searching a physical wonder. And like I said just now, some even think it takes the form of a white powder, but they never answered their quest. They never found it so they called it a myth…" She was now laughing. "And yet it has been in their hands the whole time." Her laughter got the better of her. She was now convulsed to the pit of her stomach.

I was considerably taken back by her account but, nevertheless, curious. Had she really meant what she was saying? Could this method truly heal and prolong live. Western medicine, I knew would disagree, but the Chinese are known to use similar strange methods like acupuncture to help the flow of Chi around the body. Correct Chi flow is said to be able to cure all sorts of illnesses. So could this method of hers truly heal and prolong life?

"How old would you say that I am?" she asked suddenly.

She looked to be early seventy, although, if this was so, she did seem to be in fine form for such an age. Despite having long grey hair, her face was full of life. She may have even been younger, plus she was articulate and appeared to be of sound mind. In any case, I had been taught from childhood never to ask or guess a lady's age.

"I am not sure," I replied coyly.

"I will be two hundred and twelve next birthday," she said.

I was about to laugh but the look on her face stopped me. *Either she is lying,* I thought, *or what she had told me about this Philosophers' Stone had to be true. Either way, I could never be sure. How could she prove such an extraordinary claim?*

However, under the circumstances, I decided to give her the benefit of doubt, what else could I do? Then again, in retrospect, I think that the decision was more of hope than judgment.

"This is nothing new," she went on laughing. "While it is true that some failed in their attempts and some even died trying, alas there were a few successors. Among others, many of the wise old alchemists that had mastered the technique, managed to control the force and could send it to every part of their body. Just as you have done by raising the force in the palms of your hands, so they would fill their entire body and more. They would be continually charged, and when needed, completely at will, they could send the force to any part of someone else's body thus healing them of their ills. Some of these adepts were alleged to have lived twice my age."

I was speechless. Here was I trying to come to terms with the idea that she was two hundred and eleven, making her tremendously older than she looked, and now she professed that not only was it possible, but people have lived to twice that age, that had to be a myth. I was not convinced. The old girl had to be deluded.

"How am I to meet Jak halfway?" I studiously implored, changing the subject.

I had stopped her laughter dead. She peered at me sharply, like a rattling snake at its prey, her eyes, so green, had a hidden power that seemed to reach in through my body, infiltrating my spirit, searched and as if touching the back of my neck, my spine tingled with fear.

"Do not mock what you know nothing about," she snarled. She was clearly irritated. She quickly looked away to brood over the hot embers.

I sat motionless, glaring at her in dismay.

The fire's light flicked in her eyes bringing fresh life to her changing thoughts. "I am sorry, but I feel so passionate about my craft," she expressed in a low soft amiable voice. "Of course, this is not what you are here for."

She looked back at me with a warm smile. "Would you please accept my apology?

"There is no need for you to believe in these things, but in order for you to meet Jak halfway, there are certain things you will need to practice."

I sighed with relief, for she was a dear old lady, and I really did not want to upset her. On the other hand, she may not have looked physically strong, but I could sense that beneath that frail exterior lurked something very powerful.

"Now then…for you to meet the 'Great One' halfway, you will need to learn the ancient art of separating your soul from your body. This will be your next step on the path to wisdom and is generally known these days as astral projection."

I was all ears. I did not mean to be unappreciative to Lucinda since I was sure that she must have been wise beyond her years— however old that might have been—but I was so keen to get on with my chief calling which was to me so sublime. I leant forward expectantly. "Astral projection is an art not so easily accomplished. Some adepts spend years trying to experience this phenomenon, and yet others never could and never will manage to do it. However, you have an advantage over them. You have done it before, so you shall do it again, only this time you will be in full control. With practice you will be able to project your soul out of your physical body into the world beyond. That world is called the 'astral plain', and it is in the 'astral plain' that you will find Jak."

I smiled and nodded eager for her to press on.

"There are many ways to accomplish astral projection, and like all old arts, there are many disciplines. There are also many books on the subject which you might like to apply yourself too, should my method fail you.

Anyway, that aside, to project using my method you need to build up a concentration of life force. There are three ways of creating this force. The first is by focusing your mind, the second by drawing it in with your breath and the third, is to create it naturally. The first method you have already tried when you created the stone. The second I will explain in a moment, and the third is produced naturally when the body is in action.

Most people that exercise in a gym on a regular basis will report feeling good after training, they should because they will have created some life force. But alas, they may have created some force but would have spent a great deal of it doing the actual physical movements. So, the best two methods are to focus your mind and the other is to draw it in with your breath.

The method I will be explaining to you is the same method that I was taught by my mother at the tender age of nine. We will need to swap places for this. It is important that you are completely relaxed and comfortable." She got me to lay on her sofa with my head comfortably resting on a pillow.

I felt warm and at ease, waiting for her instructions.

"Please do not be disappointed if nothing happens tonight. Practice is the key. Like any other art or skill, in order to succeed, you will need to practice.

Even so, total physical relaxation, a calm mind and an out and out desire to travel are the main factors. These factors alone have sometimes been enough to project may a spirit form the body. Although, natural projection can and does occur, this is when someone is under emotional stress. The death of a loved one among other things has been known to cast out the spirit, resulting in an out-of-body experience. This could be what happened to you in the first place.

I want you now to close your eyes and relax, of all the factors here, the most important one is your mind. Your mind directly influences all the others. If you are relaxed, your mind will be calm, and you will be able to think clearly and concentrate fully. You will also need to relax your breathing, which means that you breathe in and out slowly and smoothly with your mind and body in unison. Once you have learnt to relax, you will be able to monitor the energy and eventually learn to control it.

Your concentration is the most essential thing. You must learn to control your thoughts and regulate your mind. You do this by concentrating all your thoughts on just one point. Meditation is good for this should you have problems with concentration, but I am sure that you will be okay.

For now, I want you to focus on your breathing, in and out very slowly. As you inhale, allow your stomach to physically push out and, as you exhale let your stomach muscles relax so that your belly returns to its normal position."

I did so.

"Yes, that's it…" she said encouragingly.

"You are now breathing like a baby, bring all the natural energies down to the pit of your stomach. This pumping action of stomach muscles activates and creates life force too. Like I just said, life force can also be created naturally when you exercise physically.

Keep breathing slowly and smoothly, imagine all that life-giving beautiful energy being drawn in through your lungs and down to your stomach. Now that you have learnt to create some life force between your hands, you will know the feeling of its presence. I now want you to create the same feeling in your stomach. By inhaling a long stream of air each time, I want you to imagine life force being extracted from that air and cause it to remain in your stomach each time that you exhale. By doing this, you will be building energy in that area. It is important that you focus your entire mind. You see, it was not your hands that created the force between your palms, it was your mind. Your mind is the catalyst. Your mind creates the force as well as any physical action of the body. The more you concentrate on your stomach, the more energy you will be creating there."

She paused for a moment, no doubt, waiting for all this information to settle and mature in my mind. And then she added,

"The feeling you had of the block between your palms is symbolic to a foundation stone for the building of a great edifice that edifice being a spirit body, and that spirit body will house your soul."

I am sure that what she was saying was quite simple in context, but it all came across as being really spooky, making me feel uneasy. I sighed.

Sensing my frustration, she drew closer and said softly, "Try to relax. For best results the energy must be positive. To create positive energy, you must think positive. So I want you to picture someone or something that you dearly love."

This was easy. Sharan sprang into my mind intently, and I had always been very close to my family so I pictured them all as a loving group.

"Now hold that loving feeling—it is energy in itself—and direct that too, the entire thought mass at your stomach. It is difficult at first, but you now have to try and combine all these qualities together. Hold that concentration and breathe in the natural goodness of the air, filling any empty void in your stomach with a mass of kinetic energy, bringing with it unmistakable love. You may see it as a bright light illuminating your soul.

This will all take practice, but in time, you will master this feeling, and you will know how to create and hold this energy in this area of your body. It is where food for your physical body is stored, and it will be where food is stored for your soul.

Now remember to breathe in and out slowly and smoothly. If you are concentrating all of your attention on that spot, you will feel the soft force getting stronger, like the feeling you had with the stone. And remember, this must be a positive energy so infuse it with love.

I will leave you now to make some tea. Keep concentrating on your stomach."

This was a lot of information to take in, but somehow sensing that I had done something similar at a time long forgotten, like a duck to water and trying to focus, I closed my eyes. I heard her gentle movements as she limped into the kitchen.

I really wanted this to work, so like she had suggested, I tried to clear my mind. I was uncomfortable though, so rearranging myself on the sofa, I tried again. This time it was much better. Then picturing my loving group, I captured the feeling of positive energy and directed it to my stomach. I breathed in and out slowly trying to concentrate all my attention and extracting more and more energy from the air when I blow out. After each outgoing breath, I felt its soft presence growing. I imagined it to be full of warm, desirous, unmistakable love. I have no idea how long she had left me in this state. It was a pleasurable feeling so I didn't care one bit. I lay there totally engrossed and all attention to the area of my stomach.

Once again, I had not heard her return from the kitchen. It was only apparent when I heard her soft voice saying: "Now turn that energy into a bright white light."

I did so. I could see it very clearly in my mind's eye.

"I now want you to imagine this energy growing larger, getting bigger in size. I want you to expand it, making it larger, filling your whole body with a bright white positive light. This light must be so bright that it illuminates the entire room."

I concentrated more and just as she had mentioned. I saw the room as I imagined it to be in on a bright summer's day, full of life and vigour.

"When you have done so, I want you to imagine it expanding even further. I want you to become as big as the room."

This was easy because I felt to be already there. But as she said it, I instantly grew bigger and bigger, and with all that energy, I expanded beyond the confines of my own body filling the room, I could sense and see the entire room at 380 degrees.

"When you are as big as the room, you will expand further beyond this room. I want you now to become as big as this large house, filling its dark rooms with the pure positive light you have so rightly made. When you have done so, imagine growing and expanding as big as the local area. Now expand and grow across the country until you are as big as England itself and beyond as large as Europe and as big as the entire world."

She paused for a while allowing me to create and expand this mass, the quintessence of my new rapidly growing spiritual body.

And then her soft voice returned. "You are now the world, and the world is you. I now want you to go beyond Earth to the outer reaches of our solar system and more to the cosmos. You are now at one with the universe...you are the universe."

I felt wonderful, as if, like she had said, "At one with the universe." I lingered there waiting for her guidance.

"You will now reduce in size, bring all the positive energy that you have just received with you, down to the size of Earth again. And then to the size of Europe, to the size of England, to the size of the country and the local area, feel that wonderful energy you have captivated and reduce, compressing it to the size of this house and to the size of the room, to your body on the sofa and the beautiful glowing feeling in your stomach."

She paused allowing me to concentrate.

"You now have an abundance of positive life force teaming in your abdomen. Well done, it is so bright I can see it with my psychic eye."

I felt really good, so wondrously alive. I could actually feel the power resident right there in the centre of my body.

"Don't move," she whispered. "Stay focused on that small bright ball of light. Because now I will teach you how to make an astral body, a kind of spiritual shell to house the essence of your soul."

With anticipation I awaited further instruction.

"From that ball of energy, I want you to project a small stream of light like an umbilical cord to about ten feet above you. This will be a continuous flow of energy creating a large egg shape at the top, the size of your physical body."

I projected my thoughts and a stream of energy relinquished itself, forming, as she had suggested, an egg shape of energy attached to a thick vaporous cord which connected both of us in unison.

"Now turn that egg into the same shape as your body so that it is your double."

I had no problem with this and delighted in sensing a kind of twin brother, hovering above me.

"Just allow yourself to become accustomed to this image. Imagine all of its features as your own, your hair, your face and all the contours of your body. Now clothe it, just as you like to be dressed."

She paused. There was a silence whilst I gave detail to my double.

It seemed quite content hovering there. It almost had a life of its own. "The image of this double should be so strong that you feel part of it. It is as much a part of you as you are a part of it."

Once again she paused.

I did exactly as she had suggested but now suddenly something had changed. I felt lighter, and then I felt a floating sensation. In my mind's eye, I could see the twin that I had created, but there, to my absolute delight, now some ten feet beneath me was my physical body lying on the sofa. I saw a vaporous cord connecting us both at the area of our stomachs. I then sensed Lucinda gazing up at me. Her image must have been so unexpected, that in shock or excitement, I know not which, I lost my concentration and snapped back into my body. There was a sudden jerk as I opened my eyes. I looked straight at her.

She was sat there in her arm chair, calm as you like, with a wide-eyed smile.

"I did it," I said, "I actually did it."

"I know ducky, and I am so very pleased for you."

I sat up, leant over to drink my tea. It was stone cold.

"That went cold ages ago, my dear. I would make you another, only it is rather late."

She was right, it was midnight by the time I left.

"Keep your stone topped up," she advised as I was leaving. "Even if you stop astral travelling, creating the life force is good for your mind, body and spirit. Good luck. Come and see me again sometime."

Chapter Thirteen

At last, I now had the means and the know how to contact Jak, and I resolved to use them to my full advantage. With this in mind, I was to practice all the exercises Lucinda had kindly imparted to me. I was feeling excited, for it was the first time since all this strange stuff had begun that I truly felt in control. No longer would I have to wait for the ghost to contact me. At long last, I now had found a way to contact him. It would take practice, a great deal of practice, plus drive, willpower and perseverance, but sooner or later, I knew that with dogged stubbiness, I was bound to succeed. I prayed to God to keep me safe and steadfast.

I felt sure to succeed, but I still had one obstacle to overcome. To me, there was only one thing holding me back, and it would prove to be extremely irritating. It was a question of timing. Lucinda had already warned me that, "Owing to low energies, it would be difficult or impossible for a contact in mid-winter." Yet the drive and cheer tenacity that I held inside was not going to prevent me from trying. I couldn't wait until spring. Even if I failed, I had to at least give it a go.

With this determination, each night I would practice projecting myself out of my body, and each night, for many weeks, I failed miserably. Although I fought so hard to stay awake, I could not concentrate and fell asleep every time. To make things worse, I suffered dreadful nightmares. This, I assumed, was due only to the lack of sleep, but later I had realised that this was not the case. To increase the probably of a favourable outcome, I was trying to control these nightmares, only this caused more exertion, misery and fear. I had many encounters with all sorts of demonic entities. The demonic attacks, I reasoned, were due to fear alone, for my own negative fear seemed to be attracting these negative entities.

Lucinda had told me to keep my thoughts positive, full of love and compassion for other spirits. "Alike attracts alike," she had said. Jak was full of positive energy, so to attract him, I would have to think positive. No sooner had I done this, my nightmares changed to dreams of wonderment and pleasure. This helped me to sleep, and I was no longer exhausted, but I still could not project out of my body. Like Lucinda had advised me, I need not have bothered at all. I had persisted, determined against all the odds but had failed miserably. To my disenchantment, it appeared that Lucinda was absolutely right.

Weeks had turned into months, and spring was in the air. One early morning, my mother had got up, and I could hear her in the garden cutting grass for the first time since autumn. My mother's grass was so green from the many days of April showers there was nothing like the smell of freshly cut grass. All plants faced east anticipating the rising of the morning sun. Even cut grass follows the sun across the sky.

I watched as gentle air currents moved leaves on shrubs in a simultaneous flow around the garden's edge. They waved in unison at the landing of a small bird. Quickly, it searched for a worm, then sensing danger, it flew, and the leaves waved its departure.

I could distinctly hear a bee working on bluebells in the garden next door, and I swear that I could smell the sweetness of the nectar that it was so joyfully collecting. The bee's black and yellow stripped coat was covered in a thin layer of white pollen. It didn't seem to mind though, it was a kind of barter, for it understood full well that plants used him to help with pollination.

Buds had appeared on plants and trees whilst some flowers had already opened. Birds were singing the opening of spring, and down below my bedroom window, fully bloomed with their trumpet-shaped heads held high, a yellow mass of daffodils. Like all plants, they too faced east towards to the rising of the sun.

Were it not for the sun, I would not have seen all the colours nature can bring forth. What beauty, what pleasure it was to see nature recovering after a cold, cloudy wet winter.

Another bird landed on the lawn. I honed in on it. It was anxiously looking for food, I could distinctly sense the twitching movements of its body. Then I moved in further and sensed its fast beating heart. *Its heart beats as fast as its short life,* I thought. There was a tremendous surge of energy, and the bird took off, leaving me on the grass. "I shouldn't be able to do this," I suddenly said to myself.

What trickery is this? I mused and then, somehow sensing that there was a great deal more of me, like the lens of a camera I zoomed back my focus. And there I beheld the most surprising sight ever. For a split second, I found my spirit halfway through the exterior wall of my bedroom. I was horizontal and must have been some 12 ft. long. I seemed to sense the lower half of my spirit inside my physical body which was lying in bed. This was anchoring the top half which was protruding through the wall. I was now facing down looking at the daffodils below. The shock instantly snapped me back into my body.

"Yes…yes," I squealed with excitement. "I've done it. I've actually done it."

This was the beginning. It had taken a while, but things were starting to happen. This was good because my determination was defiantly waning. I would now continue to practice projection. I did not manage to do it at every attempt, but about once or twice a week, I found myself floating around my bedroom.

Concentrating on building energy throughout my entire body, each day I would charge my spirit, every morning. Then using the same method Lucinda had taught me, I projected into by double. From there, I spent most of my time just learning how to move and generally familiarising myself with this extraordinary talent that I had acquired.

It was quite difficult to move at first. Unlike moving my physical body, which takes us humans many months to accomplish as a child, to move in the astral plain requires pure thought alone. If I wanted to move to a different part of the room, I would imagine myself being there. A mere thought was enough, and my spiritual body, that which I had made, would move to that spot. Learning to control the speed of my thoughts was the key. A passing memory, a flashing thought or reflection could so easily send me into a dream or another dimension completely.

The main thing that I had to learn was how to stay out. The slightest thought or sight of my physical body sent me back with a snap and jerk. No longer did I have a fear of not returning, staying out proved far more difficult. Yet, when I was successful, the rewards would be worth all the efforts.

I was quick to realise that to stop myself from snapping back into my body, I needed not to see myself. Therefore, so as not to see my physical body, I learnt to project myself to another room of my parent's house. This would normally be the lounge. It was there that the fruits of my capabilities were developed. I could expand and contract at will, stretch and distort into all kind of shapes. I would shrink if I felt bad and expand if I felt good. I was a glowing mass of energy made from billions of colourful sparkling particles that moved in mass when and where my thoughts provoked them to be.

On one such an occasion, suspended in the lounge, I saw something faintly glowing in the corner of the darkened room. It was not as bright as me but, nonetheless, glowing. I inspired a long arm to explore. I found it to be a vase of flowers. I could sense their petals, their stems and thorns. They were a bunch of roses and their collected life force was diminishing. I concentrated on them until they glowed so bright that they matched the brightness of my spiritual hand which now cupped them so dearly, a loving embrace.

Casting my thoughts to the centre of the room, above the fireplace, I approved of myself in a large mirror. Something that resembled me was a translucent body of white, a glowing mist that took the shape of my being. It looked like me…only, it was much, much more. I smiled, and the image blushed with excitement.

My thoughts moved jubilantly through a wall into the next room and out through the glass of a window at the back of the house. I was met by the glimmering rays of a full moon. It bathed our garden in a white sentient light. Its subtle influence had a magical air which made the spirit of each plant gleam impulsively. Not only could I see this light. I could actually feel it.

I looked up. It was a clear night. The stars twinkled in a beautiful, dark blue, twilight sky. I heard and felt the vibrations of a choir of angels singing the opening of the heavens. My soul purred with the remembrance of such a scene, so long…long ago forgotten. Next to the moon, brighter and larger than any other, a star held my spirit captive. Its light so beautifully bright, it had a supernatural presence that seemed to cleanse and embrace me with pure subtle passion. My soul quivered in pleasure as I delivered a return of gratification. I asked if this was Jak's star. It shimmered a positive light. Complying, I returned a complimentary thought full of love, compassion and a request to see him.

Instantly, seemingly from nowhere, I was collected by two dark shadows. Guided at lightning speed, we moved up towards this mystical star.

Although I could not see the two entities that had collected me, I could certainly feel their power. It was not a physical contact for we had no physical bodies but contact, hold and guide me they did.

Curious at what or who was in control, I tried communicating with them, but their response was simply, that they were 'collectors or delivery beings, nothing else'.

On and on we travelled, at times, it seemed at great speed. I had no way of telling how fast or how far. My concept of time had been blown away with the very air that we shot through.

On and on we travelled, along the smoothest, most direct route that I had ever experienced. No resistance and no friction, as smooth as silk, like sliding of an angel's wing, we moved swiftly on.

On and on we travelled. For a few minutes, a few days, a few years.

I had no way of telling. "Through time and space, we travel in hast," I heard my guides singing.

On and on we travelled to where I had no idea. "I wish to visit Jak. I wish to visit Jak," I expressed to my guides but received no reply.

On and on we travelled, so warm, so swift, then, without warning, all traveling ceased. There was no sudden halt or jolt, as smooth as the journey itself, all concluded in a pure, bright, white light. My guide's relinquished control and I hovered, like once before, in a quiet motionless void of bright white mist.

I waited patiently.

Then an intense white light, far brighter than the surrounding hue, appeared directly in front of me. So bright was it, it burnt my psychic eye. I tried shielding myself but without eyelids or physical hands all attempts would be quite useless. Not accepting failure, I willed my spirit to match its intensity.

Then as if he were at some distance away, I heard the wonderful sound of Jak's laughter, a low affable sound that gently echoed through the ether.

"You have done well, my boy. I congratulate you on your honourable quest."

My spirit reeled in anticipation.

He must have sensed my discomfort for the bright light dispersed, and there seated in a gloriously colourful meadow on a carpet of green grass and scattered wild flowers, being the summit of his world, Jak sat commanding all life, he was surrounded by birds, rabbits, mice, sheep, deer, all kinds of insects, including beautifully, coloured butterflies and the reddest of ladybirds. Like moths attracted to light, not excluding me, he charmed one and all.

He had long, white, silky hair that ran down his back and a long, white, silky beard that flowed in large coils to his lap. Matching his hair and beard, he donned a long, white, silky robe that covered his entire body. Like a Roman god on his throne, he smiled. Then holding up an arm in one soft swift movement, he compelled a white dove to perch on his hand. I moved closer and watched as he raised his white 'tufty' eyebrows. His blue eyes lit up, and he laughed at me.

I felt belittled, but I would show him that I had control of myself. So, like the birds, I circled around him, fast and slow, then returning I settled some distance in front of him. I held up an arm and imagined a dove landing on my hand. No sooner had I done so, a beautiful white one perched thereon.

Feeling proud of my accomplishment, I looked at Jak with a smug smile to equal his.

He roared with laughter, then slowly lifting both of his arms, his white silky robe turned into thousands of white butterflies that scattered, leaving him seated naked on a giant-sized mushroom. I was astounded and lost control. My dove, was shocked and like the butterflies, all animal life, fled.

I was stunned and baffled at why he would have done such a thing.

Again, he laughed and then said, "You have equalled me with the control of the dove, so I thought that I would return the complement and appear like you. Did you forget to give yourself some clothes?"

I looked down and was horrified to find myself completely naked.

Somewhat embarrassed, I look back at him.

Jak was now in stitches. He could always make a mock of me. Mortified, I could feel my soul shrinking.

"Hey, no come back," I heard him say. "Don't worry, boy, nakedness is just a frame of mind in this realm. Here…"

He raised his hands, and we could both be seen wearing white silky robes.

Feeling better, I opened up.

"Come sit down, pull up a mushroom," he said, still laughing.

Looking around, I sat next to him on a huge mushroom that had suddenly appeared.

"Where are we, Jak?" I asked curiously, for we could not have been on Earth.

"Mmm…here come the questions. Is it not obvious? Take a look around you," he replied.

I scanned my surroundings for a clue. As bright and as clear as a summer's day, the vivid green meadow, full of colourful flowers, stretched as far as I could see and perceive from all angles of my being. Surrounding this wonderful meadow was a medley of tall trees, mountain peaks and forests. It was very similar to a landscape that might be found on Earth, so why would it be anything else but somewhere on Earth.

I looked back at him. "I have no idea," I said, "somewhere in the countryside suppose."

"Look again," he said with a mischievous smile.

I looked to find that all the colours of the entire landscape had changed. The green meadow was now a yellow one. Shocked, although I should not have been, I returned a look of surprise.

"You are in my world now," he said tittering joyously. "It is a world beyond the physical plain. When we met just now in your bedroom, I was visiting you in your world, and I must say how very depressing it was. Now you have come to visit me in my world, and I hope that you will have a much better experience than the one you gave me."

"Hang on just a minute," I uttered in disbelief. "The last time we met in my bedroom wasn't just now, it was months ago, and I have been trying to contact you ever since."

He sighed. "You have forgotten. I told you before that time is a concept beholden to the physical world alone. It is governed by that mystifying sphere you know as the sun, and the speed of its light is what all earthbound spirits such as yourself, perceive as time. This you have separated into days, weeks, months and years.

In this, the world that I dwelt, there is no Sun, just expressions of pure thought. Everything here is a manifestation of thought alone, nothing else. Everything you see before you is a product of yours and my thoughts combined. For us to communicate, it is imperative that we remain on the same level of thought. I cannot abide the feelings that the lack of life force brings. This is why if you wish to continue visiting me here in my world please keep yourself fully charged with positive thoughts. Filling yourself with negative energy will turn this wonderful atmosphere sour, and doing this will result an attack of all kinds of horrific beasts out to play. So, keep your mind clean."

"I will try," I said, "but it is not always so easy."

Looking away, I saw a white mouse and could sense all of the other animals returning. The air was full of song as birds circled near and far.

"Thought energies are contagious," he continued. "Not just here. Even in the physical world, your world. If you lack life force, you will build negative energy and think negatively. You will feel sad, depressed and bad things will attract and be attracted to you. Negative things happen to negative people...you see. You will succumb to enjoy smoking, drinking, drugs and violent sports. Love will repel you. Bad people will be attracted to you. You will love the feeling that violent negative action gives you. You will enjoy things like action, horror and drama. Lack of life force shrinks the soul to the depths where nightmares reside, resulting in sleepless nights and a constant feeling of tiredness.

A lack of life force causes you to enjoy foods that are bad for the physical body causing illness and attracts viruses and all kinds of parasites to feed on the negative chemistry that your soul and body have provided. Some feel so down and depressed that they binge drink and eat too much of the wrong foods and grow fat in the process. They hate themselves and eat more."

As he spoke, I seemed to be allowed a moment of free thought, and my mind was cast back to the memories of my uncle Peter. For most of his life, he was a character full of these negative qualities. He smoked, drank heavily, and at times, he could be very short-tempered. He loved to watch boxing and always enjoyed violent western movies. My father told me that as a young man, my uncle was full of violence and always fighting. His favourite food was pie and chips, and as far as I knew, that was all he lived on.

Towards the end of his live, he mellowed, had a much softer character, and he became a very thoughtful person. He fell in love for the first time in his live and quit smoking. He also quit watching boxing and violent films, preferring to walk his dog instead.

I then sensed Jak's thoughts intervening.

"Yes," he said. "Your uncle had found a way of building life force, but it was too late for him. The bad negative parasites that were originally attracted to his negative chemistry had rooted so deep that they were able to feed on his positive chemistry for a while, but then his life was threatened and as a result, the fear of death would have struck him, draining his life force, turning his outlook negative and the bad parasites that loved the bad chemistry that he originally made, seized a final frenzied attack."

My spirit wept for his soul. "Why…oh why, must there be such dreadful viruses and parasites?" I cried out. "They are evil…sheer evil…"

"I understand your thoughts," he suddenly said, "but it very much depends on what side of the fence you are on."

"What do you mean?" I asked in bewilderment.

"Well, it is quite complicated, but all living things deserve to live."

"But a virus, like all parasites, feeds off your body," I exclaimed.

"This can make you ill and in some cases like cancer, kill you."

"I know," he returned frowning hard, "but they still deserve to live. Many lifetimes ago, you and every living creature alive was once a parasite feeding off a physical body, in effect, as a human being you still are. Do you not feed on the fat of animals? Does not man breed animals purely for that purpose alone and then gorge like a virus and a parasite on their flesh? And to top it all, you humans, together with these animals, rape Earth by eating mountains of plant life every day.

Man is, without a doubt, a virus to the whole planet, burrowing holes in its surface, polluting its atmosphere with industry, vehicles and war. You are a virus and a parasite, yet you still deserve to live and so does cancer. Like I just said, it all depends on what side of the fence you are on."

Shocked and horrified, I had nothing to say.

"I know this is hard for you to understand, but you are just another living organism, living on the planet. It matters not what side of fence you wish to be on, positive or negative, black or white, good or bad. The only thing that counts is the development of your soul. It is your choice whether you wish to be positive or negative or somewhere in between."

I was now very sad, sad for my uncle and sad for the realisation that as a human being, I was no more than just a parasite struggling to survive.

"And from the depths you like to take me, I guess you are a negative soul," I heard him say.

"Preferring the dark side to light, is there any wonder you had trouble trying to contact me. As I explained earlier, I prefer the positive side, the side of light."

I casually looked at Jak and terror, dismay, panic, all of these feelings and more had stuck me in one single moment of thought.

Jak had said that this, his world was one of pure thought. I had no idea the effects my mood would have had over what I saw. Our beautiful white silk robes were now old black torn rags. Jak's hair and beard was a very dark blue. The mushrooms beneath us were sweaty, giving of a dreadful odour that would normally make me very nauseous.

I looked around to view a dark, misty atmosphere. I sensed things creeping in the shadows, calling me to remember all the cryptic films that I had ever seen.

"You do like the dark side, don't you?" he said. "Always thinking negative, always thinking worst, and if you continue this way, you know what will happen to you when you die…don't you?"

Concerned about the future of my wretched soul, I looked up at him and found an ashen face, so very, very old, reflecting the age of wisdom and the dead fruits that many a lifetime of suffering beheld.

Not being able to accept such pain seen in a face, I quickly looked away, but regretting my action, I returned a look of respect.

His eyes captivated me, so dark, like black holes in the gulf of space, once travelled, never to return.

"Is this what you want?" he said. "Is this the path you wish to take? It doesn't end when you die, you know. You take it all to the grave and beyond. Death is a continuation of thought. Death is a continuation of all the thoughts you have had throughout your life. A continuation of all the thoughts you have ever had throughout many lifetimes, accumulated. You become a collected mass of intelligent energy. That mass will be the sum total of you. And you, as a collected mass will be predominantly negative or positive, dark or light. You may be cold, selfish and greedy or warm, open and generous. By the weight of your soul, you will be judged. You know what your soul weighs, boy. You normally feel it in the area of your stomach, and at present, you are very heavy."

I could feel a large heavy mass in the area of what would normally be my stomach.

"Yes, you feel it, don't you?"

"What is it?" I asked.

"It is the philosophers' stone that you created."

"Then I have been tricked," I said. "Lucinda has tricked me. She said that it would be good for me."

"And so it will be," he returned. "It's just that you have turned the energy of the stone negative, making its weight as heavy as lead, holding you down to these murky depths."

All around me, I could sense the shadows moving as the creepy crawlies moved closer.

I started to panic. This was not for me, and I had to find a way out, but panicking, I knew would only make things worse. I had to keep a cool head.

There was a tingly sensation around my legs. I looked down, and all around me, bugs were crawling up my spiritual body.

"Jak…please, I don't want this."

"Don't panic, my boy. You see it's like this…

As you know there is an opposite of everything, positive and negative, light and dark, black and white. I am sure Lucinda has told you this."

I quickly agreed.

There is this spirit world and there is a physical world, in both worlds everything is opposite. The sun gives light to the earth, but here light and the sun are darkness. In this world, darkness is light. That is why we have no need of the sun to see, we can see very well without it.

At present you are fearful, worried, and what you feel in your stomach area is very heavy. It is a very heavy mass indeed. In your physical body, you would feel the opposite to this, a light, empty void of nothingness.

Now in your heart area, where your physical heart would be, how does that area seem to you?"

"I feel nothing. I just want to get out of here," I yelled in distress.

"Yes…" came his answer, in a calm amiable manner. "And in the physical, you would be feeling heavy-hearted."

He then held out his hand and gestured me to take hold of it. He was a decaying skeleton and bits of flesh dropped off as he did so. I cringed as I reached out to clasp his slimy, bony fingers and was horrified to find that my own hand was no different.

"This is all an illusion," he whispered, "just a state of mind. You must fill your soul with positive energy. Think positive, and the monsters will go away. The dark creatures are attracted to your heavy negative stone. It is a source of energy to them. Imagine it getting lighter. Do what Lucinda had taught you with the exercises you have practiced. Fill your soul with love and the remembrance of pleasurable things…things of beauty."

I saw a glow of light surrounding us.

"That is it. I can see the darkness of your stone getting lighter. Concentrate on the possibilities of flying. Concentrate on how you like to see me best. Now hold that thought and follow me."

Our spirits connected, and we infused as one. Filled full of positive thoughts, devotion and life force, glowing as bright as the sun, and just as a long dark, skinny creature lunged at us, we took off.

"Hold on," he shouted. "Keep your thoughts on me, or I might lose you."

I tried to hold his image in my mind, but for a brief moment at a point, somewhere in the expanse of space and time, I was sucked back to my physical body lying in bed.

I woke up feeling angry with myself. I was angry for not being able to control my thoughts, angry for losing contact with Jak's spirit and angry for coming back to my physical body so soon. He had lost me on the way to what could only have been a heavenly place.

Then as quickly as I had returned, my mind drifted again. On an air of wonderment and thoughts of where and what it might have been.

How quickly experiences are so easily forgotten, I thought. *No.*

I forced myself out of bed. It was six in the morning, but I had to put everything down in writing before the memory of the experience became, like a flame, suddenly extinguished.

***

Towards the end of the week, one morning after breakfast, I overheard my mum saying to my dad, "These roses have perked up, normally, they would be dead by now."

I knew why the roses had perked up. I had given them a good charge of life force before being collected by the dark beings. I smiled and went off to college.

Chapter Fourteen

I could now contact the ghost at will. I was so very pleased with myself, for who would have thought that such a contact was possible, let alone have control and means to a secret knowledge. And who would have thought that such knowledge would be out there anyway. What else was there to be learnt? Could it really be mine for the asking?

I revelled in the notion of a successful return. The anger that I had felt for losing the contact that night was a mere glitch. I could always make contact again, but things would have to change. I was desperate to find out more. So next time, I wanted to be with him for a much longer period and have a pleasant experience instead of a bad one. Therefore, before I attempted a further meeting with Jak, I had to 'get my house in order', meaning that big changes would have to be made. My mind, body and spirit would have to be 'reset' and 'purified'.

According to Jak, our makeup is either positive or negative in nature. There is good and bad in us all. We know only too well of the bad people of this world, the media is full of their stories. Good caring people who I know exist must be very far and few between. Or is it just that the majority of us cannot see them, choosing only to see the bad instead. Does this say something about our own individual spirit?

I might have been naïve but I felt and hoped that most of us were peaceful loving creatures at heart, predominately good, caring, honest, moral, just and upright people of society, wherever we may live and work in the world. Yet prone are we to the dark side of life.

It is obviously different for everyone, whether we are in groups or as individuals. We all have our vices, whatever we consider them to be smoking, drinking, gluttony, greed. Still, these details are only peripherals for this side of our lives maybe considered dark or negative but I don't think that this was the kind of negative Jak was referring too.

The above mentioned vices, mainly concern our physical bodies. Yet for Jak, the physical body is not nearly as important as our spirit. His wish is for us to develop our inner being. The thing we call I or our soul, where bad negative feelings like hate, anger, greed, jealousy and resentment dwell.

For Jak, everything is about emotion. Good positive emotion or bad negative emotion. The stirring feeling that you get when you feel good and passionate about something, or the bad fearful feeling that you get when you are scared, stressed or agitated. One is positive, and the other negative.

Jak had told me more than once that he was a positive spirit, and so, to meet and hold that contact demanded more than just thinking positive. A like attracts a like. I had to, like him, become a positive spirit. I would have to be completely positive, a whole positive being, filling myself with that stirring, thrilling feeling that you get when you are passionate about something, the feeling that you get when you are in love. I had to be positive, totally positive in every sense of the word.

Like all great spiritual leaders able to accept unconditional love for everything. But how was this possible in such a dark, negative world?

With this in mind, somehow, I would have to gain control of my thoughts. This would be difficult of course, but I had to try. So, I continued building good, positive life force throughout my body as often as possible and I tried to think and act piously. I would turn away bad, negative thoughts and encourage good, positive ones. Hour after hour each day if a negative thought, no matter how small, came into my mind, I would just pass it off. Then another one would creep in, sometimes quite undetected causing a heavy feeling in my heart. When I felt this, I knew instantly that my thoughts had turned negative. And once again, I would pass it off saying, "I don't do negative." Day after day, I continued doing this. At times, it was fun, a kind of playful mind game I had with myself.

No sooner had I started doing this, something strange started to happen. I began to notice the quality in certain individuals. No longer were good, caring people invisible to me. People with good, positive outlooks were everywhere. I used to think that only bad news sell newspapers, yet I even found columns of stories about good, caring people, people wanting to make the world a better place.

I suppose you only see in life that in which you draw your mind to notice. That becomes your reality. And you only draw your mind to notice things that concern or attract you. This, I assumed, would depend on how you feel. If you feel bad or depressed, then bad, depressing things will appeal to you. Happy people will repulse you, and so, you learn not to notice them. They don't become part of your reality, they are not real to you. And so, the world becomes a dark, depressing place. All you see is bad people in a bad world.

On the other hand, if you feel good about yourself, then good, attractive things will appeal to you. The beauty in things will make you feel alive. You will notice good, positive qualities in people. Caring, thoughtful, attractive people will be more appealing to you and your life, and the world will become a wonderful place. And the more you look for the beauty in things, the more you will notice. And the more you notice, the better you feel.

An image of Jak flashed in my mind's eye, and I could hear his laughter. I sent out a feeling of warm acknowledgement.

And so, with this in mind, I tried to see only the good, positive side in everything and everybody. I noticed how often I turned to bad, horror or action-packed films and drama. Being more aware of what I was looking at, I was amazed how many ways human beings could be mentally and physically tortured, and how many programmes featured a murder or murders. My heart would then become heavy. For the first time in my life, I found this kind of entertainment boring. So I stopped searching and watching horror, blood-thirsty movies. I found richness in warm, loving, emotional entertainment instead.

I noticed more kind, peaceful, loving qualities in people. To me they seemed different because I used to see people like that as 'weak'. Thoughtful people I never gave the time of day, now suddenly, they appealed to me. They didn't seem weak anymore. On the contrary, it's not easy to be a good person in such a bad world. So to be positive can at times be very tough.

To try and encourage matters further, I looked closer at the life force that I had been creating. Life force, that anyone can raise, is a curious thing. Sometimes it would require a great deal of concentration to raise it, and other times, I would instantly feel its presence the moment I separated my hands. I also noticed it to react just like a magnetic force. It could attract my palms together or repel them apart, depending on what my mind caused it to do. According to Jak, there is an opposite to everything, so I reasoned that one must be positive and the other negative.

To settle my curiosity, I decided to experiment and find out. So for one week, I practiced attracting the force and another week, repelling it. I was right. Without a doubt, when the force was repelling and forcing my hands apart, I felt much better. This then had to be positive energy.

Thereafter, I continued causing the force to repel. It became more and more difficult to push my palms together, creating, once again, Lucinda's stone—the one she so fondly referred to as the mystical 'philosophers' stone'. It was a mighty force of immeasurable power lightly contained, outside of my body, in the centre of my palms.

I played around with the distances between my hands. I made it expand by stretching my arms apart as far as I could possibly reach. In time, I found that I could even dispense with my hands altogether and could direct it as a concentrated mass to any part of my body. Then finally, I managed to expand and direct it as a powerful force from the centre of my stomach to become an enlarged form larger than my body. My soul now felt full. I sensed it to be egg-shaped and could, at times, feel twice the size of my physical body. This gave me a wonderful sense of well-being, so much better than the first time I had raised the force at Lucinda's place.

I had not felt so fit and well in my life, and yet I knew that to reach Jak, I needed more. I had to bring my mind into order. I had to stop bad, negative thoughts from accruing. I knew that there was no point inducing a contact with Jak until I had control over my own thoughts.

I was passing off negative thoughts but some would keep on returning and others were difficult to remove altogether. This it seemed would be a problem. How does one change a habit of a lifetime?

From youth I had been pessimistic. I was always able to see the bad side in everything, never the good, positive side. Everything was a problem. I was full of ideas and started many projects, but not one did I complete. I was told more than once that I was doing well at college. "Extremely well," were the words of one lecturer. "You are truly gifted," were the words from another, but no one was able to convince me.

The death of my uncle was all that I needed as an excuse to leave college, and I would have quit long ago had I found another career path.

I was also a bit of a loner. It was natural for me to think badly of everyone. "People only want to know you when they want something," I once said to myself, and that was my attitude. Although, my pessimism had marginally improved, and I was now

211

seeing things more clearly. My changing outlook was now improving, and I was making more friends at Art College. However, this to me was not enough. I still, at times, had occasional negative thoughts. For this reason, I did not consider myself to be pure enough for Jak.

This was indeed a problem that might have plagued me for the rest of my life and would have, of course, hindered my communications with the ghost. Until one day, Julia showed me a way to cleanse my soul, enabling me to accomplish my objective.

It was one fine sunny day, Julia and I among possibly the entire college populace were taking lunch on the college lawn. Fortunately, for us, the college grounds were very large and seated in a quiet area under an old oak tree with no prying ears Julia enlightened me with a technique that she had acquired from Lucinda, who had apparently acquired it from Jak. This, of course, was no surprise as Jak was the root to the whole assignment anyway.

She told me that first of all I should, "Continue building the positive energy because that is the foundation for the next stage."

She was most surprised when I told her of my positive mind games and experiments with the force. She informed me that I had been playing with the final stages of advancement.

"You must be feeling really good about yourself," she said. "In fact, I know you are. I can see it in your eyes."

I told her of my problem with all my negative thoughts, and how I didn't want to execute a visit to Jak until I had cured that negative fault.

"Well, I can certainly help you there," she insisted. "Lay back on the grass for a moment, and I will take you through an exercise to help you change your outlook."

I laid back and made myself comfortable. She then asked me to raise the force and fill my entire body with it as usual.

"As you inhale, bring in the force, let it settle, turn it pure white, and as you exhale, keep the white mass in your body. You should then feel its presence as usual. I want you to concentrate building the force and to imagine this white force glowing full of passion, the kind you have for things and people that you love. This light should fill your entire body.

Now, only when you have acquired this state of mind, do you continue to the next stage."

I nodded in recognition.

"When the first part is achieved, you must hold on to that positive feeling and at the same time, allow yourself to bring in a memory of something or someone that you dislike. You then fill that bad memory with the love you hold so dearly in your spirit. You must turn the feeling of hate into love. Let go of the bad feeling, forgive those you hate, love all the bad tastes and smells, let all irritating noises conduct as a symphony."

She paused, no doubt, allowing me to concentrate. Then she continued.

"Everything is energy. Turn the negative energies positive. You must accept them one at a time not necessarily all in the same sitting, but in time you will turn your bad thoughts and memories pure, releasing the hatred and bonds of a heavy heart, allowing your spirit to 'breathe'.

If you have operated well, you may even have released bad ties relating to previous lives, freeing your spirit from its karmic bonds. If you have succeeded, you will feel no hate in your heart, no tight knots in your stomach, free and as light as air, your thoughts will lift your spirit to a higher level of existence. You will have become a 'positive spirit', able to love everyone and everything."

She had to be right. Fear, hatred, jealousy, mistrust and all manner of defective prejudged thoughts are caused by past experiences and are rooted in your memory. It is there where you hold your grudges, and this, of course, effects your present way of thinking.

So I had to forgive. I had to pour love and passion into my bad memories which would neutralise the hatred and in turn, change my present way of thinking, and my spirit would feel a positive relief from its negative bonds.

This made a lot of sense to me. This was just what I needed. If I was successful in creating a pure heart void of all fear, hate, jealousy, mistrust and prejudged thoughts, I would be on the way to staying in contact with Jak. This was the answer that I had been waiting for.

I suddenly remembered the old Christmas story and felt like Scrooge about to release his chains that had kept him bonded to the heavy weight, dragging him down to a dark, miserable existence. Each link of the chain was a memory of negativity, bad seeds of thoughts that had matured into dark, deep-rooted trees. To release my spirit, I would have to work on each and every link in turn. And cut off the dark tree from source.

I lost no time, and from that day on, I practiced what she had suggested and feasted on the delightful thoughts of freeing the bonds of my soul.

I eagerly pressed on and practiced for a few weeks. Every bad memory was turned into love, for each bad memory was a true lesson learnt. We should learn to love them. Like Jak had said, "We learn from our experiences be they good or bad."

I continued building and playing with the life force, and Julia's discipline complemented the energy admirably. To my surprise—although it should not have been—her method actually worked. My days were now filled with joy, and my depressions had not only subsided, they had completely disappeared.

I felt a much better person altogether and noticed more strange things happening to me. I could see the beauty in food, and for the first time in my life, I changed my diet and made healthier choices instead.

Among other things, I could concentrate much better on my work. My eyes seemed to focus more allowing me to see better. Colours in everything appeared to be a lot more vivid. Being artistic-minded, this was a real bonus.

As I was able to concentrate, my work rapidly improved. I was asked to represent the college by entering a competition, and to my amazement, I won. My work was featured in the college prospectus.

For the first time in my life, I saw beauty in everything and everybody. Girls became more attractive to me. Girls I hadn't noticed before. I so loved the beauty that you see in people's faces when you pay them a compliment. People that I knew paid more attention to me causing me to concentrate on what they had to say. I could see no bad in anyone. I had no enemies, and every stranger was suddenly a potential friend.

I lost contact with bad influential people. They didn't seem to want to know me anymore. Warm friendly people were suddenly coming to me with their problems, and I advised them the best that I could. With tender loving care I sent them away smiling.

I was more than happy to help people, because among other things, it made me feel good knowing that I was a positive light in such a dark world. I offered them a positive outlook and encouraged them to learn all they can about everything and anything, to use their skills for they are indeed a gift that other people do not have. I did not really solve any of their problems at all. I just pointed out the positive side of their lives. The side of their life that was invisible to them. The side that used to be invisible to me. They then solved their own problems.

I was more than happy to help but at times, I would feel so drained. I had no idea why, but it seemed that some would return only for me to repeat the same advice. It was bizarre, but it seemed to me that these individuals were only interested in my attention. As if my attention was more important than what I had to say.

At first, I thought that they just needed someone to off load their troubles to, but later, intuition told me that it was much more. I did not know how or why but some people can really 'take it out of you'. On certain occasions I really felt quite weak. I could not explain it. They had quite unintentionally, I am sure, drained me of all the life force that I had so patently built up. They had somehow sapped me dry.

It was for this reason that I would spend my breaks alone at the local park. It was there that I could replenish myself. Perhaps this was why great, wise spiritual leaders of the world sought out the wilderness.

After a recharge, I would feel much better, and the beauty of the world was once again reviewed. Beautiful things were very attractive to me. No longer did bad memories plague my thoughts. Love and wonderment filled my world instead. I could only see the good in everything. I truly loved myself, and I felt like an angel might on its root to deliverance.

Everywhere I went, I saw nothing but beauty:

I saw it in the clouds as they shape-shifted across a blue sun-bleached sky.

I saw it in the trees as a gust of wind blew thousands of pink petals from their branches.

I saw it in a woman's face walking her dog and the beauty in turning her back while in great concentration, the much loved companion, relieved itself in a nearby bush.

And I saw it later as flies fought over it like a treasure worth much more than gold.

Everywhere I went, I saw nothing but beauty:

I saw it on a station platform in the arms of a woman breastfeeding her baby.

I saw it in the face of a little girl as her grandfather shared his cake.

I saw it in a man giving his little boy sweets.

And I saw it in the eyes of a rat as it tore a crust from an old sandwich before running off to feed its young.

Everywhere I went, I saw nothing but beauty:

I saw it in my mother's face when I returned home safely each evening.

I saw it in the care she had taken whilst cooking a meal.

I saw it in the faces of my family as they sat around the table. And I saw it in a rainbow of bubbles as I washed the dishes.

Everywhere I went, I saw nothing but beauty:

I saw it in the moon and the stars on a dark summer's night.

I saw it in the eyes of Sharan when I kissed her red lips goodnight. I saw it in dogs and cats, so attracted, they followed me home.

And I saw it in a loving couple arguing on their way home. I was now ready to meet Jak.

Chapter Fifteen

I would guess some two months had passed since my last meeting with Jak. It was almost summer, I felt sure and ready. I longed for a return visit. Walking home from Sharan's house a full moon and bright stars lit up the clear night sky. I was followed for part of the way by the usual cats and a dog that had recently been attracted to me. I would stop and stroke their beautiful coats, so soft like silk running through my willing open fingers.

Continuing on, the air was so blissfully warm, I closed my eyes, held my chin high, took a deep breath and sighed, allowing the good, natural forces to blend with the love I felt in my heart. I was so elated I did not walk home but floated on soft gentle movements that progressed in time with the song that I was so merrily singing.

I could not wait to get home, for this was the night that I had planned to make another excursion out of my body and hopefully, meet Jak.

Once home, I quickly retired to bed. It was midnight. I lay there comfortable and warm with just a thin cotton sheet loosely draped across my body. I listened to the subtle voices of nature that filtered through the open window, surprisingly, birds and the ever present echoing sound of air circulating the world.

With full intent on leaving my body, I started the exercise Lucinda had taught me. I built up the energy in my abdomen and expanded it to the size of my body. Filling it with love and positive energy, I grew to the size of the room, then the size of the house and so on until I felt to be the size of the world, the universe and back again. This always gave me a wonderful feeling of wellbeing, connected not just with the world but to the entire universe.

Once I had returned to the size of my body. I sent out a thin stream of silvery matter ending as usual in the downstairs lounge, where I produced my double. I would then project all of my thoughts into it. This did not always work, but this particular night, I was successful. As before, I then moved through a wall to the rear of the house and out through a window, where I was greeted yet again by a clear sky and a full moon that lit up the stars and my mother's garden.

As before, I looked at a large, bright star situated very close to the moon and requested to see Jak. I waited for a while, but unlike the previous attempt, I was not collected by dark shadows. Something was wrong. It all felt different. My mind was now drifting, and I was finding it difficult to hold my concentration. I tried so hard to stay with the moment. I didn't want to shift back to my body, "Oh no…too late," I snapped back. I was so disappointed.

From then on, I tossed and turned trying to concentrate a return, but alas, I was unable too. For how long I tried I have no idea, hours must have past when suddenly, in a kind of drowsy, paralyzed state, between consciousness and sleep I felt a floating sensation.

At first, I saw many colours, and I heard voices all around me. I heard and felt myself vibrating at a very high pitch. The wonderful sensation was so familiar to me. I instantly knew that I had successfully floated out.

I drifted higher and higher, the colours turned grey and the voices ceased. There was a silence. I paid the changes no mind. I am full of love. I am made of pure positive energy. What harm can become of me?

I expressed the will to see Jak. Moments later, I seemed to open up, expand and merge with the surrounding grey mist. I sensed a cool tingling sensation like I was water vapour floating on a cool breeze. I had no idea of scale, so it was quite impossible to know what size I had become. Yet, I didn't much care, I just went with the flow. The feeling was too good to do otherwise.

I somehow sensed that I was made up of millions of colourful molecules. I had sensed something similar before, but this time, the tiny molecules appeared to be of a different shape, each one like a minute prism separating light into rainbows, reflecting all the colours of the spectrum.

There was a cool up draft, and some of the molecules instantly joined together. Then things really stated to change as we collectively touched very cold air. I instantaneously shrank and felt extremely heavy. I was unable to float anymore. Then to my horror, I started to fall. It was then that I realised I had become a rain drop.

I was much larger than the rest, and I was falling much faster. I tried to resist and pull out of the fall but all attempts failed. In a vain hope that somehow, I might be heard, I sent out a telepathic SOS to Jak for help. Then receiving no response and not knowing whether I could be helped, I howled for help anyway.

It was at this point that I realised fear was getting the better of me, turning all of my pure 'sanctimonious' energy toxic. It was by no means easy, nevertheless, due to my personal training that I managed to turn the fear into a positive thought. It was all too late. I was a rain drop, and rain drops do only one thing. I hit a hard surface and splashed.

Then I heard it, a shriek of hilarious laughter.

"Boy…you do know how to make an entrance," came the unmistakable voice of Jak.

I opened up my awareness, and there before me seated on a large Wicker throne was the long white-haired ghost. He was dressed in what looked to be a long, white silk robe. Complete with white beard, he was bent over with his hair touching his bare feet. And he was convulsed deep in laughter. This, of course, was nothing new for I had been ridiculed by him many times before. So, allowing him to get over himself, I took a good look around.

It appeared that I had just been delivered in a shower of rain which had instantly stopped the moment I had landed, for my entire surroundings were soaking wet. Yet what an awesome sight I beheld. In what looked to be a huge opening in the side of a mountain, I could see down from a large stony balcony. Below, deep in a gorge was a light blue river with water so clear, from afar I could see fish and other aquatic life.

In amazement, I cast my attention up the side of the mountain to see huge green trees growing from naturally made platforms. Platforms made from beautifully coloured plants, many I had never seen before, let alone give a name too. I could hear the constant flow of running water that formed natural fountains everywhere. There was no sun, but the sky was as blue and bright as the river below. I could smell the beautiful scent of flowers in the warm air currents. I heard the calling of exotic birds and other sounds of nature. A wondrous scene from a distant memory somehow forgotten, and yet I could recall this same feeling so long…long ago. The moment was so magical that I wanted to stay forever.

Complete with fairy tale like creatures, I was in a wondrous land that time had lost. From behind the trunk of a large tree, I saw two white mice playing happily with a large tabby cat whilst a small white hart deer enthusiastically looked on. There came music, and the atmosphere 'danced' to the rhythmic thumps of a rabbit's foot on a hollow log. This startled the cat and the white mice. They jumped to move and dance with the beat. The cat whistled through a blade of grass whilst the mice moved on to play the blue bells, and birds from all directions sang.

"Yes," said Jak, "You are remembering the moment that you were conceived in your mother's womb. You are remembering that innocence beholden only to a sell and spirit of a child. You are in 'fantasy land' where your emotions are being visually expressed. What you see is how you feel, and what you feel is what you see."

I at once redirected my attention, concentrating all of my thoughts straight at him. The music and merrymaking instantly ceased, and I sensed the animals contemplating their next move.

He was still seated in this Wicker chair that looked to be alive and had just grown into its shape. Sitting peacefully on his right shoulder was a pure white dove. Wide eyed, Jak looked at me with an all knowing smile. His smile always so warm and friendly, how could I have ever doubted such a pure spirit? It had taken him a while, but he now had my complete confidence.

"It has taken much more than a while," he said, picking up on my thoughts. "It has taken much longer than you could ever imagine possible, but it's not the time that is important though, it's the final arrival that counts, for some spirits will never experience or understand the beauty of such a feeling.

"Some spirits are doomed ever to follow the dark negative side of their emotions and will continue to crave it in death when the physical body is no more. Those spirits move on into a darkness of their own making.

You, my lad, will not experience such likes. You have seen the light. You can see the goodness inside others, and they see it in you. Because you think positive, then positive things will happen to you. You feel fulfilled, and your heart is full of love. Now that you realise your spirit's potential, it will continue on into a world of bliss for evermore. Your physical body will cease, but the spirit will live on…"

"Please, Jak, for I know that I have much to learn of these things, please explain, in a way that I might understand the nature and meaning of 'pure positive life force'. Please, Jak, how does it work?"

"Need I explain the meaning for it," he expressed with surprise. "Are you not full of it?" he asked. "And does it not make you feel good?"

"Oh…of course it does, words cannot express the feeling, but how does it work, and what part does it play in our everyday lives?"

He moved back into his chair, and I watched as he and the dove, like one spirit combined, moved themselves into a seemingly comfortable position. Settling, I placed myself a few feet directly in front of them awaiting his explanation.

He put his hand to his mouth and paused deep in thought. "Mmm…" he muttered, "In a way that you will understand."

Then leaning forward, he brought forth a finger and touched my spirit body. I winced as I immediately felt a sharp pain.

"Being outside of your earthly body you would not normally suffer pain such as this. I have caused this to happen for an effect. It is to demonstrate a point."

I felt the pain increasing until no longer could I draw my attention from it. I was about to scream at him to stop when he shouted, "look…!"

The whole of my spirit body that resembled its physical counterpart had faded somewhat, but now, in the area of the pain was a bright glow.

"This is precisely what happens when you are in your earthly body," he said.

The pain was so intense, I still could not draw my attention away from it. The inflicted area in turn grew ever brighter. I had no choice for the pain was too great to think of anything else. I was about to inform him with no uncertain terms that I had had quite enough of this abuse when he withdrew his finger. With much relief on my part, the pain instantly stopped.

I was then about to return some abuse by inflicting him with a nasty piece of my mind when he shouted once again, "Look!"

I looked and there, to my surprise, coming out of the brightly glowing area that had given me so much pain and discomfort was a stream of bright glowing vapour, now directing its way towards Jak. As I watched the vapour completely disappeared, and Jak seemed to absorb the lot.

"There," he whispered, "you have just witnessed in its purity the action of life force itself. Few beings have ever seen such a thing."

I listened in awe as he explained the whole thing to me.

"Your spirit or soul is an intelligent mass. It is like a kind of vortex that is able to control life force. Like a whirlwind it can draw the energy in or move it out. It all depends on its needs. To create thought requires energy in itself to make it. So your mind will draw in life force when you are thinking and when you are in deep thought. Concentration causes a great amount of the force to accumulate."

He looked at me as if to delve into the deepest recesses of my soul.

I could somehow feel him inside me.

"This also applies when you concentrate your thoughts outside of yourself. Wherever your thoughts go, so does the force. The more you concentrate on something, the more force your will gather there. You can feel it now, can't you, as I am concentrating on you?"

I nodded.

What he had said sounded fine, yet its meaning remained elusive. I was about to comment before his words continued.

"Have you ever had the feeling that someone is looking at you and a quick observation confirms the same?"

"Sure, no doubt, everyone has," I replied.

"That is the building up of force that you felt. The person that was admiring you whether he or she knew it was giving you life force."

I must have still looked confused.

"This is what happens when you fancy someone. You know that tingly feeling you get when a girl looks at you funny. That is you receiving some force. And when you meet eye to eye, there is a cosmic connection. You literally connect and your spirits briefly merge but, once this connection has taken place, that person becomes part of your reality…never forgotten.

This is intensified when two people fall in love. One cannot stop thinking about the other. As the energy grows between them, they become not just full of love but, it overflows. They no long need energy from other sources, and they can quite literally go off food."

"That's what people call 'living off the fruits of love,'" I said.

"Yes…exactly," he replied with a grin. "As the energy grows so does the relationship. In some cases, the connection becomes so strong that the spirits fully emerge and become as one. They will at times know what the other is thinking because they are one spirit. Unfortunately, for them, when one dies, the other can follow shortly after. This is because one part cannot live without the other. Living becomes too unbearable without their soulmate. Their mourning becomes so intense that they cannot stop thinking about the life that they had together and would prefer to be with them once again. And so often their wishes are granted."

I thought for a moment. Then with a sudden remark, I asked amusingly. "Is this why my girlfriend does not like me looking at other girls?"

He laughed. "That is correct, when you concentrate admiration in someone's direction, you are giving them force, and your girlfriend will resent it since you are not giving it to her instead.

Although girls do not realise it but, that is why they dress up. It's not always to attract a male for sex. If this be so then why do married women dress to impress? When you understand the principals and functions behind their actions, it is quite simple, they do it to attract life force. It makes them feel good.

The same applies to men also, this is why they go regularly to the gym, build up those muscles and or drive fast cars. They are out to impress and attract some 'force'.

It is your thought or thoughts with concentration that controls the life force," he went on, "And your thoughts can nourish your soul. Like your physical body needs food to survive, your soul needs life force to exist. It does this through concentration. The more you concentrate your thoughts, the more force you will create. This is accomplished through the art of concentration.

For example, some people feel good after meditation because that is what meditation is about, it causes an accumulation of life force within the body. To concentrate on parts of the body will give you more life and vitality. Thought is energy in itself, it is the building block of your spirit and the building block of life."

His eyes widened as he gave me a big smile of approval. "And you certainly have more force in you than the first time we met. You glow like a jewel, boy…well done!"

I looked around and could see all the animals nodding with approval.

"Nothing can exist without this force," I heard him say. "Every part of your physical body needs it, your mind and soul too." I looked back at him.

"This is what the demonstration was for," he went on, "I merely wanted to show you the force in action. When you injure part of your 'earthly body', that injured part needs much life force to heal. In a normal situation, to get your soul's attention, it has an inbuilt mechanism, you know this as pain. This causes you discomfort and draws all of your attention. The pain then makes you concentrate on that injured area. The concentration does not make the pain go away, on the contrary, at times, it may feel worse, but when you concentrate on something for long periods or keep turning your

223

attention to one cause, a great deal of the life force will accumulate in the required spot helping the wound to recover."

"So, when you caused me that pain just now, it was my concentration that made it glow, then?" I asked excitedly.

"Precisely," he returned.

"But what about that stream of bright glowing vapour that departed from the painful area, and whilst suddenly dimming, it went in your direction, where I saw it all go into you?"

"Yes…that again was you," he replied.

"Your concentration had changed direction and so did the 'force'. It was your anger. Anger stirs up a great deal of 'force'. Your thoughts and anger were centred on me and so that is where the 'force' went. Not being angry in return, I absorbed the lot…thank you very much," he said.

"So wherever I focus my mind, I will create life force there?" I asked.

"Well," he murmured, smiling again. "Your thoughts do not create the 'force'. Your thoughts cause a concentration of it, and when and wherever you send your thoughts, the 'force' will accumulate. This is precisely how faith healing works. It is the result of pure concentration.

Most people's minds in modern day life are too absorbed in too many things. If you were to ask them, they will tell you that to concentrate on one thing is difficult and just damn right boring. They would fine it, far too hard to concentrate on anything for too long a period. Their minds are all over the place…" he chuckled.

"The practice of mediation can improve this. Most people find it hard to concentrate for a few seconds, let alone a few minutes or hours, and most abuse their body and never give it a moment's thought. Is it any wonder that their spirit lacks life force? They send the 'force' out everywhere and leave none for themselves. Their spirits are low, and they feel empty, of course they do. No wonder modern man suffers so many illnesses. If you pay the body no mind, it will lack the 'force', and nothing can live without it."

He was now laughing again.

"Why…even a simple act of the toilet is refused concentration. Many prefer to read a book, a newspaper or even play games on their mobile phone, and they wonder why they have a trouble going…ha–ha." He could not continue for laughter.

"And then…and then…how many people do you know eat and watch television at the same time. Then later complain of indigestion. By concentrating all of their attention elsewhere, they have diverted the 'force' from their stomach, where it was much needed, straight into the television set. No wonder this media holds so much power over the nation…" he giggled. "Food for thought, isn't it?"

I thought for a moment whilst he laughed and amused himself. I looked down at the mass he called my spirit body and concentrated all my thoughts in the area of what would normally be my stomach. Within seconds I could see a faint light appearing. Then I looked back at Jak and concentrated on his stomach area. Again, I could see a faint light appearing.

"Oh, thank you," he said, "that were most gratifying."

"Can I accumulate force anywhere I send my thoughts?" I asked.

"No matter the distance?"

"Yes…! Now you are beginning to understand. Yes, anywhere in the universe, although, long distance is very difficult and takes a great deal of practice. What you have just seen appearing in those areas of thought still happens when you are in your physical body, only it cannot be seen. Yet, you have felt it right between the palms of your hands."

"Oh yes," I replied, "many times, and I have felt it grow extremely powerful."

"Good…!"

"Now, when you return to the physical world, I want you to try and feel its presence. In time, you will learn to recognise its flow from person to person."

I was not quite sure what he meant but agreed anyway.

"Now that you are aware of the 'force's' presence and how it is controlled and moves, when you are in the company of others, with practice and concise attention to its movement, you will realise how some people manipulate and strive to gain more and more of its power.

And now that you know of the 'force's' existence and how it works, you will realise why some demand attention. Attention seekers are life force seekers. They seek the 'force' because it makes them feel good.

Babies need the 'force' to aid spirit growth, so they sometimes cry for no apparent reason other than to gain attention.

Children need the 'force' to aid further growth, expand their spirit and satisfy their playful nature, so they want their parent's attention all the time. This is why parents complain of being so tired.

Their little ones are constantly drawing their attention and the 'force' from them.

Everyone needs the 'force' to stay alive, it sustains their spirit and boosts their morale. It generally makes the physical body feel good too. Therefore, everyone seeks love, affection and attention. It is merely a demand for life force."

He paused, smiled and winked. "Ah, yes," he sniggered. "That is what live is about—life force—and there is more than one way of accumulating it. Another way of getting it is from other people. If you can gain someone's attention to yourself, you will accumulate the 'force' inside you, and the longer you have their attention, the more of it you will feel gathering inside, and as you know, boy, the more you have, the better you feel...right?" He laughed on as usual. *Like any spirit would, that being full of so much 'force',* I thought. I waited patiently for him to continue.

"Ah...yes, my boy, everyone seeks attention. The more attention they receive, the more force they build inside and the bigger their spirit grows. This is why you might say that famous people seem different to the average person. They have an air or an aura about them. What you are sensing is their abundant 'force' given to them from the concentration of thousands of people. They have taken a trip to cloud nine, you might say...to second heaven.

Ask any entertainer while leaving the stage. They are on 'a high' and buzzing with life. They will tell you how wonderful it is to perform. This is why some people seek fame, want that prestige car and or the big house. They have a need to show off. They are attention seeking. They don't always know why, except that the attention makes them feel good. Ah...ah...yes, any entertainer will tell you of the wonderful feeling they get after a performance. All that attention on them, all of that force filling up their ego and spirit. Who needs drugs when you are full of life force?"

His laughter continued.

"Comedians—although I am sure they are not aware—are able to control the 'force' in mass. They can capture the attention of a live audience. Then a good comedian will whip up the 'force', conduct it like music, and when the time is right, and when everyone has invested enough attention, the 'force' will be extremely high— you may know it as an electric atmosphere—the comedian will then inject it with a funny thought causing the 'force' to infuse to rapturous laughter.

This is why it is better to go and see a comedian live. This is why it is best to be entertained with many people. It is not that the jokes or comedy is necessarily any better, but you are able to feel the 'force' at its best."

He stopped laughing as if a sorrowful thought had come over him. With a long face he sat back in his chair.

"Sadly though, as always, there is a negative side to this wonderful 'force'. As you know there is an opposite of everything. Like any spirit, I suspect some comedians and entertainers get addicted to the good feeling of the 'force', and so when their fame has reached its completion, and they no longer entertain, the intense 'force' ceases, it slowly declines to a normal level and can send the celebrity to deep depression and a pit of self-destruction…"

He looked away as if trying to gain control of his emotions. Then in deep affliction, he bowed his head. Leaning forward, he placed his head into the palms of his hands, and slowly he continued.

"I feel for them… I feel for every one of them. It is a sad truth, but many famous people die young. They cannot face life without the excessive levels of life force. Their soul shrinks, and they can no longer bear the pains of a normal life. You know of this feeling, don't you…lad? You have experienced a shrunken soul."

I agreed but could not believe that for once he was turning the whole atmosphere sour. *How ironic that is,* I thought. It wasn't me doing it this time. No…! I shouted, but it was too late.

He looked up. I was spellbound and just nodded in recognition. His image horrified me. I was shocked—although, I shouldn't have been for I had seen him change many times before—but he appeared to have aged fifty years. His face was now dreadfully grey, tears ran down old drawn-in wrinkled cheeks. He resembled the traditional ghost we all associate with at Halloween. But the eyes, his eyes were no longer blue, they were grey with shrunken black pupils. Not being able to look into those dark eyes, I turned away, only to find that all the animals of this beautiful world had disappeared with the setting. I instantly flashed back. His head had returned to the palms of his hands. Knowing full well that this hideous image he now portrayed was not a true reflection of the spirit that dwelt therein. Reluctantly, I waited patiently for him to continue.

"When a celebrity's soul shrinks, fear sets in. They start doubting themselves, and all manner of demons start pestering them on daily basis. On the street people no longer recognise them. They see people looking and laughing and assume that they are laughing at them. Afraid to be seen in public, some feel insecure and stay at home in their large mansion where the walls seem to close in on them turning their once great home really quite small. In a vain hope of deliverance from this hell, they turn to alcohol and or drugs. Their dreams are full of all kinds of dark creatures that plaque and torment them in their sleep. Not knowing whom to trust, fear of being robbed takes them over. They can't help but assume that everyone wants a bit of their hard earned fortune. And so, their home becomes a fortress. But little do they realise that by locking the world out, they are locking themselves in…"

His voice was now tapering off, and I could feel the warm atmosphere growing cold as his image began to shrink, going with it, his world was diminishing but, I heard him say,

"If only they knew of the life force.

If only they knew how to love life once again.

If only they knew that there is truly life beyond fame. They lack knowledge that's all.

Such a shame as all worlds need entertainment and all worlds need entertainers. Where would your world be without them…?"

Chapter Sixteen

The following morning, I woke up early with Jak's sinister image still on my mind. As I lay there between the warm sheets, this disturbing vision caused me to think about the night's trip to the other side. The experience was amazing and once again, very informative, but something was baffling me. It wasn't his hideous face that was bothering me as I had seen him change into something similar a few times but, the reason he had changed, that was the one thing that puzzled me the most.

Until now, I was always the one that turned everything sour. This was the sole reason I practiced the exercises of course. This was the whole reason I wanted to purify my spirit and build the life force and thereby have a longer session with him. He was always full of this 'positive force' and he was constantly the one in control. So, why had he brought the whole thing down? And why is he so sympathetic to entertainers?

I lay there pondering over this for a short while, and in my opinion, there could only be one possible explanation. Conclusion: he used to be an entertainer in a past life. Well, he did admit to experience many lives. So, perhaps he used to be an entertainer and knew all too well what it was like to be one and no doubt, what it was like to end as one. And perchance his previous life was that of an entertainer—and once an entertainer, always an entertainer—I say.

My blood suddenly ran cold, and I sensed all of my well-earned positive life force draining from my soul. My stomach was now empty, and my spirit had drawn into what felt like a small led weight in the centre of my torso. I lay there dazed with a heavy heart.

This train of thought I never considered. This train of thought I did not like. Until this point, I considered him to be like a supreme being, a deity or God of some kind, but this was different. This turned the whole thing on its head. This could mean that he was just a fiendish old ghost after all—was he messing with me? Has this whole scenario been just one big show?

I instantly sat up in bed. "No, surely not…! Have I been the butt-end of a great, big joke…? Can a ghost actually do such a thing? He certainly changed a lot and laughed the whole time. Who else would do that but an entertainer?"

And what of his world, I mused. Then, as the realisation came into fruition, I muttered, "and his world would then be a stage." I sat there, mouth open like a fish out of water, and I sure felt like a fish too, cold and shocked my hands were shaking with adrenalin.

"No…" I couldn't bare it. I got out of bed. It was seven o'clock on a Sunday morning, and my entire family was still in bed. Who could blame them? I would normally be doing the same thing only I had things on my mind, things that needed resolving, and things that needed to be finalised.

After breakfast, checking on the weather I briefly took a look in the garden. It was warm but somewhat overcast.

Nevertheless, I decided to go for a stroll in the local park.

My local park was called Black Park, located on the outskirts of Langley near Slough in Berkshire. It is next to Pinewood Studios, where a lot of the great movies have been made. It is the birth place of all the James Bond movies and many other great films. In fact, a great deal of the filming for those movies took place in Black Park. It has a large lake, and its woodlands stretch for many miles making it ideal for filming. This park being less than half a mile away from where we live, I frequented as a kid. I often went there with my friends on our bikes, and a few times, we were able to witness filming actually taking place.

On entering the park, I immediately walked to the side of the lake and stood on its bank just admiring the view. This lake with its surrounding woodlands always brought back good memories of when I was a child. At the water's edge, I was greeted by the usual ducks that appeared to have lived there forever.

Nature is a curious thing, it never seems to change. The lake with all its birds and other wild life looked exactly the same as when I was a kid. I thought about all the changes that had taken place in my short life and pondered over the changes that had taken place in our modern world throughout the generation before me. Although I dare say most of us would call it progress, the changes I am referring to are advances in technology, machinery, vehicles, planes, TV and the latest marvel of technology, computers and the internet.

I looked down, and there, before me, completely unchanged as, no doubt, for thousands of years were ducks – ducks just being ducks, bobbing up and down in water.

Inquisitively, I looked across the lake.

Wow…! How amazing humans are, and what a wonderful world we have devised for ourselves. We have, indeed, created a great deal of knowledge amongst ourselves. Knowledge we learn from school, college and books from the library. Knowledge we share and learn from TV, computers and the internet. We know a great deal about our world, and all of our collected knowledge—that which we have collated together—we are at our pinnacle. The human race has never been so advanced and intelligent as now.

And yet, we still don't know enough about ourselves. By that, I mean our inner selves, that part we refer to as me or I, the inner spirit. In comparison, we know nothing of the human soul or what controls nature. And what of the hidden spirit of nature for I was sure that there is one. At times, nature does appear to have intelligence.

Some types of plants, for example, blossom in various colours in the spring, this is to attract bees, and then, by depositing pollen on their backs, bees take pollen to other flowers, thereby helping the plant to germinate. This is part of what we call pollination. This process surely—on behalf of the plant—must take deliberate planning, and with deliberate planning, there must be intelligence. Moreover, some plants can even catch insects. They have actually engineered a trap that closes around insects, trapping them to be digested later. And the plant didn't even go to college to learn the process.

I now laughed as an image of a plant going to college reflected in my mind. This is ridiculous of course, and anyone would have me sectioned for thinking such a thing, but the question still remains. How do plants, such as venous flytrap, manage to create its trap? This can only mean that it has a spirit, an intelligent spirit that can plan, and if it can plan, then it can, of course, think. Nature can think…? I glanced up, trying to come to terms with this weird idea. Is that even feasible…?

High in the sky, I saw a few noisy seagulls. There cluttering was so loud that they caused me to focus on them and the world of birds. Birds gather in flocks or groups in autumn and fly hundreds or even thousands of miles to warmer climates to feed and breed. Who taught them how to migrate? Pigeons can travel hundreds of miles and return to their coop. How do they know where to go? They never went to navigation school. They never sat for hours studying maps and learning the routes of the roads.

And dogs too, sometimes hundreds of miles away from home, some dogs have been lost whilst on a trip with their owner. And yet, despite being all alone, somehow, they manage to find their way home. How is that possible…?

In wonderment, I held my head up high, the heavy overcast sky was moving, and I could see the sun trying to break through the clouds.

We know a great deal about our planet, and with the use of telescopes, we know a lot about the universe, but the hidden world of nature somehow eludes us. I couldn't help but feel that there is intelligence behind it all. A kind of collected intelligence, like it can think for itself.

Just then, I heard shouting. This noise annoyingly drew me away from my thoughts. The noise continued, and there was now a dog loudly barking. I looked to see what the commotion was. The dog owner was trying his utmost to control his large pet, but the dog was having none of it. Out of pure curiosity, I casually looked up to see what the dog was barking at.

And there, high in the sky, was a breath-taking sight. I stood there motionless and in awe at a natural display of birds. Due to distance, I had no idea of the specie, but they were small, one of a kind and a huge number of them. They were flying a small distance apart, almost touching as they flew in unison, like one body mass or a large marine creature moving, creating patterns flowing from one shape to another. Not being able to draw my eyes away, I stood there in bewilderment just gazing at this amazing spectacle.

"It's almost as if they are being conducted by some inaudible music created by an invisible conductor," I said to myself.

I then heard Jak's laughter and voice saying, "They are starlings…there is music of a sort, and there is a conductor…"

Half expecting to see him, I instantly looked around, but alas, he was nowhere to be seen. "He's 'flippin well' playing games with me again," I huffed.

Disappointed, I signed. But I couldn't put out of my mind the idea that he was the conductor and that he had put on this spectacle for my entertainment. "More theatrical I suppose, Jak…!" I shouted with contempt.

The dog owner looked at me in puzzlement. Well, I was shouting and talking to myself. I hastily turned and continued along the path at the side of the lake.

The pathway was an old dusty dirt track with trees that grew on the bank to my right and there were thick woodlands to the left.

Disillusioned, with head down I sauntered along this footpath. It was a while, but nature has a habit of soothing the spirit. It was summer, and the trees where full of green leaves that moved with the breeze from the lake. I could hear birds and the occasional sound of a nearby plane, probably just departed from Heathrow Airport.

A curious mix of nature and technology, I mused. And yet, nature appeared to carry on regardless. Maybe, the animals were just used to the sound, but the loud plane didn't seem to bother the birds at all. It was quite uncanny. It was as though the aircraft didn't exist. Or maybe to them, it didn't. Maybe it didn't figure as part of their world. With this thought in mind, I immediately stopped in my tracks.

Opposite me now was another small group of ducks, maybe a dozen or so just bobbing up and down in the lake? I wondered, *Are they aware of me observing them from the bank? If I approached them, they would see me and scatter, of course. Or if I throw a stone in their direction the splash would also startle them, but would they have known it was me that threw the stone, and would they have known it was me that created the splash. More to the point, would they have seen me walk the path, pick up the stone, hold it up and throw it into the water? At what point would I have become real to them? At what point would I have become part of their reality?*

Something then dawned on me. How can some birds seem so intelligent one minute and so unintelligent the next? They can navigate the skies with such precision but spend most of their lives just feeding and nesting in trees or bobbing up and down in water. They seem to lead such simple lives in their own little world. Save throwing ducks some bread, I was sure they would not know we even existed. We live side by side, but are they truly aware of our world?

I shook my head and once again, looked at the sky. What was I thinking? This thought process was deep. What was I trying to fathom out? What was it so deep in the recesses of my mind that failed to surface? It was a thought abstraction that needed to come to fruition. Then finally, the conclusion struck home. We are beings living in different worlds. We are living on the same planet of course but living in different worlds. And we being more intelligent are more aware of the animals, than they are of us. It's a question of knowledge.

Then I remembered some of the stuff Jak had told me. We think with our spirit and not with our brain and we humans are the most intelligent because we have lived many lives as molecules, plants, insects and animal before we even started many lives reincarnating as humans. We know of all these other worlds—the animal kingdom as we call it—because we were once there in their world. The penny had finally dropped. I'd finally acknowledged the obvious. I stood there in awe as the concept reached its peak in my mind.

We are worlds living side by side. We are worlds coexisting, but we are not all aware of each other. I looked down into the dark green water and there I could just make out a fish swimming. I now wondered if that fish in its own little watery world was aware of the world of the ducks on top of the water. And although having their webbed feet in its surface, were those ducks aware of the creatures lurking about in the wet world below? Due to knowledge, understanding and intelligence we are aware of these two worlds, of course, as we are aware of all the animal kingdom,

This all seemed rather obvious even a child could have worked this one out, but what if we were living next to a world that we were unaware of…?

If this seems inconceivable, then let me inform you that until the end of the last century, there were people living in the Amazon Jungle, tribes totally unaware of our existence. This does not make them unintelligent, they just lack knowledge about us. And yet, they understand the Jungle far better than we do. They live off the land and hunt wild animals. They have their own customs, belief systems and to all intense purposes, are living in their own little world.

What if…! What if we lacked the knowledge or were just too damn ignorant to perceive another world, an intelligent world far greater than our own, living right next to us on the same planet. Like the tribes in the Amazon Jungle, what if we were so preoccupied in our own little world or too proud, thinking that we are the most intelligent beings in the universe, to even consider that there could be a higher form of life beyond our perception.

Then, as the realisation struck a chord somewhere deep in my psyche, I shook my head once again with this reiterating thought. Jak had said that our spirits reincarnate and we started as molecules, plants then progressed to higher entities, such as insects, fish, birds, other animals and finally, humans. And through each, step we would have experienced the world of each creature in turn, gaining more and more knowledge and becoming more aware and more intelligent throughout the various worlds. Moreover, even as human beings we tend to live in our own little world. And all this knowledge we can take with us for the next step and the next world.

We are very aware of all these creatures that live next to us in their own little worlds, but what about the next step? What about the world next to us that we cannot perceive?

"Is that even possible…?" I suddenly said to myself. But I knew that to deny this other world would mean to deny the existence of Jak, and that I could not accept.

I glanced back at the ducks. My mind flipped back to the idea of the perception of those ducks. At what point, if at all, would the ducks perceive me observing them from the bank? Or, due to lack of knowledge and or understanding would they not perceive me and just be startled with the splash from the stone?

I then had another wild idea that caused goose bumps and a tingling sensation that ran up my back. What if I could not perceive Jak, and that a lot of the time he was observing me from afar? And what if the spectacle he created with the birds was his way of making a connection. What if the barking dog was his stone and the flock of birds was the splash. If only temporarily, by throwing a stone in the water, I would have made the ducks aware of my world as, no doubt, Jak was trying to make me aware of his world.

I then heard Jak's laughter, although, I was not sure whether it came from my head or the atmosphere around me. "This is not entertainment…" I suddenly heard myself say. "He is offering me knowledge." I had been too quick to jump to conclusions. I had no idea why he had turned the last meeting so sour, but instincts now told me that it was not for my entertainment.

"Oh…my…God! What and who is this Jak? Is he just a clever old ghost or perhaps an old spirit that has lived and gained a great deal of knowledge from so many lives reincarnated? Sharan had intimated about such being on the day at the park. She was questioning the existence of advanced souls, but referring to living souls, advanced souls still alive today. He may not be alive, but perhaps he is one of those advanced souls. Could I even speculate and say that he was one of the first to live and started reincarnating millions of years ago…?" He changed so much, I had no way of telling what he was. I had to find out. I had to find out his true identification.

And what of his world, the other side, the world of spirit?

Was it a world we and science choose to ignore, or was it a world so beyond our understanding that we could not possibly perceive until the next step of our spiritual learning and awareness? Was this the world I was only now beginning to perceive? And with a perception only obtained after so many lifetimes' reincarnated.

I sighed and moved closer to the water's edge. Seeing me approaching, the ducks naturally moved away as predicted. I sat down under a huge oak tree and made myself comfortable on some of its large roots that were jotting out of the side of the bank. *This is where it all began,* I thought. It was not the same lake, but the atmosphere and setting was very similar. I peered over the edge of the bank. And there in the clear water, I could see my image just as it appeared on that day at the park with Billy. Only now I felt wiser but not content. I was unhappy and somehow felt lost, like there was something missing.

I looked at the sky and there moving from behind a large cloud was the sun and its rays radiating energy, lighting up a blue sky that reflected like jewels off the surface of the lake. It was then obvious what I was lacking. I was lacking Jak's life force.

I closed my eyes and immediately began building this wonderful force in my stomach, and then on completion, I caused it to spread over and outside my body, to the world and the universe and back again. Once again, I felt alive and not just an empty shell anymore but a whole spirit again. I peered back into the water. My image had taken on a glow. I now looked alive, teaming with energy. I smiled and the reflected image smiled back.

I reminded myself that it was a Sunday and so time was unimportant. Without a care in 'my world', I continued gazing amusingly at my image there in water. It was a while, but as I did so, something quite unexpected happened. The image suddenly changed. I was now an old man in the darker days of his life. I was about to look away when it changed again, this time to a young man in a First World War uniform. I also sensed the hardship of his time and experiences. I saw it change again and again into many people, women as well as men. I saw the image of an old mariner with deep lines in his face from many years of harsh weather on a Galleon at sea. I could even remember the name of my matchlock gun that was by my side during the day and in my hammock at night. I named her 'ebony' as she was so black.

I could now remember so many lives, so many memories of lives forgotten. I wanted to savour those memories, be they good or bad, for they were me, all of me. Like parts of one whole now coming back together. I felt to be a whole soul and a complete spirit

I closed my eyes and continued building the life force with the memories of those past lives, filling them with love and understanding offering thanks and gratitude for the experiences. Tears ran down my cheeks.

Opening my eyes, I once again gazed at the present image of myself. A young man in his prime and a whole life to look forward to, not in war but in peace time, time I had fought so hard over so many lifetimes to accomplish.

There was a splash, destroying my image and thoughts in its wake. Assuming it must be a duck or a kid throwing stones, I looked up. It was neither. An acorn had dropped from the tree. The acorn had surfaced and was now floating in the water close by. I looked upon it in a semi-conscious state. I felt shocked and cheated out of a wonderful chronicle moment with my spirit.

It was whilst I was gazing at this acorn, I sensed his presence. I sensed him observing me from afar. Some distance away in the trees behind me. He was always able to read my thoughts so I asked him to come closer. I sensed him approaching, and he stopped a few feet away from me. I turned, and there was Jak, bold as life, right there in front of me. He had taken the shape of an old man in what looked to be his seventieth year. The way he was dressed, most would assume that he was a local in a t-shirt, jeans and trainers. But I knew different. It was him alright, I had learnt and could sense his spirit anywhere.

"Was it you that made the acorn drop from the tree?" I asked in a calm, friendly manner.

He smiled and nodded,

I was so pleased to see him, like a long, lost friend, I wanted so much to hug him, but composing myself, I gestured him to sit with me, and he did so. There was a silence as I took a moment wondering what to say.

"You want to know if on your next spiritual step, at the time of your death, you will enter my world instead of another turn in this wondrous world of learning."

I nodded in eager recognition.

"That would very much depend on you…" He returned with a friendly smile and a wink. "That depends on how you spend your time here. If you spend it wisely, who knows, you may indeed be eligible for such a merit."

Somewhat puzzled, I looked away. *What could he mean? I thought? How was I supposed to spend my time here?*

"You have much to learn," I heard him say. "Not just you but humanity as a whole. All souls in the material world are in their infancy, and until they graduate, they will forever remain shrouded in obscurity, caught up in a never-ending circle of rebirths. But you,

237

my boy…you have already learnt a great deal, and so, you may just succeed, you may indeed graduate and become one of us."

"So there are more of you then…?" I asked hesitantly.

"Why…sure there is. There is a great many of us in fact."

I was about to ask who and what he and the others are when he held up his hand saying, "Yes…I know what you are thinking, all in good time, all in good time. Your spirit is delicate and can only take on board small amount of information at a time otherwise it will go into spasms."

"No…!" I shouted, and like a spoilt child, I stood up, turned, walked away a few steps whilst saying, "Jak you are talking in riddles again. This is ridiculous…I have had enough."

But then I heard him quite unexpectedly say, "Are you not forgetting something?"

"Mmm…more riddles," I mumbled. What is he referring to now? In a sharp hasty movement, I returned a glance but was completely unprepared for what I was about to see, for there was I, still sitting next to him, seemingly quite content, my physical body was asleep on the rough roots under the large oak tree. In disbelief, I looked up at the sky, and once again, the sun was shining through a small gap in the clouds only this time creating visible rays of light, like a film set, they shone brightening up my scene with a radiance befitting a spirit I now knew him to be.

Then he uttered words I will never forget. "Yes…you only see the light when you are not shinning bright. Come…sit for a while, I will teach you more."

His presence was so alluring, my entire soul ached with a yearning for his knowledge. In the true meaning of the words, I was a lost soul succumbing unto its master. And so, once again, I found myself captivated by his enchanted will. I moved closer and came to rest next to my body but not too close as I knew from experience it might snap me back.

He then held up his hands, and with both palms facing me, I felt a surge of energy filling up my spirit. "There, you were not as full as last time we met so I thought you could do with a top-up."

"Thank you." I returned with a warm smile of gratification. This seemed to amuse Jak and he burst into laughter. I waited patiently for him to finish entertaining himself. Then I asked curiously, "What happened at the last meeting, Jak? What made you so upset that you lost control and turned the whole scene sour?"

"Oh…yes, I must apologise for I just got carried away and caught up in the moment. I became too engrossed with their 'grand spirit' and temporarily became one of them."

"What…!? I am not sure what you mean, can you explain?"

"Yes, of course, the key to it all is the life force. This force is kind of electric, although, not to confuse it with the electric science is aware of but, nonetheless, it has currents that permeate through everything in the universe. It's made up of an infinite amount of what we call 'grand spirits', but I believe science refers to them as wavelengths, fields, realms, and I think you like to use the term worlds. Different names for the same thing, it matters not what you call them. Putting it simply, they are divisions or part of a whole."

I must have looked confused.

"Okay…well, it shouldn't surprise you to know that all living creatures are intelligent. If it lives, it has spirit, and all spirits are conscious. From the moment of conception no matter how big or infinitely small you are, you will have a spirit. Nothing can live without a spirit. Each species of animal, plant, insect, etc. from the moment of conception is an individual spirit but connected to the rest of its species by a link. This link connects the individual spirit to the rest of the species as a whole, and collectively that species will have a 'grand spirit', something that controls the whole of that species."

He paused and seemed to be deep in thought, then captivating an answer he continued.

"I know that lately you have been questioning the intelligence of birds."

I nodded but felt my spirit draw in a little as I realised that he had been observing me after all. This was a bit eerie to say the least, but I let him carry on anyway.

"Like all living creatures, every bird is born with a spirit and that spirit is conscious and has intelligence. This is always an inherited intelligence with an onus deriving from the individual spirit of that bird. And if it has an inherited intelligence, then, of course, it has a memory. However, each spirit is connected to a higher entity called a 'grand spirit' and, every species of bird has its own. This 'grand spirit' represents and is the grand total of knowledge relating only to that species of bird. Therefore, because they are all connected, should one individual bird or a few of its friends learn a new trick, this trick or new information, after a while will spread among all other birds of its kind, and because of the spiritual connection, each individual will learn or realise this new trick. For example, if one learns a good way to crack a nut, pretty soon others will start cracking nuts using the same method. I mean even birds of the same species with no physical connection, living possibly hundreds of miles apart…"

"A kind of psychic connection, is that what you mean…?" I asked enthusiastically.

"Yes, that's right exactly so…permeating throughout the level of the 'universal life force' will be that species of birds' knowledge and all saved or gathered inside its 'grand spirit', an accumulation of their experiences…" He answered with a little laughter. No doubt glad that I was still following his thoughts.

"Now…you also questioned the wonderment of bird migration. Well, you may or may not know that not all birds migrate. Partridges never move from their local area. As a species that is all they have come to learn, but most of the other birds of England migrate. And some fly long distances too. Swallows breed in Europe and spend winter in Africa…"

He looked at me and winked. "I know that this to you is puzzling for they have no maps, etc."

This had all suddenly become really creepy, for not only had he been observing me, but he had been following my thoughts too. Yet again, I paid it no mind, I didn't what to be the one to turn the scene sour. So, I let him continue.

"Sometime in the distant past, one or maybe a small group of Swallows took this journey, and since then, because the information is stored in the Swallows' 'grand spirit', the entire species is able to do this journey every year."

Trying to make sense of all this information, I looked across the lake, and there, still in their own little world were ducks being ducks, bobbing up and down in water. "Yes…!" I heard him say. "They haven't learnt a new trick in a while. Their last new trick was finding out that when clothed creatures appear, they may throw some white stuff that tastes nice. This thought form was very conducive to its species and was an immediate success up and down the country. Bread is not a natural food for any animal. It is manmade, but now, all ducks will eat bread, no matter what lake they are born in."

Accepting his notion, I glanced back to Jak with an unexpected thought, and as this thought materialised in my mind, his face lit up.

"So…does this apply to humans as well?" I asked.

"Naturally," he returned in anticipation.

"So…when you turned the last meeting sour, you had connected with the 'grand spirit' of all entertainers?"

"Yes…my boy that is exactly it. Entertainers live in a wonderful world, but like everything else they have a dark side, and that is where I got caught up. I apologise."

Excepting his apology, I continued, "If entertainers have a 'Grand spirit', then surely every human has one too?"

He laughed and said, "Well, humans are not quite as simple as that, they are highly evolved beings. Each human spirit is the product of many lives reincarnated. Therefore, each human spirit has had the pleasure of connecting to a great many 'grand spirits'.

Now, what you have to remember is that when each life was ended, you took away with 'you' personal knowledge plus knowledge of each 'grand spirit' or world that you experienced. That is why as a human you understand more of the world that you live in, by that I mean the physical world, the world you all refer to as reality. It is all thanks to those 'grand spirits' that taught you."

"Wow…!" I suddenly remarked. "There must be a lot of these 'grand spirits' if every species of animal has one?"

Jak burst into laughter, "Oh you kill me, boy. A lot there most certainly are, you have no idea." He went on laughing, then calming down, I looked as he pointed to my physical body lying next to me.

"There in that body live great many cells, trillions in fact and every single cell is alive, as alive as you and I. And what I have said before, 'if it lives, it has a spirit'. There living in that body of yours are trillions of cells with trillions of spirits. Each and every cell has a spirit called a 'Billimous spirit' and like all living things, they are all conscious and very intelligent. In their own little world, each one is given food in return for work. They all have jobs and carry them out to the best of their ability. They work for the good of the whole and for the good of your body, After all, that body is none other than their planet. And every living cell is guided by its' 'Billimous spirit' who is guided by their very own 'grand spirit' called a 'Compillion spirit'.

Furthermore, every living creature whether they be a plant, insect, animal or human being all possess trillions of cells with trillions of 'Billimous spirits', and all are being guided by their 'grand spirits' or 'Compillion spirits'."

I could not believe what I was hearing. This was insane…!

I turned and focused back on Jak. His eyes widened, but he was not finished.

"Like it or not, viruses have 'Compillion spirits' too. Each time your doctors come up with a new medicine to alleviate the symptoms of a disease, the viruses and bugs will find an alternative means of attack. They do this by consulting with their 'Compillion spirit'. And I don't just mean the 'Compillion spirit' contained in one individual physical body. All individual viruses have a connection to a 'Compillion spirit' which has a link to other 'Compillion spirits' on the outside of the physical body and a link to a level of the 'Universal Compillion spirits'—what you might call a 'grand spirit of viruses', and every species of virus is guided by at least one low level of 'Compillion spirit'. These viruses work together, and so when one individual bug or a few of its friends learn a new trick, all others will soon find out, and people up and down the country will fall ill seemingly at the same time. Have you never wondered how or why millions of people can fall ill at the same time? Hospital files are full of such documentation. Plagues have been noted in old manuscripts, and new viruses breakout even now in your lifetime. In your period, viruses have broken out in Africa and many parts of your world."

He paused and smiled. Then a funny thought seemed to take possession of him, he chuckled and said. "Have you never wondered how or why flu and the common cold can strike so quickly in December, and at times, millions of people can catch a sickness bug immediately or in just a few days…?"

He had now blown my mind. I could not move. I could not think. Anchored to the spot, I stared at him in wonderment. And what did Jak do, he laughed of course, he laughed to the pit of his stomach, assuming that he had one, for I still had no idea what or who he really was, I was about to ask when he said,

"This is too much for you, isn't it? I did warn you…!"

He was right, but not wanting to admit defeat, I looked away, and with my head held high, through the trees, I held the sun and a bright blue sky in my regard. So bright and beautiful, it immediately relieved me of some strain set in motion by the desire of my quest. I didn't want this to end, but it seemed that I was at my limit. Could my spirit take on more? Was there room in my soul for yet more knowledge? I pleaded to the sun that I may be restored. I looked down at my spirit body, and there as if my wish had come true, it glowed. It was now glowing brighter than I had ever seen before.

"You really have got the hang of this life force, haven't you boy," he said.

I held up my spiritual hands, they seemed to glow brighter than the actual rays of sun shining through the trees. Once again, I looked at Jak in amazement. "Just how powerful is this 'force'?" I asked.

With a wide grin of approval, he said, "very well, my apprentice would like some more. Yes, it is very powerful...very powerful indeed."

I remained still, just admiring this amicable old spirit. I was mesmerised and transfixed to an endless flow of information that appeared to just pour from this 'kinetic being'. Half of the time, I didn't even see his lips moving. But, I had to remind myself to saver the moment, and not to forget any of the information that was so faithfully being imparted. The world that we were in seemed effortless. And it was a world where communication appeared to be fast and direct,

"You talk a lot of this 'life force', Jak, but what is it really? I find it an enigma, nothing and yet everything."

"Ha ha...you are asking for the secret behind life itself. It is indeed an enigma, my lad...an enigma indeed. However, it will be told. You will know of its secret. I did promise you as much."

"And...just how strong is this 'force'? You make it sound very powerful."

He looked back at me with a mischievous grin. "Why it is, lad? That it is." Then holding out his palms, he leant forward and gestured me to take hold of them. I was about to offer my hands but hesitated, for the last time I touched one of his hands, he inflicted pain in me.

I looked deep into his eyes, they were a serene blue, the kind of blue you see in a clear blue sky on a clear summer day. Contemplating my next thought for I knew very well that he was reading my mind, I gazed at his face in anticipation, and then, as if time had somehow slowed down my question, it was finally relinquished. I gave heed to his agreeable face as it positively lit up, giving me the reassurance that I was now ready for such an answer, his entire spirit appeared to glow with delight.

He moved back a little, and no sooner had he done so, the image of the seventy-year-old man was no more. Then I watched in awe as he seemed to expand, growing possibly ten feet in height and brighter as he did so, he became so bright, my own spirit took on some of its radiance. And there before me, appeared the most beautiful being I had the pleasure to bestow. His eyes were the same 'sky blue' and they housed the same pious spirit for sure, but his face was much younger—no wait—'her' face was much younger, I could not be certain, although, the body appeared to be naked but lacking great detail as it was so bright and transparent around the edge. Then, quite unexpectedly from behind this 'grand spirit', unfolded the most spectacular pair of white wings imaginable. Fluttering with a bright radiance of a pure white hue, they moved with a life and energy seemingly possessing their own spirit. At that point, time for me ceased. I was, once again, mesmerised by the sheer presence of this immortal being.

"I am a watcher and a messenger…" he said. "I am a 'Celestial spirit', an 'Angelus', or what you would probably call an Angel."

There was only one thing to do, and that was to hold his hands which were again stretched out before me. I expressed the thought, and I watched as my tingling spiritual hands connected with his, no sooner as they did so, I felt myself swelling and growing much larger than I was originally. I felt my whole existence as it was expanding and then quite suddenly, we exploded. And for a brief moment at a point somewhere in the expanse of space and time, I felt stretched at what could only be the speed of light. Then expanding to the outermost limits of existence, I saw a tunnel and a bright light. Moving towards and through this bright light, I saw billions of suns with orbiting planets circling our Milky Way and then in an instant of glory I was able to sense the entire universe. There was a flash, and for a brief moment, we were separated then re-joined and all became one, I…we had become everything.

In remembrance, I drew back to the beginning of time where consciousness first realised itself. I was the singularity physicists endeavour to seek. I was the love that poets so beautifully define. I was one with all so beautifully sublime. In that instant, the eternal, the anonymous, the unknowable had been exposed to me, an incredible certainty.

Then my entire existence was instantaneously reduced to a single speck. And there teetered on the very edge of Earth's atmosphere, I admired our blue planet at its entirety.

I then heard Jak's familiar laughter. "There, you know what 'pure positive life force' is now, don't you, boy?" I was absolutely speechless.

"There…" he continued, "you have just remembered the feeling of dying for you have done this many times, of course, after each lifetime. At death, if you have lived a good life and invested in the feelings of others, then many people, friends and family will mourn for you. Their concentrated thoughts will have accumulated a great deal of the 'force' leaving them emotionally drained, allowing you to receive their final gift. A gift of all the feelings you had given them in the past. All the feelings you have given them whilst you were alive get returned in one mass of affection resulting the ultimate send off and look at you. You shine so bright like one of the stars that surround you."

He smiled. "Don't worry, I know what you are thinking. You are not dead. Yes, that is what all…the fuss is about. That is why every living entity seeks the ultimate high, the height of enjoyment and the ultimate climax. This is why people want fame and fortune. Some people have sensed it on stage, others have sensed a glimmer of it in passions of love, and still others sadly seek it in drugs. Yet, no matter how little or more you have sensed or experienced, you will always crave for more. It is the elixir of live itself. Kings have sent armies to the ends of the earth in search for it. Modern man seeks it among the stars, but what they cannot understand is…"

Then, laughter, as always, took possession of him. I watched as he tried to gain control of his convulsions, and how so gracefully his wings moved effortlessly securing him to the moment.

"What, what they don't understand is that it's all around them. They are…you are…everyone and everything is swimming in the stuff, ha…ha…" his laughter continued.

I looked around me, trying to get to grips with this wondrous experience. How could everything possibly depend on one energy source? I could sense the thin atmosphere, the ever, present force, which appeared thin, yet, although being thin, it held me firm and suspended. But then my spiritual body was like thin vapour too. *So, why wouldn't it support me,* I thought.

I gazed at the stars. I looked down at the huge blue mass below me. What an awesome sight the earth was from my vantage point.

"Yes…and it holds the planet Earth firm in its orbit too," came his soft voice.

"How's that…?" I asked with a chuckle. "It can't be that strong."

"What stops the earth from dropping or falling out of the orbit? Something holds it in space, something invisible and very powerful holds it in space. Does this not sound like the great force I have been talking about? It fills all space and all matter. It might be invisible and hard to detect by modern methods, but its power is ever present and everlasting. And your spirit is a concentrated form of it.

"I know what you are thinking, if you can see the concentration of it in your spirit body, then why can you not see it holding up the planet Earth? You can, if you look close enough, it's just so spread out and so far away for you to sense it but, I assure you, it is there!

Many tons, thousands of feet above the Earth's surface, it can support a huge aircraft in flight. It guides meteors around planets, and it is so strong that it holds the planets in orbit around the sun. It has strength so powerful, it supports the billions of stars that move around the Milky Way and of course the galaxies that expand the universe. And yet…more to the point of your existence, it has such subtle features that it can also support all life forms and spiritual bodies too."

He paused and gave me a loving smile.

"It is in everything. Yes, even hard earthly matter is made up from compressed life force, I tell you, it is everything, nothing exists without it."

Again, he paused and looked at me searchingly, no doubt, making sure that he had my full attention. With gratification, he gave me a warm smile. Then continuing, he held out a hand gesturing me to look out to an endless expanse of space where the blackness of the universe staged the billions of stars that glistened so bright, I blushed as they seemed to credit me with a blessing.

"Everything started as one single mass of the 'universal life force' with a gravitational force so strong nothing could escape it, not even time or light itself. Then everything exploded, and everything was blown apart but alas, hear this nothing was separated. Everything was and still is connected."

His voice ceased, and we remained motionless, just hovering there in space, so warm and calm, it was a delightful feeling. It was whilst we were floating amidst this force, something occurred to me. "You say that this force contains many spirits, and that they are all conscious and intelligent, and that all answer to their 'grand spirit'. Do these 'grand spirits' have 'grand spirits', and if so, what controls them…?"

He chuckled with approval, and with one swift movement from his huge wings, he circled around me.

"This force is split up into a hierarchy, a system of spirits arranged in a grand order, rather like a pyramid form. At the bottom of the pyramid, there are cell spirits or Billimous, then further up, there are many levels of their grand spirits or Compillians, then many levels of body spirits called Souls and then many levels of nature spirits or Deities and so on. Even planet Earth has a 'grand spirit'. We call her 'Tellus', but there are many above that almighty presence. Some are like me. We have our own grand order too, within the universal grand order of things. It all seems a bit complicated, I know..."

"And who is at the top level, that must be God, of course...?" I said, jumping in enthusiastically.

Jak chuckled. "You are quick to jump to conclusions, but no. First of all, there are no levels. No one spirit is better than any other spirit, no matter where they may be among the hierarchical pyramid. From the bottom to the very pinnacle at the top, we are all equal and equally learning.

And yet, you are quite right, the universe, just like everything else within it has a 'grand spirit'. And this 'grand spirit' reigns supreme. Being the ultimate 'grand spirit', this spirit is the supreme spirit of the universe. Everything is connected to this universal spirit. It is conscious and highly intelligent. It is energy, and that energy lives. It moves and is constantly moving, creating more energy as the universe expands. This is what we call 'universal life force', but alas, the supreme spirit has no name or..." he chuckled, "He just won't tell us."

Once again Jak had me in awe. What could you say to an answer like that? At least, I now knew what he was. He was clearly a 'grand spirit' of some kind, and where he fitted in with the hierarchy, I didn't much care, although, I suspected him to be high ranking.

"The life force is in everything," he went on. "It is everything, and although seemingly weightless, it is what you are. It is the makeup of your spirit, and it is what connects us to other spirits making things like telepathy possible. It also connects time. The past with the present and the present with the future, all is one."

He suddenly stopped and for a brief moment the atmosphere drew quiet. He seemed to be contemplating something. Then in a soft voice he said, "you know that even written words have the life force and reading them connects you to the 'spirit' of the writer and then to his 'grand spirit', that being me."

I felt my spirit wane a little. He had picked on my worst weakness. I suffer with dyslexia, and all through my childhood, I suffered the ridicule of my class mates. Sensing my affliction, he offered me a warm embrace and smiled like a creature to its solitary kin.

"Now, you've defeated that weakness, have you not...?"

This being's warm voice was so sincere and full of passion, it emitted a capacity to captivate anyone's soul.

"Besides, it wasn't a weakness anyway. You were only learning a new skill that you hadn't picked up in a previous live. This is nothing new, many spirits are learning how to read for the first time. Until recently, only religious scholars or nobles were taught the art of reading. And most books then were religious or philosophical in nature. You should feel proud that you have learned a new skill.

No, this is not at all what I was referring too. In any language words are made up by many symbols. The meanings of those symbols were taught to you as a child. They are illusions. When these symbols are placed in the right order your mind can follow them creating patterns of thought, pictures and feelings. Words are symbols, an illusionary gateway, directing thoughts on a pathway to an experience. A book can do that. A good book can have a discerning way of evoking your spirit, enticing it from the body and connecting it to an experience. That experience is a thought form created by a spirit which has a link to a 'grand spirit' that being me. A concentrated thought creates life force connecting all forms of spirits to the ever present immeasurable gulf where time cannot reside. And this force infuses with the 'great all present universal force' connecting you with us."

I now realise who my invisible friend is, "It is you…"

"Across time and space our spirits are indeed connected. As everything in the universe is connected, so are our thoughts and the spirit that has been following these words. Yes, it is you my friend, the one reading this book, and you are the most welcome soul. Whether you realise it or not, your thoughts and spirit have been enticed from your body. You have been out with me, out with us on a spiritual journey. Do you feel the connection? Do you feel haunted by what you have learnt or perhaps a tingle of excitement or disbelief? You are touched and blessed by the love of an ancient spirit, a 'grand spirit' of old. I have existed since the dawn of time, and you are most welcome, my new apprentice.

I know that you have tried and sensed the force between the palms of your hands but if you continued practicing the exercises that I have taught you thus far, you will not just have sensed the great life force between your palms, but you will have felt it in your body. But more importantly, to receive the most benefit, remember to fill it with love and compassion. And if you have been practicing regularly, then you should be full of it, and you will be feeling blessed to have done so.

Should you wish to learn more, it will be available to you when you are ready. It was once said by an enlightened one a 'grand spirit' of ancient times, "When the spirit is ready, your guide will appear."

Like plants grow, so shall the great knowledge, the knowledge of yourself. Time is the key—my apprentice—time is the key.

"Fashion it in gold or silver, let it appear in a ring on your finger or a pendent around your neck, tattoos are fashionable. You may now wear your initiation symbol, the three moon phases, a circle flanked by two arcs, as thus)O(.

Throughout many lifetimes, you have gained much knowledge; had you not done so, you could not have followed these words, for you would not have been able to read, and they would not have had any meaning for you. You could not have connected with my thoughts. I am your 'grand spirit'. You are a part of me, as I am now a part of you. The things you have learnt came with an energy, and that energy resides within you. You cannot undo what you now know. But don't worry, for you do not have an apprenticeship with a ghost that would be far too sinister. You have an apprenticeship with something far more superior. I am 'pure positive life force' acquainted with love and compassion for all forms of life and positive spirits.

I will now leave you with a question. You are developing and you are gaining more knowledge about yourself all the time. You are a very wise old spirit, but you are not alone. There are many wise old spirits in the world today. Things are developing. The world is developing and spirits are gaining more knowledge about themselves all of the time. The question is this, what is all this knowledge for…?"